ond Seventeen Vagabond Seventee

Potter's Field

by
Chris Dolan

Vagabond Voices
Glasgow

First published in September 2014 by
Vagabond Voices Publishing Ltd.,
Glasgow,
Scotland.

ISBN 978-1-908251-32-9

Printed and bound in Poland

Cover design by Mark Mechan

Typeset by Park Productions

The publisher acknowledges subsidy towards
this publication from Creative Scotland

For further information on Vagabond Voices, see the website,
www.vagabondvoices.co.uk

*For my brother Paul, who helped with this as he's
helped with so much else throughout my life*

Potter's Field

The days were centuries long, the air like parchment. The town endured in its valley, like the rocks on Monte Capanne – patient, dry, waiting. Spring sun, autumn sun, a little rain, the odd wind, nothing changed for more than a moment.

So many generations have made a living here; too many. The earth is red and sore from being forced, overworked, tugged at; the hillsides rudely naked since the vines failed and the soil became bitter. There's so much past there's no room left for any future.

There's a man walking towards a village. He doesn't know it for sure yet, but his future doesn't lie here. There are two boys playing outside the house the man is heading for – a plain cottage overlooking the sea behind. On an island this size, the sea – the only means of escape other than hot earth being laid over you – is never far away.

One of those two boys will only ever know this island; the other will discover a whole new world. But he'll bring his island with him. He'll wear it like a shell. Wherever he goes that house by the sea will be with him – the house and the heat and his brother and the man who has arrived at the gate now and stretches out his sure and dependable father's hands.

I

A peep of a breeze sounds through the cherry trees and showers Maddy in pink blossom. This morning Kelvingrove could be the Tuileries; the Jardins du Luxembourg. A sky as fresh as a mermaid's breath, and greens so light you feel the sun might be shining from under the grass.

"Hey, Maddy!" Even Bob or Billy or whatever his name is, gleams crisp and sharp in his dark, smart uniform. Spring actually living up to its name is so rare you want to cel-ebrate it. Cry off from work, put on floral summeries, and open a bottle of something as sparkling as the morning air. Lie under that huge cherry blossom on the hill and let the petals smother you pink.

Instead – this...

"Couple of parcels for you this fine morning." Detective Inspector Alan Coulter has a face that belongs to a rural parish minister. Fifty going on thirty without a line to show for the endless stream of horrors that unwinds daily before him; no furrows for the hours, years, spent with squat, squashed spirits. Not even a pucker for the strain of family life. Maddy keeps walking towards the centre of everyone's attention, a square fenced off like a boxing ring, police tape bunting in the sun.

"Heels, stockings and jacket? Respect." Coulter has teenage kids who if nothing else keep him linguistically in vogue. "Takes more than a cloudless sky and a tropical sun to impress a lassie frae Girvan."

Maddy smiles at Alan, but actually she's just misjudged. An image of herself comes into her mind: a kid's drawing. A big black line around her, scrawled crayon picking her out from the background. Beyond the line – brightness, airiness, shops opening in the distance, the street outside the park coming to cheery life. Inside the line, a weariness of limb out of kilter with the buoyancy of the new day. Her tongue's dry from last night's smoking. A not-quite headache, from the fourth G&T, that will eventually surface. Clothes too tight and black, doleful instead of sexy, heavy for an unexpected morning like this. Shoes all wrong.

"We don't get these chaps moved soon," Alan's smile is like an invitation to a trip to the seaside, "I'll have to put sunscreen on them."

"Nobody wants to go to the pathologist with a big red nose."

They'd managed to get a van into the park and Maddy went behind it to get kitted out. Except there is no behind it – a park with a van in it is still a park. She looked over towards the taped-off space to see who was about. About fifteen folk already suited up; Adams one of them. "Keep telling you, Miss Shannon – you should wear trousers."

Bruce Adams, Crime Scene Manager. No matter how airborne a morning can be, or how loathsome the crime, Adams brings a humdrum ordinariness to it all. She looks at him now and is struck again by the dull fleshiness of him. Unfortunately, however, he's right – she *should* wear trousers to crime scenes. With trousers, you can slip on the lower part of the spacesuit no bother. A skirt you have to howk up, where it ruffles and annoys. And in *plein air* too. Twenty or so guys – crime scene photographers, forensics, tecs, Uniforms – pretending not to watch, and women opted between sympathetic smiles and faces like torn-scones. Maddy's not a professional; not like them.

WPC Amy Something helps her out. "It's a bad one," she says tenderly.

Walking towards the cordon – bunched-up skirt adding two bulging inches to her backside – another peep of wind loosened more blossom from the trees. She looked up, and a beetle fell on her face instead of petals.

Thankfully, there was no public audience this morning – this corner of Kelvingrove well chosen for its seclusion. The river slunk along quietly below, rhododendrons, delirious with joy, danced around them, enclosing them in a private little theatre.

"Hup!" Alan Coulter encouraged her over the tape. Her skirt now up at her waist, heels slurping into dewy grass, she tottered gracelessly towards the centre of activity. Backs bent in diligent work, the odd flare of a camera flash as ineffective in the sun as a kid's torch, the scratch of Biro on notepad, mobiles ringing their silly rings. Everyone moves back for the Fiscal, as she steps centre stage.

There are these moments in life. Moments you suspect will change everything, will be pivotal in some way. The egomania of the religious would have you believe that the world has been set up in precisely this way to get a message solely to you. It hasn't, and the moment will probably prove to mean nothing in particular. As if you had misread the signs, lost an opportunity

Two bodies. Lying side by side, about a foot and a half apart. Limbs splayed, lying slapdash where the boys had been dumped. Blossom-confetti decorating them like some satanic wedding ceremony. Heads twisted away from one another. Sixteen, fifteen, years old? "Neds," said Adams, and Maddy walked round the vile pietà away from him. She took her phone out.

There was something in the scene that held her. Banal enough if you're used to this line of work – the peaked caps, the trainers, the lanky limbs and hunched shoulders. She sees rangy boys like these every other day in the courts, with not much more life in them. Only this time, in those brutally crushed faces, in the montage of limbs, Maddy felt the thick black line between her and the world dissolve. Springtime ended here, in this grim little patch of hell. Her protective layer, her outline, was stripped away. She was fully in this place.

The boys' hands almost touched. The fingers of one stretched flat as if he'd just let go, or was pulling away from, the half-folded fingers of the other. Maddy looked up at the fathomless blue and smiling sky and, stupidly, tried to make sense of it all.

"No ID," Detective Sergeant John Russell said.

"Chaps come out without their credit cards, did they?" There was only the simplest form of irony in Adams's quip. Russell, somehow managing to leer at the dead boys – just the unfortunate geography of a trampled face – watched his boss, Coulter, search around in the mud as if he might find a "This Murdered Boy Belongs To..." tag.

"Anyone recognise them?"

Everyone glanced down at the faces. DI Coulter laughed. Not at the poor kids' violent end – below the eyes, which were shut, there were only clumps of bruised flesh, glints of protruding bone – but at the stupidity of his own question. The boys were dressed in the uniform of the defeated. Not even hair colour was an indicator, so shorn were they both. Lads like them gave nothing away. Except, sometimes, their lives.

Dr. Graeme Holloway squatted beside them. Maddy had phoned him on her way here. He touched them gingerly with gloved hands. "Had their teeth knocked out, both of them."

"A fight?" wondered Coulter. "They do it to each other?"

Holloway shrugged. It wasn't fighting that killed them. A bullet hole each, plain as daylight, in the side of the head. "Executed." Holloway pushed one head to the side, a child looking for slugs under stones.

"Maddy." Adams approached her, the fixed grin, the opaque eyes. "Don't let us detain you."

Procurators Fiscal don't usually attend the crime scene. They can, but it suits everyone all round if they stay away till the police have done their job and committed it all neatly. But this wasn't a usual crime, even for Glasgow, and

Maddy not your run-of-the-mill Fiscal. She was standing, staring – listening, but taking little in. She had no need to. The Fiscal views the crime scene and then leaves the various police departments to their jobs. On paper, Maddy was in charge of the case, and would be, all the way through from this morning until the sentencing of the killer, or the deaths of two nonentities were filed and spiked. On paper. Cops don't like paperwork.

"One of them's got a T-shirt on," she said.

"Yes, well, they both have." Crime Scene Managers could make the PF's life hell, particularly uppity lady ones that got under your feet at the start of an investigation. Adams tolerated Maddy, which impressed female fiscals more junior than herself. He was deemed to be good-looking, in an old-fashioned way: squared hair, bristly short at the back, classic suits, tall enough. Too predictable and fixed for Maddy's tastes.

"A T-shirt with something written on it," Maddy said to Coulter. "Might help."

Dr. Holloway heaved the corpse in question up at the shoulder – an ambitiously big boulder to explore under. A once black-and-white striped shirt, muddied and bloodied. "L then an E, I think."

"Le Coq Sportif," Maddy told him.

"Le what?"

Alan Coulter liked Maddy, but not enough to give her the limelight. He got in first: "Sports gear make."

To be fair, Coulter knew more about street-culture than Maddy ever would. "Favoured by, as Mr. Adams here calls them, Neds."

"So. They're wearing what you'd be expecting them to wear." Adams smiled at Maddy: "Thanks, anyway."

She was outstaying her welcome, but couldn't help wondering, louder than she'd intended to, "Don't different tribes use different makes?"

No one responded, and Maddy began to back off from

the scene. She could stay if she wanted to. Demand notes. Shadow Coulter and Adams and Russell all day long if it came up her hump. The power of the image, though, the two teenagers splayed mute at her feet, was beginning to fade. It wasn't telling her anything she didn't already know. It's a world where two dead-end kids could die and nobody'd bother much. Those two hands, stretched towards each other, was a Da Vinci touch, a stroke of visual genius in an otherwise ham-fisted sketch. Walking away, her sling-back heels turning to clumps of mud, Maddy noticed another detail. The eyebrow of one of the victims. Thick young hair, snicked à-la-Beckham. Maddy turned her head away, hoping not to cry.

"Hey!" Distracted, Maddy was unzipping her suit, loosening the hood, before she'd stepped back over the tape. Adams was good at his job – small thing like that could sink an investigation before it's even begun. A fallen hair, confusing the forensic evidence. A broken nail. It also confirmed the prejudices of all those present about Procurators Fiscal. Post-Grad nancies who couldn't cut the mustard at a proper law firm. Pen-pushers who understood nothing about crime investigation.

The fourth floor of the Procurator Fiscal office is open-plan, made immune to spring or snow by layers of impregnable beigeness. Maddy exchanged the odd nod and half-raised hand as she walked the gauntlet of desks and phones to her glass-walled cubicle at the far end, trailing mud and cherry blossom behind her. Izzy, Manda and Dan tinkled keyboards like toy pianos, the cumulative sound like static. Izzy was in the fish-tank marked "M Shannon Principal Depute" before Maddy could close the door.

"Crown have adjourned the Petrus case till next year." Izzy was already reading from her pad as she sat elegantly down at the other side of Maddy's desk. "Complications. Even more collating, organising, classifying and cataloguing files for us." She flicked over to the next page. "*And...* Two new hospital deaths – neither of them look suspicious to me – and a domestic disturbance. Dan's looking into that now." Izzy closed her notepad and looked expectantly at Maddy. "Well?"

Isobel Kinloch, one of Maddy's PF Deputes, wasn't referring to this morning's surprise flowering in Kelvingrove. Murders aren't that much of a talking-point in here. Maddy Shannon's reputation as the Fiscal's living soap opera was much more interesting. And Maddy traded on it too often to complain when she wasn't in the mood.

"The *test?*"

Maddy cringed. "Shit. Did I do the test?"

Last night was Thursday, and Maddy was the one who'd insisted on going out. Just a drink, a bite to eat. Anything to remind her she was still alive. Maddy's section in the Fiscal's office, after all, was called the Solemn Team. She, Dan, Izzy, Manda, and one or two others that were constantly changing, had the happy task of dealing with all the murders, attempted murders, culpable homicides, the City of Glasgow had to offer. All suspicious deaths in hospitals, homes, prisons. Folks dropping suddenly in the streets, in the comfort of their own living rooms. Negligence cases – professional, corporate and personal. Suicides.

This had been a specially tough couple of weeks. Gathering and arranging court papers for the infamous Petrus case – an industrial criminal negligence claim. To date, the petro-chemical multi-national was accused of causing three deaths, two cases of cancer and a mental breakdown.

Maddy Shannon had made it a rule of her section that Thursday, six o'clock, signalled the official commencement of The Weekend. She would lead her posse across the bridge o'er the Clyde, first to a fancy cafe, Barga, to make them feel modern and chic and European, and then, inevitably, on to sloshing beer in the Scotia or the Vicky, like twenty-three generations of PFs before them. Somewhere in the midst of this process they had been diverted to the bar at the Tron theatre, where the victim – Bert? – happened to be innocently drinking.

"Matt," Izzy reminded her.

Izzy, long and narrow on the seat, gleamed like a little sunshaft that had snuck its way indoors. Yellow hair that looked advert-soft, pretty pastel dress fluttering over reedy limbs. The girl's skin was so delicate white you could see the veins. They curled vaguely up from her calves and her arms, disappearing suggestively into her dress. An uninvited sexuality, present nowhere else in the girl's physique or demeanour. "Did he pass?" Izzy closed her notepad.

Maddy, in the presence of this gentle sigh of femininity, felt heavy. Like the mud on her shoes had entered her veins.

Maddy could be a difficult boss. She could get obsessive, work mad hours and expect everyone to do the same. She could go off at tangents – start acting like a detective in cases when, really, proper collating would do the trick. She'd suddenly run off down the exciting, undiscovered path of a new case, leaving the Dans, Izzies, and Mandas to finish off older, duller work. She got away with it by making herself public. By being the office party-girl, though – as Mama was forever reminding her – she was ten to fifteen years older than her fellow-partiers. Also, her single status was a matter of concern – the human bit of the boss, the sensitive spot that made staff and colleagues feel useful. They could console, plot with her, match-make.

"Well, he passed the intelligence test."

"I'm not talking about intelligence."

"Talked about rotifers."

"Rotifers?"

"Tiny fish-like creatures apparently. They can be celibate for 70 million years."

"Good grief."

"Know how they feel."

This Matt guy had been going on about desire. Maddy said she was all for it. "It's the Italian in me. Proper women should be desperate with want at all times." That's when she signalled to Dan, and whispered to her young excited underlings that she was going to do "The Test".

It was an old double-act she and Dan had perfected years ago. When the victim went to the loo, Dan was given the nod. It worked best when there was someone present who'd never seen it done before. Last night there had been some trainee. Izzy had explained the system to her.

"Dan follows him in. To check on him ."

"Check *what?*"

"You *know*. Check him out. For Maddy."

The girl was still mystified.

"If he's up to it…. "Oh for God's sake – to see if he's well-endowed!"

The newbie was dutifully scandalised and exhilarated, the rest all whooped with laughter. "What if the guy catches Dan looking?"

"They never do – Dan's an expert," Manda explained. "Years of practice."

Maddy, sitting repentant now behind her desk, felt a flush of disgrace rising in her cheeks. Izzy sat back in her chair. "So? We never heard the final adjudication." Maddy opened her mouth to speak, but, thankfully, the phone rang. She quickly agreed to see the boss straight away and got up from behind her desk.

"Maddy! Tell me."

Maddy had headed Dan off last night. When he came out the gents, she moved quickly, diverting him out the door of the Tron bar. There was still warmth in the air, the swelter and noisy mess of the east end. Maddy scrabbled in her bag for her ten-pack and lighter. The setting sun had lodged itself between two tall buildings, an old red sandstone bleeding thickly in the light, the other all chrome and steel and glass, disappearing into its own glint. The laughter from inside the bar, the nicotine hit... Forget about corpses and estate agents; her city had better things to offer.

"You don't really look, Dan, do you?"

"Might."

But now Izzy wasn't going to budge from the door until Maddy told her.

"Minnow. Told Dan to throw him back."

Leaving the cubicle, she caught sight of herself in the glass – dark, a shadow of a woman. And smaller shadows floating around her. Two dead boys.

At the far end of the open-plan blankness, she stood and waited for the lift to come. She looked back down towards her section. Dan, impeccably dressed, on the phone, businesslike. Manda bent over her keyboard, fingers flashing, like she were gutting fish. Izzy, back perfectly straight on the chair, only the single document she was working on on her desk.

For all the nights out, the imprudent pranks, the gossip, they worked hard. Their profession was the centre of their lives. Some of that early missionary zeal, the decision to get paid less in the service of the Fiscal rather than make a mint in private practice, never left them. It burrowed itself in deep, under the jokes and the attitude. Companies killing off their employees in order to make a few quid more; negligent professionals letting unimportant people down; youngsters executed and dumped behind park bushes... somebody had to do *something*.

They felt the horror and meanness of every case, though they worked hard not to show it. Worked hard to make sure the police didn't cut corners but conducted investigations properly, found the right culprit. And once they had him, she and Izzy and Dan and a hundred others in this building like them, toiled night and day, to collate, precognose, present, prosecute, prove. Get the bastards behind bars.

Maxwell Binnie – *the* Procurator Fiscal. All the rest of them were Principal Deputes, Senior Deputes, Deputes. To prove he was *the* Procurator, his chair was higher, so visitors to his office had to peer up at him. He was in his fifties, tall, one of those men who grow better-looking with age. And authoritarian – he spoke to senior staff like Maddy as though they were trainees.

"Take me through it, Miss Shannon."

"Unexplained violent deaths. I've ordered the bodies to be removed for autopsy."

"Bullets to the head, I believe?"

"Both from the same gun? We can't tell if the victims were held down, if they struggled. I recommend we inspect organs for drug and alcohol content – were they insensible at the time of death?"

"Risk of HIV or hepatitis infection?"

"High I'd say. These two wouldn't have been sipping Merlot and nibbling Camembert."

"Age?"

"We'll find out. Seventeen? Younger?"

"How long do you need the bodies signed over for?"

"Long as possible."

Binnie jotted on his pad, like a dissatisfied school teacher. "Who's handling the case?"

"DI Coulter."

"C Division. Crawford's little gang. Good. I think you'll find Crawford will allow a little more PF activity than normal. We both sit on The Consultative Steering Committee on Delinquency and Crime. If these victims turn out to be under sixteen – even if they're not – we'll have to report to the Scottish Executive and the Press on it."

Maddy groaned inwardly. Binnie was clearly going to be on her back throughout the whole case.

At the afternoon session in Division A's incident room, disinclination fugged the air the way smoke did up to the ban last month. Scotland of all places leading the way in health and bad habits. The butt end in the ashtray, Maddy knew, was her. Bad form, a PF worming her way into a briefing. Inspector Coulter hadn't explained his reasons for inviting her, no reason on earth being good enough. Probably he wasn't even sure himself.

"If it's unhelpful, I'll go..."

"Nice to have a lady in our midst," Adams smiled. Which couldn't have pleased DS Amy Something, or the incident room co-ordinator, Trisha. The rest were men: four CID personnel, two of whom she recognised, the other two giving her the narrow-eye treatment. In the corner, the cheery Uniform from this morning – neither Billy nor Bob, she remembered now. Patterson. Patterson Webb. A cruel fate, ending up a Glasgow polis with an Edinburgh advocate's name. Then there was Simon, another Uniform she'd worked with before. Okay guy. They were waiting on Doc Holloway (all the jokes had been used up a very long time ago) and – Holy of Holies – Chief Constable Crawford Robertson himself. Why on earth would *he* make himself available at such an early point in an investigation? It was like turning up at a party without knowing it had a Grand Lodge theme. Another plain-clothes detective – who had the perfect disguise of looking more violent, boorish and stupid than your average hit man – entered late. Coulter got the meeting started, turning to DS John Russell.

"Okay. Re-cap. John?"

"Bodies found at 7.20 AM this morning, April 30 2005, by a jogger with a mobile. Pat – Constable Webb – was at the scene by 7. 30. DI Adams informed at that time, Crime Scene protocol in effect by 8.00."

"The jogger?"

"One James Docherty. Saw nothing else. Just the bodies, and he didn't take too close a look at them." Russell put his notes down. "Too busy spewing."

"Where is he now?"

"Was taken up to the Western. We have all his details. Merchant City address. Works at home – something in graphics."

Russell sat down, and Coulter walked to the middle of the room. "The park's being finger-tipped?"

"Half the force there with tweezers," Russell replied.

"Door-to-door?"

"The other half are ringing the bells of every house from Bentinck Street to Park Gardens."

"Extend it. Byres Road to Charing Cross. The path along the river – any other early-morning runners or cyclists out? If the victims made their own way to the park, or were brought – did anyone see them?"

Russell nodded, and wrote the instruction down.

Holloway finally arrived, in the company of another overweight middle-aged man, John MacDougall. All that was missing now was Maxwell Binnie to make up the four-ball. Maddy felt a sense of solidarity with the policemen around her. Suits like Binnie and Robertson were bad enough, but at least they had worked their way to the top. Political appointments like MacDougall just drove everyone mad. The Highlander – there was no mistaking *that*: he wore his accent and Island air like battle medals – had been appointed by the Scottish Executive to look into the problem of teenage delinquency. The School Czar the tabloids called him. Everyone in this room, though, suspected him of being just another overpaid senior manager, out to make their work harder.

"I hope you don't mind me listening in, gentlemen. I'll be as quiet as a mouse here at the back."

They did mind him listening in. He made Maddy feel

downright popular. Holloway reported only what everyone at the park this morning already more or less knew: two teenage boys, shot point blank in the side of the head. Holloway guessed .38s by the size of the holes and the charring.

DS Russell – always happier to contribute when the big boss was around – reported that he'd got a check put on the Missing Persons list. Somebody, somewhere would miss the boys sometime. The other CID officers of varying ranks selected their areas of enquiry. One had links into the gang scene; another the crack-cocaine/heroin market; a third the sectarian wars.

Maddy picked up her bag. They half-waved back. If there was any further information, they were waiting until she was safely out the way.

The morning's sweetness had curdled, the sky a simmering grey gruel. Maddy, heading west, waded against the flow of Sauchiehall Street shoppers. She'd worked till ten on Monday, had taken enough files home on Tuesday to bury an elephant, gone in early Wednesday and worked late last night. She could afford a little time on a Friday afternoon to tidy up her flat before the estate agent came.

Her route took her past the southern edge of Kelvingrove. There was nothing to connect the tranquil greenery, the perpetually dormant bowling greens, with the little corner of horror deep in the park's belly. Boards outside shops blurted the deadening news. "Bodies Found in Kelvingrove'".

Glasgow spreads like a stain, weeping along the least line of resistance in every direction, between mountains, down valleys, draining into the sea. But there's a secret geometry to it, a nervous system that makes death in the west felt and feared as keenly in Easterhouse or Giffnock. Today's double portion was pretty much on Maddy's doorstep. An incursion into her heartland.

At Lorraine Gardens she admired the street, as she always did, before opening the door. She'd been here for ten years, the only house she'd ever owned. The HQ of the private Maddalena Shannon, hybrid woman. A Mediterranean kitchen – terracotta tiles, colour-washed dresser, pots, pans and dried peppers hanging round the hob – that somehow looked absolutely nothing like a Mediterranean kitchen.

"White's the problem," Dan had said. He'd run his hand over the paint daubed straight onto the plaster, to give that Mexican adobe look. "Blue-based white doesn't work in the north. Looks great in Andalusia, looks like dogs' piss in Glasgow. What you need's a yellow-based white."

She'd salvaged from her childhood bedroom in Girvan a saccharine picture of Christ The Shepherd. Golden-locked boy in a soutane stroking a lamb. The irony hadn't come off. The whole house was a botched blend of attempted modernity and beefy auction-house furniture. She'd considered making a move, selling up, finding somewhere new. Roddy Estate Agent looked around the flat and said: "Declutter. One little word, one big task. But worth it."

Inspecting each room in turn, he'd propped himself up against the door jamb as if the vision before him might overpower him. He had the smile of a man consoling a bereaved but distant acquaintance. "Get rid of the books. Only leather-bound volumes sell a property."

Unread books, in other words. Hyndland had changed. When she had arrived, she'd sneered at the dusty pretension of the place. Lecturers, doctors and dentists with clapped-out bangers rusting between Doric pillars in driveways. Art collections clustered behind unwashed windows. Patched elbows and unkempt haircuts reading on threadbare sofas. The violin and piano practices of a screech of Gails, Robinas and Leos. Maddy had shaken her head at it all, yet here she was, a decade later, mourning its passing.

It was Roddy's area now. His soft-top silver sports car not conspicuous anymore outside her window, winking between SUVs and Beamers. At 36, Maddy was Old Hyndland while Roddy talked interactive tellies and surroundsound. Maddy blamed footballers. Once, they stayed safely out of the way in the southside and Bothwell. Since they'd started migrating from warmer climes they preferred the liveliness of the west end. She'd spoken the thought out loud to Roddy Estate Agent, and immediately wished she hadn't.

"Bulgarians, Hungarians, Australians." Roddy had rapped on her theme. "I've sold houses to Czechs, Latts, Poles, Danes and Swedes. Organised mortgages for Spaniards, Germans, Portuguese, Uruguayans and Geordies. Makes you wonder why our teams aren't doing better than they do."

"Cause they're all too busy poncing up their west end flats?" suggested Maddy. And putting them out of her price range. Still, they looked nice, the thick-locked and dark-curled foreign footballers, outside the cafes.

Roddy scanned his eyes over her bedroom like a client making up his mind in a Bangkok brothel, his gaze resting for a moment on the open-topped Moroccan laundry basket, tastefully bedecked with a pair of yesterday's knickers.

"Roddy," she'd said pleasantly. "Could you do me a favour? Could you get yourself to fuck out my house? Thanks."

She had been the PF in charge of a murder last year. A woman a little older than herself who had taken a knife in the stomach from a husband who had been kind and faithful for fifteen years. Moving house, apparently, had pressed the hitherto unknown button in his brain.

Maddy was walking the house with a cardboard box and a bin bag. Roddy had put her off the idea of moving in the near future but, bless him, he was right about the decluttering. Ornaments, pictures and old CDs that might fetch some charity shop a tenner were going in the box. Old letters and junk mail, general crap from ten years of living alone, in the bag.

She sat at her favourite window, the bay looking out onto a copse of trees heavy with themselves. She remembered one of her first cases. A twelve-year-old girl, snatched on a street between home and school and left all but eviscerated in a wood forty miles into the Lomond Hills. Maddy had spent nights then in this very seat at the window, weeping violently. But no tears would come now for these boys. Their hands reaching out for each other. Boys like that *never* reach out for one another, do they?

Walk twenty minutes in any direction from this house and you'd be in their world – Wyndford, Yoker, Ruchill. Twenty minutes to the next galaxy. Young feral males addicted to destruction, the sons of earlier feral, destructive males. They were hard to cry for. That in itself should have made her cry.

Jim Docherty came in from the kitchen and handed his wife a fresh-brewed coffee in a white china-bone mug. "Sure?"

"Any more caffeine," Alan Coulter said "and I'll need beta-blockers. I trust you've recovered from the shock?"

"Take up jogging they said. Do you the world of good." Docherty half-laughed and shook his head. A man in his late thirties, John Lennon specs, baldness disguised by a no. 1 haircut. Below an ironed shirt and smart trousers he wore a stained pair of slippers.

"Must be nice, working from home." Actually Coulter thought it must be hell. The flat was an expensive Merchant City job, so cramped for space that the bedroom was on an open mezzanine above their heads. For some reason – although there was no sign of ruffled sheets or underwear lying on the floor – Alan felt it was embarrassing.

"Yeah, it is. No rush-hours. Everything you need to hand."

The room they were in served as lounge, dining area and study, as well as bedroom overhead. There'd be a bathroom off the narrow hall outside and a tiny kitchen somewhere. Place would have cost them a fortune, though. Being ground floor, it didn't even have a view, and there was a pub right next door, which must be noisy at night.

"Are you a runner yourself, Mrs....?"

"Elaine. No. Gym girl." Elaine kept glancing up at the mezzanine too. Perhaps feeling the same embarrassment, or worried that it wasn't properly tidied. Coulter thought he detected a wistful glance – as if she'd like nothing better than to crawl back into bed. She didn't look as if she could muster the energy to even *get* to a gym.

"You're a graphic artist, Jim?"

"Not quite. Or rather, I am, but it's not what I currently do. My business partner is the artist – I do a bit of touching up, a veneer job for the clients."

"Who are?"

"We produce high-quality brochures, specs, ads, portfolios, whatever, for a range of clients." He had gone into business auto-pilot. "Anybody from the Council to big companies and political parties, to smaller stuff like indie bands, community organisations."

"And this company of yours is called...?"

"Sign-Chronicity."

On the easel at the moment was a series of coloured blocks intersecting at angles; amidst them could be made out a rough impression of a couple about to kiss, a figure behind them scowling.

"Who's that for?"

"Community radio station. Local kids making a soap opera based on their real lives."

"Whereabouts?"

"Moves around. The station sets up for a month in various deprived areas, puts on a few shows, including a soap-type drama, then moves on elsewhere."

"Where have they been recently?" Sergeant Russell had finally found his voice. He seemed, till now, to have been stupefied by the modern art paintings on the walls – semi-blank canvasses, or montages of dirty greys and browns – and the languorous slouching of Elaine.

"I've no idea. We just do the posters. Elaine here sometimes gets involved." He smiled towards her, but she didn't smile back. "Elaine's a designer."

"Yeah? What do you design?"

Mrs. Docherty answered Coulter's question as if she could hardly remember herself. "Play areas. Parks. Common rooms—"

"Always for youngsters?"

"I seem to have ended up doing that most, yes."

"Who advised you to take up jogging, Mr. Docherty?" Russell asked.

"Martin. Martin Whyte."

"Your business partner?"

"He's out every morning without fail." Docherty was smiling, swirling the coffee in his cup, but there was something reluctant in his voice. "Half an hour, morning and evening. An hour or more, Saturdays and Sundays. If I was as fit as him I'd not have been the one to find those kids."

"Sorry – how's that?"

"I don't go fast enough to pass anything without noticing."

"You weren't running alone yesterday?"

"No. Well, yes, when I found the bodies. I was trailing way behind Martin. When I saw the kids, he must have been a half a mile up the road."

"Did you inform us of this at the time?"

"I've no idea what I garbled into the phone that morning."

"Tell us more about Mr. Whyte."

When she was a rookie junior, Maddy could get the office to herself in the mornings. Hung over or not, the taste of reckless kisses, whether sour or sweet still on her mouth, she could shuffle her shoes off, tie back her hair with an elastic band, and get down to work. Now it was a race to see who could be at their desk first, showered and groomed, arranging power-breakfasts. Izzy was there already, at 7.05. Dan had been in and gone again. Manda would make up for them by arriving at least an hour late.

Alan Coulter had left, sometime over the weekend, a voicemail. "Our jogger wasn't alone. Work partner with him. Unfortunately, said gentleman is presently out of town on business."

Also a wifie up by Kelvindale with a view over the canal had seen several men walking along the cycle path at six o'clock the morning of the murders. They weren't winos and they didn't have fishing rods. "Can you believe that?" Coulter cackled on the answer phone, betraying a smoking habit from some time before Maddy knew him. "She sees dads regularly taking their kids angling at the crack of dawn. What for? Wild tellies? Freshwater condoms?"

One person was walking alone and the old dear thought he might have been a youngster. He had a stick he was trailing along the ground. Then there were two more people who she thought were older. She supposed they were all on their way to work, or coming back from work, or maybe a party. She wasn't clear about any peaked caps and track suits.

Coulter had been made Detective Inspector on one of Maddy's first cases. They'd taken to each other. The gaps in gender, age, background and outlook working to their mutual advantage. He was a married father of four; she a singleton increasingly unlikely to have kids whether or not she wanted them.

"That canal path's hoaching with arse bandits." Alan, she knew, only spoke like this outside the house. She'd been invited there a couple of years back for his daughter Lauren's eighteenth. The entire Coulter clan – even the black sheep, Ben, were pleasant-natured, bright-eyed and clean-living. Almost too polite.

He suggested lunch and signed off as Maddy was opening an attachment on her email. Doc Holloway's initial report.

The beatings the boys had received around the head, neck and torso, were not random – their wounds were remarkably similar. In particular, they each had deep incisions made around the area of the mouth. Under the bruising and blood lay carefully inflicted wounds. A slash across the cheeks so deep the under half of the face had fallen away the moment the bodies were moved. A second slash extended from the septum to under the chin. The attack was vicious or manic enough to have crushed the front teeth of one of the boys. Holloway couldn't be sure yet, but thought the knifing might have been inflicted before death.

No signs of struggle? Those lads wouldn't have stood, or lain, there and let someone do that to them. They'd have kicked out in pain, terror, if not in fury. There was no sign of drugs or alcohol. But the cadavers gave little indication of struggle. The whole drama had taken place in a few square yards – Holloway had appended notes from his colleagues at Forensics. The victims, more than likely, had fallen to the ground under the beating, and the gun was fired from the assassin's standing position. Whether one or more men had applied the beatings and the bullets, it was too early to say. A single long, black hair had been found on one of the corpses. DNA testing would go ahead first thing next week. Maddy hoped to God it wasn't hers.

Why hadn't they fought back? Because they knew it was hopeless? Or, they took their punishment like men, presuming that was an end to it. The gun was produced as a surprise addition – a magician's trick. Were they already unconscious when their executioner(s) stepped forward?

Maddy caught her reflection in the glass. Better than last week. But her clothes still looked like they'd been taken from another woman's wardrobe. She'd never intended to look like this. She thought: I dress myself like a stranger.

She managed, mid-morning, to get a hold of Dan over at the High Court. As dogged as ever, not allowing some posh advocate to muck up a case he had prepared without at least sitting in court and giving him the evil eye. "Here we go again," he said. "A vicious bastard's about to get away with murder. Literally." A taxi driver had backed over a client he'd just a minute earlier overcharged by several pounds. "One of these wee fly-by-night companies, carting folk around in vehicles fit for the knackers yard. Driver's famous for his racist rantings, and the hire just happened to be Asian. Despite a near-perfect precognition – though I say it myself – they can't make a murder charge stick."

"Maybe it wasn't murder, Dan. Maybe he just meant to break the legs. Culpable and reckless conduct? Who's defending?"

"Deena Gajendra."

Maddy smiled. "You've had it boy. One flash of those legs and any judge is a goner. Even if she's female."

Dan sat down and closed his eyes. "All that work, and my man'll get a ticking off, a fine and a spot of community service."

She prodded Dan on the shoulder to get his eyes open. "Tell me, Schemie Boy. Le Coq Sportif – and save the jokes – give me a profile of the average wearer."

Dan perked up. "There are a number of different models. The serious sportsman, all square-jawed and sweating manfully. That's the ones Le Coq pay to wear their gear. The ones who fork out the moolah, as ever, are skinny little squirts who get pregnant at fourteen or end up splattered in corners of parks."

Dan was sleek as a seal. Tall, fleshy, broad shouldered, thick black locks carefully sculpted around his neck. The kind of man who carries weight well. *Bien dans sa peau* as the French say. Suits – a different one for each day of the year it seemed – hung well on him. His surplus fat shouted health and wealth, not hamburgers and crisps. Maddy wondered if, de-suited, the effect might not be quite as acceptable. Were there 32C moobs flapping under his silk shirt? Still, he managed to look professional and affluent on a restricted salary, as only a particular breed of gay men can.

"Any particular gang?"

"*Crew.* Please. Can't say, but I have noticed a preponderance of Coq Sportif in the Drumchapel area. South tends more towards Nike. Easterhouse teams, Reebok. But underclass streetwear is a notoriously capricious niche." Despite the suits, the confidence, his rich voice, Dan McKillop was a child of the Schemes. He grew up in the less classy streets of Clydebank, among a likeable but deeply dysfunctional family. Three kids, three fathers, mum McKillop a monster of irresponsibility, talkativeness and fun. His dad all but killed him when – via local gossip – he found out that his boy was a shirtlifter. When Dan spoke flippantly about pregnant fourteen-year-olds, he wasn't being condescending. His sister had been one and was probably the dearest human being to him in his life. Wee brother Pat ran with boy racers south of the river (therefore wore, presumably, Reebok). How Dan had survived all that to become a respected and efficient Depute Fiscal, an assured and settled gay man and dependable friend, was a wonderful mystery to Maddy. Astonishing, too, that he still lived in Drumchapel – albeit in a big stone townhouse in the old village.

"Couldn't ask around, could you? Anybody gone AWOL recently? Any reason why anyone should? Who's playing with .38s?"

Dan took the print-out of Holloway's report Maddy had on her lap.

"Slashed," Maddy said. "Across the mouth. Vertically and horizontally." She made a little "X" an inch away from Dan's lips. "That mean anything? Omerta?"

"You've got to do something about that Sopranos fixation."

27

"*Both* of them. In exactly the same way. Deep enough to cut through gum, teeth, and, in one case, tongue. That's not a random act. Had they spoken out of turn? Were they about to? The cuts might have been made just before or just after death – either way, there's a message in it."

Dan got up to go, his hearing about to resume.

"That canal path leads to Drumchapel, Dan. There must be *something* you can find out."

"Are you suggesting that I have links with the criminal underworld, Mz Shannon, just cause I live in Drumchapel?"

"You might know a man who does."

Dan sighed, handed her back the report and promised to ask around. "After I've watched Ms Gajendra release a homicidal racist back out onto the streets."

"You have to admit – she's got her good points. As it were."

"Not my type."

"True, *I'd* go for her quicker, if I buttoned up different." She tried to smile but the muscles in her face were too taut. Two boys dead. Crosses scrawled over mouths like Stop signs.

A meeting with Adams wasn't giving him much to work on. Coulter listened to Adams making a meal out of very little. At this rate, he was going to miss his lunch with Maddy Shannon.

No weapons had been found. A killer who executed with such precision and dedication would hardly be daft enough to throw precious guns away in the immediate vicinity.

"There are traces of footsteps leading up to the patch behind the rhododendrons. One of the boy's trainers matches perfectly." Adams deduced, from the fingertip search and early forensics, that the boy approached the murder scene in the company of three others – the second victim and two unknowns. Probably males. That didn't quite match with the account the woman hanging out her window had given.

Nothing Coulter learned led anywhere – literally. The boys seemed to have been walked around a bit before ending up behind the rhodos. Perhaps with the intent purpose to hinder detection. Similar footprints had been identified on the canal path. But nothing precise – the surface of the path, dry as dust after a rainless week, was too disturbed by late evening runners, walkers, prams and bikes, to track the fatal journey far. The prints found furthest from the scene were to the west of the park itself.

The single strand of hair represented a glimmer of hope, but might just as easily belong to a victim's sister or girlfriend or someone next to him on the bus earlier that day.

It was 12.50 when the meeting finally broke up. Ten minutes to get to the west end for lunch. Just as he got to the door, Russell called after him. "Something's come in."

Alan wasn't quite through the doorway enough to pretend he hadn't heard.

"Nice to be held in such esteem." She was sitting at an outside table, sun specs, reading files, her hair a charcoal blur.

"Sorry. Got held up."

"Of course. You've an important big boy's job. I've got all the time in the world."

Coulter knew from experience not to keep fencing with her. He sat down across from her, his back to Byres Road. He hated eating outside. Cars blowing exhaust fumes all over your salad; the noise, the flies, the sun in your eyes, burning up one half of your face. He wanted a table and tablecloth, walls with wallpaper, peace. He'd never been in the Lochan before – but looking in the window, its interior was cool and inviting.

Maddy put away her file. "Anything new?"

"Let's order our organic pomegranate on bran oatcake first, eh?"

"Piss off. The grub's good."

29

She shouted on a waiter. A little too brusquely for Coulter who smiled twice as hard at the young man. He ordered black pudding and poached pear. Maddy didn't even look at the menu. "Steak and chips. Rare. No blue." She grimaced at Coulter. "That way you might just get medium in this city."

Coulter ordered the same and sparkling water, Maddy a large Semillon. He settled back in his chair, the table rocking on the cobbles with the slightest movement. Maddy took her shades off. "Okay, let's be civilised, then. How's the family?"

She meant it ironically, but he wanted a bit of space before she got worked up about the case. "Helping Lauren rid her house of Artex. Jennifer's studying day and night for her finals. Bethany's got a boyfriend and we're all hiding the fact from her mum."

"And Ben?"

"We don't talk about him. How's your family?"

"Do I have a family? Let's see – mum's trying to out-lonely and out-passion Judith Hearne. Granddad will be 92 next month, and he's still younger than I am. He's turning into a veritable study of beautiful old age, Nonno."

"And your dad? Still living it up in Tuscany?"

"We don't talk about him."

The waiter brought them their food and drink – lunchtimes move fast these days.

"So? Can we get on now?"

"This case is really pulling your chain."

"Pulling my *chain*? That one of Beth's? Not sure you've got the usage right."

"Stop avoiding the question. Two hoods clobbered in a park. Your nephews and nieces and all the nephews and nieces in all the world are all a little bit safer for it." Coulter took an envelope out of his pocket, slid it clandestinely over the table to her. She knew it'd be pictures, and if she wanted to look at them she'd have to peek inside. Peering at images of a double murder while sipping wine in a pavement café seemed inappropriate. The boys, cleaned up in the mortuary, blood scraped from their faces, lower jaws stitched back on, and with the help of professional photography, looked more like real individuals. One of them, she could see, was a shade gaunter than the other.

"Micky and Eddie. Micky's on the right, with the snicked eyebrow."

"Micky and Eddie?"

"Blood Brothers. That musical. Russell's idea. Never seen it."

"Me neither."

Micky was darker-haired, judging by the shadow over the skull and the eyebrows. Smaller-eyed than Eddie who, somehow, even pictured in this state, looked the more innocent of the two. Shorter, a hint of baby fat in what cheeks were left him. Their clothes were still blood-stained but, dug up from the mud, you could tell they were smart – according to their own code – when they ventured out yesterday morning. Mum would have had their tops and trackies all nicely washed. In one long-view shot, Eddie's trousers looked like they had an ironing crease down them. Both boys' shoes looked brand new.

The boys looked even younger than she had originally thought. If they walked up to their table now, sat down beside them, it would be difficult to know their age. These kids carry thirteen-ness right into their twenties – in their frail frames, suspicious eyes, hunched shoulders. At the same time, they had a depth of experience, a weariness that gave young teens the quality of ready-made men. Pre-chiselled, hardened for anything.

The brutal axles over their mouths were perfectly obvious now. Neat, considering how much force was needed to score through skin and flesh and bone. Micky's tailed off at one end, like slapstick on a miserable clown. Eddie's crisscrossed evenly up and down, splitting the septum and extending down under the chin, the vertical cut almost ear to ear. The waiter put Maddy and Alan's plates down on the table.

"We have a missing person report. Woman saying her son went out Wednesday evening and hasn't returned. Out of character."

"Where?"

"Govan."

"Who?"

"Don't know yet, Maddy. Just got the briefest of details from Russell as I was coming here."

She knew he knew and he wasn't telling her. She could insist. But not here, not yet. A social lunch on a Saturday, Coulter with Police Department pics that should never have left his office.

They both ate in silence for a moment. Then Maddy spoke without looking at him. "There was a guy at my school. Stevie. Stevie Chalmers. Wired to a Mars Bar. In trouble with everyone, about everything, all the time. Ran with the bullies, but wasn't one. Got slapped about by his own mates when some mad sense of injustice grabbed him and he stuck up for the spotty diddies."

"One of each in every class."

"I was a chubby girl, you'll be surprised to hear."

He wasn't. Maddy was still unfashionably, and temptingly, hearty.

"Stevie comes up to me one day and goes "All you need to do, Maddo, is run around the block a few times. Gie it a month and you'll be pure skinny.""

"Such wisdom."

"Next Saturday morning, I came out and wheezed my way round the park. Guess what? Out of nowhere comes Stevie Chalmers, all shorts and legs like knotty string. Kept me running for nigh on twenty minutes with his daft patter and stupid jokes. Did that every Saturday for weeks."

"And did you get skinny?"

"Does it look like it? I made a friend, but. A lanky hiss of piss whose future was mapped out in his brothers in Borstal, his Da in jail, on the crushed expression on his face when he wasn't making other folks laugh. A Micky. An Eddie."

Alan forked up the last bite of his black pudding – which, irritatingly, was also his second – then put it back down again. "Our jogger who discovered the Blood Brothers? Yesterday was the first day he'd ever jogged in his puff."

When she and Packy Shannon separated, Rosa di Rio bought a flat in the southside. Maddy managed to persuade her that she couldn't afford the west end – having your mum next door was hardly conducive to living a riotous life. Payback came on Sunday mornings when Maddy had to go cross the river and chauffeur her mother around. Sundays, feast days, holidays of obligation – plus regular coffees at Fazzi's, lunches at Sarti's, groceries at Peckham's West End, and a daylight robbery of a dress shop on Hyndland Road. Maddy went, picked Rosa up, saw to her spiritual and earthier needs, took her back home and, if she spent an hour with her there, could get away with only one phone call between trips.

Rosa was a lesson in how to be 65. Slim, elegant, as pained as a teenager, naturally silver hair you'd pay a fortune for at the stylist's. She hung on Maddy's arm going up the steps of the church. Not because she needed the support but because that's the way you entered church in the old country. The old country! Apart from childhood holidays – the scene of her One Great Tale, starring Marco and Irish Packy – Rosa hadn't lived a single day in Italy.

She hadn't always been so classy and slim either. The transformation happened when she finally ditched Maddy's dad. All those years working in the chip shop – Maddy's training ground for the world of commerce, petty theft, malnourishment, Eddies and Mickies – Rosa was an apron-wrapped, grease-stained, strongwoman. Biceps to shame a weightlifter from humping sacks of tatties and fat-filled chip vats around. She developed a voice powerful enough to defeat the explosion of batter being thrown into boiling fat, after-pub sing-songs and school dinner rabbles. She still had the voice.

"Not up the side aisle, Maddalena! In the middle."

At every visit to church Maddy tried to hide, as she had done since a kid, in the pews at the side-altars. Rosa liked to be where she could be seen. She would take out her rosary beads, sing out loud, and respond enthusiastically. Maddy was sure her mother was no more religious than she herself was. Matters of personal morality, the communion of saints, metaphysical concerns, never intruded on Rosa's life at any other time. Church was only part of the continuing war between Rosa di Rio and Packy Shannon, now waged across oceans and frontiers.

After the separation, Packy struck with a *coup de théâtre* that took the wind out of everybody's sails. *He* was the one who went back to Italy. Donegal Packy bought himself an old farmhouse on a hill in Tuscany, not a kick in the pants away from Rosa's ancestral lands.

With every foot that Packy put wrong – coming home from the pub drunk, late, arguing, not arguing, talking too much and talking too little, frying the fish too much, making the batter too heavy – Rosa threatened to "go home". That Italy had not been the Di Rios' home since 1919 was neither here nor there. That Rosa could survive a single day alone south of Girvan was unlikely. It didn't matter – she was simply letting Packy know that she had made a big mistake in her life – him.

"Marco would never have let me suffer like this!"

So, what revenge! He probably hated it over there, Packy. He'd never learned Italian, and coffees and brandies on pavements were surely no match for big frothy pints and solid oak bars, shouting the odds about Ireland and socialism. Maddy refused to visit him, so it was possible he was living the life of Riley, but she doubted it. Sweet vengeance kept him going on a daily basis. Her mother's only response was to stop talking so much about Italy, but *become* more Italian, in a B-Movie kind of way. The Gina Lollabrigida of Shawlands; Sophia of St. Catherine's.

The Mass was said by a different priest than usual. The old guy with the stutter must be ill, or at the nineteenth hole. Shame. Maddy liked the show he put on – gruff and bad-tempered and more quintessentially an oul' Oirish priest than any minor character in Father Ted. There was a young zealot on the altar instead this evening. Almost good-looking, like a failed audition from The Thorn Birds. Unusually, Scottish. Maddy – Maddalena Benedetti di Rio Shannon – thought all priests were Irish or Italian.

The priest's sermon was a hideously happy series of silly anecdotes involving cute kids from the local school, his own auld granny, and Great Celtic Football Players of the Past… all of them shoe-horned together to reflect the meanings of biblical parables. Father Mike, as he matily called himself, was a self-satisfied bore, but Maddy was envious of him. She was envious of everyone who had it taped. Her dad and his socialism. Dan McKillop and a philosophy invented entirely by him: humanistic cynicism. Izzy and her private conservatism, public benevolence. Even Coulter must have *some* philosophy that helped him create his near-perfect little family. Maddy had never found a system that Explained Everything. She drifted off to Father Mike talking some nonsense about suffering little children; the face of the shepherded lamb in her living room becoming Eddie's – torn, battered, but still serenely smiling.

DI Alan Coulter and DS John Russell were sitting in the living-room of Anne Kennedy – a woman with small dark eyes like peek-holes in a long, flat door of a face. A door, Alan thought, she'd no intention of opening. Her house was a Govan new-build, poky rooms, sparsely furnished and decorated, but still more of a home than the Docherties' Merchant city pad would ever be.

"Your son's name is Simon Kennedy."

"Sy."

"And he's what age?" Coulter wanted to hear her say it.

"Thirteen. Fourteen in ten days."

Holloway's lowest guesstimate had been sixteen to just under. This woman – long and lank even sitting, as if hard times and stress had stretched the elasticity out of her – couldn't be the mother of the murdered boy. At least, not *their* murdered boy. "Sy done this before, Anne? Disappear."

"This time's different. He used to live wi' his daddy. But now I've got myself sorted. He's never bunked off from here."

"In how long?" Russell asked.

"Near a year now."

"D'you mind me asking Anne – sorted from what?"

Her dress was bright yellow, new or washed specially for the police, plain like an overall. Her hair was a rich solid brown, pinned back behind her ears. "Not drugs, if that's what you're thinking."

"Weren't thinking anything, Anne."

But Anne Kennedy had her case for the defence at the ready. "I had Sy when I was sixteen. Everyone went mental, so I did too. Me and Tone – Sy's daddy – got back together when I was nineteen. But it was on and off, you know?" Coulter wondered if this was the longest speech Anne had ever made. "In my twenties I acted like I was in my teens. Anyhow, I've settled down now. Got a job. This place. My Ma and me are talking again. Tony and me are history but he does his bit for the boy."

"When Sy went missing before," Russell was being more direct with this worried woman than Alan thought necessary, "where did he go?"

"There was a kids' home up by Shawlands. He was in there for a while, when Tone was down south and I was

being an arsehole. He made mates there. He could hide
in their rooms, even get fed, without the staff realising he
was around."

"Down south?"

Anne stared at Russell. Coulter sighed. Russell had no
idea what it was like to have kids. Coulter, with four of
them, couldn't imagine what it'd be like for a son or daughter to go missing. "Anne, if your husband was in prison, it's
best we know, the more we can find out about Sy...."

"Saughton. Five year. Armed robbery. Wasn't his fault.."

"But he's out now?"

"Eighteen month ago."

Coulter wanted to get the subject back onto Sy. "He
was put into care, you say? Why? What did Sy do, Mrs.
Kennedy?"

She steeled herself. "Shoplifting. Bit of cheek to the
teachers. Sy's no' a bad kid, mister, just a bit wild at times."

"Have you checked with the home if they've seen him?"

She nodded, then shook her head.

"Which school did he normally attend?"

"Cross High."

"Tell us about the last time you saw him," Russell cut in.

"Wednesday evening. He was fine. Nothing special.
There's five-a-sides over at the sports complex. I assumed
he was going there."

"Did he take his kit with him?"

Anne Kennedy looked at Coulter when she answered, as
if Russell was just a voice in an earpiece, a translator. "His
kit and his clothes are the same thing. Plays in trackies and
trainers. Gets a shower when he comes in."

"Except he didn't. Come in."

"The boy's father, Mrs. Kennedy—"

"Tony. Got his own house over in Partick."

"He be there just now?"

"Doubt it. He bought himself a van. Set himself up doing
deliveries. Gets a lot of work. London even."

Russell smiled at Coulter. "Wonder if the Inland Revenue know."

Coulter frowned. "We're not taxmen, Mrs. Kennedy."

"Aye, you are," she said, matter-of-fact. "Anyway. Tony does his bit for the boy."

Life, Coulter reckoned, was working out just fine for Tone, after his wee stretch for violent crime. It was Anne who had been pulled out of shape – all the recoil chewed out of her. Coulter pretended to write in his pad and, not raising his eyes, asked as casually as he could: "Just out of interest. What make of trackies?"

"His newest. Coq Sportif. Like he wanted."

He wasn't sure if the woman had noticed the wince he tried to hide. "What about friends, Anne? Had a special mate he hung about with?"

"None in particular, no."

"What's your theory?" Coulter finally said. "Where do you reckon Sy is, right now, Anne?"

She looked out the window – a reasonable view from the Kennedys' second floor flat. Lots of bright cloudless sky. "He's in the shit. Life that boy's had... mister – those bodies found in the park...?"

Alan told the truth. "We think they're older than Sy, and probably from north of the river. But right now – anything's possible."

"If it is him, my wee stretch o' sanity's just ended."

The Fiscal, Maxwell Binnie, was visiting his underlings one by one to show off to his new Committee pal, John MacDougall, the School Czar. "You'll be dealing with the Kelvingrove case, I hear?" MacDougall asked Maddy at the door of her office.

"If they ever catch anyone."

"So you take nothing to do with it until there's a court case?" MacDougall had been a teacher or lecturer or something. Nothing to do with the law or the police. He'd been drafted into the Steering Group on Youth Crime and Delinquency because of a lifetime's dedication to young people. Maddy couldn't imagine him ticking off a naughty first year, let alone shouting the odds in the Scottish Parliament. Not with an accent designed for kindly remarks and reciting poetry.

Maxwell Binnie got in an answer, even though MacDougall had clearly addressed Maddy. "The police will keep us abreast of the progress of the investigation but, yes, you're right, John, our real work comes once there has been an arrest."

"And what do you do then?"

This time Maxwell allowed his underling to respond. "We study all the evidence. Sometimes re-interview witnesses. Precognose the case—"

"Precog...?"

"Question witnesses, collate the data, bring all the productions – evidence – together, decide on an argument, have everything ready for the prosecution."

"Which you yourself then present in court?"

Maddy looked at Binnie, who shuffled for a moment. "It's not usual. Although Miss Shannon here is a solicitor advocate." He gave his best patronising smile. "Passed her exams a year or so back. There's a general feeling, however, that if you've been involved in the precognition of a case, you're too close to it to prosecute properly."

"In which case," Maddy said merrily to MacDougall, "we pass on all our hard work and months of preparation to an advocate who follows our advice for five times the money."

MacDougall looked at Binnie. "Does seem a shame, doesn't it? No chance of this delightful lady prosecuting the Kelvingrove case?"

Binnie walked away. "We'll see."

Maddy smiled broadly at the retired schoolteacher, and he waved as he turned to follow the Fiscal.

She returned to her fish-bowl cubicle, her email

pinging. Coulter. Had Maddy ever come across a home for kids called Lochgilvie? She emailed back that she hadn't, but would ask a colleague who'd done a lot of work with children's panels. While she waited for a response she discovered that Lochgilvie House had its own website.

The place appeared rather grand, set back a little off the street, two typical southside townhouses knocked into one. If you looked closer at the photograph, however, and you could see most of the windows have cracks in them, one completely boarded up. All the curtains had either been torn or torn down. The garden was like a little muddy patch of the Somme.

The text that went with the proud photo was determinedly jaunty. "Glasgow City Council have a long standing and deeply held commitment to the youth of our city – especially in their time of need." It listed a variety of services it offered young people – counselling, training, school taxi service, family links, ecumenical church projects, community involvement schemes.

There was a picture of the Home's director, a Mrs. Janet Bateman, with two of her staff, an older man and a younger woman. They were smiling – stalwartly, Maddy thought. She minimised the site, took out her Petrus files. But put them straight back again when Dan knocked and entered.

"Report, ma'am, from the desolate land of Drumchapel, far oe'r the sea.."

"See? You do keep bad company."

"There *is* a certain excitement in the neighbourhood. Groupings of young gentlemen surrounding older, better-dressed ones at corners. Talk of some generalissimo from London spotted loitering round local closes. Amazing what you can find out at the check-out of the local Home Bargains."

"Hey, you're looking at the chip-shop queen here. All this wisdom you see before you was acquired over the judicious sprinkling of salt and vinegar. Haven't the police noticed anything?"

Dan picked her pen up off her desk and began clicking it annoyingly. "Possibly. There's been a heavier presence of late."

"God – do CID and Uniforms never talk to each other? Coulter's never mentioned any of this."

"Probably no connection. Just some internecine skirmishing."

"How many connections do you need!"

"Oh dear, I can see where this is going to lead. Maddalena Shannon – Caped Crusader."

"Or just trying to do my job?"

"Or alleviating crass bourgeois guilt?"

Maddy's email chirped again. She stuck her hand out towards Dan.

"Pen."

God loves alcoholics and workaholics – He lights the way though they make no contribution to the journey other than moving their feet. Coulter was at Tony Kennedy's door within minutes of hearing the man had reappeared. Half eleven at night. DS Russell stood beside him, staring at his shoes – this could've waited till tomorrow.

Before Tony had finished opening his door, in a close backing nearly onto the Clyde, he'd clocked Coulter as the filth. Coulter could tell. "Take it easy. I'm not here to give you hassle."

A moment, and then Tony asked. "Sy?"

"What makes you think so?"

"I don't know."

Coulter brought the man up to speed, following him into his kitchen. Spick and span – the way a man learns in the army. Or in pokey.

"Disappeared?! How d'you mean, disappeared? Nobody told me nothing."

"You've been away, Tony boy," Russell snapped back. "Where were you?"

"Dundee."

"Can you prove that? Order forms, invoices?"

The knee-jerk clenching of the fists was quickly followed by Tony suddenly paling. "Fuck. The boys in the park. I heard on the radio."

"It's okay, Mr. Kennedy. There's no direct link. It's unlikely that your son has anything to do with Kelvingrove."

He'd be, what – five foot nine-ish? Thirty-three years old. In prison from twenty-four to thirty. He and two accomplices stormed a pub after hours one Saturday. Daft have-a-go-hero barman got himself killed. Not at Kennedy's hands – one Billy Mitchell, well known to the police, had the gun. Mitchell gets himself shot in the subsequent chase. Dies, to everyone's delight, even his own family's, in hospital a week later. Anthony Kennedy got ten years, served six.

"You've no idea where Sy is?"

Tony sat at the kitchen table and stared at the salt cellar, as if it held the answer.

According to all the documents Coulter had read that day, Kennedy had been a model prisoner. Liked by inmates and screws alike. Once out, he never broke his parole. He negotiated – with the help of the parole office and a voluntary prisoner support organisation – a loan for a second-hand van. Paints "A Van & A Man" on the side, and goes touting for business. Folk hire him for flittings, moonlightings, shifting washing machines or dryers from parents' houses to kids' flats. He undercuts parcel delivery services, breaks the speed limit to get farm produce into town. Has even delivered fresh-caught seafood from up north all the way to Glasgow and London. "What Anne's told you'll be right. She knows the boy better than I do."

"I need you to do something for me, Tony." Coulter sat down in the chair next to him.

"What?"

"Just go see. Belt and braces job. Elimination purposes. It won't be pleasant, but it'll clear your mind and help our investigation."

The clouds hadn't burned away yet, the morning woolly and colourless. Maddy walked along Argyll Street, passing other somnambulant workers. Tony Kennedy was waiting at the door of the mortuary when Maddy turned the corner.

They hardly spoke as they made their way inside, through the hospital and chemical-plant smells, the disinfected corridors; cold tiled. The entire building a monument to the shortness of life and the banality of death. She didn't need to be here; she was like a moth to a flame with this case. Kennedy with his little legs had to take two steps to every one of hers, but keeping a little ahead. He looked so alone. "I telt her, No point, Anne. I'll go alone. You'll only upset yoursel' for nothing."

Maddy hoped, and believed, he was right. Pathology's report wasn't enough to put some poor guy through an ordeal like this. Sy Kennedy was too young to be either Micky or Eddie. "They telt me it'll be a bit full-on," Tony said, not really to her. "Not good at blood and stuff." She stopped herself from saying that must be a drawback for an armed robber.

They were met by WPC Dalgarno, Doctor Niven and a mortuary supervisor Maddy had come across before. They entered the already prepared room in silence, like Kennedy was being led quietly into the electrocution chamber. Two beds had been set up. Both bodies covered. The supervisor turned down the first sheet. A face so bashed and bruised you'd think it would be impossible to identify. But there was no need to pull back the second sheet.

The Greeks, Etruscans, Romans, French, you name it, each

in turn had wrenched the best out of Ettore's home ground, and left him with dust.

Ettore is walking back from Portoferraio, where he managed to get a day's work unloading supplies from the mainland. He sees Antonella, outside the house half a kilometre away, tending the herb garden. He hears the boys' shouts, Vittorio and Carlo playing happily, home from school. The local priest is forever saying Count your blessings, Ettore. Maybe he's right. But how does a man know when it's time to stop counting, to do something that'll earn you blessings in the future.

His grandfather had tended vines here, like his fathers before him, never suspecting that a disease was slowly rotting them. When Ettore's dad returned from the war and the mustard gas cleared from his nostrils he smelled the sickness in the earth.

On this island, men have been taken away to die in wars they never understood or cared about. They'd died in fields, on foreign mountain tops. At sea, in boats that needed repair. His father had taken bullets in his leg in Africa, thirty years ago when he wasn't much more than a boy. Ettore himself, only a year ago, had just escaped death at Austrian hands at Caporetto. A flesh wound he thanked God for, as the army had sent him home and had never recalled him. Those who escaped fighting for king or prince or government stayed at home and kept up the battle with the earth.

They had kept on tugging at the soil, pouring their lives into it, because Elba had given them good things. Rich times when no one came to demand their lives in battle, when the sea was calm and abundant, and the earth green and moist. Any day now, Ettore's little patch of land might send through more shoots. Any day now he might be able to feed his boys, his wife, more heartily.

But the big war that had half the men of the world shooting each other, dying in holes in the ground, in planes that singed the sky, was ending. Any day now, friends and family who had survived would return. And look for work on Portoferraio harbour, where there was hardly a day's shift for Ettore already. Any day now, the ground might cease to give him anything at all.

Ettore remembered childhood meals composed of wild berries from the bushes further up the hill. Those bitter little pills still managed to live when the grapes and the olives and even the beet had died. Berries and thistle-leaves, water from the well – that was their dinner, and breakfast. Perhaps a small fish his father had pleaded with a fisherman not to throw back in. Things had got better since, but the pendulum seemed to be swinging back again. It looked so beautiful, his island, but a fickle, mean little heart beat under its surface.

"Ettore. Where would we go?" Antonella wasn't happy as far away as the other side of Campo Nell'Elba.

"Where Roberto and Vincente and Vito and Tonio and the rest of them went."

Milan and Rome and Spain and France. More, of late, as far as England. The Benedetti family over by Nisporto were getting mail back once a month or more from Scozia.

"Where's Scozia?" Carlo had asked him one day.

"Near America," his mother had intervened, though Ettore didn't think that was right.

"Let's give it another year," Antonella will say tonight, if he speaks about blessings and worries and plans. Ettore didn't *want* to go. His home ground was like a dying, miserly old man, hanging onto its last few paltry possessions. But the view down over the sea! The warm little house, his friends up in the village, Vittore and Carlo laughing in the sun...

If they left, Ettore would be the first not to make a life for his family in San Piero dell'Elba, with its little stream lingering carelessly through their field and slice of hillside. For all Ettore knew the Di Rios went all the way back to those Greeks and Etruscans. Settled men, happy to stay on their island home, run back to it the moment peace was declared. Yet there was Tommaso making a living for himself in London. Sending money back to his family. He said there was more work there, and all over Inghilterra, and in this Scozia. A man can either stay and watch his sons grow weak on a diet of memories and pride, or he can come out fighting, find another way to live.

Carlo came out of the house and walked towards him. Ten years old and already only a head or so shorter than Ettore. But thin, so thin. Even when he clenched his muscles, his limbs weren't much broader than pine-tree twigs. A new decade was looming. What would be right for Ettore di Rio and his family in the 1920s? He didn't really believe in God – why the hell should he – but he prayed anyway for guidance.

Carlo remained quiet by his side – even when six year old Vittorio came running up shouting and singing and spinning round and around like a swallow at dawn. Older brother and father looked at him with serious faces, until at last the child broke Ettore's troubled mood. Ettore laughed and Carlo chased Vittorio back down the hillside, the two of them arms akimbo like swooping hawks.

Matt or Bert – the guy she'd done the test on – was in the same coffee shop as Maddy and Rosa.

"Why do they have to give you such big cups?" The coffee her mother had was officially a medium latte but was the size of a soup bowl. "On the Continent you get a nice dainty little cup."

On the Continent. Holidays in Italy as a kid – where she would have been very unlikely to have been in many cafes – and one holiday in France. Eight years ago, in a mad last bid to save their marriage, she and Packy had gone to Paris for four days. The way she referred to the Quartier Latin ever since you'd think she nipped over every second weekend.

It had been a tough week. Petrus had continued to give Maddy the run-around – reports that obscured proper information, complaints about her department's approach. A negligence case that had been pending for months finally went her way, Wednesday afternoon. Then on Friday morning she had to lift tough Tony Kennedy off his knees on a mortuary floor.

Names changed things. Sy Kennedy. A punctured-sounding name. But it gave Victim A, "Eddie", a history, flesh, a direction down some inevitable path that led to being murdered in a park on a sunny spring morning. Numbers made the equation different too. Fourteen. Sy Kennedy was only fourteen years old.

"Nonno's party's only a month away, Maddalena."

The celebration of her grandfather's Big Adventure. The Di Rio family's very own Holiday of Obligation, the sacrificing of chickens for cacciatore, whole yields of peppers for home-made ciabatta luscious and slippery, entire legs of Parma ham, vats of imported Ligurian wine and extended family gossip. Maddy looked forward to it every year.

The guy – Matt – had spotted her. He smiled and gestured he'd come over in a minute. Maddy got out her phone.

"Can't you sit for a minute without talking to somebody who's not here?"

"Dan," Maddy said, smiling at Rosa, "guess who I'm looking across at?"

"Your mother. You told me."

"No no. I'm looking past *her*." Rosa looked round, mystified and annoyed.

"Let me guess – any one of a string of guys who you profess interest in but about whom you'll do nothing."

"Matt... Thingy. From the Tron. Did you really *look?*"

Dan sighed. "A slightly under-proportioned male."

"*Grazie, collega.*"

She put away her phone. Her mother glared at her, and Matt nodded over again. But he looked a little anxious at the smile she gave him, and got deeper into conversation with his male friend, glancing up at her furtively. "What was *that* about?" Rosa demanded.

Maddy changed the subject back to Nonno's party. Dan was right, though – she was as bad as her mum, endlessly playing a role. Lusty Latin lover, always ready with a wink and a suggestive one-liner. It was becoming pathetic; a parody of the woman she imagined she'd be when she was a child.

Jim Docherty was the business side of Sign-Chronicity and lived in an arty pad in the Merchant City; Martin Whyte was the artist, but lived in pebbledash land in East Kilbride. Not even any pictures on the wall.

"You don't work from home, Mr. Whyte?"

"Got a studio in Glasgow. WASP."

"At the Briggait. I know it," DI Alan Coulter said, easing into the interview.

"Where were you this week?" DS John Russell said, going straight for broke.

"You know where I was. You phoned the office, my mobile, sent emails and text messages."

"You weren't keen on replying."

"I was busy."

Russell flicked through his notes. "At... Artizan plc?"

"In London. They deal in paper, inks – all the stuff we use. I go down twice a year."

"Must be important if you can't return a call from the police asking about a murder."

"Tell us about the morning of the sixth." Coulter decided going for broke might be easier after all.

"I met Jim at quarter to seven."

"Mr. Docherty tells us you were very keen on him jogging. Why's that – get lonely out there alone?" Russell really wasn't taking to Martin Whyte.

"Jim was out of condition. He was sluggish around the office. He was the one that suggested I get him running."

"Go on."

"We met at the bridge at Kirklee. It's easy to park there. That's where I always start. We spoke for a minute or two and then went into the park to start running."

Russell brought out an OS map of the area around Kelvingrove. "Could you trace your route, Mr. Whyte?" Russell laid the map on the coffee table, and the three men moved closer round it. "We came in at this gate here, ran down onto the river." He traced his finger along the lines of the path. "Crossed over it here. The Ha'penny bridge. Then I normally do a little loop round this green here—"

"Why?"

"Because I like it. and the entire run takes exactly half an hour." He went back to the map: "We came up here, alongside Garrioch Road, kept going southwards. Around... *here,* I lost sight of Jim. I'd been keeping the pace down, encouraging him along, but he seemed to be doing fine, fitter than I'd expected, and I kind of forgot about him. Sped up into my old rhythm."

"And here," Coulter pointed at the map, "is where he found the bodies."

Alan Coulter's phone rang. He walked out into the hallway, keeping one ear open for Whyte's replies.

"You must have run right past them," Russell continued.

"S'pose so."

"How much ahead of Mr. Docherty were you?"

"Couldn't have been much. Three minutes? Five or six at the most."

"How could you not have seen two dead bodies?"

"I don't know. I know that route so well, my mind's on my work mainly."

"Mr. Docherty saw them."

"Jim was out of breath. He stopped. Unluckily for him, just beside the rhododendron bushes."

Coulter stepped back in the room looking a different man to the one who had left a moment ago. Both Russell and Whyte clocked it, and moved a step back from him.

Coulter took a minute to study Martin Whyte closer. Reassessing him. Lean, small, scrubbed. Fingernails short and spotless, clean chinos, ironed shirt, neatly cropped black hair.

"Jim said you run twice a day. The same route?"

"Usually. Why? I sometimes change – just for variety."

"Did you run the same route the night before you and Jim went out?"

"Can't remember offhand. It's possible."

"Do you live alone, sir?"

Whyte matched his new formal manner. "I do."

"When was the last time you had your hair cut?"

A pause, then, "Monday."

"This Monday? Three days ago?"

Russell stiffened. What had Coulter learned on the phone? Not a DNA match with Whyte – forensics would take longer than that. Did Whyte have previous? Whyte himself didn't react in any visible way, but stood staring at Coulter.

"Where were you last night?"

"Here. Working."

"Alone?"

Maddy wasn't too keen on Semi Monde. Up-market, Ibiza-chic drapes and hefty furnishings, background trip-hop, teeming. Glasgow trying to imitate what it thinks Reykjavik or Prague might be like. Age range from barely legal to verging on creepy (Maddy knew which end of the spectrum she was on). Not out-and-out gay, but pretty fruity, though the sex is all show. No one's quite as rich, or glam, or gay, as they're trying to make out. The conversations are about bosses and holidays and last night's telly.

So when she spotted Alan Coulter at the door searching for her she was relieved – she's better these days at professional woman than party girl. Until she caught the look on his face: a picture of hunched misery. Only something deadly serious could bring Alan to a place like Semi Monde. She walked past him out the door into the damp calm of the street.

"Sorry," Alan said, arriving by her side, keeping his gaze on the opposite side of the street. "Maybe this could have waited till morning."

"Clearly not."

"Had to tell somebody." Coulter turned around, not towards her, but until he was staring in the window at the laughing, noisy, overdressed customers of Semi Monde. "There's another one. Found this morning. Same deal. Beaten up. Bullet to her head."

"*She?* Same age?"

Alan nodded. "Not very old anyhow."

"Cross on the lips?"

"Don't know yet."

He was looking in the window, but he was seeing corpses. "Who the hell goes around executing fourteen year-olds?"

II

The girl lay on a gurney, Maddy, Coulter and the pathologist assembled round her, like a macabre nativity scene. She
was covered up to her neck in crisp white cloth.

"A week," said Dr. Erina Niven. "Entomology will give
us a pretty accurate time, but I'd say we're several generations of blow-fly down the road. The warm weather may
have speeded things up. And unfortunately she's been got
at." Niven glanced down at the girl's covered side. Maddy
looked up enquiringly at Coulter. "Foxes," he whispered,
guiltily.

The face was swollen, discoloured, but still there
remained something of the real girl that had inhabited this
battered casing. Her hair was pulled tightly back into a
pony-tail which bounced, childlike, as the pathologist – an
older woman Maddy had never worked with before – pulled
the sheet further down her neck. The mortuary wheezed
around Maddy. A place of death yet with its own deep, slow
breath. The stale gurning of machines, air-con, struggling
lighting, sounded like a repressed growl.

Dr. Niven displayed the girl's neck and shoulders like a
magician's trick. "No cuts to the lips or jaws. Bullet to the
left hemisphere splitting the parietal."

Maddy tried to keep looking only at the eyes. Closed,
like a statue's. The girl had been found, like Sy and Micky,
amongst flowers.

"No signs of struggle?" Coulter asked.

Niven shook her head and covered the girl up again.
"Very close range."

"What age?"

Niven sighed and stared at the covered shape of the girl.
"She could be as young as fourteen."

Alan Coulter put his hand gently on Maddy's back as they walked out of the room.

"I could come with you."

Coulter handed Maddy an envelope – more details of a crime that wouldn't normally be in the Fiscal's hands at such an early stage. "Whyte's in the station, Maddy. You'd better stay away. For the good of your case."

There were a couple of decent pubs near the mortuary still open but neither of them suggested a nightcap. They stood out in the street, the air spiky cool under a merry sky of stars. Maddy fingered the ten pack in her jacket pocket. "No news of the other boy?"

Coulter shook his head. "Nobody's got a clue who he is."

"No one else reported missing?"

Coulter shook his head. "Doesn't match any missing person report the length and breadth of Britain."

She didn't *feel* tense. Nausea and gloom were natural after a visit to the morgue. If anything, she felt lax, disconnected. She'd been part of the Solemn Team for years now, up to her oxters in murders and corpses. But Sy, and now that poor girl... and only a quiet graphic artist in the station to explain it. Whyte a murderer? Not from what Coulter had told her of the man. Hardly sounded like the demon who was turning so much young flesh into dull putty. An unassuming professional from suburbia. No record. Likes jogging. "All you have on him, Alan, is a careless shortage of alibis?"

"Damn sight more than that. He ran right past the boys' bodies!"

"Probably another dozen joggers did the same."

"Ran past the scene of the crime the night before."

"What – casing the place?"

"Maybe."

"From what you've told me, he doesn't sound like the type who could strong-arm two sturdy teenage boys into being shot."

Coulter and she were genuine friends – but this kind of thing would always divide them. How the Prosecution look at a crime, and how the police look at it. Once they had a suspect they convinced themselves he was their man.

"He was out running *again* the night the girl died. He has black hair—"

"Jesus Alan! That puts me and half of Glasgow into the frame!"

" – Which he got cut just before the police came calling. He works with kids. His partner's wife designs playgrounds." Coulter looked away. He hated falling out with Maddy. She didn't understand that you needed something in the bank; some sense of forward motion. A suspect gave you some kind of bearing, some *in* into the murders. Coulter and Russell and everyone involved in the case needed Whyte.

"But *why*, Alan? Why kill kids? Does he buy drugs?"

"Not that he admits to."

"Does he kerb-crawl? He'd have to be into both boys *and* girls—"

Coulter shrugged - you couldn't out-guess the mess of some folks' lives in this city. Sy Kennedy was no angel. Shoplifter. Seemed he pocketed almost anything he passed – hi-fi equipment he had no use for, jewellery which, when he couldn't flog it, he threw in bins, women's clothes, ornaments, stuff he didn't need. He ran with the Young Team; was a nightmare in school. For fourteen years old, nothing hugely criminal, but heading that way. Sent to Lochgilvie House for problem kids. What else he and Micky X got up to was anybody's guess.

"We've no reason to suspect that Sy or that poor lassie in there got up to anything that'd lead to their murder," Maddy said.

"You have to admit, Maddy – chances are she won't have lived the life of a saint." Coulter started buttoning up his trenchcoat. It was hardly cold enough for a coat let alone button it. They walked aimlessly towards town. "No point in shutting avenues off – he's the only lead we've got."

"The words garden and path spring to mind."

"You do *your* job when it comes to you," he snapped.

"Because I'm shite at doing yours? Thanks. Only trying to help."

They stopped at a corner. She caught him eyeing the reports he had given her, regretting it now. She clutched them tighter. To hell with him. She marched off up a side street that brought her no closer to home. He waited for a moment and went off in the opposite direction.

It was still warm enough to open the living room window, the night breeze moving the leaves in the trees. She put on Art Pepper, made a pot of tea and took her briefcase to the chair. "You'd Be So Nice To Come Home To." She closed her eyes. Pepper's sax stirred up autumn leaves on Girvan streets. There had been a jukebox, in the family shop, kept up to date by Nonno until dad took over in the 70's. He never changed it.

Nonno had two themes in his selection. Big Songs – Gigli arias, Mario Lanza, Presley. Big blowsy orchestrated ballads with overblown lyrics that, nevertheless, made you weepy in an empty shop. She could still hear Nonno belting out those daft big songs, his voice nowhere near as good as he liked to think, frightening off the already remote possibility of sit-in customers.

Way better than Presley or "My Way" were the cooler, jazzier selections. Sinatra: Under My Skin. Tony Bennett. Sarah Vaughn. Ella. Bobby Darin. Nowadays she liked instrumental jazz even better. When Coltrane's sax rumbled deep down low, she could smell hot oil; when Dizzy Gillespie peeped at the top of his range, she could feel the cold west coast wind cooling her down behind the fryers. Getz rolling out a stately samba was the sound of the Atlantic from her girlhood bedroom.

She glanced at her notes on the Petrus Case – new evidence about their dumping practices. Cutting corners on safety. The storage walls of the dump not thick enough, the shaft not deep enough, the sealing shoddy. A third man had died, allegedly, at their hands. Forty-two-year-old father of three. A second woman had contracted a horrible skin disease. Four Petrus employees were claiming their cancers were caused by working close to the dump. One of those cases that'd take years.

She tore open Alan's envelope. Micky X was still resisting identification in grand style. Sy, the police were convinced, could only have met him through Lochgilvie House for problem kids. Nobody on the staff recognised the boy, and none of their recent past pupils had gone missing, but they agreed that a home for disruptive youngsters attracts a lot of visitors to the lanes and closes nearby. So much for the System coming to the rescue. If Sy had never been sent there, neither he nor his pal would now be the silent subjects of a massive murder hunt.

Star Eyes hummed lazily on the CD. The shadows of trees outside brushing in tempo. Maddy, dozing off, found herself repeating a childhood mantra. "Now I lay me down to sleep..." She let the file slip from her lap and her mind into a sad blue dream.

The killer – or killers, if there was more than one of them – had a penchant for good weather and pleasant surroundings. This time, the back garden of a Bearsden mansion. A staunch sun shone steadfastly, toughing it out up there no matter what little horrors lay below.

"Back garden" turned out to be something of an understatement. Acreage, grounds, fields – simply making it plural to *gardens* would be a better description. Maddy had passed the top of this street hundreds of times, along the main artery from Glasgow out west towards the Lomond Hills. She knew there were fair-sized piles up this way – but nothing as grand as this.

She had left her car in the street, walked up a driveway to a large porch and a main door built for a race of giants, eight foot high and reinforced with iron brackets. The hallway was castle-like, staircase vanishing up into the gloom high above. Through a door on the ground floor she could see a little old lady being interviewed by DS Russell and Sergeant Patterson Webb. If you'd passed her at the shops you'd have considered helping her with her bags and discreetly bunging her a couple of quid. Russell stood leaning against a marble fireplace as high as he was tall, wide and deep enough to roast a pig in. All the rooms and the hallway were panelled in dark wood nearly up to the level of Maddy's shoulder. Alan Coulter came out of another door at the back of the house, a massive slab of wood nearly half a foot thick.

"There might be a lot of coffee in Brazil," she smiled, "but there can't be a whole lot of mahogany left."

If he had any bitter after-taste from their little street argument last night, he didn't show it.

"Time of death of victim – a week last Friday. Five nights before the murders of Sy and Micky." He kept his voice even, the tone light. You've got to watch your step with information like that. Get it wrong and everyone would go home to bed and never get up again. They walked out into the garden via the back door. Coulter kept talking, giving information. "The hair we found at Kelvingrove? Not even bloody human. Dog."

"It's taken all this time for Forensics to distinguish between a human hair and a dog's?!"

The house might have been big, but the garden was ridiculous. She was following Alan down off a little raised terrace bordered by intricate iron filigree, onto wooden decking which twisted past a little pond onto a wide, flat lawn. "They've known all along. But, I don't know, a report went missing somewhere, and in a meeting lines got crossed... Basically, all this time we've been assuming we're dealing with human evidence. They've known for a week we're not."

They walked across the grass – Maddy wised-up for once, wearing flattish shoes – and still it took a minute or two before she could even *see* Coulter's colleagues. Amazing that ten, maybe twelve, experts of various sorts, plus uniforms, could get lost in someone's garden. "So my reasoning last night – about Whyte getting his hair cut was—"

"Was perfectly reasonable, given the information you understood you had."

They smiled at one another. Truce. A new day and a fresh sun. As he led the way towards Bruce Adams and the rest, Maddy noticed that grand as the gardens were, they didn't look quite as pristine as she guessed they once did.

"Think your woman back there could afford a better gardener."

"I imagine they don't stay long – if they keep tripping over corpses."

Adams, Crime Scene Manager, looked up, hearing their approach. Maddy didn't have to feel self-conscious about being here – a PF's presence at a murder scene was required. And, as well as the sensible shoes, she'd been at her girl-guide best this morning and put on a proper pair of light trousers. At the patch at the end of the garden where the girl had been found, Bruce Adams smiled at a wayward pupil who'd done her homework for once. "You can suit up inside if you like. Amy'll give you an overall."

"No need. I'll just stay here and listen to what you experts tell me."

Adams turned abruptly away. Maddy wondered at her own contrariness. Heels, skirt and stockings, and she puts on a crime scene jumpsuit; flat shoes and proper trousers and she decides not to. No wonder the police despaired of PFs.

The far end of the garden was lined with a knotted row of hydrangea and then a column of tall, narrow trees, standing to attention like soldiers on guard. "Corsican pine," Adams said proudly – and probably incorrectly, Maddy thought. The girl's body had been found between the bushes and the trees. No surprise, really, that it had lain there for a week and a half without being found. Even if the place was tended to by a part-time gardener. A Mr. Ian Lennon. He had been working on the beds at the top of the garden, and the fencing to the west side. Only came down here for a stroll while he was having his tea.

When he found her – he yelled. No wonder. Nine warm days, barely covered by earth. He ran into the house, shouting on Mrs McKay to phone the police. Now, only a few broken twigs, some crushed blue petals and the slightest impression in a patch of soft earth were all that testified to the girl's intrusion into private property.

"You'd have thought the ground would be soaked in blood," Adams said to Coulter. The two men, who usually made a point of keeping their distance from each other, stood together nodding and wondering. Could the execution have happened elsewhere? Or was she dragooned here, to be executed? The same questions they still hadn't answered about Sy and Micky X. "Pathology reported no sign of a blow powerful enough to have knocked her out."

Maddy moved back towards the path. It led to a set of concrete stairs. There was a door in the green wooden fence at the bottom of them. Alan Coulter came up towards her. "She was probably brought in this way."

Through the gate lay, not a back lane as Maddy had expected, but another road. It took her a couple of minutes to see the full picture in her mind's eye. Bearsden and Drumchapel backed on to each other. Of course they must do – she'd just never thought about it. Mrs McKay's palace of a house was one of a row, all of them with gardens sloping down to this frontier road. On the other side, an expanse of green belt, No-man's-land. Beyond that, the backside of a dowdy clump of Council housing. Drumchapel and

Bearsden, two extremes of Glasgow life, not quite facing each other, their backs turned in a huff. As if no travel or trade ever took place between them.

"Except at night," Coulter said. "And then it's the Drum boys running home with Bearsden silverware under their oxters. That's what Mrs. McKay says anyhow."

Ian Lennon had been brought to the garden to go over his precise movements the night before last. Coulter and Russell found him at a flower bed beside a shed at the side of the house, getting on with some digging while he waited.

He looked like he'd been gardening his own face. Big bruised mushroom of a nose half-buried in stubble black as earth. Lips as cracked as a month without rain, furrows like tractor tracks on his forehead. According to his files he was fifty-six. He looked, and sounded, like some ancient ogre from a mile below the earth's crust. Coulter thought better of making any jokes about cauliflower ears. Russell had already interviewed him down at the station, the night the girl had been found, but – despite the colourful history they had dug up on the unusual creature – had got nothing crucial from him. Judging by how his side-kick was cowering behind him now, Coulter got the impression he didn't want to aggravate Lennon in any unnecessary way. The policemen perched themselves on a flimsy B&Q garden bench. Lennon carried on weeding.

"Why were you in prison, Mr. Lennon?" Coulter asked.

"Isn't it manners to go in for a few insincere niceties first?" Lennon had a faint Northern Irish accent. "Like Good morning, Mr. Lennon, how's the weedin' goin'?" His vocal chords sounded as though they were located somewhere in his feet.

Coulter smiled. "Fraid I know nothing about gardening. What were you in prison for?"

Lennon found a clump of weeds to dislodge behind him, so that he had to turn away from his inquisitors. Coulter interpreted the move as defiance rather than dissimulation or anxiety. Lennon stuck his hefty arse a tad too directly at the visiting detectives. "You've got the file. You tell me."

"Gun-running. Arrests under the Prevention of Terrorism Act. General violence."

"So why ask?"

"I wanted to look you in the eye while *you* told *me*."

Lennon swung his arse out further. "No' doin' very well then, are you?"

"You work here Tuesdays and Fridays. The kid you found – she was killed a week last Friday."

"I wasn't down that end of the garden."

"Did you kill her?"

"No."

"Do you know who did?"

"No."

"She was just lying there when you walked past."

"Aye."

"Not much blood. We reckon she was killed elsewhere and taken there. Not long before you found her."

"Could have worked out as much myself."

Russell was being unusually quiet. Not doing his normal jutting in on Coulter's questions, heading off down totally different lines of enquiry. Lennon must really scare him. It wasn't just the bashed-up face, the big gardening arms and hands, the impressive case history. It was the air of settled intelligence, a more than physical sense of force.

"How did you get this job?"

"Through prison. Parole suggested it. I like places without people." He looked back into the expanse of the garden. "When I was wee they used to send me to my uncle's to work on his farm. Feckin' hated it. Every day of every summer from the age of eight to sixteen. But I learned a bit about growing stuff."

"You were in Saughton. Ever come across a Tony Kennedy?"

The gardener shook his head. "When was he there?"

"You must have overlapped. Two, three years back?"

"There are over a thousand in Saughton. Half of them could be called Tony Kennedy for all I know."

"What about the canal, Lennon? Kelvingrove Park. Ever go up there to get away from it all?"

He turned back to his digging. Coulter could read nothing from his movements – not deception, or pity. He had skin thicker than tree bark. Coulter stood up to go. Russell jumped up, too, eager to get away from the man's slow brutal energy.

Maxwell Binnie dragged out his meeting with Maddy to bridge the gap until the start of his Steering Committee on Delinquency.

"I'm suggesting that we keep the press only minimally informed."

Binnie drummed his desk with his sterling silver fountain pen. Maddy doubted he could actually write with it. "Tough one – they love it."

The tender age of the victims made for good copy; the brutality of the executions, gruesome headlines. "The hunt for Micky X has become a national quest. Just what editors like."

Maddy nodded. Especially the editor of the *Record* – a personal pal of Binnie's, and a man her boss liked to be on the right side of. The press were an important part of a career plan.

The tabloids were "doing their bit," searching Britain and beyond for the name and family of the murdered boy. They were "working" with organisations for the homeless, drop-in centres and Childline. In fact, all they were doing was keeping the story on the front pages. And trying to force a return of the death penalty – this time for child-killers.

"Their coverage could lose us the case before we even have a suspect."

Binnie nodded vigorously, but Maddy knew he'd do nothing about it. He checked his watch, and ran his fingers through his thick, attractively graying hair. Time for his next meeting.

We're all too used to the deaths of kids who live on the edge of things, she thought going down in the lift. They're forever falling into canals, or under cars. Drinking or OD-ing themselves to death. As for someone actually setting out to kill the youngsters, maybe the good and decent folk of Glasgow who'd had their cars broken into once too often, who had put up with cheek in the street, might even feel a guilty touch of sympathy.

Her mother knew not to come out with such sentiments in Maddy's company. The sun hung stubbornly to the edge of the evening sky as Maddy made her way to Sarti's. Rays slanting through sandstone, glass, chrome, granite. Glaswegians became Milanese for the night – strolling, chatting, hanging jackets over their shoulders. Maddy entered the cool and candlelit restaurant, and found there had been no need to hurry. Mama was not alone.

It wasn't unusual for Rosa to pick up a companion. She hated being alone, even for the ten or fifteen minutes she sometimes had to wait for Maddy. But the young priest from church the other night was a bit much. Maddy just didn't get the curate thing. In her experience they were testosterone-free zones. Generally pleasant enough, good-willed, if smug. Too dull to be either the perverted villains of modern mythology, or delectable forbidden fruit.

"Maddalena. This is Father Jamieson. He's kindly agreed to help advise us on a little service for Nonno's party."

"Please, Rosa, if you insist on the 'Father', make it Father Mike."

To be fair to priests, there was really nothing they could say these days that didn't sound like a comedy line. He stood up to shake her hand.

"Hi." Maddy wasn't going for either the "Father" or the "Mike".

"It's a privilege meeting your family," he said to Rosa. Then to Maddy: "Your grandfather, Maddalena, is an extraordinary person."

Maddy had occasional doubts about her own profession. It could be too easily corrupted; the law in general was no longer held in high esteem, and lawyers in desperately low esteem. But what must it feel like to be a Catholic priest these days? The majority of folk around you didn't even believe in the premise on which you built an entire career. At best, you were an irrelevance; at worst, a madman. Have to hand it to them – there's some kind of courage in facing a disinterested or openly hostile public each morning.

"He is, Father, I know."

"I had assumed it was his birthday we were celebrating, but your mother told me the extraordinary story."

Nonno and his Great Adventure. It wasn't all that uncommon, but it never failed to impress. The rest of the family, even two generations down the line – besmirched now by bog-Irish peasant blood the colour of peat – benefited from a little reflected glory. There must be a trace of the grit and courage and perseverance in them all.

"What an example he is! Not often you hear of that kind of courage and bravery."

"Oh, I don't know, Father. Look closely enough and you find little examples of heroism everywhere."

"You're right, Maddalena. The problem is, we don't celebrate them. And we do have to look very hard to find them. Stories like your grandfather's should be brought to our attention. Put in the newspapers. Published—"

"I've often told Maddalena," Maddy could mouth the words with her mother, "she should write his biography."

"Memoirs of an Ayrshire Chip Shop Dynasty."

"I agree with your mother, Maddalena," Maddy found

it breathtaking – the man was half her height, a decade younger, yet he spoke to her like a wise old teacher. "I think you should, too. What a role model your granddad could be."

"Braehead Revisited."

Mike didn't seem to get the joke.

He allowed Rosa to persuade him to stay for a glass out of the new bottle Maddy ordered. The sharpish, tingling Alto Adige must have been recommended by a waiter – her mother knew nothing, and cared less, about wine. In her day she had been a soft-drinks connoisseur; could distinguish at a glance Irn Bru from Iron Brew, Tizer from Cherryade, which bottle got threepence back and which six. Her interests had never extended to fine wines.

She was playing a fine game with the little priest. Somewhere between a charmingly mature Sophia Loren and a devout, ageing Italian Bernadette. She wasn't coming on to the poor guy, just trying to impress him. She had developed a slightly saintly smile Maddy had never seen before, and a vaguely earthy line of chat.

"Maddalena's thinking of moving house, Father. I think trying to stay one step ahead of all the ex-boyfriends."

"I've told you, Mama. I'm not moving any time soon."

Fr. Mike, though, was more interested in the boyfriends than the housing market. "Who's the lucky man these days, Maddalena?" He sounded like an old favourite uncle who'd been unavoidably out of touch since school days. And a girl doesn't want to disappoint a prodigal uncle, so averagely endowed Matt was, on the spur of the moment, promoted to Boyfriend.

"Matt. Short for Matthew…?" Father Mike was trying to confirm if the Boyfriend was of the Catholic fold.

"Don't think it's short for anything, Father. His mum was a Matt Munro fan I believe." That was maybe pushing it too far. A look of doubt darkened Mike Jamieson's eye. But he nodded tolerantly while Maddy happily made up more nonsense, the term "spiritual atheist" catching his professional attention.

"Now what might *that* be?"

"I think he doesn't have *beliefs* as such. He's prepared to let anything he's learned or come to accept, be challenged. Believers, by definition, can't allow their doctrines to be questioned."

They both knew she was talking about herself. Bad move. She sounded like the worst kind of pompous, half-educated lawyer, and it allowed Father Mike to embark upon a long and boring proclamation of the nature of Christian knowledge. Probably, the man was quite clever. But it didn't stop her mind wandering to Alan Coulter. Out there right now on the trail of Sy's and Micky's and the little girl's killers. She told the priest a few gruesome details not even the worst tabloids had printed. "Now *there's* knowledge. The facts of our broken little lives. Corroborated, Father, by dead flesh, broken bones, scarred lips."

He didn't deserve that. He was only doing his job. Maybe even he's right. We need some kind of religion. Mystical, political, whatever. A sanctuary in which to house our vulnerable humanity, a tabernacle that, if not good in itself, at least keeps the evil out.

Far from motoring hard on the heels of killers, Alan Coulter was bored out his wits at an evening meeting of the Scottish Executive's Consultative Steering Committee to investigate the growing problem of delinquency. That committee, if Coulter was getting the fascinating history right, had taken it upon itself to set up a practical, applied arm in conjunction with the police. Chief Constable Crawford Robertson had of course managed to wangle his way onto this shiny new quango. They were meeting in the evening, Robertson said, "because we're all busy men and women and this coming-together of minds is of a vocational nature, not part of our nine-to-fives."

Coulter had to attend because he was the Senior Investigating Officer in both the Kennedy and Mullholland cases. The only thing that made the boredom tolerable was counting the scapegoats. The Scottish Minister for Education and Young People blamed the telly, the papers, and the parents. The Shadow Scottish Minister for Justice blamed the "liberal establishment" and computers. Only MacDougall the Czar from the Islands seemed to have trouble thinking one up. He had a reputation for being a hard but fair history teacher, then Heidie in schools from Caithness to Lanarkshire. The kind kids feared and loved in equal measure. Modern life was hard, he said in his singsong voice. "My heart goes out to Simon Kelly and his family. An atrocious waste of life."

Robertson quickly got things back on track. "But the sad fact is we will doubtlessly discover that Master Kennedy and his mystery companion were, to a degree at least, architects of their own downfall."

Some worthy Coulter couldn't place agreed wholeheartedly: "It's the society which allows that process to take place that we must tackle."

Coulter automatically wanted to rebel against whatever these talking suits said, but he knew there was a grain of truth in it. Sy and Micky X hadn't been picked up off the street and executed for nothing. They'd been involved, somewhere down the line, with their killers, or with their killers' line of business.

Whatever, the Island school master, the Assistant Chief Constable, the Fiscal, this whole damned meeting, were all getting in the way of Alan Coulter catching one, or maybe two, sets of murderers. Martin Whyte, sitting in the station at this very moment, needed speaking to. Jim Docherty needed speaking to again. Ian Lennon. The kids' school teachers, pals... it all urgently demanded his attention. He stood up halfway through Maxwell's Binnie's tuppence worth of outrage.

"It is of the utmost urgency and consequence, moving forward, that we ascertain the identities of both the boy in Kelvingrove and the girl."

The room fell into silence as DI Coulter shut his briefcase, and marched to the door.

Coulter didn't believe in gut instinct. He had a hunch, though, that that was why his marriage was outwardly perfect, privately problematic. Not because he lacked the intuition to know when Martha needed company, or wanted left alone. But because he didn't believe there was any such intuition to lack in the first place.

Most policemen's hunches were, to be generous, simply reasonable deductions from the available information. More grudgingly, they were wildly inaccurate guesses that totally ignored that information. Female intuition was also bollocks; attributed to any woman who happened to be proven right about something, and ignored when she wasn't. DI Alan Coulter had a tendency to state the truth as he saw it, too bluntly and too often. And that from a man who suspected that the very idea of the Truth might be bollocks too.

So, looking at Martin Whyte sitting in front of him and Russell didn't do anything to Coulter's waters. He didn't get a sinking feeling, or a tingle. There simply wasn't enough reason to keep the guy longer than was necessary.

"Should I have a lawyer?" Whyte asked, almost as a matter of interest.

"If you want one."

He shook his head. "Carry on."

"Sign-Chronicity did some work for Lochgilvie Home."

"Couple of years ago now."

"Tell us about that," Russell said.

"Really, it was Elaine's project. We did some signing and publicity. She upgraded their outside spaces, helped the pupils design a common room and a play area outside."

"When Sy Kennedy was attending."

"I never knew that."

"The Home's director says you involved the kids in your project," DS Russell was forever getting hunches. He trusted them more than he did statements, interviews, productions.

"We wanted their suggestions."

"Who did?"

"Elaine and I, mainly."

"You talked, apparently, to Sy himself."

"Did we? I'm sorry. I really don't remember."

Coincidence? Like Whyte's company name – synchronicity. A man runs past a murder scene several hours before the murder takes place. Then he runs past the victims the next morning. The bodies are spotted by his business and running partner. He has no one to corroborate his alibi the following week for another, possibly related, murder. Through further investigation – and with no help from Whyte – the police discover that he might actually have *met* these boys.

Coulter watched Whyte coolly – innocently? – sipping his tea and remembered his daughter Lauren's theory of the Six Degrees of Separation. Everyone is connected to everyone else on the planet within six moves, if only you knew where to look. Whyte is connected to a Masai tribesman, though he doesn't know it. His uncle, maybe, lived next door to the father of a Church of Scotland minister who went to college with a boy who became a missionary and went to Nairobi, where one day an envoy from the tribal chief arrived...

In a city like Glasgow it took only three moves. Less. Nothing remarkable in coming across, though work, a pair of lads and then running past them in a park two years later...

Russell was staring hard at Whyte, trying to discern the elusive pattern, the blueprint he needed to connect the graphics artist to the killings. Coulter wanted to say that if you stared at anything too long, you just lost all perspective. Like a kid saying the same word over and over again until it becomes meaningless, a nonsense sound. Stare at anyone's life long enough and you'll see chance, luck, absurdity.

The fact was that their clincher piece of evidence, the clue that made both Russell and Coulter sure they were on a path leading somewhere, had gone. You can't keep a man in jail 'cause he might have patted a dog sometime. The hair wasn't Whyte's. No motive for him killing anyone could be found. Nor could a weapon, or any previous record, or nefarious connections.... Nothing but coincidence, and the cold feeling that Whyte gave off. A hunch.

Maddy sat in the middle of a den, hemmed in by walls of cardboard boxes. She'd been preparing to move for weeks – collecting all the boxes and bags she'd thought she might need. Do as Roddy Estate Agent said: declutter.

Years of Stuff. But it was pictures of Sy – alive and dead – and Micky X that she held in her hands. Both of them lying beaten and dead on the mortuary table; smiling family snaps of Sy. A broken and bloodied mannequin come to life.

At the time the earlier photograph was taken, Sy hadn't had his Number One haircut. He'd preferred the front worn a little longer and gelled down. Half the kids that traipsed through the courts in front of Maddy sported this fashion. It gave them a just-hosed look, as if they had been driven with a cattle prod through a car wash. A sheen of metallic wax on their greased-down hair, their glossy skin. Sy was smiling a little inscrutably. Just at the edges of the crop you could see Sy's living room, a leg and a shoulder belonging to a man. The smile might be shy or forced, or just one of those insincere grins anyone would put on for a family snap.

70

Micky X was the taller and darker of the two; the one with the snicked eyebrow. Having seen Sy photographed alive, Maddy could imagine his pal better. Pathology was sure that the unidentified victim was a good year older than the Kennedy boy. Micky, she guessed, was the harder of the two – physically, and possibly mentally. Sy's face was all angles. Micky looked more complex, somehow.

Maddy could *hear* the two of them. Sy would have one of those skinny voices, as lean and tapering as his long sallow arms. His speech full of expletives, vocal jerks, a time-lapse effect to both his talking and his living. Micky would be the quieter one. That husky vocal texture you get in Southern Italy. You probably had to strain to hear him at all. And she could imagine their movements. Sy's histrionic, eye-catching; Micky's slow and unsure. She couldn't pretend to herself that she would have got on like a house on fire with either of these youngsters in life.

She put the photos down. The whole point of getting stuck into decluttering was to rid herself of those two shiny, spectral boys. But she kept them near as she began sorting through her piles of books and CDs and stuff.

Putting books and domestic miscellany in boxes is like filing away old dreams. Bits of previous Maddy Shannons that had left evidence of themselves in corners of cupboards. Books she'd loved but couldn't remember much now. Old CDs, vinyl. Maps of Europe with red lines drawn on them, an earlier Maddy's plans for a Big Adventure of her own, in the family tradition. A time in her life when dreaming seemed closer to the surface than it did now. She felt a pang of loss, putting item after item in a box destined for the city dump. She had beached up in a duller reality than she'd meant to. Like an object in water that had floated to the surface, too lightweight to return any deeper.

Victor Jara records. Billy Bragg. The Levellers. A leftwingery she had forged for herself; that was *hers* and not a version of Packy's. Georges Brassens. Durruti

Column. The Manics. She remembered an anti-Fascist concert in Rome. Only seventeen. Candles, matches and lighters being held aloft – before Barry Manilow got his grubby hands on the idea. A glow of hope mingling in the southern dark, rebellion curling up into the air with the black scented tobacco smoke. Beautiful hazel-eyed young people in the musky night. Maddy's Left – freedom and passion and *grappa*. Not Packy's rantings. Not the new left that seemed to have more rules than her old parish priest in Girvan.

Her phone rang. She tripped over a box of unmarked videos, stepped on and broke an old framed photograph of Uncle Dan. Dad's side. Mad guy, spent half his life in prisons. All she remembers is a laughing giant of a man who used to swing her around the beach at Girvan; the scratchiness of his beard, the smell of smoke.

She limped halfway out the room towards the hall and the nearest phone, just as it stopped ringing. She heard her own voice, trying to sound friendly, inviting people to phone back. Whoever it was didn't leave a message.

She still had a photo in her hand. Who would have thought that Micky X – the bigger, harder, cleverer-looking of the two – would have been the one to have reached out to take little Sy's hand?

Elaine Docherty didn't go in for the languorous look this time, either because her husband was out or because Russell was accompanied by WPC Amy Dalgarno. Or maybe he and Coulter had just caught her at a bad time before.

"You have no memory of Sy Kennedy?"

"I'm sorry. I really don't. If he was at the meetings I held at Lochgilvie he never said much, I'm sure."

"Did Mr. Whyte spend more time with the pupils? Could he have met Sy separately?"

"I have no idea. We saw the boys on separate occasions."

Russell caught Elaine glancing up at the mezzanine floor

where the king-size bed was. For a second he had a vision of himself and Elaine tussling naked together. Elaine clocked it, he was sure. So did Dalgarno. He looked away, faltered, the flow of the interview lost.

This wasn't a development he'd been keen on anyway. Elaine was never a murderer. A nice case had been piling up against Whyte. Coulter was dismissing it out of hand – just because he couldn't make all the pieces fit. Coulter reminds Russell of a woman shopping – sees what she wants, then spends the whole day looking for something better, ending up where she started off.

Amy was showing Elaine the photographs of Sy Kennedy. "You recognise him?"

"Yes. From the papers."

Russell put a photograph of Micky X on top of the one of Sy, trumping Dalgarno. "What about this boy?"

Elaine shrugged. "All those kids look like him nowadays."

"You have no memory of seeing these two boys together?"

"At Lochgilvie, I never had a clue who was an inmate, who was staff, or family. Just a bunch of unruly, untalkative young guys. I felt quite threatened, actually."

Maddy hated going into the meeting rooms for the public. Windowless. Painted a cold blue. Hardbacked school chairs. Couple of cheap prints on the wall. One of the bridge over the Clyde – which you could have seen in the flesh had there been a window. Another of a dolphin. Who *took* these design decisions?

Maddy nodded at Anne Kennedy, sat hunched over the desk, as if she were reading runes hidden in the grain of the polished wood. Tony Kennedy stood in a corner staring at a poster claiming Strathclyde Police had cut crime by 17% in the last quarter. Sy's parents in together, and each of them utterly alone.

"My deepest commiserations."

When the woman was younger, Maddy thought, before

the shittiness of her life had turned her bones to rubber, she would have been tall, hazel-haired, straight-backed. Proud looking probably. If she pushed back her shoulders the way Mama always told Maddy to do, that long face of hers might even look aristocratic. Tony was small, a bird-like quality to him. Like his owner died or got fed up with him, let him free to flit off and fend for himself.

"When can we have him back?"

Maddy had seen every response to bereavement poss-ible. Wives who could hardly speak, sometimes for months. Young children bored, or intrigued, by death. People pre-tending to feel more than they really did. Tony Kennedy's voice was even, but she knew he was in as black a place as his estranged wife. And Maddy was going to make things worse for them. "Has nobody explained this to you?"

"Got legal aid. They said you won't let him go?" Anne Kennedy looked up at Maddy as though she were gazing on the countenance of some terrible potentate.

"I'm afraid I can't release Sy's body."

"Why not?!" The dad lost his evenness of tone for a second; Maddy could feel the furor coming off him. The jaw held tight, specks of saliva at the corner of the mouth. How else could you feel when someone, for no reason you can imagine, takes your boy along a canal path, shoots him dead, then carves up his face?

"Defence – if and when there is one – must have patho-logy access to victims. For evidence. I'm afraid we have to keep Sy in the mortuary a while longer."

"You keep us from burying our boy so when you find his killer you can cut Sy up all over again to help get the bastard off?"

Fifteen years' experience and seven years studying, yet Anne Kennedy, probably without a Standard Grade to her name, had summed the situation up more accurately than Maddy could.

"How long d'you keep him for?" Tony ventured out of his

corner, but immediately looked exposed, frightened. "What if they don't catch anyone for months? Years?"

"If, after three months, the police are nowhere nearer to making an arrest, then the Fiscal have it in our power to release the body. Please God we won't have to wait that long." Evoking God gave authority to the law's unpalatable and confusing rules and regulations. "When a suspect has been apprehended, I'll be working much closer with you. My name's Shannon. I'll be compiling the case against your son's killer or killers."

"Will you be working with the other boy's Ma and Da as well?" asked Anne. Maddy nodded. "Poor bastards." Strange how pity for others can gleam through your own personal darkness.

"I'll do everything in my power to get justice for Sy."

Anne hauled herself out her seat, as though her muscles had ceased to function. Tony scurried to the door, in case a bigger bird swooped down and caught him.

The girl's name was Frances Mulholland and there was no obvious connection between her and Sy. She came from Drumchapel. She had no family in the Gorbals, and apparently no connections with the Kennedys. Nor, for that matter with a graphics company called Sign-Chronicity, or any charities they had worked with. She was a pupil at St. Catherine's and no one in her family had ever heard of Lochgilvie Home.

The Mullholland family hadn't reported Frances missing, or heard about a body being found in a garden. The police had found them by accident. Two PCs, one of them young, both of them new to the Drumchapel beat, had been sent to Coulter this morning to tell him about it.

"We responded to requests to look into a domestic disturbance at the address indicated in the report."

"As a potential ASBO—"

"You can speak English with me, guys."

"Sorry, sir. Anti-Social Behaviour—"

"I *know* what it means, Constable! Just tell me in nice short words – what kind of a disturbance?"

They stiffened, straining now for casual English. "Raised voices—"

"Shouting."

"Shouting, and noises that indicated – I mean seemed to... *suggest*... physical violence."

"A fight. In other words." Coulter groaned inwardly. All he wanted was the basic details. But people don't like giving the basic details, especially if it's part of their job. Makes everything look too simple.

"And the requests for the police to visit the Mulhollands came from neighbours? Do we know if this is a frequent request?"

"Yes."

"No."

"One of the neighbours said it *had* happened before, but not for a long while."

"When we went in, we found Mrs Mulholland under the influence of alcohol—"

"And perhaps drugs."

"In a bit of a state. There was a man there, who had also taken drink and possibly drugs—"

"He looked glazed."

"They admitted there had been a fight, but it was all settled now."

"A young boy was crying in a bedroom next door. We asked Mrs. Mulholland if she could bring him through."

Eventually, Coulter got the whole story. The visitor was Ricky Graham, a local dealer; one who had been helpful to the police in the past. He had no reputation for violence, but both he and Jacqueline Mulholland had been drinking and dropping speed, never a very peaceful combination. It turned out she owed him money, which he, in the usual domino pattern, owed to *his* masters. The boy, Darren, was brought out for inspection. There were no bruises or cuts or obvious signs of abuse. The uniforms had noticed photographs of a second child, and Jackie Mulholland herself had mentioned the name Frances. It was the boy who said his sister hadn't been home in two days.

"How come? How come the mother doesn't notice a thirteen year old missing for over a week?"

"We never got much sense out of her after that."

"The girl often stayed over with friends she said."

"Mrs Mullholland started wailing, sir, shouting out for Frances, shaking Ricky, screaming if *he* knew anything."

"Did he?"

"Only to suggest that he had assumed that the girl – Franny they called her – could have been coming and going as usual. She'd often get in at night before her mother and be out before anyone in the morning. We got the impression it's a pretty disorganised household, sir."

Jacqueline and Darren Mulholland were now being looked after by a relative. Jackie hadn't been officially informed of her daughter's murder, but she knew the minute the cops started asking about her.

The officers then visited some neighbours to get an impression of life *chez* Mullholland. Darren and Frances got up and went to bed at all kinds of hours. They spent as much time in pals' houses as they did in their own – ate better and more regularly with some of them. Both children were in the habit of sleeping over, sometimes for more than a night, at more settled, warmer, safer houses.

"The boy. Darren. What's his story? His sister missing for a week and he does nothing?"

The two policemen looked lost for words. Anything was possible in a house like that. And they shuffled off to write their reports.

"Completely unrelated murder," Russell insisted afterwards. Coulter thought he was probably right. Hoped he was. The implications otherwise were terrible. If Frances and the boys truly had nothing to connect them, yet were killed by the same hands, then Glasgow had a serial killer on its hands. A serial killer of children.

Antonella was inside the house, shouting on Vittore over the din made by her mother and Ettore's parents and by the boys and a few villagers who were hampering progress as much as helping. Ettore was tying up bundles and stacking items that would be left with parents and neighbours either until the Di Rios returned, or sent for their things.

A kitchen table with its legs dismantled. Pots and pans that no one wanted to use in the meantime. Old tools – hoes and spades and hammers and an old blunt scythe – tied up with rope. Sacks full of the boys' clothes – not to be stored away, but to be delivered to Antonella's parents' house along the road at Procchio. A single suitcase lay by the door of the house, alongside an old army kit bag, a large seed-pouch, and Ettore's regimental belt, good for carrying the few coins and notes to begin their journey.

"You'll need this." His mother came out the house holding up his army coat. The war had ended and no one ever came back for his military gear.

"It'll be cold in the north."

"It's too heavy to carry."

"Then wear it."

"Some days it'll be too hot."

"It'll be good for bedding, if you have to stay out a night."

He took it, folded it, and stuffed it into the seed-bag. Ettore wasn't sure if they'd ever have a roof over their heads again.

Carlo was helping. Bringing out sides of wood from the dresser being dismantled by his grandfather and uncle. Vittore was supposed to be helping, too, but was really just getting in the way. Every time Carlo, the oldest, came out with a flattened drawer, or a slat from the dresser's back, he caught Ettore staring out to sea.

"That way?" the boy asked.

"No," Ettore said. He pointed northwards. "You'd have to walk up and right round the cliff tops. And then you'd have to be tall enough to see over France and Spain."

"I'll be tall enough."

Ettore smiled. Carlo was holding his shoulders high, to make him seem bigger, manlier and healthy, and clenching his muscles, holding his soul in, straining not to cry. He'd hoped up until the last minute that his parents would change their mind and take him with them. Just a year or two older, his dad had said, and they might have considered it. And anyway, with his coughs, this wasn't the best time. They needed Carlo here to help look after Vittore.

All day, Carlo had helped out, almost wordlessly. Resigned. Steeling himself for the moment when his parents would walk down the road towards Portoferraio, away from their farm and their house, perhaps never to return. Headed for some land that the boy could not begin to imagine. He had hoped his mother at least would have stayed, but then worried that, without her, his father might fare worse.

Ettore couldn't put his arm around his son – the slightest contact might bring on the weeping in all of them. Behind them, Antonella was coming out of the house for the last time, ahead of the procession of mothers, aunts, uncles and neighbours. Ettore's father sat in the shade under the slats of the roof. Antonella had Vittore in her arms. As Ettore came towards them, she held the child out.

Six years old, though he had hardly grown since he was four. His face was full of confusion. The tumult of the day, the presence of his entire family, the noise and activity and dismantling of everything had excited him. Ettore could see in his eyes that the lad knew some crucial moment had arrived. He took the boy from Antonella. "Hey, my big soldier."

The sky stretched out over them, almost white; the sea below them, black out in its depth. Carlo hung tight to his father's side, Vittore to his neck. The same sky and sea that

reached as far as *Francia* and *Inghilterra* and *Scozia* where
one day, if everything went well, the boys would follow their
parents. Right now, though, that sky and the sea were steal-
ing his mamma and papà.

"Look after Vittore. You're in my place now."

Both boys looked back at him through dark, wet eyes.
Nobody moved. Not Ettore, or Antonella, or any of the
dozen friends, family or neighbours. A single step seemed too
big, too decisive. Vittore clung on hard, and Carlo clenched
his muscles tighter. If either one of them relaxed for a second
it would be their fault that their mamma and papà were leaving them behind; their fault if they never returned again.

Maddy didn't normally take her car into work, the subway
going from door to door, with less than five minutes' walk
either side. This morning, though, she had filled the boot
and the back seat with stuff for the charity shop. Her recy-
cling duty done, the afternoon was still bright and the evening would be long – summer solstice just around the corner.

Coulter had gone to ground. Maybe they were getting
close to an arrest. Maddy should start getting to know the
details of this case. The faces. So far she had only met – of
the living – Tony and Anne Kennedy.

She had seen photographs of other people attached
to the investigation, in files that Coulter had slipped her
earlier than necessary. The blank – frankly boring – faces of
both Martin Whyte and his business partner Jim Docherty.
The heavy-lidded carnality of Elaine Docherty. Though
perhaps Maddy was just imagining that – hardly surprising, after the way Alan had described the woman, slouching suggestively at him and Russell, flashing her undies.
Wishful thinking no doubt. Maddy knew that some colleagues and a lot of policemen talked about *her* in those
terms. Single. Goes out. Wears high heels and makeup.
Takes a drink. Down at Division A she'd be gagging for it.

Then there was the photo of Ian Lennon. A face hewn

from the living rock. His picture shouted in her hands, though Coulter had said he'd been quiet-spoken. His eyes were set so deep set they seemed to belong to a face hiding inside another. Skin the colour of Aberdeen granite, crevices and gorges in it worthy of Cairngorm. Lennon was fast overtaking Whyte as the police's front-running suspect. Ex-jailbird, IRA hit man – of the mercenary type, apparently, rather than the politically dedicated. Lived alone, gardened alone, had no one to corroborate his alibi for Sy, and was in the garden the day Frances was killed, possibly around the same time.

Now that Maddy had decided not to get rid of her house, she wondered if she should change cars instead. Get rid of the little Mazda sports; everyone commented on it. Flashy, tawdry, yellow. Her mother hated it – though Maddy knew Rosa would have loved being seen getting in and out of it when she was younger; when her legs worked better. Outside the church at Procchio. Marco and all the village boys looking on.

Maddy wanted to glimpse the places of the story so far. Where the Kennedys and the Mullhollands lived. The gardens, other than Mrs. MacKay's, tended to by Lennon. Lochgilvie House. She drove over the Kingston Bridge. Glasgow's skyline brittle like a cracked eggshell, the late sun's yellow yolk dribbling down into its streets.

Lochgilvie looked pleasanter in real life than in the web photograph. A glowing red sandstone building, only one window cracked, and a couple of kids standing outside, chatting and laughing. Moments like these, she could almost believe in progress. In the law managing to help the vulnerable. She tried to imagine Sy and Micky X standing there talking, laughing. About what? After all the time she had worked with kids in this city, all the times she'd served the local bad boys chips, she still couldn't imagine what they said to each other in the privacy of their own company.

The big difference between the photograph of the home and the reality, was the garden. It had been a patch of mud on the website. Now it had a lawn – a few divots and holes in it, but still a lawn. At one side, a basket ball hoop; at the other a giant chess set. Those pieces must be chained to the ground. Benches had been provided at either side of the door. A flower bed at the front looked well tended. All of it the work, presumably, of Sign-Chronicity.

A woman – of fantastic girth – had clocked Maddy from a window and within a couple of seconds was standing staring at her from the front door. A good sign – staff picking up on strangers hanging about. Maddy got out to introduce herself.

The woman looked askance at this designer-suited stranger, skirt half an inch too short, lipstick tenth of a millimetre too thick, getting out of a yellow sports and clacking her heels on the pavement.

"Miss Bateman?"

"Uh-hu."

"Maddalena Shannon. Procurator Fiscal."

"Follow me." Janet Bateman, perfectly small and fat, wheeled along in front of Maddy to her office. Popped behind her desk, she looked globular. Her eyes were strict and tired, narrowing behind thickish lenses. "Fiscal. Thought you don't get involved until there's an arrest."

"Usually. But I was passing, and as I'll be working on the case soon enough—"

Bateman waved away the procedural protocol. "Sy was sent here for menacing behaviour—"

"I thought it was shoplifting?"

"As well. Like most of our youngsters in here – Sy was out of control in most areas of his life."

Maddy nodded. "As would be the other, unknown, victim?"

"I've spoken to the police about this. He's not one of ours."

"Could Sy have befriended someone outside the Home, during his stay?"

Bateman took off her glasses. "Let's not be romantic, Miss Shannon. My clients are capable of secret lives that would astound you. Having said that, Sy Kennedy wasn't one of the worst. Came from a better home than most. Father around, in some shape or form. Confident enough boy. He could easily have met someone locally."

"Did he get into trouble often, in here?"

"Boys like Sy don't have to go *looking* for trouble. Trouble finds them. Like a mangy dog that follows you home. Trouble's everywhere. This building's a magnet for all sorts of low-life. Yours isn't the only sports car to sit out there."

"What others?"

"Gangsters looking for errand boys. Posh men in tailored suits with enough dosh to tempt careless laddies into doing whatever they ask. Big brothers, and ex-graduates of the home on revenge missions. Local kids – some of them well-educated and nicely-spoken – bored and looking for adventure. Fifteen-year-old private school girls looking for a bit of rough."

"Do you have any idea, Ms Bateman, which of those threats might have led Sy Kennedy to Kelvingrove that morning?"

Janet Bateman replaced her glasses with a sigh.

"You're understaffed here."

"Pool of seven. Only three on at any given time. Fifteen, sometimes seventeen clients. Admittedly, others come in to help. Some local volunteers."

"Like who?"

"The local Minister. A few socially minded neighbours. The parish priest, one or two parents..."

"How do bad boys get on with do-gooders?"

"Men like them can be better with boys than you think. Get them to turn up for football games. Putting a team together is nigh on impossible, though. The players are only here a few weeks, and then they end up in borstal, or, if they're very lucky, back home, or...."

"Dead."

DI Coulter, DS Russell by his side, gave an update on the case so far to the Chief Constable. Not a task he ever enjoyed; even less so today. Martha was at home having one of her worse headaches. They could go on for days, weeks. Where they came from, nobody knew. Not classic migraines. They'd had tests done over the years for everything any doctor could think of. For a while they suspected ME, but she had none of the symptoms between attacks. That left the sole probable cause, Alan reckoned: him.

Nobody was in the mood for this meeting. Chief Constable Robertson had never mentioned Coulter's walking out in the middle of Maxwell Binnie's speech at the Youth Crime Committee. He didn't need to – the facial expression of a maltreated pit-bull sufficed. "'Some loose ends', Coulter? You're a master of understatement."

"Not enough of them, sir" – he never called Robertson "sir" but thought on this occasion it might be politic – "to make me think Whyte or Docherty are responsible for very professional executions."

"You'd call the Mullholland girl's killing *professional*, would you?" CC Robertson was itching for a fight.

"Possibly. But we're not even sure it's connected."

"Docherty and Whyte *had* done some work up in Drumchapel, three, four years ago." Russell spoke as if he were in full agreement with Coulter, but was just having a couple of niggly difficulties. "We know they worked directly with Kennedy."

"Whyte ran past the murder scene twice...." Robertson flicked through Coulter's report as though it were covered in slime.

"We've checked the Dochertys' and Whyte's medical records," Coulter soldiered on. "Driving records, financial history, passports, credit cards, family background… Nothing. I think we need to look closer at Ian Lennon'

"The gardener."

"Ex-IRA hit man. A hired hand, we think. My guess is Mr. Lennon doesn't believe in *anything*."

"He had the opportunity. Alibis?" Robertson asked, while Russell shifted in his seat. Any talk of Lennon, Coulter noticed, seemed to unnerve his junior.

"Lennon's a loner – he never has an alibi. At least no corroboration. When he's not alone in his house, he's at the back of somebody's garden somewhere. He doesn't make appointments, just turns up and works, calling in once a month to get paid. Consequently, none of his employers know when he's around and when he's not. He knew Sy's father in prison. Governor at Saughton said they often sat together at meals, but claims he can't remember him."

"Motive?"

Coulter remained silent. Robertson met him directly in the eye. "So basically we have the same problem with both the Lennon and the designers theories? No sniff of a half-way decent reason for shooting three kids."

"Lennon had no more reason to kill the Mullholland girl than Whyte did the boys," Russell nodded gravely.

"I think," Coulter said quietly, knowing that his opinion didn't count for as much as it should, "that Ian Lennon is capable of things Whyte could never be. He knows a dark side of this city that Whyte has no notion exists."

Maddy stood next to Jackie Mullholland as the mortuary assistant brought in the gurney. The woman was proof of chaos theory, a splat of ill-fitting mismatched clothes, Medusa hair, involuntary movements and sounds. She had black rings under her green eyes, looked as if she hadn't slept in months. Smoker's skin, but a young, red, un-lip-sticked mouth, long artistic fingers.

The mortuary assistant was a young man, very professional in his bearing. Apart from the earring – but that was
probably a generation thing. Anyone ten years younger
than her probably wouldn't even notice. Jackie Mullholland
stared at him as he stepped back, towards the door. Maddy
took hold of the sheet.

She felt, as she held the cover down, that she was doing
something pornographic. Leeringly exposing something
private. The girl had been tidied up for her mother. Jackie
hopped from one foot to the other, glanced at the dead
child, then at Maddy, then somewhere unknown, unthink-
able. Maddy kept holding the sheet down off the fading
face, the greenish tinge of death like makeup. Jackie
glanced down again, and her eyes flared momentarily, her
fists clenched. You could see her fighting for breath. She
gave Maddy this strange little nod – almost eager, like a
child in a class with the right answer.

When, with Frances covered again, Jackie followed
Maddy to the door, her presence was somehow lighter.
There was less of her. The wild hair and edgy movements,
the little coughs and red lips, all muted, washed away by
uncryable tears.

Alan Coulter sat in the little cubicle sectioned off from
the rest of the noisy office by sheets of thin cardboard. He
had his daily "to do" list in his hand. Progressing well for
midway through the morning – phone calls, reports, meeting with Robertson, all ticked.

He was a rule-bound creature. His kids told him, regularly. Maddy once said it. Not disparagingly, he didn't think.
A man who followed orders, in his personal and professional life. Martha needed rules as much as he did – maybe,
way back, when they first met, it was one of the things that
brought them together. Certainly now, with her ill-health,
she needed order, regularity. Any departure from the daily
routine developed over years of being parents, could start

up one of her headaches. Holidays, social engagement, kids' school outings, his own long and unpredictable hours were all potential crises.

Sy Kennedy, he thought, might have been a rule-follower, of sorts. Micky too. At school Sy was a wild kid, but his final hours suggested he was disciplined, biddable. He had met someone, as arranged, agreed to be taken to a deserted patch of park at dawn. It was just a question of whose rules you followed.

Frances Mullholland on the other hand was probably a breaker of everyone's rules. A genuinely feral kid. Everything they knew about her school life bore that out: constantly in trouble, cheeky with teachers, excitable and unstable. "Thick as two short planks," one teacher had confided in them. "Mad as a March hare," said a neighbour. The sort of thirteen-year-old girl that could go missing for a week and a half and no one thought it strange. Friends thought she was with other friends. Family didn't seem to care much. Someone gave that lassie a rule and her instinct was to smash it, scream blue murder at it.

He'd switched his mobile to vibrate only for the meeting with the boss. It buzzed against his leg now – one of the strange new experiences modernity has brought. Not work: everyone knew he was here. He sighed – one of the kids wanting something. Then again, could be Maddy, suggesting a drink. More likely, Martha in a panic, or – it was always possible – ill.

"Coulter here."

A pleasant surprise. Jenny Tate from the Press Office. And with some info. "Came across it almost by chance." She was going to read whatever it was out over the phone, but he told her he'd come down. In this job you had to savour these moments.

Maddy was walking back from the High Court, enjoying the fresher turn the weather had taken.

Work in the law and you'll know that anything can happen on the High Street. A worn thoroughfare spiralling through Glasgow's history, it runs from the Cathedral to the Gallowgate where smugglers and cut-throats and reivers and chicken-stealers used to get hanged. The official border of the East End, until Yuppies moved in around Bell Street and the fringes of Bridgeton and the Saltmarket. Now there was old crime and new crime combined. Wide boys mugged naive owner-occupiers; fatcats sold upmarket drugs behind juice-bar counters. All the same, you don't expect, as a highly esteemed PF Principal Depute, to get knocked to the pavement by a shabby middle-aged man jumping off a bus.

"Sorry," Coulter mumbled. "I was going to get off at the next stop when I saw you."

Maddy, having got over the shock of a detective falling out the sky directly onto her, thought the situation quaintly old-fashioned. People used to jump off buses all the time, in the days when they were open-backed.

"Driver had kept the door open, seeing as how it's sunny."

"You should have arrested him."

"I'll phone ahead, catch him further down the line."

Even with Alan, Maddy was never quite sure if policemen were joking or not. They were scarily zealous about rules. He took a hold of Maddy's arm. They had become quite close colleagues, friends even – but never to the point of physical contact before. Coulter's mind was clearly very far from social niceties, however. Something was exciting him, and it wasn't the touch of Maddy's flesh.

A door in that stretch of the High Street could have led into almost any kind of establishment – cappuccino bar, piano bar, trendy club pointlessly open in the afternoon, old-fashioned tea shop. As luck would have it, it was one of the more traditional hostelries. Invisible veil of cigarette smoke as you went in; whisky and flat beer fumes mingled with human smells that made you regret the smoking ban – sweat and farts and feet. It was quiet, though, despite the pub being half full; folk murmuring, keeping their voices down. They could clock a polis and a lawyer in seconds flat.

"D'you want to go somewhere else?" Coulter looked around.

"I'd have thought this was right up your street."

"Bit manky even for me."

"Get us in a drink. I get the impression you have something urgent to say."

He moved towards the bar, and flinched. "Shit. I'm going to have to order a couple of fizzy waters. In *here*." But he went about the unsavoury business like a man.

"How's Martha?" she asked when he came back, unscathed if a little flushed in the cheek.

"Having a bad week."

It was seldom, it seemed to Maddy, that Martha had a good week. "Sorry to hear that. Right. What?"

Coulter produced from under his jacket an A4 envelope.

"Did you have that stuck in your belt?" He did; Maddy burst out laughing. "What – instead of a six-shooter?"

Coulter smiled, humouring her, and took out the contents of the envelope. A newspaper, which she recognised as being old, the paper too limp to be today's. "You know what Potter's Field is?"

"The field bought with Judas Iscariot's thirty pieces of silver'

He looked at her, astonished. "Is it?"

"Is this a trick question, or did a sudden need for Biblical trivia come over you? Judas, on a guilt trip after the event, took the silver back to the temple, but even the high priests wanted nothing to do with the blood money – that's probably where the phrase came from now I think about it."

"What's any of this got to do with potters or fields?"

"They put the money to good use. Bought a field from the local potter… Do potters have fields? Well, this one did. And they made it into a graveyard for paupers and strangers."

"That's the connection."

"To what?"

"Is that where the story ends?"

"Story, Inspector? This is divinely inspired doctrine. Didn't Judas then hang himself from a tree in that same potter's field? Don't quote me on that bit."

"How d'you *know* all this?"

"Convent education. That and shining my shoes so highly the boys can see the reflection of my knickers. I'm pretty sure this is the strangest conversation I'm going to have all day, Alan."

He put the paper in front of her. An odd size of page; unusual typefaces. The headline didn't mean anything to her. "Signs of the Times". Not a front page scoop. She checked the top of the page – page 16, *New York Times*, January 2005. She found the article hard to read, the light being dim, Alan staring at her, male drinkers glancing at her from all corners. Slowly, however, she got the gist.

Potter's Field was also the name of a graveyard in New York. Deceased paupers and unidentified bodies were buried in the cemetery run by the city – an astonishing number of unclaimed cadavers and lonely deceased buried every year. Like the high priests' field of blood. Coulter was getting impatient waiting. He tapped a paragraph towards the end of the piece. Typical flatfoot, ignoring the outer layers of information, gagging for the quick hit of hard facts.

In the last decade there has been a series of distressing killings. Seven young men, or boys, murdered in as many years, one as young as eleven years old. Only two were identified by family members. The killings might not have been connected – simply the sad reflection of a violent city in violent times – were it not for another gruesome link. Each of the victims had knife-wounds across their mouths. Pathology indicated that the wounds were inflicted either just prior to or moments after the victims' deaths. The actual causes of death vary from case to case. Four were shot – summarily executed. Two were stabbed through the heart, and a sixteen-year-old black youth was beaten to death. Only one of the victims was Caucasian.

Commanding Officer Casci of Brooklyn Court Section told The Times last year: "The only elements that link the murders are the age of the victims and the wounds received to the face. Each of the individual cases is being kept open and will continue to be kept open until a perpetrator for these brutal crimes is behind bars."

Officer Casci went on to say that they are working on gangland connections. The knife-cuts across the lips are probably a warning, or punishment. An "Omerta" sign out of Mafia film lore. However, two of the victims are thought to have been involved in "wilding" – kids high on drugs and alcohol running amok through Central Park and other civic spaces, attacking anyone they meet. Many "wilders" caught in the past have turned out also to be drug dealers. Major narcotic cartels are thought to be behind...

"So my Omerta thing wasn't so daft after all."

"Excuse me?"

"Dan McKillop wasn't convinced by my gangland revenge theory."

Coulter pulled the paper away and put it back in the envelope. "These are your copies. There are five other articles in the envelope about the same murders."

Murders, exactly like at least two in her own city, but in New York. Seven of them over ten years. That strange brew of emotions bubbled up inside her – disgust, a sinking feeling; but at the same time, a rising of hope you get with the discovery of new information. She and Coulter sat quietly, their brains working overtime, eyes exchanging knowing, wondering, glances. Like a pair of addicts, ashamed of themselves while lusting for more.

"Hey, maybe we'll get a dirty weekend in the Big Apple out of it," she said at last.

Seven kids dead. Joking was all a respectable person could do. Coulter got up to take the glasses back to the bar. Maddy took the *New York Times* back out of the crushed envelope. There was a picture of Potter's Field, looking rather attractive, expensive even. A serious-looking authority figure – mid forties? – was labelled Officer Louis Casci. A sad looking young black boy, Derrick Braithewaite, was one of the few named victims of the New York murders.

III

The original plan was to send Coulter off to New York – economy travel, second class B&B in some no doubt naff part of Queens. But the Kelvingrove and Bearsden murders were becoming a national and media obsession and, by extension, the whole issue of delinquency. John MacDougall, chair of the Committee on Youth Crime and Delinquency was forever being interviewed, consulted, invited to conferences. He had already spent a week each in New York, Boston and Washington, and accepted an invitation from Gracie Mansions to return to New York later in the year. The Committee feared that sending a mere working copper over, B&B or nay, might smack of a junket. Which is how New York ended up footing the bill and sending Commanding Officer Louis Casci to Glasgow instead.

Maddy watched him, standing leaning on a fence, a look of utter disbelief on his face. Casci and Coulter, she thought, were near enough interchangeable. Louis maybe four or five years younger than Alan, thicker-haired in that Italian way, bit stouter. But they were about the same height, had the same unearned youthfulness about them, a kind of innocence despite their shared profession. Both were easy men to be with.

"Are those *real?*"

Maddy had taken over the weekend tour guide shift – Martha wasn't well, so Alan couldn't come out to play; Rangers were at an end-of-season climax and John Russell had got himself an away-ticket. Commanding Officer Casci of Brooklyn District clearly wasn't important enough for Crawford Robertson or any other top brass to spend quality time with. Alan had asked her to steer clear of talking shop – the poor Yank could do with a break.

"Of course they're real!" she laughed.

Louis had nodded politely at the exhibits in the Burrell Collection and Pollock House. But he clearly wasn't really as interested in pre-history or early modern painting as he'd claimed when she'd suggested the trip. Driving back through the park grounds, though, the man nearly had a fit.

"Holy *fuck* – what is *that*?!"

Maddy had stopped the car and let him get out, intrigued by the American's mouth-gaping awe. "Highland cattle."

"*What*?"

"They're just hairy cows."

"They're *yaks* for chrissakes. Or bison or something. They're *Scottish*?"

Maddy remembered being overawed by a simple olive tree in Liguria – the weird, neanderthal way it curled round itself, like a gnarled, bad tempered little man – to the ill-concealed boredom of a handsome young Lothario who didn't hang around much after that. Wasn't only Americans who became wide-eyed babies abroad. "You've never seen these before?"

Who would have thought that the one truly surprising and inspiring thing about her country would be Highland cattle? Next time she gets to go on a conference somewhere, forget the pipes and clarsach CDs, the Gray and Vettriano postcards, the Colin Baxter landscapes. A couple of plastic-framed photos of hairy cows and she'd be Miss Popular.

They were deep in the heart of the residential south side of the city, but the scene in front of them was like something out of Brigadoon. Pity Casci hadn't been around the last few weeks. The heatwave had passed its climax and was guttering out. Maddy liked these kinds of days better. The heaviness taken out of the air; everything softer, still warm enough and a hint of sea-spray even in the metropolis. Casci managed to pull himself away from a Beatle-mopped heifer that seemed just as mesmerised by him.

"She's never seen a New York cop before," Maddy grinned as they walked back towards the car park.

"So. Procurator Fiscal – you're like a prosecuting attorney, yeah?"

"Right now I'm just a friend of a friend who's showing you the delights of our humble little city. But, since you ask, a Fiscal's *much* more important than any old common or garden prosecution lawyer."

At the car, she got in, but he stood by the door. He leaned down to talk in to her. "Take me to Kelvingrove?"

"Surely DI Coulter took you?"

"I'd like to see it again."

"Okay."

Casci got in the car, pulling his legs almost up to his chin. He looked out appreciatively at the woodlands in the middle of a grimy city, well-tended lawns on one side, prettily boggy fields on the other. The breeziness of the modern Burrell ahead; solid Scottishness of Pollock House behind. "That's where you're different from us," he said, still looking around. "You go to great lengths to hide the misery and the shit."

They were halfway through a *thali* for two at Mother India's Cafe – Louis lapping up the contents of every cute little dish – when the waiter brought a distracted-looking Coulter to their table.

"That looks good. I'll just ask for an extra plate and cutlery, shall I?"

"Back off, buddy. This is a meal for *two*."

Coulter smiled, but Maddy saw he was pissed off. She asked the waiter to keep the dishes coming, from now on enough for three. Coulter sat down, dragging his chair back from the table, separating himself from his companions by a matter of inches.

"So. You two had a nice day?"

"You ever seen Highland cows? Jesus."

"I heard you were up at the murder scene."

"How d'you know that?"

"We keep an eye on the place. You were spotted."

"Impressive. Perp revisiting the crime scene sort of thing?"

"Sort of."

Casci and Coulter, Maddy decided, were too alike to get along. One at a time, they were calm, easy company. Double them up and the effect was mutual suspicion. Coulter looked directly at her. Perhaps more accusingly than he meant.

"I like to get a feel of SOC," Casci said. "You know what I mean?"

"And...?"

"We okay to talk in front of the prosecution?"

"Have either of you talked about anything else all day?"

"No."

"That's not true, Louis. I told you about potato scones and Iron Brew, and the Scottish Colourists, and Highland Cattle."

"Big fuckin' hairy things. Jesus."

"Could we forget the cows, please! *Did* you feel anything of interest, think of anything?"

Casci pushed aside his dish. "You know, I think I did. Five of my seven victims were killed in out-of-the-way places—"

"Aren't most people?"

"Only two taken out on city streets. In the middle of the night. A third in a derelict building. One in Central Park, in a kind of hidden recess behind trees, not unlike your Kelvingrove scenario. The most recent, on a river bank, south of the city."

"That leaves two?" Maddy asked.

"One on an island, upstate. And, curiously, a girl found in a rich man's garden. You asked what I *felt* was different, Alan...." When they had got to the clearing in the rhododendrons this afternoon, Casci had fallen silent. He wasn't the most garrulous of men anyway, but he had gone particularly quiet, pacing out the little patch of grass like a prisoner in a cell. "Today reminded me of a couple of my murder scenes. Not just it being out of the way." He stopped to take a sip of his Indian beer. "In fact, you'll have noticed that there are better-hidden spots right close by."

Maddy looked to Coulter, wondering if he *had* noticed. She hadn't, until Casci had pointed them out. There were gaps deeper in the rhodos, away from the track that both Whyte and Docherty had run along. The killers could have taken Sy and Micky closer to the river, further away from the road and any tracks.

"It's as if the killer *liked* the spot. The thought's occurred to me before. Down by that river bank. On the island. Next to a Japanese garden area in Central Park. Or the garden the girl was found in – like yours, it was the best garden around."

Coulter was normally an enthusiastic eater; but he had balanced a forkful of spiced courgette all the time Casci was talking. "Hang on. You mean a hired hand, a practised killer, takes his victims to less than perfectly safe places, just because he likes the *look* of them?!"

"Or because he likes the *feel* of them."

Derrick Braithewaite was the most recent of the victims; body found August 10 2004. Driven in a large 4x4 on Highway 9D to a drop-off point between the villages of Cold Spring and Beacon, around fifty miles north of New York City. From there, Derrick was taken on a rowing boat to tiny Bannerman Island a few hundred yards out. There's an old castle on the island, with a caretaker. The caretaker doesn't live there, but crosses over on his boat every morning. Derrick was shot in the back – as if he were an escaping convict, or slave, gunned down. A .38 bullet penetrated his lung and his spleen, a second lodged in his stomach. He took a long time to die. Maybe he'd had just enough energy to call for help when Jim Tickell, the castle caretaker, arrived around 7.30 the following morning. But he couldn't get enough volume behind his cry, or his windpipe was too full of blood. Whatever, Tickell didn't hear him. Braithewaite wasn't found until the day after that, Wednesday; time of death estimated at 12.00 midday, Tuesday 9th.

Hopefully, he had been unconscious. If not, he shivered through seven hours of damp and darkness, heard Tickell arriving, and a group of reconstruction volunteers working on restoring parts of the old castle. He'd have heard the rush-hour traffic across the narrow stretch of water, and heard it again, lunchtime. He'd have drifted in and out of consciousness. Would have seen the sun rise along with his hopes of being found, and watched it disappear again behind clouds, a summer shower falling unexpectedly and heavily. Wiping away all forensics, footsteps, fibres.

"There's a connection for you," Casci said, suddenly breezy. "Bannerman Castle. Not really a castle at all, actually, but an arsenal."

The evening streets had an end-of-term easiness about them; it was after ten but there was still a glow in the sky, a lilac blush in the air they were breathing. Students called to each other across Woodlands Road, arranging trysts in bars up town, exchanging information about parties. Coulter, Casci and Shannon – they sound like a law firm, Maddy thought – took up the whole width of the pavement, each enjoying their own space. Anyone passing would have taken them for a bunch of old friends. A couple and a brother-in-law maybe, out for a quiet drink on a warm night.

"The island's real name is Pollopel. Old Indian name. It's called Bannerman after the castle which, according to the stuff at the visitor centre, is built with turrets and walled garden and moat in the old Scottish baronial style."

"Why?"

"The original Bannerman – so the story goes – was the only MacDonald to escape those other guys at that place."

Maddy laughed. "I hope your criminal investigation details are a little more exact, Officer Casci. The Campbells? Glencoe?"

"That's them. He was called Bannerman, because he saved the MacDonald banner. Carried it over thistles and shit, Campbells showering him with bullets or spears or whatever. Even escaped those crazed Highland cows."

They turned into University Avenue, the big limes and horse chestnuts on Kelvin Way turning their heads slowly in the night breeze, silver birches silent. Three people laughing – minutes after hearing how Louis had seen a sixteen year old lying dead in a hollow of earth and rocks and tree-roots, executed on a barren island. Maddy glanced, ashamed, up at the trees. Then corrected herself: mustn't beat yourself up for laughing. If there was a heaven up there somewhere, maybe Derrick was in it, laughing too, the worst of it over.

He remained unidentified for more than six months. They couldn't match any missing person's details to him. Finally, with no leads as to who murdered him and no family or friends to inform, they buried him in Potter's Field. Almost as soon as they had, Cheryll Braithewaite arrived from Canada.

"She'd been searching for her son for months," Louis said, kicking an imaginary stone on the pavement. "Family were Barbadian with cousins in Toronto."

Cheryll, raising Derrick, his two young sisters and little brother, on her own, on the salary of a sales assistant in a Bridgetown travel agent, had managed to save enough to send him to Canada to enrol in an engineering course. Thanks to a perfectly innocent family misunderstanding – the Canadian cousins hadn't expected him until September, just before college started – Cheryll didn't even know he was missing until a month after he was dead. The last place she'd thought of looking was in New York. Derrick had flown directly from Grantly Adams airport to Toronto. The Braithewaites had no connections anywhere in the States.

"Derrick was the exception." Casci wheezed, the hill through the university taxing his beefy build. "On a number of counts. The only Bajan. The other black males were Haitians." He regained his breath as the hill slipped back down towards Byres Road.

"Sure, he'd been running with a few of the bad boys in the 'hood' back in Bridgetown. One of the reasons Cheryll wanted him out. But nothing serious. Also, he came from a family who, though not exactly rich, could afford, and cared enough, to have him exhumed and given a decent burial."

"Back in Barbados?" Coulter asked.

Casci shook his head. "Couldn't afford that. But a better district of that heavenly metropolis, Potter's Field. And the proper C of E rigmarole. A few cousins down from Canada. A nice headstone."

They had names for only two of the other black victims. "Henri-Charles Lespinasse and Ti-Guy Plissard. Both New Yorkers from the Haitian community, sons of known and convicted criminals. And both with impressive records, for a fifteen and a seventeen year old."

"I thought everyone in Potter's Field was unidentified."

"Plissard and Lespinasse, too, for a month or more. Families like that don't go to the authorities, not even to collect their dead."

Of the seven victims mentioned in the *New York Times*, Louis Casci reckoned two were completely unrelated to each other or the rest. There had been dozens of unidentified young cadavers buried in Potter's Field since the first of his cases, nearly a decade ago. The *Times* said that seven of them had been slashed around the mouth.

"Not so. One – older than the others, maybe as much as

twenty – had been slashed around the lips and cheeks all right. But he'd been slashed to pieces everywhere else as well. As manic a knife-attack as you'll come across. That doesn't match up with the cool professionalism of the others. Cut *only* around the mouth, and *after* being shot. Or, in Plissard's case, being stabbed in the heart."

The other case Casci discounted was the only girl – to this day still unclaimed and unidentified. Like Frances Mullholland, found shot in a rich man's garden in Staten Island.

"Shot in the head, and then slashed. But on the hands as well as the mouth. For me, she doesn't fit the bill."

So, five New York victims: Braithewaite, Lespinasse and Plissard. A fourth, unidentified young black boy; around seventeen, dressed more in Jamaican garb than Haitian. Killed in parkland in Queens, six years ago this month.

"And the fifth's the Irish kid?" This was the one Coulter wanted to know about.

They were standing at the end of Ashton Lane, throngs of summer revellers all around them, heading for the bars where you could stand outside on the cobblestones, lean on upturned barrels, sip and talk and watch the night thicken. Maddy knew Coulter wouldn't join them for a drink. He'd jump on the Underground here, get back to Martha and the family.

"Goodman Lane."

"That's an *Irish* name?" Coulter looked askance.

"Well it ain't Haitian. Goodman – named after Bono."

Coulter stared at him, confused.

"The lead singer of U2?"

Coulter was none the wiser. Maddy helped him out: "Forgotten your Latin? Bono, meaning good."

A large group of young people, babbling some language incomprehensible to any of them, washed around him, hiding Coulter from view for a moment.

"Not an IRA supporter was he? Goodman."

"Goody was too spaced-out, lobotomised by crack, jellies, uppers and downers to know what *day* it was never mind foreign political movements."

Coulter nodded and turned away, looking lonely.

"His old man knew, though," Casci kept talking. "Bernard Lane. Laundered IRA cash through a club he ran, supposedly for aficionados of songs from the old country."

Coulter searched in his pocket for the Underground fare. "Let's chat about that tomorrow. Have a nice night."

You told me again, you preferred handsome men. She'd always liked that line. Maybe Janis Joplin got the choice more often than Maddy. Anyway, Maddy found her definition of "handsome" shifting these days. Certainly a young Leonard Cohen – even an *old* Leonard Cohen – would have fitted the bill. An old fantasy she'd forgotten about: deserted Greek island, retsina and black tobacco, a white-walled room with one small, single bed. She and Leonard in it. Dawn beginning to bloom outside; the hot, sad smell of jasmine and juniper. *But for me you'd make an exception.*

Louis Casci was a reasonably impressive catch. Italian-American, hot-shot in the NYPD; tailored, clear-featured, powerful-looking. Exotic; at least, until he took his clothes off. Few people can retain exoticism in the buff. Common humanity wipes away most traces of singularity. Flaws make us all familiar – the paunches and scars, knock-knees and bald bits, the blemishes. Our bodies make us nobodies.

But for a while there last night, the magic had worked. For once she had hit upon precisely the right combination of drink and food, jokes and conversation. It all went smoothly. One more Semillon spritzer in Bar Brel after Coulter'd gone off. Then, at Louis's clever suggestion, a coffee in Tinderbox. The two of them rediscovering their Italian-ness together. Her joking about Italian immigrants to Glasgow thinking they were in New York.

"Didn't they realise they hadn't crossed a great big ocean?"

"Story is, they got to Liverpool, bought tickets for the boat, were sailed round the Isle of Man a hundred times and booted off in Glasgow."

That old chestnut; she didn't believe a word of it. She did, of course, believe in Nonno's Great Adventure, but didn't mention that to Louis Casci. They tried out together their limited language skills in Italian. They walked through cool midnight air. He might as well crash at her place, they agreed – her floor couldn't be any more uncomfortable than the cheap hotel he was staying in. A G&T in the sitting room. Left unfinished. . . .

She hadn't felt awkward and she didn't back off. She didn't mind when he shed his shiny, tailored skin and became just another forty-something man; had he been beautiful all the way through she'd have felt plainer and inferior. She was delighted at – emboldened by – his ordinariness.

She was a little darker-skinned than him. Somehow that helped. Helped her fade into the night, the unlit sheets. It was warm enough to keep the window open and that made her think of films set in New Orleans or LA. They slid easily together, she and Officer Casci. They could both do with losing a few pounds, but she felt lithe and strong, graceful even, in a solid sort of way. When their eyes met – and neither went in for too much of that – they smiled. No one was pretending to be overwhelmed; no one's life was changing.

The incident room is never deserted, not even on a Sunday. At the very least, there's the HOLMES supervisor, or one of the deputies, at the door. There are usually one or two indexers, too. Kids almost, same age as Coulter's eldest two, squeezing every last penny out of overtime, desperately trying to get on the house market merry-go-round.

It's hard to find a place to think. Too much going on at home, what with Martha and everything... He didn't have an office any more, just a "station" in an open plan, a "hot desk". The relative emptiness of the HOLMES Room was the best he could hope for. After a few sociable comments – the Old Firm and weather, a bit of shop-talk – he got past the supervisor. A geeky indexer was gawking at his computer screen, totally uninterested in him.

Coulter hated HOLMES. It turned policing into accountancy – a career full of folders and files and passwords and permissions, instead of leads and labyrinths and the intellect. They didn't trust detectives to *think* any more; they'd rather that was done by machines. He even hated the name – Home Office Large Major Enquiry System. The bad Sherlock acronym was cringe-worthy enough, but they couldn't even get it right. *Large Major?* The whole approach was a way of restricting professionals; a form of social control. You couldn't speak to *anyone* – not a witness, or a victim, or a self-confessed gangster, or a psycho in prison for smashing folks' heads – without getting the go-ahead from the HOLMES supervisor, who inherited *his* authority from The Computer. They were all in thrall to it, even on a Sunday morning like this; its ghostly whirr, the banks of terminals where there used to be walls and whiteboards and real writing. The flashing cursors.

There's info in there – Coulter was staring blankly at a screen that, equally blankly stared back – on every serious crime in the country in the past twenty years, and a goodly number of crimes worldwide from Asia to the Americas. He pressed a key, expecting nothing. Millions upon millions of little pieces of information, floating around in cyberspace, coming together at the touch of a button. Amongst them, his own little current cases: The Kelvingrove Executions (password Red Rhoddo); and the Bearsden Garden Murder (Tall Trees).

He'd spent a month now, talking again and again to Sy Kennedy's family, his friends, schools, neighbours. Ditto Frances Mullholland. He, Alan Coulter, personally, in the company of DS Russell, or WPC Dalgarno, or some other colleague, had spoken to residents as far as six streets back from the addresses of the known deceased, and a mile and a half around their places of death. Yet the "Statements" with his name against them were a drop in the ocean. The guy at the door, the HOLMES Supervisor, had told him that so far there had been over 3,000 statements taken, on the Sy and Micky X case alone. Nearly the same for Operation Tall Trees. Every bobby on every beat, it seemed, had a little bit more data to throw into the HOLMES' den. The system had a hunger for any kind of information.

Three thousand pieces of information – and not the slightest sniff of Micky X. A perfectly healthy young man is found dead, in the company of a pal about whom they now knew almost everything, and yet there's nothing to link him to some kind of lived life. Not to a parent, or to an uncle, not even a school or borstal, a football team. Nada. HOLMES droned and hissed, whispering to itself, like it was keeping something back. They gave it everything they could – Micky's height, weight, snicked eyebrow, Coq Sportif gear, estimated time of death, estimated time of arrival in Kelvingrove. Zilch.

Who *was* the little shit?

He called up the image of the victim's face. Coulter felt that he knew him. That face, even in death, was local, he was sure of it. The cut of the jaw, that particular shade of pinkish skin, the scraggy neck. A wee Glaswegian hard man if ever he saw one. The gear, the expression of sour guardedness, even in death. Maddy Shannon reckoned that his hand was stretching out, looking for Sy's, reaching out for a final human contact. Coulter disagreed. Micky was pushing Sy away – solitary to the bitter end.

She'd almost forgotten. The Sunday before Nonno's party; she'd agreed to go to Mass with her mother, so that they could speak to Father Jamieson. Make arrangements.

"I'll go with you," Casci said.

"To *Church*?" She'd scooped her clothes up and jogged to the bathroom. Without the emollient of G&T, midnight ambience and horniness, her Yankee copper wouldn't be quite so forgiving about the state of her. She had to shout quite loud. Roddy Estate Agent had said the house would have got an extra twenty grand if she'd put in an en-suite. Thank God she hadn't: this morning, that would be a proximity too far.

"I was going to ask you anyway."

She came back into the bedroom – brushed, washed, covered up. Louis had taken advantage, too. The moment she'd left the room, he'd jumped up, pulled on his kecks and shirt, obliterating all memory of nakedness and intimacy.

"Ask me what?" She sat in front of her dressing table mirror. She liked this pose; like something out of Jane Austen. The lady brushing her hair in front of her gentle-man companion. Joan Fontaine in *Rebecca*. The old-fashioned, low-level eroticism of it. Loretta Young in *The Bishop's Wife*.

"Where I could catch Mass."

She looked round at him in amazement. "That's a joke – yes? Where you can *catch* Mass?"

"I'm not sure what's amusing you." He was smiling, but uneasy. "The way I speak, or the fact that I go to church?"

"*Do* you go to church? Or is this just some weird way of thanking a girl?"

"Do *you*?"

"Only if mummy insists."

"I go sometimes. The shit you face every day. You want to believe something. Then you get there..."

"And it's all nonsense."

He smiled; turned away.

"Today's one of the days you want to go?"

"Why not. You're going."

She nodded; hoping it was boredom pushing him towards St. Catherine's, not guilt.

They got into church late, the only pew available one up from Rosa. The poor woman had to sit through the whole service – including an overly long sermon by Father Mike – glancing back at her daughter and the strange new man.

When it was finally over, Father Mike stood at the church door in his full vestments to greet his parishioners, like he was the Doge of Venice. When Maddy and Louis arrived, he gave one of his warmest welcoming smiles. "Good morning! Maddalena. Thank you for coming. This must be... Chas?"

"Matt, Father."

"The spiritual atheist?"

"Actually this is neither Chas nor Matt. This is Louis."

Her mother stared in turns at Maddy and the unknown man. Where, in conversation in Sarti's, she'd liked the idea of her daughter having an adventurous love life, it was quite a different matter inside the chapel door. Particularly when there seemed to be three of them on the go at the same time. Chas, Matt and Louis.

Louis putting on a smile every bit as charming as Mike's and probably every bit as habitual. "Lovely service, Father. Thanks." Then he bowed slightly: "Signora."

Slick enough to make Maddy wonder if she'd been more of a victim to the seductive arts last night than she'd realised. This morning the guy was a genuine expert. The accent suddenly seemed more Kennedy-like, the voice deeper, gravelly. But *thanking* a priest for saying Mass? Calling her mother *signora*? These were touches of genius. Maddy didn't know whether to feel a little proud in the reflected glow, or creeped out.

"You sound American, Louis?"

"Product of Father Duffy of County Tyrone's strictest of schools. St Joseph's Sunnyside, Queens, New York."

"What kind of strict school, Louis?" Rosa asked, fearing borstals.

"For altar boys."

Bang on the money. Father Mike and Rosa laughed loud and heartily. Louis, like an old pro, knew he'd scored a direct hit, and left the stage quickly and elegantly.

"I'm going to see if I can pick myself up a *Sunday News*. See how the Yankees got on."

Another round of handshakes, another little bow for Rosa, an acceptably intimate nod for Maddy, and he was off. Glasgow's very own Bill Clinton for a day. Maddy waited for the swell of interest in him to die away, answering her mother's and the priest's questions about who he was, how long he was here for... She remained dignified and hesitant, giving as little away as possible.

"Just a colleague." But she heard the note of coquetry in her own voice; felt a flush in her cheek. "Now, what about Nonno?"

As she asked, the Parish Priest, Monsignor Connolly, joined them. Maddy's little sunny moment was over. Mike Jamieson she could take – overly matey and simplistic as he was. Connolly was that other kind of priest, straight out of central casting: old, hairy-nosed, dandruffed soutane, bad-tempered. There was no priest so ugly, however, that her mother didn't immediately flirt with him.

"I'm so sorry you can't make the celebration, Father."

It transpired that, actually, he wouldn't be in time for saying the Mass at Nonno's house, but might just be able to make it along in time for coffee and sandwiches after, and a wee drink.

"That'd be wonderful, Father!" Rosa was over the moon. *Two* priests at her little party.

"And you must be the granddaughter." He stared at Maddy through hazy, perhaps cataract-shrouded, eyes. He had the look of a man who was forever a moment away from tears – either of anger or despair. He was taller than Maddy, uniformed in black and magenta, a High Priest of an ancient and arcane order. But that wasn't what made him scary. Something else; a darkness, a feeling that he'd seen things no human wants to see.

"Maddalena." She put out her hand. Well, *she* had seen things too. Had Monsignor Connolly watched as a pathologist turned over two dead boys like they were pebbles? Seen the smashed jaws, the slashed, dead skin? They looked at one another for a moment, then Connolly turned away, spoke to the mother.

Maddy tried to keep an interest as the little trinity around her talked times and numbers of guests, the crockery needed for a house Mass, candles and cakes and donations. Monsignor Connolly took Rosa into the sacristy so he could write down a few crucial details. Nonno's name, age, the date of his Adventure, the names of all his children and grandchildren, dead and alive.

Maddy was left alone with Mike, waiting for Louis's return.

"He scares young children," Mike laughed.

"Scares *me*."

"You don't have to live with him!" Then, gravely: "Joking apart. He's as good a man as ever I've known."

"Is he? In what way?" She wouldn't have spoken so cheekily to Connolly himself. The old man intimidated her; Father Jamieson merely irritated her.

"Most of us live on the surface of things. Going about our jobs, eating, sleeping, watching TV…"

"I seldom get to watch TV, father. And you ought to try my job for a day or two."

"I wasn't meaning *you* personally, Maddalena."

He was good at this; might even have made a half-decent lawyer. And he was, in a way, right. Izzy and Manda could deal with the same cases as Maddy, yet were capable of leaving behind the murdered prostitutes, revenge killings, wives battered to death, and go happily home to Marks and Sparks microwave meals and *Friends*.

"Monsignor Connolly I think of as older in every way. Deeper. You know – I think of him as a deepwater fish."

A weird line – one that could only be leading somewhere in particular. They both saw Louis returning, crossing the road, leafing through a *Sunday Mail*. Maddy hoped he'd come over quick – Jamieson was about to deliver some well-practised homily on her.

"Unbelievers are like fish, too. Not big, ancient creatures like Joe Connolly whose eyes can see in the darkest deep. Most agnostics – like you and your friends, Maddalena – swim in shoals. God is the water. He's all around you. You need Him to breathe, to exist, yet you have no notion of His presence."

And with that, he was off. His little lecture – which had the feel of being both learned from someone else and repeated at every opportunity – completed.

As she and Louis walked away – the policeman still flicking though the paper, genuinely trying to find the result of a baseball game – she put her hand through his arm.

"How seriously do you take this stuff?"

She nodded back at the chapel. He shrugged.

"You're a mackerel."

"*Excuse* me?"

Ian Lennon was somehow always outside. Even in the blank airless box of the interview room, he brought in a whiff of earth and root and callous nature. The smart suit and leather shoes didn't tame him. His was a wildness that didn't just threaten but got into your bones, like a snell shower. Russell leaned forward reluctantly, a man bending into a headwind. Casci peered the way a tourist would at an old mossy castle in the mist, or at a bleak and craggy view.

"Aye I've been to New York."

"To do what?" DI Coulter didn't feel frightened or frustrated by the gardener; he was a puzzle he had to solve. How to disentangle the creeper from the husk of the old, empty tree.

"To see the Statue of Liberty."

"Three times?"

"And the Twin Towers. And where they used to be."

"I'd appreciate it, sir, if you wouldn't make light of that tragedy."

"Sorry, pal. Never liked those buildings. And you see worse things on the telly every night of the week. Just, unfortunately for them, not in America."

Casci had been playing interested onlooker until now. He drew his chair closer to the table. Opened a folder. "Information was recorded about your visits."

"So much for the land of the free."

"The third and last visit you made – according to our intelligence – was November 1996—"

"Before the Good Friday Ceasefire," Russell interjected. No one made any comment on the observation.

"You stayed with a Mr. Toby Lafferty in Washington Heights. You made two inland trips. One by train to Chicago, where you met with Mr. Jack Burton and a Mr. Enrique Gotzone. So far correct?"

Coulter watched Lennon closely as Casci read through the notes. The gardener was a man who'd been trained in the "whatever you say, say nothing" school. His instinct was to stonewall, obfuscate, mislead. Even when he didn't have to it came as naturally as breathing.

"If you say so."

"Messrs Lafferty and Burton are both Irish Republicans," Casci said. "There's no point in you denying that as we know—"

"I've no intention o' denying it. Most Yanks have sympathy with the Irish over the colonial English. Almost anybody I'd meet would fit that bill."

"They were *active* Republicans."

"True. Toby liked his golf."

"It might interest you to know, Mr. Lennon, that since your last visit to our country we've apprehended Mr. Lafferty. And become quite friendly with Mr. Burton."

"So I've heard."

"You'll know a Mr. Lane as well?"

"What is this? A memory test? So far we've got a Burton, a Lafferty, now a Wayne."

"Lane. Bernard Lane. Collected a lot of money for your cause."

"The Bring Back Dana campaign?"

"What do you know about Enrique Gotzone?"

"Names are getting harder now."

"Joseba Gotzone. Pal of Jack's."

"Jack. Lafferty?"

"Burton."

Coulter was impressed by Casci: he showed no irritation at Lennon's attempt to confuse. He kept a serious face and didn't take his eyes off his prey. The pair of them following in the slipstream of each others' flow, like birds wheeling together in the air.

"Maybe I had a beer with him and a few others. In Chicago."

"Gotzone is also a fundraiser for the Chavez regime in Venezuela."

"Chavez. Definitely never had a drink with him. That a Cork name?

"Fundraising mainly done by money laundering. Gotzone is a Basque name – does he have ETA connections?"

"No, now I'm totally lost." Lennon eyed Casci, then Coulter.

"Must take you back, Ian," Coulter tried to mirror Casci's insouciance, "to the good old days with Charlie in the Empire and the Cottars." Lennon didn't react; Casci did, though, turning to Coulter inquisitively. "First we ever heard of our good friend Mr. Lennon here," Coulter explained, "was way back. Before I was out of uniform. He used to run for Charlie Dempsey–"

"So you say. Proof?"

Coulter kept talking to Casci without glancing at Lennon. "Dempsey owned a couple of pubs in the north of the city. From the Empire Bar and the Cottars Arms he organised a protection racket for every other pub north of the river. Ian here used to collect – and clean up any messes–"

"You're talking shite."

"But you've got to hand it to old Charlie, he wasn't an out-and-out crook and bully. Some of the dosh from his pubs and ancillary services went to good causes."

"Let me guess," Casci said. "Good causes based in Northern Ireland."

"Exactly."

"If you had proof o' any of that," Lennon smiled, "you'd have Charlie in jail. At the very least you'd have closed him down."

Still Coulter ignored him; continued talking quietly to Casci, as though only the two of them were in the room. "Young Charlie, who's taken over the business from his dad, has lost the old man's hunger for good works."

"It's a demise in community concern we've noted in our country too, sir. No one works for charity any more."

Now Coulter turned to Lennon. "So Mr. Gotzone's activities would hardly have been a mystery to you. You were in the States collecting funds for IRA coffers." Lennon said nothing; hardly blinked. "What was the deal with Gotzone? Swapping dirty cash? Sharing contacts?"

"What has any of this got to do with the lassie whose body I found?"

Russell was scribbling in his notebook – pointlessly, given that the tape machine was recording. Casci closed over his folder – he knew the rest of the story from this point on.

"Enrique Gotzone is now in a penitentiary in

Pennsylvania. He ran not dissimilar operations to Charlie Dempsey senior *and* junior. Was a link in a gun-running chain, too, shipping defective arms from Ohio ammunitions factories to Central America and, more recently, Afghanistan. His work brought him into contact with Yardies from Jamaica, Barbados, and Haiti."

"*So?*" Lennon seemed genuinely puzzled.

"Several Haitian kids have turned up dead. Shot in parks, their faces slashed."

"Thought I was helping you wi' enquiries into the death of Frances Mullholland?" Lennon directed the question to Coulter. "Not the boys in Kelvingrove." He turned back to Casci. "That lassie wasn't shot in a park."

"One of the boys – a Goodman Lane – we can connect with your old buddy Jake Burton through the boy's father, Bernard. Ever come across *him*, Ian?"

"I am seriously confused here, officer."

"And a girl was found in a garden. *You* were in the New York area at the time of Goodman Lane's death. *And* at the time of the murder of a Ti-Guy Plissard."

"Who's he when he's at home? It all sounds like a big mess to me. If you don't mind me saying. gentlemen."

Lennon stared hard at Coulter. Then he turned his stony look, for the first time all afternoon, on John Russell. Russell looked startled, moved back in his chair, like a child accused of something he hadn't done.

Later, he wouldn't remember so much the difficult days. The cold nights high up in Piedmont moving from farm to farm, some not much bigger or better than their own, hoping to pick a few grapes, dig a field, clear a well. The hot days under a dogged French sun that seemed to sit lower in the sky than in Elba, burning your skin by being nearer rather than hotter. The long treks, sore feet, uncomfortable cart rides, sleeping some nights on the bare ground, others in cheap hostels dirtier than anything the ground had to offer.

For years to come Ettore would remember how the absence of Carlo and Vittore created an emptiness inside him, like a belly swollen from hunger. But he'd never talk of it. Nor of the worry he felt, wondering if Vittore was growing at last, if Carlo was getting any stronger. A sense that time was running out; that he and Antonella were like long-distance athletes, people from an ancient world with an Herculean task to complete in order to save the lives of their sons.

But in the years that followed, when it was over and what was done was done, what he talked about and, mostly, what he remembered, was the adventure of it all. Walking through valleys in the Alps in soft summer afternoons, side by side with Antonella, like they were young sweethearts again. The freedom of being without roof or sink, no children tugging at their skirts and sleeves. How the walking seemed to refresh Antonella so that he'd look at her once again like he used to. How at night they rolled together in unexpected places, foreign rooms, beaches, on trains, like a pair of illicit lovers.

They discovered towns together. Cuneo. Then Pinerolo. Then the poverty and bad language and cheap food of Torino. The pass across the border from the snowy valley of Aosta. Then *Francia*, a whole, new, strange country.

"I don't think they really speak like that," Antonella said after a day or two. "They do it for foreigners. But when they go home, they speak like everyone else." For the first time in years they found the ability to laugh.

Somewhere beyond Grenoble they found work in a smart hotel undergoing refurbishment. Ettore helped clear a whole wing of all its furniture and break everything up. Antonella got serving tables for a week while the full-time waitress was ill. For Ettore it was back-breaking and for Antonella, humiliating. She wasn't a natural attendant. But the food was better than anything they had ever eaten before. In decades to come, the best meals they ate were likened to the Alpine Spa Retreat's restaurant. Ettore could have got another week's work out of them, but they had money for a train now, and to keep them in rations for nearly a month. And besides, Antonella was in danger of being dismissed for cheek to the high-station clientele.

For the rest of their lives they entertained people with their stories of that Great Adventure, and particularly their four months in Paris. Stories about singers and entertainers they met and found out later were actually prostitutes or thieves and not the slightest bit ashamed of it. About gamblers, and speculators, and Americans, and barge-owners who made their lives on canals. They met circus acts and philosophers whilst Ettore worked at the Gare d'Austerlitz and Antonella cleaned houses and museums.

But Paris wasn't the end of the journey

"So why didn't you stay?"

Because the trek hadn't ended. They had the name of a cousin – Mario, from San Piero – who was waiting for them in London. That was the land of work. Pinerolo was beautiful; Grenoble was healthy. Paris exciting. But *Inghilterra* was where a dream could come true. They had two boys waiting for them to carve out a new life. Across the water lay a land where hard-workers could build something solid. They didn't need to discuss it: Ettore and Antonella just knew they had to cross the water, take the last bend in the road.

Maddy threw her keys into the top drawer of a tallboy that had temporarily served as a hall stand for ten years, went into the living room and slumped down in the chair by the window.

What constitutes a bad day? She wasn't sure any more. Anne Kennedy and Jackie Mulholland had pleaded with her all week to release their children's bodies. But she didn't have the power to let Sy or Frances go. Or Micky X, had anyone come looking for him. The police needed time to find a suspect and let his or her people do their own pathology. Just one of the less pleasant tasks a senior PF had to do as a matter of course.

Things wouldn't be so bad if her own boss didn't put his fat carcass in the way of her career plans. She had hoped that by now – all the necessary exams passed with flying colours – she would be given the chance to present in court a case she had precognosed. The Petrus brief, for example. But Binnie, a man of humble Glaswegian origins, was in thrall to over-enunciating Edinburgh advocates. He wasn't talking too hopefully about the Kelvingrove or Bearsden cases either. "A triple murder, Maddalena? I'm not sure we should be experimenting with such an important matter. We'll get you in court sometime soon. Promise." Like a sleazy old friend of the family offering sweeties. She even clocked his eyes glancing at her bum as she left his office.

He was jealous of Maddy's fast-track career; the publicity she would attract if she were to win a big case. She got up, poured herself a glass of red from last night's half-empty bottle, and put on Ella singing Ellington. The smoky sound of late-night New York. Louis was being treated by police department boys to a night on the town. If that doesn't have him running back to Brooklyn quick style, nothing will. They hadn't repeated their night of love in nearly a week. Maddy didn't think she was upset by it. She hadn't detected any sign of indifference in Louis. They had met for a cosy lunch, he had phoned. They just needed the co-incidence of being together in the evening, and professional schedules simply hadn't allowed for that.

She felt more anxious at being left out of the loop on the Sy and Frances cases. Not even Louis told her much of where the investigation was going. She could push for more information but that wasn't advisable. Waiting on the sidelines wasn't where Maddy di Rio Shannon liked to be.

She wondered if she should get herself a cat. For company on an evening like this. Just then she glimpsed a fox skulking in the trees outside. A pussy cat wouldn't last a week, even in the leafy west end. She took the *Herald* out of her bag to catch up on the latest outrage to public safety, headlines screaming panic-stricken. Normally, a new high-profile crime took the heat off an ongoing case. But on this occasion, it only made matters worse. A group of kids had gone berserk in some godforsaken town in Lanarkshire. Ella's soothing voice sounded like it came from a different universe, not Louis's city where even worse things happened.

An elderly couple had been walking down the street around dusk. A flock of teenagers – fifteen or twenty-five of them depending on whether it was a broadsheet or tabloid report – had settled at a corner. When the couple approached, some of the gang shouted jokes and obscenities at them. The man, father and grandfather, ex-merchant navy and voluntary youth worker, checked them.

He told them to behave themselves. The youngsters all retreated into themselves, murmuring their insults and laughing quietly. All except one: a tall gangly boy of fifteen stepped up towards the old man and told him to fuck off.

The man stood his ground; the boy advanced. They argued, the man calm and the boy agitated. But the old man became increasingly outraged, his own language getting more offensive, which made the boy quieter, meaner, more determined. The woman kept pulling on her husband's sleeve. The gang behind the lead boy split: some stepping back from the affray, a few leaving the scene altogether. But a small band stood staunchly behind their leader.

"For a generation we've let this plague fester!" Pat Lovell, the newly appointed Minister for Education and Young People, told the media.

The front pages and TV bulletins were covered with pictures of John and Moira Baxter, and furry images of gangs of youths.

"We've stood by and done nothing," said the First Minister for Scotland. "In the name of charity and goodwill, we've watched our children become lost and angry." Even the soft-spoken Schools' Czar MacDougall felt compelled to fall into line. "We've made *ourselves*, society, vulnerable to that anger. It's time we found a response."

Conservatives and Labour alike called for a curfew. The leader of the Tories called for special phone lines. Labour propsed new radical school discipline measures. A parents' charter. There were appeals in public phone-ins for special police powers, amendments to the stop-and-search laws.

The incident took place in an old Lanarkshire mining town, Stratheaton, under a red evening sky, raw and chapped. It ended badly. Whether John Baxter hit out first, as the youngsters and one onlooker claimed, or the ringleader did, wasn't the point. As far as the papers and the Youth Crime Committee were concerned the old gentleman had put up with enough abuse already. Wasn't he protecting his elderly and infirm wife? Whoever struck the first blow, the old couple were rounded on. John Baxter received severe bruising over 70% of his body from kicks and punches and being hit by some unknown implement. Moira Baxter was nearly as badly bruised but, probably because of a previous medical condition making her bones more brittle, her leg and her arm were both broken. She died in hospital the following night.

John MacDougall, the Youth Crime committee convener, proposed that a national debate be initiated in the press. "And amongst ourselves. In school staff rooms. In churches. Round the family table. We should examine our consciences with regard to how we treat our children. How we let them dress when they're going to school. The hours that they keep. The programmes they watch and the computer games they play. This tragic situation is as much our fault – as teachers, politicians, parents – as it is theirs."

Other, more ferocious, politicians managed to change the tone of the argument about the death penalty. The tabloids, until recently, had been demanding capital punishment for child killers. Now it was calling for the return of the birch and, without quite saying so, even suggesting death for young offenders themselves.

She met Dan on the stairs to the office. He always climbed them to keep fit; Maddy was only there today because the lift was broken.

"Keeping fit for Louis?"

"Wheesht. How's court Number Two?"

"All the fun of the fair. Not helped by tirades like this," he waved his *Scotsman*.

He and Izzie had been assembling a case for months against a known cartel of drug dealers operating in slum estates in the north of the city. They had been using teenagers to push the stuff on the streets. One young man had died in a shoot-out. "You can see the jury suddenly switching their attention from the real bad guys to the kids they use up front. Nobody under the age of twenty's got a hope in hell in any court in Scotland now." He paused at the door of their office. "Your Micky X fellow. I was thinking about how you can lose a kid entirely from the system."

"Go on."

He yawned. "I took statements from a girl in a case last year. Took me some time to find her. She wasn't on any school roll, and she wasn't living in the house where she was officially supposed to be resident. She had moved. Simple as that. She and her mum had been living with her granddad, so the name on the door and on the electoral register didn't change. The girl's school was supposed to send stuff onto her new school, but either they forgot, or it got lost in the post. Whatever, it meant that she could play truant for the rest of her scholastic life – no school or authority were on her case anymore."

"It's that easy to slip out of the system?"

"The system's pretty keen on losing certain types of folk, it seems to me."

"But to find a Micky or a Minnie you'd have to go

through every school roll for pupils who left to attend another school—"

"And see if they ever arrived."

Maddy opened the door. "That could take forever."

"I don't know," said Dan. "You might be lucky. Micky was with Sy Kennedy, so there's probably some connection with one of the schools Sy attended, or at least some school or home in the area."

"The area being the whole of Glasgow."

"Or West Central Scotland. I've got a new contact now in the Education Department. Sunail. Dark, slim, very well groomed. Anyway, I asked him, *en passant,* about Micky. He checked the records. Nearly a thousand kids moved out of schools in the last four years. And that's just the primaries. My guess is Micky's never been in the secondary system, at least not in Glasgow."

"A thousand!"

"You can discount over seven hundred straight away. At the push of a button Sunail managed to confirm that at least that many re-enrolled immediately in other city schools. The problem arises with the three hundred who left to go further afield."

"Three hundred's still a lot."

"Little Miss Negative. Eighty or so went abroad. Or returned abroad. Let's discount them for the moment, though we may need to go back to them later."

"Micky doesn't strike me as a jet-setter either."

"Subtracting all those Sunail can account for, we're left with around sixty-odd who left to continue their schooling elsewhere in the UK. Sunail has ways of following them up. It'll take him into next week."

"This isn't like you, Dan."

"What? Being punctilious and exhaustive in my research? Thank you, Boss."

"You're forever telling me to stay away from cases until they're properly ours."

"We gotta clean this city up." His American accent was woeful. .

Coulter was pleased to see that Casci wasn't enjoying himself delivering his little lecture. All the key people involved in both Red Rhoddo and Tall Trees had been assembled to hear him speak. The entire divisional CID, senior uniforms, press department boys, top brass from neighbouring constabularies, even a Met head honcho up for the day.

"I hasten to add that there's not a specific Haitian gang problem. The Haitian community are law-abiding respectable folk for the main part, but those that are involved in crime tend to link up with various forms of Yardies, or other such African-American criminal organisations."

His audience were happy enough to be there, if quickly bored by what he had to say. It was a change of routine sitting listening to someone who did your job in another country. In New York of all places. There had been lots of jokes about Hill Street and Kojak, and some less geographically accurate stuff about Dirty Harry and Sam Spade.

Louis showed photographs of victims, crime scenes, bullet holes in foreheads. He gave brief details of the background to the killings of Ti Guy Plissard and Henri-Charles Lespinasse, and two other still unidentified young, probably Haitian, victims. He retold the sad, mysterious story of Derrick Braithewaite found dead on Bannerman Island.

"Then we have a female victim. I had discounted her case from being related in any way to these others. But the fact that you have a similar situation here—"

"Not necessarily related," interrupted MacDougall, who had become an annoying fixture at every internal police meeting with more than three people at it.

"That's correct, sir. I'm merely pointing up that a young female was found executed, and in a garden. I'm not even convinced she's connected to other New York cases. As for your situation here, it's not my place to comment."

"Nonsense," Coulter said. "You're obviously a highly respected detective, working one of the toughest beats in the world. We have you here, we might as well get the benefit of your experience and insight."

Casci eyed him as if the statement might have been intended as a veiled insult. He gave a quick run-down of the Goodman Lane case, the possible Irish link with Ian Lennon. Then he treated his audience to a selection of the theories thus far explored by the NYPD – turf wars, vengeance killings, silencing junior members of gangs, racial discord.

"I've left a sheet at the door. It has my contact details in New York. Please get in touch if anything new comes up over here – anything at all. There are a couple of web addresses on it. For Potter's Field, internal NYPD stuff, and a public noticeboard I put up asking for information about the mysterious deaths of these young people. Thank you all for listening."

As the room cleared, Casci took his time collecting his papers, and Coulter loitered, until they were both alone. "The turf wars theory," Coulter asked. "Do you go for it?"

"Black mobs traditionally took over Mafia interests from Harlem Central. They came into conflict with the old Irish territory around Queens. The city's nowhere near as cleanly carved up as it used to be, but there are protection rackets and vice rings that are broadly speaking black and Bronx-based, and white mobs with similar operations to the south and east of them." Louis stopped to arrange his documents correctly. To Coulter he looked more like an academic, with his shiny brief-case and colour-coded folders, than a working policeman. "We know that Lane's father ran protection for bars and shady businesses. He gave some of that money to the Irish Republican cause."

"Which Lennon collected from him."

"Strictly speaking, all we know is that Mr. Lennon had

some contact with Lane and Lafferty and Burton. Also with Gotzone."

Coulter nodded solemnly, trying to hide that he was lost in all these names and new information. "Possible connection with Basque terrorists."

"Leaving that aside... White and Irish interests collided with the black gangs a few years back. Couple of months of mayhem."

Both men fell silent for a moment, Coulter working out the implication. "Lespinasse, Plissard and Goodman Lane being fallen footsoldiers?"

Casci nodded.

"Why didn't you tell *them* that, here a moment ago?"

"You're the guy on the ground, Alan. Those fucking senior blow-outs are nothing but methane sources."

Coulter laughed and walked towards the door of the conference room. "Do you think Lennon's our man, Louis?"

"Even if by some chance he wasn't – that there's *another* guy that links your victims with mine – Lennon's ass is worth locking up for a long long time."

"Difficulty is, Lennon's visits to the States don't always coincide with your killings."

"As far as we can tell." Casci clicked his bag closed and followed Coulter to the door. "I'm not saying he personally pulled every trigger, wielded every knife."

"Want to grab some lunch?"

"Can't. Sorry."

"Meeting Ms Shannon?"

Casci half-nodded. Coulter smiled. "Why didn't you mention these turf wars to me before?"

"Only takes a minute to spot the ball-breakers and the jerks. Got to spend some time to know the stand-up guys."

Coulter went back to his desk feeling the holder, somehow, of a consolation prize.

Barlinnie – despite laws and rules and regulations, prisoner support groups and charities, an enlightened approach to the penal system – might still just as well be in Siberia or Burundi. It breathes horror into the most upstanding of souls. To Coulter and Russell it's a regular visit. Yet, as they entered, both had to work not to betray their dread. The cold and the echoes, the electronic doors, brutal bars. The pretended normality of conversations with the sequence of prison officers they meet the deeper into the building they go. Eventually they're led into a room that's a triumph of barrenness and where a small man is sitting waiting for them.

Jim McArthur is incidental. Not only to this particular case, but in general. Coulter thinks as he sits across from him, that the man must know it. How life has just nudged him about, knocking him into jail and barely noticing it: life had been concentrating on something else at the time. McArthur gets out every now and then and, with perfect comic timing, like a man slipping on a banana skin, two minutes later he's back inside. There'll have been a theft, a fight, an implication, but nobody is really quite sure why Wee Jim's in jail, least of all Jim himself.

"You were in Saughton with Ian Lennon, Jimmy. Did Lennon know a Tony Kennedy in prison?"

Jim McArthur shrugged, non-committal.

"Did you know Kennedy?"

Another shrug. "Came across him."

"Did they do any business together, Lennon and Kennedy?"

"Could have." McArthur wasn't playing with them. He didn't know how to. He wasn't looking for some kind of deal. Small, bald, stubby-fingered, he had learned that deals didn't exist for him.

"What kind of business, McArthur?" Russell was showing everyone he wasn't a patient man. "Did Lennon involve any of the inmates?"

McArthur paused, then shrugged. "When people got out. They got messages to do."

"What kind of messages? Information? Letters? IOUs?"

"Dunno."

"Did Tony Kennedy get a job when he got out?"

The slightest of pauses, then: "Might have."

"Might's not good enough, Jim," Russell growled. But all of them knew that mights and maybes were as good as they were going to get. McArthur's *around*, not in the know.

"What about you, Jim? You get a job to do?"

The little man still looked sad and said nothing. The big boys don't play with him.

"Funding the Republican cause couldn't have gone down well with around half the population in Saughton."

McArthur looked at Russell, surprised. "Everyone knows Big Lenny *used* to work for the IRA. Not anymore, but. Not for years."

That's as much as they would get out of him. Information the Maddy Shannons of this world could do nothing with in court. Uncorroborated hearsay by an unnamed minor crook. But at least Coulter and Russell now knew that Ian Lennon had favours and paying jobs to hand out; and that one of the people he'd dealt with was Sy Kennedy's father.

She hadn't seen him since Sunday afternoon. She had kept her distance from him as much as he had from her. That was fine. In a way, she might have preferred it if Louis had gone home already. They'd got on well. Laughed, talked and worked fine together. Slept well together. Nothing too bowel-churning, and so far no embarrassments. No truths they'd rather not know surfacing. She didn't want to find out now if he was the father of six, or four-times divorced with a cruelty case behind him. Maybe tonight was going to be a mistake.

He looks good, though, studying the menu. Not too tailored. Not too combed and cologned. There are different kinds of Americans, Maddy thought. Irish-American.

Black-American. Louis Casci's not just Italian-American, he's near enough Movie-American. Might as well enjoy the show while it lasts.

She'd taken him to The Sisters restaurant. An unfashionable part of town, not quite West End. Lorries and buses strained up Crow road. Trains shrieked across a loose-sounding bridge nearby.

"Great place," Louis said, and he seemed to mean it.

Maddy had skate, Casci steak. The eponymous Sisters were the daughters of an old friend of her dad's. Pauline the kitchen matriarch, Jackie front-of-house.

"NYPD?" Jackie turned from Louis to Maddy. "He'll not be wanting the poteen then on his steak." Then, heading for the kitchens she called out. "Pauline, tell the dancers to put their clothes back on."

Maddy decided she had chosen right. The place cosy and friendly, the food amiable and spirited. Louis let her choose the wine and she did what she always did – third bottle down on the list. Louis doubled up with beer. The tables were packed close together and, although the hum of general conversation covered their own talk, they still felt the need to keep their voices low, as though they were having a slightly furtive assignation.

Maddy explained about Petrus and petro-chemical poisoning. How the company was, ultimately, American owned, but being so supra-national, any national court could only take bits of it to task. No doubt the illegal dumping went on all over the shop, but they could only do anything about it here. "Company as big as that – they'll move their garbage all over the globe."

It was okay, talking shop. They weren't skirting round other stuff; it wasn't a conversation with subtext. Work had brought them together. They were both married to their jobs – and, in the lack of any mention of another kind of marriage, Maddy assumed Louis must have nothing to tell. They compared notes, talked about the Potter's Field and the Kelvingrove cases. She sipped her Merlot, he took gulps of his pint. They felt relaxed, normal.

Ten years ago, a night out in Maryhill's Cottars Arms would have been the social equivalent of a birthday party in Barlinnie prison. The clientele, even the decor, the atmos, the same. It had been given a radical makeover since then – new carpet and wallpaper, high stools and tables, polished wood and prints – Scottish Munros and the Mcgillycuddy Reeks – freshly hung on the walls. But the underlying smell of embattled poverty, of cheap drink and fags, seeped slowly from behind Ben Lomond and the Cobbler, like fog, like damp rot.

Coulter and Russell marched up to the bar where a tall cumbersome youth, pulled up to his full height – six four at least – stood glaring down at them.

"A coke and mineral water, please," Coulter said. The usual reaction to that in a pub like this was a fleeting moment of disbelief, then the dawning that they must be polis.

"Sure, mate. Sparkling or still?" the barman said, unfazed. Glasgow was becoming a confusing place. Since when did bushy-tailed young Australians work in dead-end bars in Maryhill?

"Your boss in, son? Tell Charlie there's a couple of old friends here to see him." Coulter paid for the drinks and watched the barman lope towards Dempsey's office. He went to sit down, when he noticed that Russell had stopped in his tracks. In a snug, behind the entrance, sat Jim and Elaine Docherty. A man had his back to them, but Coulter and Russell both knew that delicate frame, that incipient bald patch. Coulter put his drink on the table and strolled over.

Elaine clocked him first – Docherty and Whyte still deep in conversation. She never quite lost that lazy look about her. But, behind the tired eyes, her face registered surprise, and perhaps guilt. Only for the quickest of seconds, but enough for Martin Whyte to pick up on it, and turn around. Coulter beamed broadly at them. "Martin. How are you doing? Elaine. Jim." He sat down like he'd bumped into his dearest old friends. "John, bring over the drinks, eh?"

Russell scowled and waited for the Coke and water. Jim Docherty shifted in his seat. Elaine sat up a little straighter. Whyte didn't even look at Coulter.

"I know this place has had a job done on it, but I still wouldn't have thought it was quite the design centre of Glasgow."

"We happened to be nearby," said Whyte, as Russell returned.

"You're not friends of the landlord by any chance, are you? Charlie. Known him myself for years."

Whyte turned round in his seat until he was facing Coulter directly. "We happen to be working with an architect on a housing association new build. We had a meeting with the community in a public hall round the corner. This was the nearest place to sit down."

"Mr. Whyte, the only public hall round here is quarter of a mile that way down Maryhill Road. If you mean the new flats going up over towards Summerston, that's a mile in the opposite direction. I can think of several pubs and even a cafe in that area. None of them great, but no worse than this."

"This is the one we happened to come across. We left our cars in the Tesco car park."

Coulter saw Dempsey's "Staff Only" door open. The big Australian barman came out and gave Coulter a thumbs-up. Coulter got up from his seat. "Small world, isn't it?" was all, lamely, he could think of saying.

"Isn't it just," said Whyte, dismissing him by mimicking the banality of the remark.

The Cottars Arms makeover had been even less

successful in Charlie Dempsey's office. No amount of cheap paint could stop it being a store-room with a desk and a couple of chairs. Pine air-freshener not enough to mask the reek of stale alcohol and loose morals.

Charlie looked like several different men stuck together. His prematurely white hair was a veritable halo, but his eyebrows were as thick and black as the devil's. He had long, thin fingers, but a big round belly. His legs seemed too small for the rest of his body. Coulter had known him for years, but still felt as if he'd just walked into a room full of strangers.

"DI Coulter. Been a while. You here to give me a certificate of good behaviour?"

"D'you deserve one, Charlie?"

"Course I do. Who's the new little helper?"

Charlie better watch himself here. Detective Sergeant Russell was a more violent man than Dempsey imagined, and liable to fly off the handle.

"Don't give us it, Dempsey. You've come across me often enough."

"Have I? So sorry." He turned to Coulter. "What?"

"You've taken to chilling with the creatives, Charles."

"Come again."

"Graphic artists. Designers. Messrs Whyte and Docherty."

Charlie shrugged. "I make it a rule not to consort with anybody who drinks in *here*."

"Not even Ian Lennon."

"What about him? He's a gardener now. Found that wee lassie – what more d'you want? Let me guess – you're giving him dog's abuse just because he once worked for my dad?"

When Old Charlie was alive, he used to admit that *his* old man had been a bit of a bad lad, but he had cleaned things up now. Young Charlie took the same tack. He'd gone further – giving the impression at least that the Cottars Arms had gone legit. No longer a social hub for thieves and racketeers, a cover for dirty money and IRA backhanders. To be fair, it was a long time since the Arms had appeared on any police report. Maybe Young Charlie was a better operator than Old Charlie.

"He's worked for you, too."

"Nothing to do with me. He was my dad's man, not mine. Doesn't even like me."

"How *is* the old man, Charlie?"

"Not so great. Prostate cancer."

"Ach," Russell said. "That can take years to kill you."

"No way your old man and Ian could still be up to their old tricks again?"

"Don't be daft."

But there was a flash of doubt in his eyes. Chances are, Coulter thought, that young Charlie genuinely *is* more or less clean these days. Not because he's a reformed soul, but because the rough boys don't respect him enough to work for him. They'd still respect his father, though.

"My old man's dying, Mr. Coulter. He's not up to running protection rackets, and keeping an animal like Lennon on a leash.."

"Sorry to hear that, Charlie." Russell looked at Coulter, wondering if he meant it.

"Tony Kennedy, Charlie. Know him?"

"One of the Kelvingrove boys' father, no?"

"So you can read," sneered Russell.

"Aye they've got newspapers in Maryhill too, these days," Charlie hit back. "Never come across the gentleman myself. Poor bastard."

Charlie Dempsey had been brought up on secrets and falsehoods and fabrications, telling different versions of every story to his friends, his colleagues, the Polis, himself. Smoke would come out of a lie detector.

Louis had gone on through into the sitting room. Maddy was in the kitchen, making coffee, running through her messages. About six from Mama. Better phone her back – the big day being tomorrow, Sunday.

"Don't know why you're thinking of moving!" Louis shouted through. "This pad's terrific. In New York, it'd be worth a fortune."

The next message was from Coulter. "Sorry to bother you. Tell Casci Lennon's looking deeper in it with every passing day. Amy Dalgarno found out today that one of the houses he gardens for has two big Labradors. Both black. And hairy. Lennon was working there the day before the boys were found. Amy's round there now with Russell, chasing these dogs around trying to get samples. Anyway. Tell Louis, if I don't see him, to have a good flight. If you bump into him, like. Talk to you Monday."

He sounded so sad. Every case hurt him in new ways. First the not knowing, then the knowing. One was as bad as the other. All that and Martha to deal with too. Alan was phoning from home, she could hear the television on in the background.

The coffee pot began to gurgle. Maddy turned the flame under it down, slowing down the percolating till she phoned her mother. Before pressing the last number in, she called out:

"Louis? What you doing tomorrow?"

"Nothing planned. My Work Here is Done."

"Want to go back to church?"

He laughed. "You turning into some kind of religious nut? Or do we have to go every time we…" He tailed off. There was no guarantee he was going to end up in her bed tonight. She smiled, imagining him squirming next door, putting his foot in it.

"Not church exactly," she said, returning. "But you may have to put up with a few preliminary prayers and litanies and stuff."

He had loosened his tie and she thought of Sinatra asking Joe to set 'em up in the wee small hours, which made her think, confusingly of sexy strangers at midnight, and her granddad singing tunelessly along in a chip shop in Girven. By the look in his eye, Louis's thoughts weren't so complicated.

Alan Coulter came home at the back of ten and still no one was up. He sat in his own living room as if he were waiting for the dentist, flicking through Sunday supplements. Lauren and Peter usually come round on a Sunday but Lauren, the eldest, had developed the radar years ago to sense when mum was having one of her turns. Jennifer was sleeping over at a friend's after a party. Beth was sleeping in. Martha, too, would still be in bed, but not sleeping. She never slept when she was not well, but lay still as death in the curtained darkness.

Alan had already been out to work and back. The first time he'd met Tony Kennedy he saw an anguished father, hopping around like a bird whose wings had been damaged. This morning, the tragedy of Tony's son's murder had ebbed someplace deeper inside him, and the natural mistrustfulness towards policemen of a man who hadn't always managed to live inside the law came back to the fore.

"Mr. Kennedy. We've visited Barlinnie. We understand that an Ian Lennon gave you a job to do when you got out."

Tony flitted about, denied it a couple of times, then stared up at his interrogators. "Is this off the record?"

Russell had been shorter-tempered than usual, desperate to get to a Rangers early kick-off. "There *is* no off the record, Tony."

"If Lennon finds out I told you..."

"He won't find out from us." Coulter had tried to sound convincing, but Kennedy gave in to the inevitable. "Week I got out, back in '03, he gave me a note to deliver."

"To where?"

"Private residence."

Shit, everyone spoke in jargon these days. "To *where*, Tony?"

"House up in Maryhill Park."

"You remember the name?"

"No."

"The address?"

"Somewhere up in Maryhill Park."

An area that had recently gone stellar on the housing market. Professionals out-pricing themselves in the West End had moved a couple of miles further out. Those who didn't have the dosh for Westbourne or Cleveden, and weren't old enough to move out to Milngavie.

"Come on, Tony, give us a name, or we'll be here all morning." They'd arrived before 9.00 AM, surprised to see Kennedy up and dressed and about his business.

"Can't remember. Ross?"

After they left Tony Kennedy, they phoned in the paltry information to the research boys and Russell scuttled off to change for the game. Coulter, back home now, threw the supplements aside and couldn't stop himself from checking Ben's room. Every weekend he hoped his son might make an unannounced appearance from London. Not this weekend. He went back down and started preparing breakfast in the kitchen. He was cracking eggs into the scrambling bowl when the phone rang.

"Mr. Coulter?"

Sales call, or he wasn't the only man working early on a Sunday.

"This is Dan McKillop."

It took a moment for Coulter to place him. The big Assistant PF in Maddy's office. Tailored to within an inch of his life, bent as a nine bob note and reeking of cologne. Coulter had never taken to him.

"I've been trying to get in touch with PF Shannon."

That was the kind of false formality that irked Coulter. They both knew her as Maddy, for Chrissakes. "She's at some family party, I believe."

"I know that. But she had her mobile turned off."

"Is there something I can help you with?"

"It's just some information. Might not be important. Maybe it could even wait until tomorrow." A seldom-seen crack in the lawyer's self-confidence. And unless he had acquired photographic evidence of Sy and Micky and Frances being killed and a signed confession from the killer, there wasn't actually much that couldn't wait twelve hours or so.

"I've been looking – in the course of preparing another case altogether – into the records of children who have left the school system in Glasgow and not shown up anywhere else."

Why did Fiscals all think they were natural born gumshoes? Maddy was the same. But at least she was a teamworker. And better looking.

"I've an appointment with Mr. Sunail Shehadeh in the Education offices first thing tomorrow morning."

Wasn't McKillop being disloyal to his boss here? Maddy always swore by him. Best Assistant she'd ever had. Coulter reckoned he was the ambitious sort who could dump you easy after years of friendship.

"But I'm almost certain Maddy might not be available tomorrow morning." There was a note in his voice… "In court or something."

She'd be with Casci. McKillop was being tactful – whether to protect Maddy's professional name, or because he suspected Coulter was jealous, Coulter preferred not to dwell on.

"So?" Coulter couldn't quite get a grip on this conversation.

"I wouldn't want the Fiscal's office to be accused of trying to hide anything, or hold things up. We might have a name."

Coulter waited patiently through the dramatic pause. McKillop knew he had earned it; he knew how crucial identifying Micky was. How much Coulter had tried to identify the mysterious boy lying next to Sy Kennedy.

"Paul Pacchini."

Coulter was disappointed. Pacchini? Didn't sound right. Micky was a Johnstone or a McRae or a Jones if ever he saw one. Not even the first name sounded right. He'd had him down as a Malky or a Joe, or possibly a Jason or Justin. He said thanks to McKillop. Hung up, and went for his coat, forgetting about the eggs waiting to be scrambled. Paul Pacchini. He crept out the front door. Paul. Pacchini. Trying to get used to the name, like a new pair of shoes.

"Here, Nonno, let me help."

Maddy took her grandfather's arm and bore his weight as he struggled to get out his chair. In fact, there was little weight to bear. Nonno had never been a bulky or a tall man. When she was growing up – Nonno must've been in his fifties and sixties – she thought of him as a dancer. Fred Astaire rather than Gene Kelly: diminutive, neat, always exquisitely dressed, foppish even in shiny brown leather shoes and dark suits, cravats and ties and big 70's collars. He'd move boxes of lemonade around dressed like that, sometimes even served chips, his suit on under his overall. By that time, of course, it was her parents doing most of the work, Rosa serving, Packy frying. Nonno would sit at one of the tables screwed to the floor, listening to Sinatra or Dino on the juke box, looking over the shop's paperwork.

She helped him from the kitchen to the living room. He was ready now to meet his public – all the people who had come to celebrate his anniversary. Di Rio cousins and Benedettis, the Cochranes who had lived across the road for three generations, two priests, local Labour Party hacks, several old fogies Nonno had picked up. Even a Shannon or two apart from herself. Cousins who had sided with Rosa over the separation. Louis Casci took Nonno's other arm.

The hall door had been left open – it was a grey but warm day, people coming and going all the time between kitchen and garden. Maddy glimpsed out at the Girvan coast. She saw the land of her childhood for what it really was: another dreary town, half empty, the wind rattling the *Closed* signs, the sea damp and dull and cross.

"So, hey, Mr. Di Rio," Louis said, "eighty years since your family came to live in Scotland. That's quite something."

"No no," the old man protested. His voice was still steady, and he spoke like a man thirty years younger. "Eighty years since *I* came here. Eighty-*five* since the first Ayrshire Di Rios."

Maddy glanced at Louis. He couldn't be expected to see the importance in the difference between those five years.

"Maddalena tells me you're over here about those boys' murder. Terrible thing."

Father Mike Jamieson saw his chance to get away from a particularly talkative Bennedetti aunt. "A life as long as yours, Nonno – you must have seen many wonderful and terrible things." The poor man couldn't help it. Every word he uttered irked Maddy to the bone. It wasn't the brat-priest's place to call him Nonno. And he didn't need to talk so loud – Nonno wasn't so deaf. Nonno looked the young priest in the eye. "And you men of the cloth should dwell more on the good than the bad."

It was a peculiarity of both sides of Maddy's family to privately condemn all things religious but keep up a public front. The Irish side were even worse. "The trouble with being a young man is everybody wants you to die for them. The Church," he glanced mischievously at the embarrassed Fr. Mike. "Country. Powerful men. Women. Young men's blood is like nectar to them all. Can't get enough of it."

Uncle Gerry came and stole Nonno from them – some old friend had arrived. Mike, undeterred by the old man's treatment of him, kept by his side. Louis and Maddy stood in the doorway looking in on the opening of another present.

"How come your family were here five years before *he* was?" Louis asked, perplexed.

"It's a long story."

"It's going to be a long day."

But Maddy didn't feel like delving into the past. It was such a crucial tale – events that took place more than half a century before her birth had forged who she would become. She changed the subject. Now wasn't the moment. She didn't want to think about the trials of youth, about families being ripped apart. About what makes one young man survive into successful beloved old age and another get shot before he's barely out of puberty.

She led Louis out to the garden. Her childhood home was a big rambling townhouse that Nonno should have sold years ago but had neither the heart nor the energy. We all hang on to things for too long, Maddy thought. That's why she should be selling her own flat. Stop getting too attached to things. Places. Louis was a hit with the Aunties, laying out food on trestle tables for a garden picnic. Fell over themselves offering him home-made treats and too much wine. Mama had made her little *bruschette* and savoury *chouquettes* with cheese and strips of Parma ham. Auntie May and her daughter Lizzie, in true Irish style, had heated up a mountain of chipolata sausages and little tasteless pastry puffs. The Italian aunts, on the other hand, were using Louis as the current judge in a lifelong cooking competition.

"It's juliennes of chicken breast rolled around spinach and slices of mushroom."

"Delicious."

"Aubergine with balsamic vinegar and sun-blushed tomato. You'll need a fork, Louis."

"Tortellini salad. I got the recipe from a friend in Siena. You ever been to Siena, Louis?"

"Never been to Italy."

"Away!"

Maddy watched Nonno through the window. Too tired to talk now, but smiling benignly at old friends and great-grandsons and, despite his supposed anticlericalism, sitting next to Monsignor Connolly.

"Tiramisu, Louis?"

Slowly, the harem of portly ladies bearing cholesterol and sugar waddled off to muster the family for lunch. That would take an hour, minimum. Louis and Maddy sat outside, the sky brightening.

"Nonno made his money from fish and chips. Very English, no?" He was still curious about her family background, but had picked up that she wasn't going to talk about the personal stuff.

"The fish is *pesce alla milanese*. The chips are Belgian, Nonno says. His father had seen other Italians put the two together in London. The story goes that when Benny – that's my great-grandfather – first tasted the combination he screwed up his face and swore it'd never catch on. A year later, they were selling shedloads of the stuff."

She sipped her wine and looked out over the fence at the sea, calm and stretching into infinity. "Great granddad Ettore was fighting the Austrians in the Alps when he was sixteen. Nonno there was helping his dad set up in business at the same age. By the age of ten he had walked through half of Europe. What were you doing at sixteen?"

Louis shook his head and smiled. "Kicking about the streets smoking shit and talking more shit. Christ, I couldn't even wash my own shorts and socks."

At least he wasn't getting killed in parks or rich folks' gardens. This could be her last day ever with Commanding Officer Louis Casci. Don't go spoiling it with depressing thoughts. She's proud of her family today. They're the soul of hospitality; all of them genuinely grateful to Nonno for what he had created for them. Teachers, married ladies, mums and dads, business people and professionals. Not a bad crop from a grudging piece of dry earth on a distant island most of them had never visited.

It was a year now since they had left their two boys at the base of the hill, the sea whispering in the background. Carlo would be eleven, Vittore eight. Please God they were fine, stronger – the way boys are able to grow and fill out on a handful of berries, a few leaves of cabbage. The way Ettore had.

Paris had been big and noisy and the night seemed to fall earlier than anywhere else, and lift later. But Ettore and Antonella were speaking French well by the time they got there and could talk to all the strange people they met there – a circus of rich and poor and happy and sad, talkative and taciturn. But none of it was any preparation for England, a land so unreal and faint, that it felt like they were living through a story.

The language sounded like it was spoken though cotton wool – muffled, like everyone had a cold or wooden teeth. It was spoken in a steady drone and reflected the appearance of the place. Fixed and pale. Ettore got the impression that no day quite got started. The sun never burned away the clouds; they just faded and drifted down from the sky, until the whole world felt thin and watery. Like you were looking at it through a veil. And it was cold. Not the same kind of cold you got high up in the Aosta valley, or in Grenoble. A softer coldness. Wetter. It could be dry for days and your clothes warm but somehow you felt damp inside.

For the first week, he watched Antonella stare at this bland new world. He felt a little separated from her – as if the muslin of the air, the cotton wool of the language, had gotten between them. The light here made *her* fade somehow. He worried that he too might peter out. Until they met Mario from San Piero. Meeting a friend from home reanimated them, put laughter back in his wife's eyes and a smile on his own lips. The three of them talked about chasing hogs and racing along the beach, the big boats moored at Portoferraio. They talked about friends and family – di Mambros and Rossis and the folks at Procchio and up at Campo nell'Elba. Mario and Ettore swore at that bitch of the land that hadn't given them enough to stay and prosper. They complained about the wars the old country was forever asking them to die in, and then they remembered good times, and kind neighbours, and their own families still there.

They took to meeting in pubs – places with huge walls, a ceiling so high you could barely see it, and great shiny bronze beer pumps and pictures of horses, women sitting at tables. Every time it would take Antonella a good hour and a few warming sips of the men's porter to feel comfortable. The war wasn't long over and Londoners welcomed them as friends who had helped topple Kaiser Bill. The three of them huddled in snugs and talked for hours. Antonella remembered lots of little stories about Carlo and Vittore. Mario talked about Maria Grazia, the Sansoni girl from the farm just north of Procchio. He had promised he would return to her with expensive wedding gifts. Now, he confessed, he was about to marry another girl.

"Molly's Irish. Mama will be happy – she's a better Catholic than anyone in Elba! Well... not in every way."

And they all laughed, including Antonella, though she and Ettore were sad for Maria.

"She'll have forgotten me, eh? Gino was just waiting for me to go."

That was true, and Gino Romani *did* make his move not long after Mario had left. But Maria flatly refused him. Just as she had refused every other boy – and there were many. Maria Grazia was pretty. She was still waiting patiently for Mario, secure in the unshakeable belief that he was working his way back to her.

"Raise your glasses, my friend. To Gran Bretagna! This is the place to make money!"

Ettore and Antonella got jobs within a couple of days of arriving in London. Both of them with the tram company – he labouring out in the roads, on a gang, lifting and straightening and replacing rails; she in the depot making the chrome and copper of those magnificent vehicles shine even brighter, so that they'd glow in the fog. They found digs in a street beside a big park, near the centre of town. They had never seen so much green in a city before.

They met after work, when Mario wasn't around, in a little coffee house run by an Italian from Lombardy. They were amazed at how Mario made his money – shipping in Italian foodstuffs. Ettore couldn't believe English people would pay good money for Italian food. Pasta and oil and tuna fish – the things they had escaped from. The café-owner served plates of white fish in batter with slices of fried potato. Such an easy dish to prepare, and the *inglesi* couldn't get enough of it. The two of them sat long together rather than return to their dingy digs, as dusk fell and London looked even more dream-like than ever.

"I'm getting used to it here," said Antonella. "We could find a way to live in this country. You don't get hot and sweaty, and the people are well-mannered, don't you think, Benny?" She had taken to calling him by the name they used in London for him. "The warm rain and the soft earth. I think anything could grow here." Her eyes shone with emotion. "I think Vittore and Carlo could grow up strong and healthy in a place like this."

He looked at her in the silky light. She was a different colour here – more olive-skinned in these dimmer days than brown. Her hair looked downy and her eyes softer. She had lost weight over the journey. Both of them had. It was like she had lived another short lifetime: returning to girlishness when they first set off, and becoming a woman again here in England. She seemed curvier, leaning against the table, sipping her coffee. He looked around, stretched out and quickly touched her breast. She glanced about, anxious, then laughed.

"You won't be able to do that soon. Once we have our boys back."

But not quite yet. There was an opportunity, Mario had said, to open a cafe and eating-place just like this. But not here in London. There were already too many of them. Mario had a friend further north. A fellow with money and contacts. They should go to him. One last lap of the journey, to a place Ettore had heard talked about and could never quite imagine. *Scozia*.

Coulter had called in as many of his team as he could muster on a late Sunday afternoon. Russell, piqued at being torn away from post-match pub analysis. Pat Webb and Amy Delgarno – who Coulter had managed to co-opt full time – had been about to sit down to family dinners. Trisha and Gordon, the HOLMES co-ordinators, were both happy to come in. Two other CID bods, Barclay and Turner, were on duty anyway.

Patterson Webb was the one who'd been searching for a paper trail for Micky. He was hacked off that McKillop had got ahead of him. "Another couple of days, I'd have had the same information. Who's this Sunail Whatsisname?"

Coulter shrugged. "Education department. Friend of McKillop's."

"Gay Mafia," Sergeant Webb muttered. He and his indexing boys were coming up trumps now, searches responding at last to the name Paul Pacchini. As well as HOLMES, they were trawling various sites they had special access to: HMSO Census, Glasgow City, Social Work Department.

"An eleven year-old Paul Laird left Taylor Primary in 2000. His father, or at least the guy living with his mother, was called Pacchini – quoted on forms as second next-of-kin. The local secondary was notified that Paul Laird wouldn't be joining them from primary, but there's no mention of where he *did* go."

"Taylor Primary? That in Govan? Did Sy Kennedy go there?"

"No. Holy Cross."

"2001. That would make Pacchini or Laird around fourteen now. Sounds about right. No other mention of him?"

"This could be him." Pat Webb swivelled a computer screen so that Coulter could see it – official papers, peppered with the name Pacchini.

"A Giorgio Pacchini was arrested for possession of class B drugs two years ago. In Manchester. Mentions that he's 'at present' guardian of a son. Doesn't give the boy's name. Report's a year old."

"What sort of a show are they running down there?"

"I've traced Giorgio back to Glasgow." It was Amy Dalgarno's chance to shine. "Sure enough, there's another drugs charge. Just possession, of cannabis. The thing was dropped – Giorgio seems little more than a dope-head, not a dealer." She handed Coulter a file of print-outs. "Look at the page I've earmarked, there, you'll see there's a request to Social Work to check on the accused's son. This time named Paolo, not Paul; Pacchini, not Laird. Riverdale Street. Catchment area for Taylor Primary."

Coulter looked through the heap of pages. Amongst the computer guff – addresses in blue, endless lines with flèches, parentheses, backslashes and underlines – were little glowing embers of precious information.

"The mother kind of evades the system, I'm afraid. A problem these days – some women changing their names on marriage and others not. In *her* case, I suspect, using both, throwing us off the trail. Can't find any marriage reference for Giorgio."

"Common-law marriage."

"No such thing."

"Bidey-in, well."

"My guess is she did a runner before Paul or Paolo left primary school."

"He and his dad stay here in Glasgow for a few months, then they go to Manchester."

"Why?" Coulter leaned against the window, the glass giving a little behind his back. He came off it – the office was seven stories up. "The mother can't have eluded the system altogether." But there was a note of doubt in his voice. He picked up Amy's file. "Father still in Manchester?"

Patterson Webb shouted across from his computer screen, reading from an internet document. "Giorgio's no longer with us, I'm afraid. Snuffed it. Car accident, end of 2004. Seems he was drunk, wandered out onto a main street…"

"And the kid?"

"Paul or Paolo's faded away from the paper trail. Why nobody checked back on previous reports, I don't know, but there's no mention of a kid in the documentation of his father's accident."

Coulter shuffled through the papers. "Died nearly two years ago. Paul – or whatever you call him – has been living off his wits since he was *twelve*?!"

"Looks like it."

"Or someone else is looking after him."

"His mother?"

They all looked up at the incident board. At the picture of Micky – possibly now, Paul – dead in the park. Dark hair. Could have Italian in him right enough. But was he rough enough to survive the streets for two years? Maybe. Product of an alky da and a broken home? Absolutely.

Where did he get the new tracksuit from, though? The money for the haircut, the snicked eyebrow, the trainers? *Somebody* was looking out for him.

Maddy felt she was inside some film scenario. She's in a hotel lobby with her New York cop, saying good night, engine still running in her yellow sports car outside where two black-cloaked priests sit waiting on the shagpile seat coverings.

"The old one's like something out of Lord of the Rings."

"Sauron or Gandalf?"

Louis shrugged. "You mean good or bad? Guys like him, it's hard to tell the difference."

"It's the young priest I can't take," Maddy said.

"I know – the enthusiasm of youth. Drives you crazy."

She looked at him, all offended. "Don't include a young thing like me in your grumpy old man act. That's it – you're getting your goodbye peck now, and no nightcap."

A jokey hint. She had no idea if he intended spending his last night of junket with her. At least she hadn't heard of him going to shops to buy presents. No significant other then. No kids. Either that or he was a mean bastard.

"What you going to do with the shamans now?"

"Drop them off at their temple, and get back quickly to the simple life – warm room, drink, book if necessary…"

"I've got a real page-turner by *my* bed."

"Has it got etchings?"

"Come back and see?"

She went out to the car, smiling. He was as awkward as she was – but just as keen. The two priests seemed embarrassedly aware of her distracted state and said almost nothing on the trip between hotel and parish house. Crossing the river, Mike squirmed in the back seat, fishing keys out of a pocket deep in some black fold of his suit. Arriving at St. Catherine's, keys found, he had to wait for Monsignor Connolly to squeeze himself free of the low-slung Mazda.

Maddy got out her seat and stood with her car door open to wave the boys farewell. Before he turned around to leave, Connolly looked her dead in the eye: "Maddalena. The job you do, the life you lead. It's too much to bear without support."

"You mean, metaphysically?"

"In every way. You have a wonderful family. Don't stray too far from them. But spiritual support too, yes."

"My family aren't really very holy, Father. Mama only goes to Mass to show off new outfits. I've no idea why Nonno goes. He doesn't seem to be a fan of the church generally."

"You're too sophisticated a person, Maddalena, to be deceived by such shallow anomalies."

What did that mean? Perhaps the old man knew her grandfather in some way that she didn't. Perhaps it took one ancient man to really know another. He walked slowly towards the parish house. Probably no more than his early seventies, she thought. Just one of these men who age in a spectacular way.

"Should you need help," he said as he kept walking, not looking at her, "from an old man. You know where to find me."

"Thank you."

Mike, in the glow of the house lights behind him, waved. "Have a nice night now."

The statement irked her as she drove away. Was he being sarcastic? It made what she was about to do in Louis's hotel feel sinful. She speeded up, wipers on full, suddenly burning with desire.

Summer rain. The papers had been crying out for it, when they weren't panicking about the morality of our youngsters. Coulter was in the front of a marked car, driven by a Uniform. Russell in another car behind him. Together they headed up a little convoy of six, growing at every crossroads. Coulter considered telling them to put on their sirens, jump the red lights. Sometimes he was in the mood for that kind of stuff.

But the night drizzle was having a calming effect on him. It fell steady, speckling the passenger window prettily, the little beads glowing in patterns when car headlights passed. The city looked shiny black. He remembered his gran, blackleading the range in her kitchen till it gleamed sharply.

Tony Kennedy had remembered the name correctly. Ross. The man he had delivered a package to, on behalf of Ian Lennon, in Maryhill Park.

What exactly Colin Ross – whom Coulter and Russell had just interviewed – had to do with Ian Lennon, let alone three dead juveniles, was still a mystery. The main discovery was that Mr. Ross owned two big, black Labradors.

If he's wrong, Chief Constable Robertson will kill him. But if his reasoning works out, Czar John MacDougall and the whole political system will embrace him like a brother. Coulter's not sure which is worse. Colin Ross's wife had no memory of any package being delivered almost two years ago, but was happy to state that Ian Lennon was once their gardener. Lennon, then, was the only link between Tony Kennedy, the father of one of the victims, and a black Labrador hair found at the scene of the crime. Quite apart from his possible American exploits, the bastard had also found Frances Mullholland's body in a garden where he presently worked… Coulter wanted him safely in custody, with a few charges stacked up against him. He'd invent them if he had to. Tuck him up in a nice warm cell tonight. Let the bastard sweat.

The rain drips out of a glowing dawn sky. A greenish tinge to it, as if the city is slightly corrupted meat. The drops fall slowly through the air and run down Louis's hotel window. He and Maddy asleep, backs turned, but close, buttocks just touching.

They fall on a police station where a clutch of men and women work behind closed blinds and a computer system never stops humming, hunting. In the basement Ian Lennon, if he'd been awake, wouldn't have seen the drops, or heard them in his windowless cell.

The raindrops form a pattern, like kids' join-the-dots, on the bedroom window of Alan and Martha Coulter. Martha's in bed alone. Asleep, but frowning, still feeling the pain, even unconscious. Alan's downstairs, dozing on the couch, drifting off.

And on it falls. Turning sandstone into the deep wet red of flowing blood. Dropping into the rivers, panning out gently to the hills that cradle the city. Nourishing the soil, the earth, in fields and gardens, and early-morning parks.

IV

Tuesday morning she kicked off with two double-shot skinny macchiatos and a fag begged from a stranger. The only way Maddy knew how to drown out dead yesterdays. She had taken Louis to the airport first light for an awkward farewell then back to her flat for moping and self-criticism and avoiding mirrors. Now she was faced with a grim-looking Alan Coulter.

"Let me guess. Your Irish fella." She was still standing in the café doorway, sucking the last drop out of her illicit ciggie. The air was still clean after the rain, and the sun looked as if it might make a reappearance. He took her by the arm and led her to an out-of-earshot table.

"Correct," Coulter said. Maddy tried to click her fingers rapper-fashion the way Manda could. She failed. It looked she was trying to get something sticky off her hand. "Two charges of murder. Paul Pacchini and Sy Kennedy."

"And he didn't try to save Frances Mullholland. He killed her."

"That's my contention."

"And your proof for the Kelvingrove murders?"

"The black hair. Belongs to the dog of someone he works for and whose house he was in the day before."

"Why? Why kill kids? Why slash two of them but not the third? Why bring attention to himself?"

Coulter sighed and went to get himself a tea. They were playing to different beats this morning. Maddy aware of her own speed. She had a million questions and she wanted to ask them all at once. She had a pile of work warm on her desk waiting for her teeth. She was itching to get onto the next stage of the case, happy to escape families and free time and fleeting love affairs. Alan, on the other hand, was being serious-minded, considered, and in the mood for milky tea.

"He's a professional leg-breaker," he said, sitting back down with his cup and a warm croissant, the smell of which made Maddy feel slightly sick. "He's killed before and—"

"Do we *know* that?"

He ignored the question, so clearly he didn't. "He's got connections to similar murders in the States. He discovered Frances's body *and* was working at the scene of the murder the day she was killed. Now we can place him in Kelvingrove too. He has no corroboration for his alibis. He works the Glasgow underworld. He knew Sy Kennedy's dad. What else do you want from an underfunded, understaffed police force? We've done *our* bit...."

"*Looks* pretty monstrous. In the photos I've seen. I'll grant you that."

"Thank you." He wasn't finding her easy this morning. Probably wished he hadn't set up this unofficial meeting.

"Then again, Al, *I* look monstrous in every photo."

"Maddy – don't start! We'll get all this shit from his defence."

She laughed. This is what she loved. Getting to the bottom of things. The heart of the matter. Inwardly she promised Sy and Paul and Franny that she'd get the bastard or bastards who killed them. If it was Lennon, she'd make sure he never saw the light of day again.

"You'll get the official call later this morning. I want you on this one, Maddy. I'll make that clear. Just, don't go playing funny buggers."

She got up to go but he hadn't finished his little lecture. "Don't go chasing shadows. We've got the killer in our sights. I've given you the rod and the bait. Reel him in."

Things didn't go much better with Maxwell Binnie. She'd tumbled in late in her boss's office like a bluster of spring wind, files and papers and hair in uproar, the caffeine giving her adrenaline a jagged edge.

"Not this case, Maddy."

Binnie had never qualified as a solicitor advocate, thus could never himself prosecute a murder case in the High Court of the Justiciary. And he was only fifty-five – fully intent on ten years more as Procurator Fiscal. From his point of view, Maddy Shannon's career was advancing too quickly, closing in on him. She could be tipped for the top job – his job – in a few years. Sooner, if she got a result in a high-profile trial. He was jealous, no doubt about it. He thought her an upstart, vulgar. Right now she knew she was a little too fleshy for her tight jacket, too mature for this length of skirt. A sexual woman at a dangerous age who wasn't the least bit interested in *him*. She leaned forward. "Then what was the point in me taking the advocacy exams?"

"That was your decision."

"You didn't say they would be taken in vain."

He leaned forward. He was the one with the power. He smiled condescendingly. "The Petrus case. I think that might be a better opportunity to try out our little experiment."

She got up to go. The Petrus case might take years to come to court, if ever. No point in keeping arguing. As ever, she'd have to do all the hard work and let an outsider take the glory. She went to the door, aware that Binnie was ogling her. Back on her floor, she skirted past Manda and Izzie. "I need to talk to you," Dan said before she could close her fish-bowl door.

"Paul Pacchini. Coulter told me."

"Sorry. Didn't think it should wait."

"Course not. You done good." But there was a hardness in her voice she didn't think she had intended.

Maybe some lawyers have a system; do things in a time-honoured, tried-and-tested kind of fashion. Maddy Shannon just jumped in, anywhere. Not because she was disorganised or haphazard – famously, quite the reverse.

But because she had learned there *is* no beginning. No clean process. You could spend half your life looking for the proper starting point.

She fired off a few emails to the august offices of Barnes Nugent Barnes Solicitors, where a certain Mr. Mark Alexander worked. Flash bastard wasn't much older than Maddy, coining it in out there in the private sector, yet he was to be trusted over Maddy in pursuit of the prosecution. She didn't bother to attach a friendly wee note to the necessary documents.

Her own inbox was ringing out every couple of seconds, as impatient as she was. Coulter sent through report after report, from which she learned very little she didn't already know. Except that a publican, one Charles Dempsey had come up trumps for Ian Lennon. He must be doling out a lot of cash to hire, on Lennon's behalf, one of the rising stars of the Scottish courtroom, who in turn had immediately got Lennon bail. Dead on cue, Deena Gajendra's office was in touch. Maddy replied immediately detailing access conditions to the victims' corpses. Gajendra was as sharp as a field full of foxes. She was also half a foot taller than Maddy, half a decade younger, aristocratically confident, slinky and seductive. Maddy had said to Dan McKillop, "I'd go for her myself if I buttoned up different." Actually she could anyway, regardless of buttons.

The paperwork done, she headed for Lochgilvie House. The Home where one of the victims had spent time and where now the authorities in their wisdom had sent Darren Mullholland, brother of another murdered child. Within two hours of banging her boss's office door shut, Maddy was sitting in a classroom with a traumatised waif of a laddie, and a silent, grim-looking social worker. Janet Bateman was supposed to have been there too, but so far hadn't turned up.

Maddy and Darren had already spent the best part of twenty minutes in near-silence, but Maddy prided herself on having a way with problem boys. All those years behind a deep fat fryer, hearing woes. "How is this place?"

Darren looked like a boy out of a different era. Long blond hair spilled over his forehead and face. Small for sixteen. Pale, thick lips, ill-fitting clothes. He looked like a street urchin from some old black and white movie. A Bowery Boy. Angel with a dirty face.

"How's your mum?"

He held her gaze. Fringe falling over his eyebrows. His anaemic mouth seemed poised to say something important at every moment. But he kept silent, and still.

"I'm the lawyer, Darren, who's going to try and make sure the man who killed Frances is punished."

"What kind o' punishment's that, d'you think?" His voice was deeper than she expected.

"Ah – that's not up to me, Darren. That's up to the courts. My job is just to make sure—"

"Know what I'd like to do him?"

"Tell me. If it helps."

He looked at her askance for a moment, then shook his head, sat back in his chair.

"What was she like, your sister?"

Darren just looked at her, waiting for a question he was prepared to answer.

"You got on well with her?"

No response.

"Miss her? Normal kid I suppose?"

Now he smiled. "Depends on what you mean by normal. Normal enough for up our bit. Ran riot, swore and drank and smoked skunk. Normal for our family. I know for a fact she was shagging a wee arsehole loser."

"At fourteen?" Maddy had stopped wincing a long time ago.

"She's been getting felt up for a lot longer than that."

154

"She smoked marijuana, yes? Anything harder?"

Darren shrugged. Either he didn't know, or didn't care to tell her.

"You ever come across an Ian Lennon?" Maddy put photographs of Lennon on the table between them. Classic mugshots. Lennon, face-on, looked exactly like a killer. In the profile shot, though, there was a flabbiness that made him look less of a hard man; the skin around the eyes and under the chin sagged. Darren picked up this photograph up and looked at it hard.

"Why would a man like that want to hurt Frances?" Maddy asked – herself as much as Darren.

"Everybody wants to hurt everyone else."

The completeness of that little philosophy chilled her. "But why this man, and why Frances? Why that night?"

Darren shook his head very slowly.

"Where had she been, Darren? Could she have gone on her own to Bearsden?"

"Franny went where she liked, when she liked, and with anybody she liked—"

"Like who? Who were her pals?"

"Wee posse of them. Pure mad." He sighed. "Try Sophie Turner. Carol Ann Christie. Misha someone – don't know her name."

Misha Donnell. The police had interviewed all the girls Darren mentioned. None of them gave them anything new. "School pals. She didn't go to school too much though, did she?"

He laughed, shook his head.

"You used to try and make her go,though, didn't you, Darren? You were the one who tried to keep the house running." Darren replied with that unflinching cold stare. "You made the breakfasts, the dinners, every—"

"Ma did what she could!"

"You tried to get Frances—"

"Franny."

155

"Franny. To go to school. To dress properly. Come home on time. That's a lot to ask of a young boy."

He flicked his hair away from his face. His eyes glowing. "She was a laugh, Franny. Say what you like, but she made you laugh. She was off her fucking bonce, but funny wi' it. And pretty. Specially first thing in the morning like that, before the make-up, the…"

He couldn't find the word, but Maddy knew what he meant. Before the hardness; before snapping her jaw into position, like slamming on a helmet.

Darren couldn't help himself. His body shuddered and jolted, went out of his control. His sobs were gulps as he sucked in mouthfuls of air. He smothered his head in his hands, clenched his body so tight Maddy feared he might asphyxiate. The social worker stood behind him; put a cold, sanctioned hand on his shoulder. Maddy remained frozen for a second, until the only possible reaction kicked in. She went round the table and took the boy in her arms.

"I was delayed at the Education Department." Janet Bateman, director of Lochgilvie House, made it sound like the inner sanctum of the White House.

"Well, Darren Mullholland got into quite a state, and I'm not trained in that kind of work."

"Perhaps you shouldn't have gone ahead with the interview."

They nodded a truce at one another. The little round lady opened a drawer and took out a stapled bunch of photocopied papers. "I've been instructed to give you everything we have on Darren." She handed the papers over. "You're going to see his mother, I believe?"

Maddy flicked through the neatly-collected papers. Social Work reports, school notes and reports. Most of it she'd already seen – maybe all of it. But you took everything you got, in case a paper, a report, a note on the back of an envelope, told you something you *didn't* know.

"There's something that's not in here, not written down anywhere, so therefore probably not of much use to you...."

Maddy looked up at Bateman, perched on her cushions. "Go on, please."

"This is purely anecdotal... One of Darren's old primary school teachers is a friend of mine. Darren was always tired at school. Never slept enough. You'll have gathered already that it was him who kept the house running. He collected the child allowance, made sure it was spent on food before his mother could get her hands on it to buy drugs..."

"How long was he doing this for?"

"From what I can gather, several years. Darren made sure the child allowance didn't go on his mum's habit, but he still needed more money, for the family to eat, buy clothes... So he was out late at night."

"Sorry. I don't follow."

"He helped Jackie out in the streets." It took a moment for it to dawn on Maddy. "Darren was his own mother's pimp."

The only person she couldn't see was Lennon himself. Not until court. She thought of her job as a kind of puzzle. She had to get to know everything about a man she wasn't allowed to meet. Like a piece kept deliberately back from a player. If she was to nail the killer, win the game, she had to discover his psychology, his motives, habits, reasoning, through every other piece on the board.

Helena Mackay was every inch a Bearsden widow. "All the money is tied up in the house. Actually, I'm one of the deserving poor."

The house was like a mini Doge's Palace – sell off a couple of the Tiffany lamps on the marble mantel, the fancy porcelain on the Queen Anne table, and you could rectify Helena's shortage of readies, *and* wipe out poverty in half of Easterhouse.

"I've only been on holiday once in the last four years. And that was a bus trip to Torquay."

"You can afford a gardener." Maddy smiled sweetly.

"Only because he comes cheap."

Helena's contribution to charity and the health of the nation was her interest in the penal system. Along with several other women in the area she sent Christmas and birthday cards to inmates and their families, visited prisoners, and baked cakes to raise money for their children.

"Of course I used to be a lot more active, but I don't get around so easily any more."

She had even campaigned for prison reform in her time. "You know those men were still slopping out their own cells until a year ago?" Maddy was beginning to thaw. Especially when the old woman was honest enough to offer the reason for her concern. "When Ronnie was arrested I remember thinking that death would be immeasurably preferable."

Maddy had read all about Mr. Ronald MacKay.

"He was innocent." Helena said. "I say it so often it must sound pat. False even."

Mrs. Mackay's husband, managing director of a precision tools company wholly owned by a much larger corporation, had been jailed for seven years for embezzlement, back in the mid eighties. He was only in his early fifties, but he didn't survive his time inside. The case caused a little flurry of tabloid outrage because the money that went missing wasn't profit or takings, but donations his workforce thought they were making to a Third World charity.

"You told the police," Maddy changed the subject, flicking though her notes, "that Ian Lennon was not one of the prisoners you visited."

"That's correct. As I said, I haven't been visiting for some time now. However, all my gardeners are rehabilitated prisoners. They've come recommended to me by my associates in the WPRC."

Women's Prison Reform Committee. Helena used to be its treasurer – clearly her comrades didn't believe that the crimes of the husband tainted the wife.

"You must be very trusting. Mr. Lennon looks rather fierce in his photographs."

"That's only because you now associate that face with a series of dreadful crimes."

Maddy hated being lectured on her job by amateurs. Especially when they were right.

"Otherwise, Mr. Lennon's face, while not, I admit, particularly attractive, is that of a common man who has had, like many, a hard life."

The thaw Maddy had felt began to freeze over again. Common man!

"You might even have said, given other information, that his is a kindly face. If you were told, for instance, that he had grandchildren whom he took to the park, you would say that he was gruff but kindly."

"But he doesn't. Take grandchildren to the park. He's been a hit man, an enforcer." Maddy bridled at Helena looking down at her over the top of her glasses. "Mr. Lennon came running in here, the day he found Frances Mullholland's body. You don't keep it locked?"

"Never. He lets himself in each time he comes to make himself coffee and fill a pail of water. I usually go out to say hello after an hour or so. That's what I did that day, then came back in here and went on writing letters."

"And when he came in shouting?"

"My hearing's not what it was. But I heard him eventually. When I got into the hall, Mr. Lennon was coming out of the kitchen. He was very pale. He asked me if it would be all right to use my phone."

She and Maddy were sitting in the drawing room, a huge bay window looking out onto the small lawns that bordered the driveway. The old lady glanced out fearfully, as if the lawn could at any moment erupt into blood. "I've lived in this house most of my life... and now, suddenly, I despise it."

"But you still don't suspect Ian Lennon in any way?"

"I didn't say that, my dear," said Helena Mackay getting up.

At the front door, Maddy stuffed her notes back into her bag, and remembered something. "Just a thought. Your WPRC stationery, you don't happen to remember who designed it?"

"I should. I dealt with them at the time. Strange name..."

"Sign-Chronicity?"

"That's them. Very Freudian."

"Jung actually. Synchronicity." You have to put these posh old biddies down every now and then.

Maddy went to her car – the yellow sports looked comfortable in a big broad driveway. She didn't know why she'd asked about the stationery. Lateral thinking maybe. But it had paid off. No one at the police had made the connection.

She was like a gladiator waiting for the lions to be released. Through the frosted glass, two big, black hulking creatures, howling not barking. Crazed with blood lust. She imagined their fangs, their drool, the red light of movie death in their eyes.

A small, slight figure loomed behind them, shouting at them to be quiet. The man managed to negotiate a place for himself between them and the door, and opened it just enough to speak to Maddy. He smiled happily.

"Miss Shannon?" he said. "Are you afraid of dogs?"

"I'm afraid of *those* dogs."

One of the beasts managed to bulldoze the little man out the way, and take a mad leap at Maddy.

"Heidi, no!" screamed the man. The creature knocked her off her feet, and covered her in drool.

"She's a big baby."

Walking up a hall with one bouncing dog trying to slabber you to death and another playing with your feet was an art Maddy hadn't acquired. Which dog was it, Maddy asked herself, whose hair turned up on the body of Paul Pacchini? The one clinging to her for dear life, or the one that thought her shoes were biscuits?

"Heggie! Go on outside now." Their owner opened a back door and both dogs ran out into a neat little garden, then stopped and turned to see if Maddy was following them out to play. Colin Ross just managed to close the door in time. "Heidi. Heggie. Stay out there!"

"Nice names."

"Short for Heidegger and Hegel. German philosophers. Coffee?"

Come the revolution, Mr. Ross will have pride of place in front of the firing squad. She shook her head.

"You'll want to know about Ian Lennon. We were introduced to him by the previous owners here. We've told the police all this. A rough diamond, I know, but we've always found him terribly pleasant. Perhaps even a bit of an *idiot savant*." French accent and everything. One brief blow to the back of the head... "The Hendersons – the folks in here before us – emigrated to Australia. I believe *she* had some connection with the prisoner-rehabilitation world and that's how Ian Lennon came to—"

"Do you have an address for them?"

"The Hendersons? No."

"You told the police that Mr. Lennon was here on the morning of the fifth of May."

"The day before the Kelvingrove murders, yes."

"He wears an overall to work?"

"Yes. I told the police that too."

"The police asked you about a visit you got, maybe two, three years ago, from a Mr. Kennedy?"

"They did. We wondered afterwards. Kennedy – that's not the father of the murdered boy?"

"Your wife said that you and Mr. Kennedy spoke in private, but she never knew about what."

"Carolyn doesn't take much interest in the garden. I do all the cutting and pruning and mowing and planting—"

"The garden?"

"That's why that Kennedy chap came to see me. Gave

161

me a note from Ian Lennon, some advice on gardening. We had just moved in back then and the garden was at a crucial stage."

"You're joking. You still have the note?"

"Sorry."

Maddy's mobile rang. She went out into the hall, listening to her voicemail and called back: "Thank you, Mr. Ross. I'll let myself out."

He wished he was better at taking time off. In the mornings, when Martha wasn't having one of her bad turns, it would be nice to sit down at the table, take his time over toast and tea, chat to Jenny and Beth; Ben, when he was up from London. Stable, successful kids. Well, maybe not Ben.

Beth handed him a cup of tea. "For mum."

He stopped at the door. "Do you think *we're* part of the problem? When she's sick, nobody challenges her. We all just accept it. It's like we *encourage* her to be sick."

"Just take up the tea, dad." Beth took the cup back out of his hand. "I'll take it."

Midweek was a drag. He drove to work on autopilot, worrying about Lennon out on bail, and protected now by a big-wig lawyer, paid for by Charlie Dempsey. Either Young Charlie had more to do with these murders than met the eye, or someone was hiding behind him. Whatever, it meant that the perp was out on the streets, and could steal away. Coulter had brought in the PF, but there were still too many loose ends, too much that could go wrong. He wouldn't be able to relax until the bad man was behind bars. And by then he'd be stressed about the next case.

The Pacchini thing worried him. They had managed to find someone who remembered the kid from his schooldays. A mother of a pal at the time – though the son could barely remember him at all. The parents were off their heads, the woman had said. Not bad or vicious, just disorganised.

Too many worries, crowding in on each other. He arrived

at the station without managing to think any one of them through, and was faced straight away with a new one. Or perhaps he was being negative. An opportunity. He didn't have to say much to Maddy, other than "Yes" and "Okay" and "Well done". Nobody had picked up on Whyte and the Docherties' connection with Helena Mackay. Maddy had been nice about Sign-Chronicity designing the old woman's charity stationery – but he knew she'd enjoyed her scoop.

"We keep finding all this stuff out about you," Russell was strolling around Jim and Elaine Docherty's main room, used to it now, "which you could easily have told us."

Jim Docherty was following him around, glaring. Elaine sat at the computer, poised to type, but looking up at the three men.

"Now look here – yes, we once did do some work for the Women's Prison Reform Committee. And, yes, we have a couple of letters on file with Mrs. MacKay's name on them. But how you could expect us to make the connection with the house where a girl was killed—"

Coulter could see both Russell's and Docherty's points of view. Follow one logic and there's little to stop you accusing Whyte and the Docherties of perjury, perhaps aiding and abetting. Possibly even murder itself. Take the other route, and you have three innocent people, who just happened to be there or thereabouts. As innocent as anyone in any city could be. We all rub along, cheek-by-jowl, one step away from being shot in a park, or connected to someone shot in a park. You ride the subway along with all sorts, work next door to strangers; you're never aware of the shadow that tells you death is approaching.

Jim Docherty and Martin Whyte run past dead bodies. Then it turns out that they worked in a home where one of the victims had once lived. They were caught drinking in a pub owned by a gangster who is helping the man accused of triple murder. Now they know a woman who knows a man who has a dog whose hair was found on a corpse in

Kelvingrove Park. The Theory of the Six Degrees? Ask the right questions and Coulter himself, Russell, Maddy Shannon, anyone in busy Cadogan Street out there, could be connected to the murders. On that basis you could arrest the whole city.

"0 2 report. Day off. Scotch pasta. Nuff for 2. CU."

She'd had to teach him text language. Louis came from what was supposed to be the world's most modern, out there, edgy city. Actually, he seemed to have stepped out of some quaint sleepy village. She'd never been to New York, but her idea of it now, thanks to Commander Casci, was a place stuck somewhere in the early 1970s.

She stopped at her car. It would be easier to take the bus from her place to the office but the thought of all that human contact so early in the morning was too much to bear. She reread Louis's message. He had sent her several since leaving last week. *Scotch pasta.* Too many Mob movies had made Maddy assume that Italians in America sat around eating *bolognese* in string vests listening to Puccini. Not Louis. He had moved away from his roots, geographically and culturally. Preferred sushi, fajitas, burgers. He associated pasta with Scotland now. Apparently there was enough for two, and he was inviting her around… then he must be alone. The message made her both happy and sad.

She texted back. "2 many carbs. Working. Got2Go. Soon. X'

She walked back to her car and listened to her voice messages. Only one, from Mama. Maddy knew even before she had spoken, just by the rhythm of her breath, she was upset. Maddy was all familied-out after last week; wanted to stay clear of every relation for a month at least. Family problems in particular held a dread for her, and she knew that tone of her mother's so well.

"Maddalena. I'd rather talk to you in person. But… Nonno's taken ill."

How ill was anybody's guess. Rosa's sense of drama could make a slight cold sound life-threatening. At Nonno's age, though, a cold might very well be.

If Shannon lost the case against Lennon it wouldn't be all her fault. Coulter knew he hadn't given her nearly enough to nail him. "The boy's mother has to be *somewhere!*"

All they had was a paper trail, and a pretty tattered one at that. Taylor Primary, the last school in Glasgow to have a record of a Paul Pacchini, had been merged with another school. Nearly all the staff had moved on. They finally managed to track down a teacher who took Pacchini's class in Primary 4. Pleasant enough boy, was all she could remember.

The old head mistress had only the vaguest recollection of either the boy or his parents. "Don't think I ever met the dad. The mother, so far as I can recall, didn't make much contact with the school either. Small woman? Young – if it's the person I'm thinking of. Must have had Paul when she wasn't much more than a teenager herself."

They had tracked down a name and a few scant details. The mother's name was Belinda Laird. From East Kilbride originally. She'd had Paul at a respectable 19, and was married soon after. The entire family had, it seemed, trodden lightly through the world, hardly disturbing the air. Until the husband ended up dead drunk, literally, on the streets of Manchester. And the son behind the rhododendron bushes in Kelvingrove with a bullet through his head. As paper trails go, this one ended badly.

Strange, Coulter thought, how the likes of Martin Whyte and Elaine Docherty bump into everything during their short stay on this earth. They're like pinballs, colliding and bouncing everywhere, rebounding, making their mark. The Pacchinis, on the other hand, could live entire lives without anybody noticing. Belinda and Giorgio Pacchini hadn't stayed in one part of the city for any length of time, so that didn't help. Teachers, shopkeepers, neighbours, publicans and barmen in Govan, Toryglen and Pollokshaws had all come across them, if tenuously.

"I think they maybe took drugs," one ex-neighbour told WPC Dalgarno.

"What kind of drugs, sir?"

"Oh I don't know. A funny smell from their house. They *looked* like the types, you know?"

Neither George or Belinda ever worked, at least not legally, from what they could tell. So maybe they were dealers after all. Little Paul, or Paolo as some people remembered him, took a page out of his parents' book and applied the rule of Look, Don't touch, to life in general. Never a member of a football team or swimming club, library...

"I'm off to grab a sanny." Coulter yawned. But, slipping on his jacket, despite the lasting warm spell, Amy Dalgarno came in waving a piece of paper. "Dundee. Belina Pacchini, née Laird. She's living in Dundee. The Hilltoun—"

"The Hilton?!" Patterson Webb asked incredulously.

"Hill*toun*, Patty," Russell said. "An area in Dundee where you don't tend to find a Hil*ton*. She moved up there three years ago. I've requested her to come down to Glasgow."

Coulter came back into the centre of the room. "Did you tell her why?"

"No. But I can't be certain the Dundee force will be as sensitive as we are."

"Make damn sure they are."

The hospital had a wonderful view of the Necropolis. Nonno had taken sick on the train to Glasgow. A couple of times a year Rosa came to fetch him so that he and a couple of his old cronies could meet up in the home where one of them had been plonked by his family.

"A stroke, the doctors said. I think quite a bad one." Rosa put on a calm voice, but Maddy could tell from her eyes she was frightened. Stone angels near the top of the hill fluttered directly across from the window of the fifth floor ward.

"The fact he hasn't stirred at all worries them."

Every now and then you got a glimpse of the old Rosa di Rio, chip shop queen of the Ayrshire coast. Tough, practical; coping alone to the point of martyrdom. It must have been rough, the drama on the train, a collapsed old man, a crowd of people, a screeching ambulance...

Maddy turned towards the bed. Nonno lay out flat, sheets pulled up tight; his breathing virtually undetectable. Monsignor Connolly came striding along from the far end of the corridor, footsteps like a sergeant major's.

"Sorry for your troubles, Missus Di Rio."

He seemed more Irish of a sudden. Not Packy's Irish; not Donegal. The accent a little flatter, sounding more Northern Irish. Maddy wished it had been the younger one. Mike was a cocky little nonce but at least he didn't have Grim Reaper eyebrows and a voice like the harbinger of doom. When Connolly knelt at her grandfather's bedside he brought death nearer.

"*In nomine Patris, et Filii, et Spiritus Sancti....* I thought Vittore would prefer the old Latin."

Maddy didn't think he would. But then again, what did she know? Did Nonno want this man here at all?

"Nearer his own language. If I knew Italian I would do it in that."

Maddy thought of making a run for it. But it was too late. She bowed her head obediently.

John MacDougall slapped Inspector Coulter's then Sergeant Russell's backs heartily when he bumped into them in the corridor. Coulter and Russell had been in since before seven, Coulter not having got away last night until after ten. MacDougall was just arriving, no doubt after a good long sleep, and for an inconsequential meeting with the Chief over coffee and scones. "Well done, chaps." The olde English phrase in a Gaelic accent sounded weird.

"Thanks," said Russell.

Coulter didn't join in with the smiles. "We've hardly got a conviction yet, sir, and there are still a few elements we—"

MacDougall, with all the self-righteousness of a politically-appointed quango convener, was hearing none of it. He told them they were excellent officers, shining examples of guardians of the law. "Keeping men like McCartney off the streets."

"Lennon, sir."

"Lennon, of course!" He strode off up the corridor.

He was fatuous and condescending, yes, but Coulter could see why he had risen in the world. The man had a certain presence, a brightness of eye that was either smart and scornful or smart and wise. Maybe a mixture of the two. His success with difficult schools was universally accepted, yet he retained a bonhomie that was difficult to resist. No, it was the way politicos like MacDougall and the rest could enter Division A buildings unannounced and unaccompanied that got to Coulter. Even visiting officers from other forces – Casci from New York – had to wear a badge. The police were too deep in the pockets of quangos and consultants these days, at the mercy of policy whims and spin.

Russell opened the door on a kind of woman neither of them had expected. They had come to anticipate the marks of poverty and despair. Extremes of thinness and obesity. Lank hair and pasty skin. Belinda Laird shone with health. Her hair was shoulder-length, light hazel, an attractive curl through it. Her complexion advert-soft; her smile, as the officers entered, serene. She was dressed simply but cleanly in a shapeless tunic – which was fine, given her figure.

"Thank you, Mrs. Pacchini, for coming all the way down here."

"Thank *you*. It's nice to be home again, for a short while at least." She gave a little laugh and neither Russell nor Coulter could stop themselves smiling back. "They say that Dundee is like Glasgow with the good bits taken out."

"What good bits?" Coulter wasn't sure if it was a joke or not.

"Oh you know, the buzz, the energy."

Coulter pulled back a chair for them all to sit down. Russell lost his smile first. "Some people might be more worried about the situation."

"I don't do worry, officer. How bad can it be? If it was *really* serious you'd have told me by now."

"Mrs Pacchini—"

"I haven't been Mrs. Pacchini for a long time. Even then, to be honest, only on paper."

"Miss Laird then."

"That'll do."

"Is there another option?" Russell sneered. Belinda thought about his question for a moment, then let it go. "What's this about? Paul?" Russell opened his mouth to speak, but Belinda answered the question before it was voiced. "He's my only next-of-kin. I'm his. And as *I* haven't done anything wrong…" She smiled. "What's he done?"

"When was the last time you were in touch with Paul?"

It was Coulter's turn to cut in. This was all going too quickly. "Hold on. I need to clarify. Sorry. Paul went back to live with you after your husband, George, died?"

"Not really. I went down there for a while, he came up here…"

"And then what?"

"He decided to go back and go on living with Veronica and Des."

"Veronica and Des?"

"Veronica's a cousin of Giorgio's. When things were bad with his dad, Paul had lived with Veronica and Des who stay down that way. That was one of the reasons I let

169

Giorgio take Paulo down there. I knew he'd be safe with Veronica and Des."

She was very clear. An accuracy in every word. There was a tougher woman behind the smiling persona, Coulter thought. One that was used to arguments. "I know it's... *unusual*. But I know also what's best for my boy. "*He'll* tell you, too. Paul understands perfectly."

At the moment of saying it, her face fell. Her eyes darkened, and she looked from Coulter to Russell and back again. "Oh, Jesus."

Coulter couldn't help his morbid fascination of the moment of understanding, the terrible penny dropping. Belinda simply, almost sweetly, put her hand to her mouth, paled a little. "You can't, can you? You can't ask him."

She stood up. Then sat back down. They all do. Then they refuse offers of coffee, water, telephoning somebody. Belinda consented to the water. Like everyone else she seemed to go through an acted grief, a performance. They flit between the dark hole they're tumbling into, and behaving according to the rules of a social situation.

"What happened?" she finally whispered.

Bit by bit, over an hour, bringing in Amy Dalgarno, they made Belinda Laird aware of the situation. Belinda had heard about Kelvingrove, but never for a minute...

Through tears, between long silences, over another hour, they got her side of the story. She and Giorgio Pacchini got married because she was pregnant with Paul. Her parents were strict and religious, old school Kirk. Giorgio introduced her to cannabis. Never any hard stuff, but they smoked their socks off. He got her into music – he played with a few bands. And he got her into new ways of thinking.

"Geo was both my Nemesis and my salvation." It had the sound of an oft-quoted phrase. "If it hadn't been for him, I'd never have wasted so much time, never have done in my head with pot. I'd've been a better mother. Then again, without him, I might never have started my journey at all."

"Journey to where?" Russell asked, but Belinda didn't answer. She never realised, she said, until he died, that the cannibis was doing something to Geo's head. She'd never have let him go off with Paul if she'd known.

"Why did you let him take the boy at all?" Russell was incredulous.

"It was best for all of us. I needed... some space. Head space, you know? Geo and Paul were great together. And they were going to live near Veronica and Des."

"What exactly is the family relationship with Veronica and Des?"

"Veronica is Geo's first cousin. Veronica Mancini. Now Kane."

"Where did *you* go, Belinda? After Geo and Paul went south?"

"A little tour." She was getting tired now. The tears had stopped flowing, and the voice flattened out. "Iona. Bit straight for me. Met someone there from Findhorn...."

Then she fell into silence.

They walked back towards the incident room. "That poor woman's going to spend the night in a cheap hotel room before identifying her son's body in the morning. You knew what you were going to tell her. She should have brought someone!" Coulter had never seen WPC Dalgarno's fury before. A legitimate fury, but he had wanted Paul Pacchini's mother fresh, unrehearsed. "Belinda strikes me as a woman with deep reserves of self-comfort," Coulter defended himself.

"Where's Findhorn?" asked Russell.

"Kind of hippy place. Up by Inverness I think." Amy swallowed her anger and returned to professional mode. "It's huge now. An eco-friendly town. Everyone lives in harmony with their surroundings."

Russell burst out laughing. "All smoking dope and living in tree-houses and going 'om'? That kind of crap?"

"Actually, I think they're strictly *anti*-drugs." Amy was warming up again for a never-ending battle against Russell. Coulter was saved from playing peacemaker by two uniforms waiting at the door of the incident room to talk to him. They jostled with one another for his attention, like kids.

"You first," he said to the most desperate-looking of the two.

"Sir. It's about Ian Lennon."

Russell and Dalgarno were too lost in their mutual contempt and walked on into the room.

"What about him?"

"He's broken bail. Gone AWOL."

"You're joking. How hard have you tried to find him?"

"Not at his residence, and he hasn't turned up at either of the two gardens he was supposed to be doing today."

"Maybe he's celebrating his release."

"We're out searching right now. He's not at the Cottars Arms."

"Lets not panic just yet, eh? Maybe he's at the flicks."

The young policeman looked at him, not sure what the "flicks" might be. Coulter turned to the second young man in uniform, looking sulky at not being chosen to speak first. "I like to save the good news to last, son. Go on."

"Martin Whyte's also gone walkabout."

"We've no hold on Mr. Whyte, officer."

"He was scheduled to meet us – about his Lochgilvie connections – but didn't turn up."

Russell came back out of the incident room. He'd obviously heard the same news. He had never actually voiced the opinion that Coulter had charged ahead too quickly with the Lennon theory, but Coulter knew. Knew, too, that Whyte and the Docherties were his sergeant's prime suspects.

"Mr. Docherty doesn't know where he is," the uniform continued. "Whyte goes off to meetings down south regularly apparently, but they've no contact address for him."

"When's he due back?" Russell butted in.

"According to Mr. Docherty he can go off for anything between three and ten days."

"And you've tried his mobile?"

"Turned off."

"Then we'll just wait until he returns," Coulter smiled, opening the incident room door. Russell stayed outside with the Uniforms, making Coulter feel uneasy. The last thing he needed was a fifth columnist inside his own team going off on another track, talking behind his back to top brass and footsoldiers. Inside, he was met with better news.

"Desmond and Veronica Kane," said Amy, pleased with her efficiency. "Pennyvale. Village, east of Manchester."

"If they were that easy to find, how come a Paul Pacchini didn't turn up on English school records?"

Any shrugged. "The whole Laird-Pacchini-Kane thing blew the system?"

Looking past her, he noticed that no one was at their desks, but huddled round a television screen. Coulter's heart sank. Even worse than the media breaking some news they shouldn't have is the media getting hold of information that he hadn't.

The school holidays had started; the drizzle had kicked in and looked set to stay until autumn term. Ibrahim "Brammer" Muhammed Khan and Caprice Fleming were walking down Alison Street on Glasgow's south side on a Tuesday afternoon. They weren't going anywhere in particular, just walking down a road which, an hour or so later they would normally have walked back up again. But, as they passed Soud's Intercontinental Fruit and Vegetable Mart, three men came running out shouting and brandishing knives and a gun, making their way to a waiting car.

Brammer Khan later told the police that he had always felt guilty about Soud's because once, as a kid, he had tanned a bunch of bananas from the pavement display and the next day when he went in with his mother, old man Soud had patted his head and gave him a free plum. In Caprice's case, experts said it was a case of fright or flight, or a combination of both. In her own words, she said she "'always wondered what it'd be like to sink high heels into some bastard's heid".

Brammer and Caprice were the nation's saviours. After a spring with nothing but bad news about the younger generation – if they weren't *being* killed they were out there doing the killing. Then along come a Scots Asian boy called Brammer of all things and a trainee WAG and foil three burly gangsters' attempt at robbery and assault. It helped enormously that both turned out, in the public glare, to be natural entertainers.

Brammer Khan had stuck his foot out and tripped the first of the men out the shop. The second man ran into the first and fell down too. It read like a scene from an Ealing comedy. The nation savoured every moment of the story. The third baddie was still inside wielding a baseball bat, about to give Mr. Soud a blow to the head, when he turned and saw the commotion. He made a run at Brammer but was stopped in his tracks by the screams of the first man.

It must have been a frightening sight, Caprice's stiletto pressing on your buddy's jugular. He wielded his bat at Brammer and Caprice and ventured slowly out the shop. Meanwhile, the driver, who had been waiting for his accomplices to return with a bag full of money – the third that morning, a newsagent's in Garthamlock and a hairdresser's in Mount Vernon – got out the car to help. He got back in quickly when Caprice came after him with her shoes in her hand. She went back to pummelling the second man, and the driver drove off. Meanwhile Brammer held off the last of the posse by chucking unripe avocados and courgettes at his head. "Brammer the Kid" and "Calamity Caprice" the papers called them. "Kid Khan". "Kitten heel Fleming".

All the TV reports and newspaper articles finished up with some version of the same sentiment: sixteen-year-old kids were better at protecting the public than the police force. Or at least, some of them were.

"*Really*, though," Dan McKillop said, flicking through the papers, "'Muhammed *Can* and Caprice *Will*.' The headline writers have gone mad. 'Story on pages 2,3,4,5,9,10,17,19,20 and 21!'"

"That's good, isn't it?" said Maddy.

"Tell you what, though. People would have preferred it if he'd been white and she hadn't been quite so common."

Maddy wasn't so sure. A slightly camp heroic Pakistani kid who spoke broad Scots, and a pouting innocent in heels... they soothed a whole series of national anxieties. "Maybe they were heaven sent, Dan."

"Definitive proof, then, that God's a gay regional soap producer." McKillop flicked through the pages of a broadsheet. "Looky who's managed to elbow his way into Brammer's moment of glory."

Maddy took the paper off him. Czar MacDougall's picture, and, elsewhere pictures and quotes from the First Minister, Chief Constable Crawford Robertson, even Maxwell Binnie. They all welcomed the Have-A-Go Heroes' glory. The worthies' various statements, cautioning against approaching armed robbers in general but praising the guts, foresight and decency of the wonderful teenagers of Shawlands, seemed to suggest that they too would have chucked courgettes and ground their golf studs in baddies' eye sockets. MacDougall in particular, the lifelong educationalist, public servant in his third age of wisdom, made not only a meal but an entire theoretical proposition out of the case.

"Children are born morally neutral," Dan read out the quote in a deep Biblical voice, "though I believe there is a propensity towards goodness." He held the paper high and walked gravely around Maddy's little glass cubicle, refining his accent to his idea of a Free Presbyterian Islander. "Whether they turn out bad or good – by which I mean, sharing in and protecting the positive values of their communities – will depend on you and me. Parents, teachers, friends, team-mates, shopkeepers, everyone who impacts upon young lives..." Dan let the paper drop from his hands.

If nothing else, Brammer and Caprice put a temporary halt to Press and Tory demands for the death penalty and ferocious public order policies against youngsters. If Brammer and Caprice had been at home helping mummy, or doing their homework, or curfewed, they wouldn't have been on the street to save Mr. Soud.

You couldn't actually see the raindrops outside the window; the air was just wringing like a damp tea towel. Maddy had a hell of a day before her – three bereaved mothers, Jacky Mullholland, Anne Kennedy and Belinda Laird. She hadn't meant it to work out that way. It was Nonno who had caused the bottle-neck – most of yesterday spent at the hospital.

"What's the prognosis?" Dan stood at her cubicle door.

"Some kind of coma. I don't know. He'll come out of it any moment now, apparently. Then they'll know what damage has been done to the brain."

The doctors were preparing the family for the worst. A gaggle of Scots Italians had gathered around the hospital. Uncle Gerry, Mr. Arcari, Uncle Dante. A few Irish, too. Auntie May. Lizzie... They sat in the canteen, or stood at the front porch. There was even talk that her dad would come over from Italy. That's all she needed – Packy stomping about in his size tens.

The door behind her closed. She watched Dan returning to his desk, sitting down and lifting his phone. Izzie and Manda were chatting, laughing. In her little booth, Maddy felt cut off. A hard shard of loneliness somewhere inside numbed her. She could feel the black outline around her thicken, detach her from the rest of the world.

Coulter was driving through warm, pale drizzle somewhere off the M6, speaking on the hands-free. "What's the story at Whyte's?"

"Nothing." Russell, he could tell, was pissed off at being left at base. "Left notes for everyone – milkman, post, cleaning lady – saying he'd be back soon. Found nothing in his house."

How come "dreich" is a Scots word when the north west of England is dreicher? Coulter had left the motorway twenty minutes ago; a piece of paper on the passenger seat was directing him through country roads to Pennyvale. "And Lennon?"

"Papers aren't through for forced access to his dwelling yet. Tomorrow? Blame the PFs."

"Better get off. I'm nearly there. See you."

The grass and the sky were both so washed out that green and blue became the same colour. But there was old-fashioned warmth in the southern air – silage, cow-dung, rain and field smells, distilled together like a good malt.

He'd left a bit of a mess back in Glasgow – and wasn't in the least sorry to be away from it all. No Lennon and no Whyte. At least, for once, he had his bosses on his side. Everyone from Crawford Robertson down was keen to get that cold-hearted Irish bastard behind bars. Even the Scottish Executive was desperate to put an end to the focus on youth and calls for belting, birching, jailing, death penalties – the Brammer/Caprice effect wouldn't give them *that* much breathing space.

He slowed down, passing the petrol station he had to look out for. One of those old ones, like out of a film. Ancient pump, a shack, and a house. Next, The Malt Shovel.... Terrific looking pub, even in the rain, all hanging plant pots and an old-fashioned sign. Local beers. Might even stop on his way back. He turned left where Amy's instructions told him. A road no bigger than a lane. Des and Veronica Kane were going to be some act. How did they manage to keep a kid so entirely apart from the system? And anyway, who accepts the hassle and expense of bringing up a nephew just to let his old dear get in touch with her inner angel?

Where did this sense of duty come from? Not from Rosa and certainly not Packy. Perhaps it had skipped a generation and jumped straight from Nonno to Maddy. This would be the third mother in as many months she had led into the mortuary, and she didn't have to be there for any of them. She had little faith in how the police, with their quasi-military training, street-battle hardened, dealt with the grieving, especially women. Or maybe it was more self-ish than that – Maddy Shannon brooding deep down what it was to be a mother.

Anne Kennedy had shown the pain more than Jackie Mullholland. The drugs work all right, for Jackie anyway. Cotton wool applied to the sore bit, a pillow *inside* your head. Still, Maddy would rather have a dose of whatever Belinda Laird was on. She was waiting in the street when Maddy arrived. A long, flowing, straight dress on. Not cheesecloth, or anything obviously hippy. A rather austere garment. And no jacket, despite the rain. Maddy thought the woman looked effortlessly elegant. More graceful in her movements, for sure, than either Anne or Jackie, as she followed Maddy and that morning's duty doc down the cold echoing corridors. Belinda glided noiselessly along, Maddy's heels beat the tiles like a workie's mallet.

When they pulled back the sheet, the woman hardly flinched. There can't be a more sickening sight in the entire world than seeing your own son killed, cut, frozen on a slab.

"Paolo."

Then she did what only a very small proportion of parents do – she put her hand on the boy's forehead. Some ask to go back to do just that, but very few find the strength to do it on first sight. Belinda kept her hand resting lightly on his brow, just above the snicked eyebrow. "Hello, Babe. How're you?" Belief in the afterlife. It always made these situations bearable. People who had never before thought about an afterlife, or who utterly dismissed it, suddenly believed, for a moment at least.

Maddy and the duty doc backed off towards the door, giving Belinda a moment. Maddy inquired if a pathologist had been given access to Sy's and Frances's corpses yet. It took a few minutes on mobiles and pagers to determine that the perfect Deena Gajendra had come to inspect the body with a pathologist, and had decided that no further exploratory work needed done – Maddy's statement of cause and circumstances of both deaths were acceptable. The paperwork should be back at the PF office this morning. Maddy walked back towards Belinda.

She was bending, kissing Paul's head. Then she straightened, pulled the sheet back up over her son's face. Then, smiling serenely, she turned to go. Some deep well of faith? Or heartless?

Coulter sat alone, an opportunity to look around the Kanes' living room. Veronica and Des were outside in the hall. Even apart from the tone of their voices, the muffled sobs, he knew what the call was – affirmation that Belinda Laird had just positively identified Paul's body. He heard the phone go down, and the middle-aged couple comforting each other before facing him again. Unlike Belinda, the Kanes had been given the full story before he got down here. Local Lancashire police had visited them last night with the news. So the phone call wasn't a surprise – but it hardly softened the blow. Their grief was genuine, Veronica sobbing in gulps, Des trying to sound businesslike.

The house was the only new one in the area. Spacious, clean, expensive. Desmond Kane was a successful enough businessman. The contents were more old-fashioned – brocade suite, chunky furniture, local artwork rustically framed stacked in a pile in the middle of the hall. The whole ground floor was in the midst of being given a repaint job. That always made Coulter's suspicions rise – guiltily now, listening to the Kanes' anguish. Veronica finally came in and looked at him plaintively.

"I'm sorry," he said. He wished he'd timed his visit for a little later. Fresh grief sometimes opens a witness up – more often it closes them down completely.

"It's our fault."

"I'm sure it wasn't."

"We should have let people know."

Des returned as she spoke, and Coulter detected the subtlest of warnings he gave his wife. An almost imperceptible lowering of an eyebrow, a momentary stare. Then again, the man had just heard positive proof that the lad he'd raised as a son for the last three years was dead. "We mustn't blame ourselves too much after the event, Nicky."

Before the phone rang, they had been explaining why they hadn't told anyone that Paul was missing. Paul wasn't legally theirs. They'd always been very aware of it. Equally, they loved him as much – more – than any parents could a real son. Belinda would never have made much of a mother, and they were the only ones who could raise the child properly. But they'd lived in fear of Paul being taken from them. Either by some unnamed, mysterious Government body, or by Belinda suddenly changing her mind.

So when Paul went out for a walk one Saturday and left a note saying he'd be back in a few weeks, they did nothing officially. They phoned locals and friends, searched the places he liked to go, and had tried to get in touch with Belinda. All they knew was that she was in the Dundee area.

"But she moves so often!" Veronica had said, trying not to show too much disapproval.

Her telephone numbers were always changing. Normally,

it was Belinda who kept in touch with *them*. "To be fair on her. She checked regularly on Paul," Des looked to Veronica for agreement.

"We received a call from Paul himself," Des turned to Coulter. "Three or four days after he'd left. He said he was with his mum. That he was fine and he'd be home as soon as he could. He sounded fine, cheerful even." For the past three months, they'd been trusting the boy who they insisted was sensible and capable. They sat next to each other on the sofa. Some couples are divided by grief, others brought closer. At least at first.

"But he was underage." Coulter kept his voice level.

Des Kane nodded. "He was older than his years. He'd lived quite a life. Drugs and hippies in Scotland. His dad drinking and wasting away in Manchester. Then putting up with two old codgers like us." They managed a smile for one another.

"The papers down here, they must have reported… events in Glasgow. Did you never think, wonder if…"

"Yes," said Des, quickly. "Eventually. It wasn't that big a story here. Middle pages. Just another killing in Glasgow. But the minute you see something like that, you can't help but imagine…'

"You can't help it, can you? Every time you hear of an accident, or see an ambulance," Veronica said, and burst into tears. Coulter wouldn't have guessed she was of Italian background. She'd presumably gone grey – Nicky, as her husband called her, was fifty-three – and had dyed her hair light brown. She was rounded, homely, but not in a Mediterranean way. Des put his hand on her arm. "You just hope it's someone else's son." Des stared past Coulter, horrified by his own words. "The descriptions were all wrong. Paul was no skinhead—"

"He left here with hair down to his collar. Lovely dark curls."

"I wanted him to get it cut. He wanted it *longer*, not

shorn off. And the shaved eyebrow – that's not like Paul at all."

"He phoned you. Didn't you dial 1471?"

Des sighed. "We tried it. Number withheld. Can you do that deliberately, or does it happen with all mobiles? I'm afraid we're a bit out of touch with the technology."

Des had told Coulter that he was a senior manager at Tesco's supermarkets, regional head of their cafes and in-store consumption. You'd have thought a job like that would keep you up to date. But Coulter himself was a senior policeman and couldn't figure out predictive texting. "What did Paul make of his mother's lifestyle?"

"Paul was more like us – even Belinda admitted that," said Nicky. "He was always happy to see his mum, and he got on all right with the people around her. I mean, they wouldn't harm a fly, these types. But he was happy to get back to real life."

Coulter took a sip of the cold coffee Veronica had made for him nearly an hour ago. "You started redecorating after Paul left?"

"No," said Des, a little defensive. "What makes you say that?"

"To welcome him home?"

Kane shook his head. "Paul was giving me a hand."

"You just recently moved in?"

Des gave a resigned little laugh. "Poor Paul. From the moment he came to us, we never quite managed to settle. We thought a house in the country would be good, so we bought one quickly – over in Odsbaston – but it was all wrong—"

"Damp," Veronica explained.

"The next year we bought again, over in Merston. We were only there – what, Nicky? six months?"

"Seven."

"Bigger this time, but needing too much work done to it."

182

"Then we found this place."

No wonder Paul Pacchini couldn't be traced – three surnames, and five changes of addresses in as many years.

"We gave it a lick of paint when we first moved in."

"Just a coat of white, to brighten up the horrible greys and browns the last people had."

"We were just starting to do it up properly, when Paul went off."

"Paul was never registered at any school – because you never settled long enough?"

"No. We never had any intention of sending him to school." Veronica was adamant.

"It meant that Paul disappeared from most state bureaucracy." Coulter met her gaze. "Tell me more about this home-schooling. I've heard of it, but never really understood it."

"Oh it's wonderful!" Veronica cheered up for a moment, then remembered.

"So you taught Paul yourselves?"

"Some of the time," Des said. "Nicky used to be a maths teacher, and I've got both French and German, amongst other skills. University of Life."

"It wouldn't work with every child," said Veronica. "Paul was a self-starter. Loved books and encyclopedias. Up in Scotland he wasn't reaching his potential in the school system."

"So how does it work exactly?"

"It's a very well developed and highly respected movement." Des got up and went to the door: "I'll show you the course books."

Veronica tried to get up too, but the weight of her grief wouldn't let her up out of her seat.

The texts and emails from Louis had suddenly and firmly stopped. The last one was over a week ago. Nothing in it had suggested a change, a retreat. He had just gone shtum.

Nonno was in some strange land between life and death. Alive to the touch, but just about dead to the eye. His breathing was so light. Was his mind active? Could he hear them – the mournful little crowd around his bed – or was he lost in some dream world of his own? Maybe he was eleven again, in another country. Another world.

"No shame in kneeling, if only out of respect." Monsignor Connolly spoke to Maddy like she were a wayward schoolgirl. There were several reasons why she didn't want to get down on her knees. One, her skirt and shoes weren't ideal for it. She had mixed gin and wine last night, talking manically about everything and nothing to Dan, so that standing took quite enough effort. Mostly, though, it felt too grovelling, humiliating. Nonno wouldn't have knelt. Mama was on her knees looking up at her, offended. Auntie Gina and her daughter Francesca were down there too – they had both arrived today from London. Maddy had no inclination to join their little band of holy willies. She remained at the foot of the bed. The only other person on his feet was the old priest, opening up his little vials and glowering at her. She tried to think of some cheekily acceptable riposte – the kind of chummy defiance her Nonno was so good at, but the only replies she could think of to a demand to get down on her knees were lewd. Not quite what the situation called for. She hung her head piously, and to avoid Connolly's stare.

"Draw the curtains, love," Rosa asked.

Maddy drew the bed curtain, encapsulating them in a tiny, too intimate space. The shamefulness of death. The deep, unsettling smells of the priest's oils made the air heavy. "*Mensa, albo lintea strata...*" The Latin sounded clandestine. A secret rite. Maddy couldn't stand it. She had been impulsive all day, working like a Trojan but taking time out to bring her team back expensive sushi before getting fractious with them all, insisting they work harder, faster. She'd called in unannounced, and fruitlessly, to Division A on her way home – Coulter hadn't got back from Pennyvale yet, and Russell had no time for her. Standing still while an old man mumbled voodoo was beyond the pale. She searched behind her with her hands, trying to find the curtain join. Reached behind her back, until she found the parting in the curtain. She'd do a disappearing act…

But she fumbled it. Tugged too tight on the curtain. Then she went over on one flare heel, pulling further on the curtain and rail. The whole contraption wobbled perilously. Mama glanced angrily. Gina and Francesca looked mortified. Connolly had a glower of such epic intensity that Maddy almost added insult to injury and burst out laughing. She managed to steady herself, recover a modicum of dignity and get out, leaving the droning and knee-shuffling behind her. "*Pelvicula cum saltem sex globulis…*"

Every city in the western hemisphere's the same, probably – in the grip of a collective compulsion to wear ridiculous clothes and shamble, waddle or plod the public highway. A more elegant age would keep the jogging urge private, like going to the bathroom.

Maddy sat in the taxi, feeling vague and tired. Conditions tonight must be perfect, bringing the joggers out in swarms. Not too warm, not too cold, not raining. Mid July, so they were either getting ready for exposing themselves on foreign beaches, or had just come back, disgusted with themselves. The ones who were thin and lean and genuinely fast, would always be thin, lean and fast. The fat, slow, and slovenly, likewise. But still they all took to the streets. They ran shamelessly past fancy bars and posh restaurants in Sauchiehall Street. Up hills and between cars. They used headphones and iPods to cut themselves off from the normal, sensible world. From her cab window she saw them tumble out of side-streets and dive up back alleys. Those same people would never *walk* along dark back streets, but put on a pair of shorts or a jogging bra, and all judgement dies. She saw them canter up towards Kelvingrove. Not even the memory of dead bodies dulled their mad appetite.

Does Louis jog? She can't imagine it. No bulging thighs or six-pack. Then again, he was healthy and vigorous enough, so who knows? Maybe he's exercising some other part of his anatomy. Not his texting or emailing finger. She got out the taxi at Byres Road. Speed-walk uphill to Lorraine Gardens – that's as much as she was going to concede to this fitness mania. Past the lit-up Church of Scotland, glowing prettily and ghostly.

He came at her like some avenging Angel of the Healthy, punishing her lack of fitness. The full kit – highly coloured Lycra, trainers that looked like something astronauts might wear for space-walking – and a thin scarf around his face. Purist who didn't want to breathe in exhaust fumes unfiltered. He came to a sudden halt right in front of her, doing this little dance, hopping from side to side, not letting her past. A score of reactions collided in her head, jamming her into neutral. Fight versus flight, a sudden and shameful desire to cry, another, just as strong, to burst out laughing at the multi-coloured, scarfed, dancing man. The result was she just stood there, bewildered. The jogger raised his hand to her mouth level – a warning that she was not to make a noise.

"I'm sorry. I'm truly sorry. Please believe me."

Sorry for what? For what he was about to do? She felt a chill in her bowels. He didn't *look* dangerous. Thin, balding, poky eyes. But then the real crazies could be the most inoffensive-looking; dull, charming to their mammies and shop assistants.

"They came to my house. I've nothing to do with those murders." He was pleading, but there was an edge to his voice that quelled the urge in her to kick him between the legs and have done with it. Also, she recognised him. Trying to remember from where stopped her taking any action.

"Get out of my way." She was surprised at the authority in her own voice. It came from some general sense of outrage.

"They're determined to get me. Blame me."

"Who are?"

"I'm not going to let it happen."

Maddy took a step back, and he took one forward. Whyte. She didn't know why she made the connection, but it was Martin Whyte. All she'd ever seen of him was a single photograph. Did the idiot think a scarf up to his nose would really hide him? Or did he want her to recognise him?

"Tell them to search *them*!" Then he garbled something that she couldn't hear. He was looking from side to side, still jogging on the spot. Maddy's pulse was thumping in her ears. She thought he said something about an exhibition, and a stick. She must have heard wrong.

Then off he jogged as suddenly and as jerkily as he'd appeared. A nervous lope. She burned with shame to think that such a man had terrified her. She turned away and walked on, trying to piece together what he had said. Someone had searched him. The police, presumably. For what – did he say? Whatever, they didn't find it, because he didn't have it. Christ, he could have given her office a phone to tell her that. *They* had it. Jim and Elaine Docherty. Did he actually say that? Did he name them? She couldn't remember, but she was sure it was the Dochertys – his pals, his partners – he was fingering. Something about an exhibition. And a stick. Or slick? Or fake, maybe. God knows.

But why did he come to *her*? The Prosecution. Well, you don't go noising up police officers on their way home, dressed in Lycra and gesturing threateningly. Fine to do it to a woman lawyer. Maddy burned with shame. Should have kneed his groin and dragged him to the police station.

She quickened her pace turning into her own street. In a hurry not so much to phone the police, which she'd get

187

over with straight away, but to get hold of Dan or Izzie, even Manda. Hit the town, let the bright lights burn away the memory. But the evening's surprises weren't over yet. Sitting on her doorstep, eyes closed like a beggar woman dozing, was Belinda Laird. She came to the moment Maddy's heels came within earshot.

"Hi."

"Mrs. Laird?"

"Are you okay?

"I should be asking you that."

"You look a bit... I don't know. Pale. Bit out of it."

"I'm fine."

"What are you doing here?"

Belinda stood up calmly as if squatting on a near-stranger's doorstep at 10 PM was perfectly normal. Paul Pacchini's mother had the ability to create a little world around herself. A simple smock on, and a haversack at her feet, but she seemed comfortable. Settled. "I'm sorry. I can't go back to Dundee and just leave Paul here. You're going to need me for enquiries anyway, I assume."

"Yes, but not tonight."

"Course not. But I'm out of touch with Glasgow. Don't know where's good – and very cheap to stay. Thought you might know."

Maddy got her keys out automatically, but didn't move past Belinda. "How did you find my address?"

"Only one M. Shannon in the West End. You looked like a West End girl to me."

"This is highly irregular, Ms. Laird." Maddy put on her most professional voice, but she could hear the tremor in it herself. She should tell the woman to wait outside while she phoned Division A. Amy Dalgarno could send a car round, find a place for her.

"The police won't be very pleased with me," Belinda said, as if reading Maddy's thoughts. "They offered a car home, but I really can't leave Paul here, jut like that."

Maddy opened the door. Wanting to stay awhile in the city where your son lies dead was reasonable. The woman was New Age. Probably didn't believe in money. Certainly wouldn't have any. No harm in finding her a cheap hotel. And the company would be nice, for half an hour. Maybe take the edge off the need to drag Izzie or Dan out. "You'd better come in for a minute." She opened the door and let Belinda go in before her. "It's a rough old place out there. Never know what might happen."

Belinda laughed. "Glaswegians love that big bad fantasy."

Coulter pinned up on the board photographs of Paul the Kanes had given him. Next to images of his bloodied corpse it was hard to believe they were the same boy. Kelvingrove Paul looked like something out of Belsen. Thin, shaved, his body all angles and joints. Despite the clean tracksuit, he was still denuded somehow. Pennyvale Paul had thick black locks, velvety lips and warm cheeks. No snicks in his dark eyebrows, both arched as if listening to the surprising answer to a question.

He didn't look like an obvious companion for Sy. Sy hadn't been changed as dramatically as Paul by death. It was clearly the same boy with the unseen man that lay lifeless, just as skinny and just as anxious. Pacchini was dark-eyed and serious-looking. Too serious? A worried boy? Or just clever. One of those intelligences that real- ises early on there's not a heck of a lot to grin about. Why would such a boy – product of a hippy mother, and solid, loving foster parents – run to Glasgow, meet up with the likes of Sy Kennedy? Some connection with his father's druggie past? But why get himself shorn and snicked and trackie'd up, like a ned, a social inclusion case? What possessed him to get himself killed in a clump of rhododendrons?

"Welcome home boss." Coulter liked the way Amy called him Boss. She crammed a lot into that little word. It was pally – a joke really. But it still gave him his place. "This him?" She leaned in close to look at Paul. Coulter sensed that she was close to tears. It happens to them all – every now and reality breaks through the professionalism, the hardened experience. A simple photograph of a real boy. A sad looking boy. "It's as if he knew."

WPC Dalgarno looked at another photograph, of Paul flanked by Des and Veronica Kane. "Uncle Des and Aunt Veronica?"

"Nicky, he calls her."

"What d'you make of them?"

What did he make of them? He wasn't sure. "Solid. Stolid. Decent. Private. Not forthcoming."

"Deliberately so?"

"Maybe. Maybe they just don't trust civic authorities. Had Paul tutored at home."

Amy nodded. "Registered him with a recognised home schooling organisation." She'd been doing her homework. They'd also previously had him registered at a primary school – in Merston?"

"Yeah. They were there for a few months. Didn't say Paul attended school there."

"He didn't. The Home School network they were enrolled with back then registered its kids through local schools. They had him down as Paul Kane. They kick over their tracks do Des and Nicky, not think?"

He'd thought of nothing else in the drive up. The Kanes had shown him a piece of paper with Giorgio's and Belinda's signatures on it, granting them custody of the then eleven-year-old Paul, should anything happen to either of the natural parents. All done *en famille*. No lawyers. That kind of set-up made Coulter twitch.

Russell arrived, later than usual. He had a pair of shades in his hand, like an MI6 agent arriving at a safe haven. The effect was ruined by a wedge of hair sticking up at the back of his head. The rain had stopped, but it wasn't sunny outside. A night out with the lads? Hiding hungover eyes. Coulter came away from the Incident Board. "Morning, John. Any word about Lennon?"

"Zilch. Strange thing, though – when we searched his place, it didn't look like the flat of a man who'd packed for a trip. Carton of milk lying on the table, half-full. Bowl of cereal. Radio on. It's not as if Lennon was an untidy man. Flat's spick and span."

"*We* whisked him away, remember? You been to see Charlie Dempsey?"

"Swears he knows nothing. Lennon came past the Cottars Arms when he left us. Said nothing to Charlie about disappearing. Charlie's not the happiest of bunnies."

Coulter laughed. "God knows how much moolah for a fancy lawyer and the client disappears up a chimney? No wonder!"

DS Russell came up to see the new pictures on the board, but he made no comment. "So, what's your theory about Lennon doing a runner?" Coulter could see he was nervous that he'd backed the wrong horse, favouring Sign-Chronicity as the bad guys over the gardening IRA hit-man. Coulter rubbed his eyes.

"Sees his chance to disappear. Decides to take a long holiday. We've got customs everywhere notified?"

Russell nodded. "Goes off of his own accord?"

"Who's going to make Ian Lennon do anything he doesn't want to?"

Maddy, slumped at her desk, wondered if Izzie – landing gently in the office like a petal floating in on a summer breeze – assumed she'd been out on the razzle. That was her reputation, after all. Not sitting up till the wee small hours discussing the meaning of life with a faery woman from Dundee.

"Have you ever seen your own soul?" Maddy asked. Anyone else but Izzie would have baulked at the question at 8.20 in the morning. Maddy had at 2 AM with a bottle and a half inside her. "Actually no. Have you?"

"Belinda Laird has."

Paul Pacchini's mum had matched her glass for glass – with herb tea. About the only thing she'd had in her knap-sack. They'd never got round to finding that cheap B&B. "Sitting opposite me one day," Belinda had said. "Nothing especially auspicious about the time leading up to it. I was in a flat where I was staying. In Findhorn. I wasn't half-asleep, or praying or anything. Someone had just left the room, and a moment later, *she* appeared."

"Your soul."

Belinda had nodded. "Exactly like me – but perfected. You know? The nose a little thinner, my skin brighter, hair shinier..." She laughed: "Imagine yourself with all the bits you don't like straightened out, perked, touched up. It sounds vain, but it's not what I mean. But I looked beauti-ful. Or rather, the fleeting glimpse I got of my soul, my soul looked beautiful."

Belinda Laird wasn't Maddy's usual type – Izzie here would have been a more natural friend. But last night she'd enjoyed the woman's company. She wondered now, back to being Assistant Senior PF Shannon, who had needed whom most last night? Belinda had needed a place to stay for nothing. Maddy had needed a calming influence. She'd been hyped up for the last week. Louis leaving, Nonno dying, a case on the go. Being assailed in a dark street by a mad jogger. She'd hardly slept for days, had been talking twenty to the dozen, rushing around madly. She recognised the signs in herself – and Belinda was a good cure. Then again, she had forgotten to report Whyte to the police. And had allowed a next-of-kin and possible witness to stay in her house.

"Did she just tell you this out of nowhere?" asked Izzie. "After identifying her son? Well, people react in strange ways."

Maddy didn't volunteer the information that Belinda had

stayed over with her. Nor did she tell Izzie about Whyte. Why not? She wasn't sure herself. She needed time to sort these things out in her head. And anyway, there was work to be done. "If you see my soul out there anywhere," she smiled at Izzie, "tell it to come home."

Izzie went off to her desk. Maddy, running through her email messages, wondered if your soul's looks reflected, Dorian Gray-like, your inner self? Hers would be a terrifying mix. Chianti-guzzling, fat. Packy's eyes and Rosa's chin, the worst combinations. She phoned Sign-Chronicity. Elaine Docherty answered and Maddy explained her business. Elaine sighed on the other end of the line. "You'll want Jim to come into your office?"

"Actually, I'll be out and about later on today. If you want, I can pass by your office?"

"Sure."

There was one report on her desk about a wife-beating and murder. Three more concerning Petrus. One of the victims poisoned by Petrus's dumping had died the night before. She forwarded the messages to Manda to deal with for the time being. She phoned the hospital to see how Nonno was doing – no change. Stable, comfortable, but hadn't woken up yet. She began an email to Louis, then scrubbed it. He was right – what was the point of conducting a long-distance relationship with little hope of any further physical contact? Her phone rang. Janet Bateman from Lochgilvie House. Darren had taken a flakey this morning. Between shouting and swearing and lashing out at staff, he had yelled Maddy's name.

Rushing out the office, she saw Maxwell Binnie coming towards her. "Maddy – can I have a moment?"

"If you don't mind, not right now." And she slipped past him out through the open plan, faces staring at her. Not the best career move she'd ever made. As the door swung slowly closed on its heavy hinges, she saw Binnie's face, pissed off.

Since they'd brought Darren Mulholland to Lochgilvie he had suffered an occasional panic attack. As if, after years of being the responsible member of the family, all the tension and fear had come to the surface. Last night he'd had his worst attack yet. David Simons, a resident social worker, had tried to restrain him. Getting worried, he called the paramedic service. When they arrived, they gave the boy a tranquilliser. Now Darren lay in his bed, eyes open and mumbling answers to any question put to him.

"The medicine should have worn off now, Darren," Janet Bateman said softly to him. "Do you still feel drowsy?"

Bateman sat at the boy's side, gently holding on to his hand. Maddy stood behind her – her life seemed to be pinned out these days by comatose people. Nonno, at the end of a long life? Darren at the start of probably a rather short one. Heaven knows why he'd called out *her* name – she seemed to be the last person he wanted to talk to now.

"What made you so anxious yesterday, Darren? Can you tell me that?"

The boy didn't move his head, but squinted up at Bateman. Then he looked away again.

"Do *you* have any idea?" Maddy asked David Simons, standing at the back of the dorm. He shook his head. "He'd been out. He's hardly been going out at all, and whenever he has, I've accompanied him. Just to the garden, or a walk round the block. Yesterday he asked if he could get anything from the shops for us. We didn't really need anything, but I sent him for milk, thinking it'd do him good."

Maddy turned back to Darren. "Did you meet anyone when you were out, Darren?" He didn't answer, but the frown that had settled on his brow since his sister was murdered deepened for a moment. "Did you, Darren? Please tell us. It'll help. Who?"

He closed his eyes. Whatever had caused his panic attack, and the reason he had called out for Maddy – not for his mother, or anyone else from his life back home – had subsided now. The safety of silence, learned over a life of living with junkies, and the after-effects of the tranquilliser, meant that he now barely even glanced at the woman he had called for last night. Janet turned to Maddy: "We think he might have spoken to someone. He came running back here, and began shouting and screaming." She squeezed the boy's hand tighter. "You know you're safe here, Darren. You can tell me, or David, or this lady here, anything you want. Nothing bad will happen to you."

Maddy thought that we promise children all sorts of things we can't deliver.

Anne Kennedy looked at the photograph and shook her head. "I'd have remembered him. Good looking isn't he? I mean, *wasn't* he. Poor soul." She handed the snap back to Coulter, who gave it to Tony Kennedy. Tony hadn't been keen on meeting the police at his wife's flat. In fact, he hadn't been keen on meeting them at all. Busy day, he said. "No. Don't know him. Sorry. Listen, I've got to rush."

They had no reason to keep him back. Maybe he was dealing with his son's murder by working furiously. He gave the photo to Russell. The man couldn't wait to get out the house. "I'll see you, Annie, all right?" Then, to the police: "You's know where to find me."

"Tony," Anne said, holding him up at the door. "You're remembering the funeral tomorrow?"

"Course I'm remembering. Fuck's sake!"

Everybody had done their work on the three bodies in the morgue – the PF, the defence's pathologists. Belinda Laird had been given the all-clear this afternoon, too. Sy, Paul and Frances could all be buried immediately.

"Is it worth trying some of Sy's pals, Mrs Kennedy?" Coulter looked at the photo of Paul Pacchini.

"That boy's never hung around these parts."

Elaine Docherty looked nothing like the woman Maddy had imagined from the files and interviews she'd read, or the way Alan Coulter spoke about her. Far from being laid back and languorous, she was smartly dressed and busy at her computer. Maybe she's what they call a man's woman. Maddy had been accused of that herself. "How can I help you exactly, Miss...?" She nodded to a seat beside her workstation in the window bay.

"Shannon. All I really want to do is go briefly over what you've already told the police."

"I understood that a man has been apprehended for the murders."

"In compiling a case," Maddy matched Elaine's curt manner, "I need to talk to witnesses."

Elaine turned off her computer screen and swivelled her seat round to give Maddy her full attention. "It was my husband who discovered the bodies, Miss Shanon, not me."

"I was hoping he'd be here. You work together from home."

"We have a project on up at Maryhill – housing assoc-iation contract. I'm sorry, I should have told you on the phone Jim wouldn't be here."

"I'll contact him later. I take it Mr. Whyte is still away?"

"I told the police, he goes off like this. No reason why he shouldn't – as far as the business goes. Usually no longer than a week."

"He's still not contactable by mobile?"

"Martin *has* a mobile, but he seldom uses it."

"Is it always work, when he goes away? We all like a little space every now and then. The three of you have been under some pressure recently."

"Martin is very work-orientated."

Maddy smiled and looked around the room, half-office, half-home. "I've just been to Lochgilvie House. I really like what you've done up there."

Elaine wasn't going to be seduced by flattery. She smiled,

pulled out a flash drive in the computer and rearranged the papers on her desk. "I have no memory of Simon Kennedy. I try my best to be pleasant and open with clients in establishments like that. But not to the point of remembering their names. It's just unfortunate that, two years later, my husband happens to discover the body of one of them. Which he reported to the police immediately." She was still on the defensive – understandably, Maddy thought.

"Then there's the Prison Reform Committee'

"That was *ages* ago. God, if you quoted every client we've done a small job for you could connect us to half the city. We're good at networking. Is that a crime?"

Maddy smiled. "The police have to check every avenue."

"But they've got their man." Her voice was still even, playing with the USB she'd pulled out the computer.

"I'm trying to get everything I can to make sure we get a conviction."

"The papers say he's gone missing."

Maddy looked at the easel at the window behind Elaine, searching the room for something that might connect to the "exhibition" Whyte had mentioned. An artist's pad was open, with a drawing of a Utopian housing estate on it. All yellows and soft pinks, children playing in a well-equipped park, friendly neighbourhood shops, cafe with terrace seats. "Looks wonderful. Did you do that?"

"Jim."

"You must have a lot of paintings and drawings from over the years. Never thought of mounting an exhibition, the three of you?"

But there was no reaction – no pause, or frown. "We're not those kinds of artist, Miss Shannon."

Maddy decided she didn't have time for any more of this fencing. Ask the question you need the answer to and move on. "Mrs. Docherty. Martin Whyte came to see me the other day." Coulter would kill her. Nearly twenty-four hours since Whyte had accosted her and she still hadn't reported it. Now she was pre-empting police enquiries. Elaine's eyebrows arched. "At your office?"

"Nothing so banal. He stopped me. In the street. When he was out jogging. He said the police were looking in the wrong place. That they should look here."

"Here? He said that? They should look *here*?" Elaine looked out the window in disbelief. "Is this the usual way a prosecuting lawyer acts? Coming to a witness's house and accusing them?"

"What am I accusing you of, Mrs. Docherty? I'm trying to help you. Do you have any idea what Mr. Whyte might have meant?"

A stick – a memory stick! The flash drive Elaine had just let drop on her desk. Could that be what Whyte was talking about?

"Then why do I *feel* I'm being accused?" Elaine was flustered. "Perhaps I should call Jim."

"Why is Mr. Whyte keeping away from the police?"

"I should call a lawyer. A lawyer of my own."

The woman was right – Maddy had no business turning up here and having this conversation. Elaine made for the house phone on a table by the door. Maddy seized her moment and grabbed the USB. She clenched it in her palm. Raised her other hand in peace, and got up to go.

Elaine dangled the phone threateningly. "How do I go about making a complaint?"

Maddy stopped and turned at the door. "Open your mouth and shout, dear." She stepped out into the landing. "Something I found harder to do when your business partner covered my mouth on a dark street."

Belinda was in the house when she got back. It hadn't dawned on Maddy that the woman might still be here when she got home, after visiting Nonno in hospital. With everything that happened today she still hadn't told Coulter either about Belinda or Martin Whyte. She'd tried to. She'd phoned his number three or four times. It wasn't the kind of thing you left a message about, and she certainly wasn't going to talk to Detective Sergeant Russell first. Belinda called from the kitchen, "I've made some dinner for you."

Seriously unacceptable that Mrs. Laird was still in her house, yet Maddy's heart rose. How pleasant to open your door and hear a friendly voice. And smell proper food – she hadn't consumed anything more than office and hospital coffee and biscuits, a sly ciggie or two in doorways, and red wine in over two days. And with Belinda instead of Louis she didn't even have to worry about how she looked or what might happen at the end of the night.

"I'll find that hotel for you."

"Straight after dinner."

Which turned out to be semi-raw vegetables in couscous. "It always seems so ungrateful," Belinda said, watching her eat, "Nature bestows such riches on us and we boil them to death."

"You've made arrangements for Paul?" Maddy asked, hesitantly.

Belinda nodded. "Funeral's day after tomorrow."

How was the woman paying for it? Maybe she'd asked the Kanes to pay. Belinda cleared the table, like a housemaid. "I'll go straight back to Dundee, the minute it's over."

Maddy felt spent. The herb tea Belinda gave her was neither tasty nor invigorating. She eyed the bottle of wine by the fridge but didn't want to give the earth mother here the idea that she was an alky. She let Belinda wash the dishes and went into the living room and turned on the computer. She checked her emails. Nothing from Louis. She took Elaine Docherty's memory stick out of her bag and looked to see if there was a port for it anywhere on her computer. None that she could see. Her laptop was newer, so she hauled it out from its drawer and found a plug that looked right.

Outside the night grew around the trees. The breeze shuffling the leaves darkly. She got access to Elaine's memory without much bother. A list of recent projects. Maryhill Housing Association, a list of city-centre shops, several of which Maddy knew; West of Scotland Anti Drugs Forum, a few more charities. Nothing as far back as Lochgilvie House though, let alone the Women's Prison Committee. All the files – about thirty of them – had been created in the last six months.

Belinda brought her the herb tea she had left in the kitchen. "Maddy? I need someone to say a few words on Thursday. At the crematorium. *I'll* say something obviously. And I imagine Des will, but I wondered if you…"

"No. Belinda, sorry. Totally inappropriate for me to—"

"I wasn't going to ask you. I know that wouldn't be right. Des and Veronica have asked if you knew a priest here, or a minister or something." She smiled. "Personally I'd rather have a white witch, but I don't think that'd go down too well."

"I'll ask my mum to get Father Jamieson. He's young and he's hip. At least he reckons he is." She punched in the number. "I need to find out how my granddad's doing tonight anyway."

Nonna had told him to go wait by Carlo.

The two brothers had covered their walls with all the post-cards and telegrams that came from far away: Pinerolo, Grenoble, Lyons, Paris, Boulogne, London. Vittore went to sleep every night with pictures of snowy mountains and motor cars, ladies in hats, children playing on grey beaches, the Eiffel Tower, aeroplanes flying. They got mixed up in his dreams so that the ladies flew over cities hanging from the tops of mountains, multi-coloured dresses fluttering. He saw his mother clad in finery and his father climbing the girders on the *Tour d'Eiffel*. For the last year and a half all the pictures had been of *Inghilterra* and *Scozia*. Pictures that didn't reveal much: more mountains, cars, an old man leaning on a stick and dressed in a skirt.

Zia Francesca came over from Procchia every month or six weeks to help them word a short message in reply. Vittore's Nonno and Nonna could manage a pen well enough, the problem was wording the notes. They wanted to tell Ettore and Antonella that all was well, that there was no need to worry, but not so well as to make their journey worthless. They missed out many events and problems, seeing no use in upsetting them unnecessarily. Everyone lived for Mamma and Papà's letters – Nonna and Nonno, Vittore, but especially Carlo.

When Vittore was nearly eleven and proud of the inches he had grown, a postcard came from Marseille. Dad was coming home. He had walked through *Scozia* and *Inghilterra*, taken trains through *Francia* without telling them so that it would be a surprise when he got near to Elba. He was taking a boat that very morning and would be back to take his boys to their new land within the week.

Perhaps they should have got word to Ettore to let him know. To prepare him. But no one was sure how it should be done, or if it was a good idea or not. Most agreed that he would find out soon enough. And soon enough was too soon.

Carlo had battled against his sickness for nigh on three years. He nearly made it, too. He lived long enough to hear that his parents had arrived safely in the place that would be their new home. He told Vittore that night that it would never be his – that Vittore was to remain strong and eat well so that Mamma and Papà would at least have one son to help them in their new world. Before the next postcard arrived, Carlo had cried away his last day and was buried. No one had the heart or the words to tell Ettore and Antonella. Not even Zia Francesca.

Giovanni Chiesa had come rushing up from Portoferraio last night to say that Ettore had arrived there. He stayed the night because it was late and he wanted to freshen up in Giovanni's house to arrive smart, ready to see his big, grown boys.

"Go on, Vittore," Nonna said. "Go down and wait for your daddy with Carlo." Nonno had insisted that his brother was buried on Di Rio land. That he was still waiting for his *Mamma* and *Papà*; that he'd never given up hope.

Vittore went every day to the graveside to speak to his brother. He did so again now, telling him that *Papà* was on his way, he'd be here any minute to see his sons again. He saw Ettore in the distance, coming up over the brow of the hill. A little smaller than Vittore remembered. Not so tousled, better dressed. Carrying a neat leather case. He was walking fast and, although Vittore couldn't see his smile from so far away, he could sense it in the man's gait. His dad speeded up when he saw him. Then slowed down. Looked at his one boy, and stopped, saw the cross Vittore was standing beside. When he walked forward again, his step was slower, heavier, older.

Factories surround the city like decrepit sentries, spindly chimneys manufacturing the famous local greyness, sending a stream of murk over rooftops. Today's a drab, dry Thursday, specially blended for a funeral.

Maddy could see the cortège below her as she came off the motorway. Wee Frances Mulholland, unheeded in life, celebrated in death for all the wrong reasons. Priest up front leading the procession. Behind him, mother Jackie and brother Darren – but Darren's walking closer to Janet Bateman, as fat as he's skinny, his state-appointed custodian. His hair blonder than the ashen light, a blur around his head, like a halo. A shilpit wee man just behind Jackie who must be the boyfriend, or fixer, Ricky Graham – a dismal streak of bad luck to spill into anybody's life. Behind that sad little trinity, a procession of near on a hundred people. Maddy left the car outside the gate and cut across old graves on foot. She didn't want to get too close, too early. Merely a professional paying of respects.

Frances today; Sy Kennedy and Paul Pacchini, interred separately, tomorrow. What's the collective noun for funerals? An argosy of coffins, she'd heard that somewhere. A benevolence of mourners. They might not all be benevolent but there's certainly plenty of them today. Young deaths always bring out the congregations. Murdered youngsters, even more. Reporters and photographers. Police. Ghouls who can't resist the burial of a young girl on a dull morning. Coulter and Russell were arriving late, coming along from her right; they must have parked by another gate. Coulter nodded to her like she was a stranger. Russell managed an unaccustomed smile.

"These things always get me," Russell said. "I mean it's sad and everything, but—" Coulter and Maddy stared at him. "Oh come *on*. Kids like Sy Kennedy are the bane of everyone's life. Can't walk past a bunch of them in the street without getting dog's abuse. Let's not get over-romantic, eh?" He didn't wait for a response, but took a couple of righteous steps away from them. Coulter coughed. Finally managed to meet her eye. "Getting all the info through okay?"

"Yup. Your people are talking to my people. A well-oiled machine. Police and the Fiscal – Together We Are Strong."

He didn't laugh, and they both looked over towards the open grave. "I heard your grandfather wasn't well."

"Stroke. Still in some kind of a coma."

"How about Louis?"

"Don't go there." She'd meant it to sound jokey. It sounded grief-stricken. Alan frowned in empathy, but Maddy reckoned he'd be happy – married people always are when singles aren't having fun. He searched in a pocket and brought out an envelope and handed it to her. "Photos of Paul Pacchini. IT are having problems sending them to you. You can give one to Belinda."

His way of telling her he knew Pacchini's mother was staying with her. Maddy felt her irritation rise. "Look. I put her up for a night or two. So what? She's leaving tomorrow."

Coulter put his palm up in peace. "Tell her we have positive sightings of her son. In Drumchapel."

It was Monsignor Connolly doing the graveside prayers. He had his back to them, a black blur amongst the sorrowful, but Maddy recognised the pompous drone of his voice. The Church had sent in a big gun for the high-profile funeral. She could just hear him saying something about the jewel of youth. Darren was staring down into the gape of the grave like he wanted to jump in after his sister. Ricky Graham, the bidey-in, useless stepfather, was sucking on a fag, leaning against a tree. Jackie stared hollowly, the daughter she'd never managed to care for, gone… where?

"No news of Lennon?" Maddy didn't think she'd meant it to sound like an accusation, but Coulter squirmed. "Not yet. You seen the papers today?"

"No."

"Your man Casci's had another murder in New York."

They stayed for as long as was necessary, and left via Coulter's car to pick up his pile of newspapers, then walked ten minutes to a greasy spoon, Coulter quiet while she read. The Herald only had a one-para Reuters report:

> The body of a further victim in a series dubbed the Potter's Field Murders was discovered yesterday in a disused car park in the Bronx district. The as yet unidentified black teenager was found shot in the head, and subsequently beaten, in a similar fashion to the seven or more previous unsolved cases.

The *Times* had the same report. The *Scotsman* had nothing. Only the *Independent* had a proper quarter-page article on the subject. The young man was estimated to be around fifteen or sixteen. There was severe bruising to his upper body and face, and evidence of a knife attack – all thought to have been inflicted either after death or during the death throes. *Where* he was cut – whether around the mouth area, like Sy and Paul – none of the reports said. Nor did they mention Commander Louis Casci. Quotes were simply attributed to NYPD or a police source or spokesman. Nor did they connect the killings to the Glasgow murders. Maddy got out her phone and began to text.

"We've been trying to get him since last night," Alan said. "Either we just get lost in the system, or we get some underling saying he isn't authorised to connect us to Commander Casci."

"Maybe he isn't."

A middle-aged woman, too jolly for the occasion or the weather, took their order.

"We are, however, in constant touch," Coulter picked up again when the woman had gone, "with Customs and Immigration, both here and across the pond."

"You don't think Lennon did this, do you?"

"Funny it should happen just when we lost track of him."

"Hang on. You had him in custody last week. Are you saying he went home, poured himself a bowl of cornflakes and had a sudden impulse to kill a black boy in New York?"

"I'm saying…"

"He'd have to skip out the country – not an easy thing to do these days, even if you're not tanned enough to be from anywhere east of Dover, and especially not if you're Northern Irish with form. He then has to get himself to the Big Apple, find someone he wants to kill, and have it all done and dusted by… when?" She checked the paper, as Coulter waited patiently for the tirade to stop. "Two nights ago. All that in four days!"

"I've never said that Lennon is necessarily the killer of the American victims. I *am* saying that there's clearly a connection."

"He knows you think that. Maybe that's why he's done a runner."

"He's the key, Maddy. There's enough evidence to tie him to three murders here, *and* to link him to the Potter's Field killings."

"Evidence? You can't even *find* him! I'm sorry, Alan. Baskets and far too many eggs come to mind."

Coulter stared out the window, his jaw stiff, while the

waitress set out their coffees. "Don't you give *me* lectures," he said finally. "You've got a witness and a next-of-kin staying at your apartment. You might have blown the case before we even get it started!"

Maddy had no defence for that. Coulter knew it, and softened his tone. "If not Lennon, then who?"

"I don't know. But I was confronted in the street the other night by another suspect you've let slip."

It took him a second. "Whyte? When?"

"He seems to think we're looking in the wrong place, too."

"You didn't report this?"

"He didn't mention any names. But he was talking about Jim and Elaine Docherty."

"Jesus Christ, Maddy! What are you playing at ?"

Both their mobiles rang at the same time. They chose to take their calls; turned away from each other and whispered into their phones. Like strangers. Or worse, adversaries.

Heading back to work, she hurried across the top of Cadogan Street, at a speed-walk pace. A police car was parked near the Dochertys. Elaine must have realised by now what happened to her flash drive. If she doesn't complain to the police, then Whyte had been telling Maddy something genuinely important. If, on the other hand, she does report the theft to the police, then that was the end of Maddy's entire career. A billboard outside a newsagent's stated in tall bold letters: "'Brammer' Khan Accused of Theft." Bastards, Maddy thought. It had taken the press a little longer than she'd expected to discredit the Have-A-Go Hero. Give it a week, and they'd have something on Caprice. Then the birching and hanging mob will have the front pages safely to themselves again.

At the office she didn't stop for niceties with Manda. Neither Dan nor Izzie were at their desks. She closed the door firmly behind her and started dialling before she sat down, struggling to take off her jacket with the receiver at her ear.

"Commander Casci, please." It was half-past one here, half eight there. Louis should be in by now. The phone rang out for ages. She redialled, twice, tried to speak to someone else in Louis's team, got two different voice messages asking her to call back, was put on hold and made to listen to tinny muzak. She dialled another number, asked for Information, and finally managed to speak to a real human being. The woman was pleasant in a professionally over-patient way.

"I'm sorry, ma'm but there is no answer from that department."

"I don't think you understand. This is an official demand from the Scottish Courts…"

"I understand perfectly. I will forward your message to Commander Casci."

At least the woman seemed to know who Louis was. "I'm sure the Commander will contact you just as soon as he is able."

She sounded black. Maddy imagined her sitting in one of those dusty, old-fashioned offices, NY's morning light shining dustily in through slats in blinds.

"We've had reports of a murder related to an investigation here. Can you tell me if Commander Casci is assigned to that case?"

"I'm afraid I cannot divulge that information."

A conspiracy theorist would say the woman was stone-walling, but Maddy recognised institutional jargon for one department not having a clue what another was doing. She thanked the woman and hung up. She sent Louis an email: "You've disappeared into thin air, Commander."

Belinda wasn't at the flat when she got home at seven o'clock. Maddy sat down on the couch for a moment and promptly fell asleep. She'd been doing that all week. Not going to bed till late, sleeping restlessly and getting up early, rushing around all day, juggling the Kelvingrove and Bearsden cases with the rest of her work. Full of drive and purpose, she felt she'd never need to sleep again. But in the evenings, her energy suddenly failed her. She'd meant to pass by the hospital tonight, but couldn't face it. She'd taken a taxi home and within five minutes was dead to the world. Except the world crept into her dreams. Holes in the ground, overlooked by a gunman in a tree, shamans chanting… It was the chanting that woke her: they were intoning, call and response like it was a Gaelic psalm, "Torna a Sorrento" – one of Nonno's favourite songs. That was too weird.

Was Lennon the true culprit? Even if he wasn't, what business was that of hers? All she had to do was compile a case. But if the case was flawed, how could she do her job properly? Why did Whyte contact *her*, and had she understood him correctly? If Nonno dies, how would Mama cope? How would *she* cope? She heard something in the room and tugged her eyes open. Belinda was taking off her jacket.

"How did the arrangements go?"

"All set up," Belinda said, as if she had organised a birthday party, not the burial of her only child.

"You got a hold of Mike Jamieson?"

"Yup. He was very kind." Belinda went to the door, presumably to prepare another healthy vegetarian diner. "You should do some exercise in the evenings, Maddy. Jogging."

"Don't mention jogging."

"Go to the baths. Swim a few lengths. I've missed two visits this week and I can feel it already."

"I hate swimming pools. I get this feeling all the men are mentally dressing me."

Belinda laughed and went off to the kitchen. Maddy looked at the copse of trees outside her window. She wondered if they were the last of the original Caledonian forest, a scrap that had somehow escaped centuries of planners, builders, road-layers. An ancient ghost of woodland in the midst of the rational city. With a groan she hauled herself over to the computer, plugged in Elaine's memory stick.

If you were gong to hide a file you wouldn't put it in the obvious place. Maddy went back to the documents menu. Finance? She opened the folder. About twenty files with boring names like MH2exps. Belinda came back in as she opened file after file, closing them again when she saw a list of figures. They knew how to charge expenses, Sign-Chronicity.

"By the way," Maddy suddenly remembered, "Did Paul have any connections with Drumchapel?"

"I don't know. I don't know anything about his time here. Why he came to Glasgow, instead of to me." If she was hurt, she didn't show it. "Why?"

"Doesn't matter," Maddy said, opening a file labeled ScotEx6. Ex for exhibition? Probably more expenses. But computer gobbledygook came up on her screen. Must need a programme Maddy's laptop didn't have. All the rest of the files were Word or PDFs. This was the exception.

"Belinda," she called through to the kitchen, "couldn't put on some coffee, could you?"

"I'm making risotto."

"I'm not hungry yet. Coffee?"

Maddy could feel Belinda's disapproval wafting into the living room, but she interpreted her silence as capitulation. She switched on her desktop again and transferred the ScotEx6 file onto CD. Wonder of wonders – she was becoming a Master of Technology, it worked. The desktop had more programmes on it. She hadn't a clue what they did but hoped one of them could open the file. The screen told her she had a new email. Louis.

"Exuse dleay."

Casci was one of these emailers who thought spelling and grammar had no business in hyperspace.

"been busy. you there now? at your compter. Not got messnger have you?"

Messenger? Yes, there was an icon at the foot of her screen. Between the spelling and the jargon, it took some time for her to follow Louis's instructions, but eventually she got the thing working. Maddy had taught Louis predictive texting, and now he had taught her messaging. That must signify something. Belinda brought through the coffee while she tapped on the keyboard, then went back to her risotto-making.

<This is fantastic. Where are you? What're you doing? What time's it? 9.30M here.> She was surprised at the time. Must have slept longer than she'd realised.

<4 30. at home. Taking some time to myself.>

<Been trying to contact you for ages> While she waited for his response she flew into the kitchen, past Belinda, and grabbed the bottle of red opened from last night. This called for celebration – coffee *and* wine.

<Sorry again. Thighs got suddenly crazy.>

She assumed he meant "things". She was aware of being girlishly pleased at being back in contact with Louis, and thought she'd better sound grown-up and professional for a bit. <Yeah. Heard about your young man.>

< Victims name is Jordan Murdock.>

<You mean Murdoch?>

<No. Murdock. and not realy a potters field case at all.>

Between messages and alternate sips of wine and coffee she got the whole story – or the part of it he was willing to divulge. They had managed to identify the kid quickly, and locate his family, so Jordan Murdock evaded the indignity of the cemetery for unknown paupers and vagrants. And he wasn't Haitian-American. But he *was* black, and he had been summarily executed for apparently no reason. <Similar injuries to the face as in your cases. and hes only fifteen.>

<There a big team of you working on it?>

<strictly speaking, Im off it. Not fitting my criteria. they're keeping me informed, as they say. Its a straight

homicide case now.>

<So how come you're so busy?>

<Don't know about you, but when I get sidelned I work all the harder. sussing out a little theory al of my own. there are conexions with two previous victims>

<Which?>

< Jordan attended the same sports club as a nephew of Ti-Guy Plissard. One of the few places Derrick Braithewaite form Barbados was reprted to have been seen bfore being killed.>

She could imagine Louis going off doing his own thing. Staking out the sports club. Sitting in a car up a sidestreet with a partner and a coffee and a box of doughnuts. Or undercover, maybe, pretending to be the dad of an eager young baseball player. Maybe she'd been watching too many American cop shows.

<You take care.>

<gewt some sleep. keeping you up too late. same time tomorrow? maybe we coudl do it in vision.>

He signed off with a few X's. In vision? A camera thingy and a microphone had come with the computer when she'd bought it. She'd decluttered them last week. In a box in the hall cupboard. And tomorrow night Belinda would be safely back in Dundee. She went to look, found the webcam and a million wires and, in a box next to it, both bound for the Oxfam shop, there were a couple of old tops. A strapped black number she'd thought she'd have no occasion to use again. But maybe for her screen debut tomorrow night…? Make that Mistress of Technology.

Coulter took his frustration out on everyone around him. He yelled at Patterson Webb to get on the hunt for Martin Whyte. He didn't bother explaining why. He told himself, rampaging back and forth between his office and the incident room, bumping elbows with innocent passers-by and not apologising, that it was because he was too angry with

Maddy. But what was he really angry *about* – that she had been in trouble, in danger, attacked in the street, and she hadn't gone to him, or because she had vital information about a suspect, Whyte, and hadn't told him? He yelled out for Amy Dalgarno from behind his desk.

"Hotels. B&B's. If Whyte really is in town and not at home, he must be staying *somewhere*!"

"*All* the establishments in Glasgow? I'll start with city centre."

"No. West End."

"Why West End?"

"Just do it Amy!"

Amy went off obediently, but he caught the look in her eye. She'd bide her time, then give him hell.

"Find out if Whyte's got relatives." DS Russell was next in line for barked orders. "Friends. Clients. Anything. Anyone!"

"I thought you wanted us to concentrate on finding Lennon?" The DS had been waiting his chance. He was being proven right – Coulter had jumped too fast at the Lennon theory.

"Free up some people, and some time, John," Coulter softened his tone. "We have to find them both."

"Can I ask why – why your sudden renewed interest in Martin Whyte?"

Coulter would have to tell him. Soon. He rubbed his eyes and rolled his shoulders, trying to relax. Maddy had been accosted, and she hadn't reported it. She had a witness staying at her domicile. Russell could sink the two of them, Principal Depute PF Maddalena Shannon and Detective Inspector Alan Coulter. At the very least put the first hole in both their ships.

She'd eaten half a plateful of Belinda's risotto, trying to make distracted conversation in the kitchen, then ran out to her computer again on the trail of ExScot6, leaving the washing up to a woman who was burying a son tomorrow.

She got to a dialogue box that asked her which pro-gramme she wanted to open the mystery file with. About twelve possibilities. She was on her tenth, waiting for something called "Real Player" to kick in. Waiting, she looked out into the dark. The trees were scarier when you couldn't see them. The darkness pressed up against her window like a black curtain. She could hear Belinda go into the spare room. Did the horror of it all get to her in the night, when she was alone? What was she doing in there – praying, maybe. Or crying to herself, public defences down.

ScotEx6 still wouldn't open. She checked in "Properties". The file seemed to be a download... There was the name of a website. She Googled in ScotEx6. Scottish Philatelic association – Elaine and Jim stamp collectors? Nah. There was a Spanish ScotEx that sold toilet paper, and a site dedicated to a pet dog called Scotex, in Brazil of all places. Two pages down, she found Scottish Exhibitionists.

Unbelievable. Men and women parading naked or scant-ily clad on the net. Fifty-year-old housewives from Perth in Anne Summers leather and lace. Twenty-two-year-old students at Glasgow Caledonian letting it all hang out – or, worse, in Speedos. Couples in Angus doing things to each other. At Craigneuk, she burst out laughing – a burly hirsute middle-aged lorry driver pictured in his wife's tiny scanties. He looked ridiculous, but happy, harmless. They didn't seem to be out to meet each other, these people. The point of the site, as far as she could tell, was purely voyeuristic/exhibitionist.

Who was she to laugh – chubby thirties single who had just looked out a sexy top for a webcam adventure tomor-row with a near-stranger on another continent. That was different from posting dodgy photos of yourself on the World Wide Net, wasn't it?

They're doing no harm, these folk – so long as their

hobby doesn't fall into the hands of the young or the weak-stomached. Some folks like to show off their bums, and others, apparently, liked to look, regardless of the state or size of the bum or other body parts in question.

Surely this couldn't be what Whyte was referring to. If he – or Jim or Elaine or, heaven forbid, a mix of the three of them – was in here, it could take forever to find them. There were pages and pages of the stuff. On average, ten new contributions a day, from women photographed, they said, by their "hubbies", men by their wives, and couples, presumably with time-delay digicams. Each file was back catalogued for *years*. There must be *thousands* of pages.

She'd try a few, see what she came up with. A fairly pre-sentable couple from Edinburgh liked to snap each other showing their pants in public places. Lay-bys, parks, the beach at Dunbar, presumably early in the morning, public flashers – the cereal row in Sainsbury's would never look the same to Maddy again. A youngish man – thirties – from Aberdeen was actually rather presentable. She ling-ered on him for a moment. Quite a lot of him to linger *on*. No wonder he likes getting his photie taken. She went back to the main menu. What was she supposed to be looking for? An association with Whyte or the Docherties. She scrolled down the file-names hoping something would catch her eye. Bert and Sal from Berwick. Ginny in Adrossan. "Strongdong" Broughty Ferry. "Silky Mum" and Rod 'n' Rita from Perthshire. Scotland was a small country and there were hundreds of these people – sooner or later she'd come across someone she knew. Good grief. Who? Manda? Uncle Gerry? Maxwell Binnie?! They were taking quite a risk, these jolly virtual swingers. Alan and Martha Coulter? Maybe they were having a better time of it than she imagined. And sharing the joy. Serene Izzie? Dan McKillop? Who knows what happens when the bedroom door's closed. Well we all do now, on ScotEx.

There's nothing like a triple tragedy for the politicos and flesh-pressers and grandstanders to get their public rocks off. Even the likes of Binnie and quango convener John MacDougall were nudged aside by bigger and slicker egos and operators. The First Minister himself, half the Scottish Executive in his trail, a smattering of celebrities – one-time footballers and half-baked pop stars. Moderators and bishops and judges and army chaps with medals. Monsignor Connolly in his black-and-magenta; Chief Constable Robertson in his navy blue-and-silver. Lined up in Glasgow City Chambers. The Scottish Establishment on parade in all its matt-finish radiance. And in the Cathedral itself. Maddy worked her way over to a side aisle.

One by one the great and the good told us sombrely about children. The wonder and beauty of them – and the terrible problem of them. It must have been the most excruciating ordeal for the families. The Mullhollands had buried little Frances yesterday. Anne Kennedy had had the longest to get used to the horror, the only one to weep openly. Bird-like Tony looked like he'd been chased by a cat – a fresh cut under his left eye and a bruise on the other cheek didn't help matters. Maddy saw Coulter and Russell clock it and whisper. Darren Mulholland, as if he hadn't had enough of funerals, was there, at the back, half out the door. He glanced surreptitiously at Maddy. Perhaps seeing other young people's graves made his sister's feel less lonely.

It was the first time Maddy had seen Des and Veronica Kane. She'd interview them while they were up here. They glared at everyone around them, probably wondering how in heaven's name the boy they'd cultivated so carefully ended up dead amongst *this* crowd. The natural mum, Belinda, sat straight and tall, as serene and dignified as ever.

After an hour of torture, the congregation filed out, each to their own family funeral, office, or television interview. Maddy nodded to Belinda, letting her know she'd attend Paul's burial too. Binnie made sure he passed coincidentally by. "My office. Minute you get in."

Tony, following his ex-wife out, was stopped by DS Russell. "Cut yourself shaving your eyebrows, Tone?" Bit much, Maddy thought, noising a man up on the day of his murdered son's funeral. He's a plastic bag caught on a tree, at the mercy of the four winds, blown around by any will stronger than his own.

She watched Belinda Laird and Father Mike shake hands. He cocked his head, listening with false intensity, nodding sympathetically. Maddy smiled – the trendy priest had finally met someone who was even surer of everything and smugger than himself. Belinda introduced him to Dés and Veronica who, from this distance, seemed less enamoured by him.

Coulter and Russell loomed up on her like muggers. "Maddy. There's someone here I'd like you to meet." Standing behind them was a short, red-haired woman with big glasses. Maddy couldn't even figure out where they'd produced her from – there had been no woman with them a moment ago. Coulter nodded to the door, and the four of them trooped back inside the grand, emptied cathedral.

Maddy's thoughts weren't on the mysterious redhead however as she followed them into a disappointingly plain room after the drama of paint and plaster and pillars of the nave and altar and reredos, but that Elaine Docherty still hadn't denounced her to the police. They would have talked to her about Whyte, and she hadn't mentioned Maddy's visit and the disappearance of her memory gadget. Maddy was onto something. If she had any sense, though, she'd hand the purloined device over to Coulter. First chance she got. Definitely.

"Miss Shannon. Aine Corrigan," Coulter was at his most formal.

Now that they had sat down around a small table, Maddy saw that there was a force about this woman.

The ordinariness she had had outside she seemed to be able to take off like a coat. She had a subtly attractive face. At first glance unremarkable, but look closer and the jaw was delicately chiselled, cheekbones high under delicately fair skin. The light amber of her eyes was made all the brighter by her small glasses; her pupils were dilated, taking everything in.

"Mrs. Corrigan has been working with the police in Dublin for some time." Coulter tilted his head in a way that told Maddy that that's all she'd ever find out about Aine Corrigan. "She has had dealings with the accused. As you are precognosing the case against Mr. Lennon, it's proper that you hear what Mrs Corrigan has to say." Coulter sat back and deferrred humbly to the red-haired woman, who turned her amber eyes on Maddy. "Ian Lennon was our finest ever sniper." Maddy was used to talk of snipers in raucous Belfast accents; it sounded strange in Corrigan's soft Dublin. The Dublin nuns at Maddy's convent school were gentle angels.

"You wouldn't think that such a big and... *individual* looking man could slip under the noses of targets and informers and police. But he did. Regularly. He would come in – from Scotland – do his homework, his preparation, set up, wait his moment, complete the task and strike camp without anyone noticing a thing. He'd walk through the ensuing hullabaloo and no one gave him a second look."

"Did he do work for the IRA in America?" Coulter was giving her rehearsed questions – the whole thing set up for Maddy's benefit. Aine was more than a police patsy, however. She didn't take her eye off Maddy. "A key operator. He kept in touch with fundraisers and money launderers."

"Was he ever employed as a hit man for you there?"

"Please don't use 'you'," she corrected Coulter abruptly. "My position within the rebel movement was rather more complex than that." In what way? Maddy wondered. Was she a spy, an accidental paramilitary?

217

"No formation of the Republican movement organised assassinations in America."

"How easily can Lennon evade detection getting in and out the country?" Coulter continued, chastened.

"It's been harder for everyone since 9/11. But Lennon is a favourite son of the IRA and will have more papers, the best forgeries, than any other operator. He'll have contacts with boats moored at advantageous spots. He'll know about changing ship mid-crossing... There was an old escape route. Boat from the Clyde coast, hopping into another bound for Wales. Taken by personal plane to the Channel Islands, and from there, private boat to the Basque Country. The whole trip, organised properly, could be done in a day and a half."

Maddy spoke for the first time: "Anything like that rumoured over the last few weeks?"

"I'm not in a position to know." There was still a note of regret. When a passionate foot soldier turns informer something, it seems, is lost.

"Tell Ms Shannon how Lennon works."

Corrigan nodded. "Two shopping bags." She paused for a moment, leaving Maddy wondering where that sentence could possibly lead. "He arrives at his location with the ordinance requisite for the particular mission, and two bags. He spends months working out in advance the equipment that will be most effective. One bag is wide, made of cloth. The other thinner, longer. Thick plastic, like you might get a new jacket in from a fancy shop." Corrigan eyed Maddy closely, milking the drama. "The first bag is full of foodstuffs. Lennon is good because he's patient. He can stake a target out for days, even weeks. He chooses his position, his stand, very carefully. A rooftop, a neighbouring window, in an abandoned-looking car, or amongst trees. Once he's collocated, he doesn't budge. He'll be perfectly hidden and he has a stillness you wouldn't believe. He can eat and drink and move his muscles minimally so that he never seizes up, or gets weak. He can do without sleep until the job is done."

"Surely a haversack would be more efficient than plastic shopping bags?" Maddy was irked by Aine Corrigan's hero-worship.

"He's developed his sytem perfectly," Corrigan dismissed Maddy's comment with a note of irritation. "He sets his sights. Readies his weapon. And waits. Waits until the moment is perfect. Until the stranger is in the *exact* spot he wants him. Until he's certain of no possible intruder or witness. When the light is just right, and escape conditions perfect... then he shoots. If it takes weeks for that moment to arrive, so be it. He never gets flustered and he never loses hope. That's why he's the best marksman in the business. The work he does for small-time gangsters here is nothing. A cover. They only ask Ian Lennon to do the top jobs. About once every five years."

"What's the other bag for?" Maddy wanted to put an end to this adulation.

"One bag for food. What goes in must come out. It has to have a tie on it, so he can seal and re-seal it. That's dedication."

Back out in the street, shoppers and pigeons had taken the places of the mourners and dignitaries. Russell rushed Corrigan off to a waiting unmarked car. Coulter made no mention of what she had said. They talked about Whyte instead.

"We're keeping an eye open but, to be honest, apart from your strange little meeting with him, he's not top of our priority list."

So Maddy has "strange little meetings" when she's attacked by a witness who is hiding out. While an ex-terrorist from abroad has them hanging on her every word.

"We went back to the Docherties. They think Whyte's just of a nervous disposition. Bit paranoid. Thinks everyone's blaming him for everything."

"There was a time when you thought he might be the killer, Coulter."

"And I'm still not striking him off. We've got men out there trying to find him. He's no Ian Lennon. He can't have got far. My bet is he's in a hotel not far from town. He'll have to use his credit card sometime. Then we'll get him."

Maddy took her leave without saying anything about Elaine Docherty's computer files. The way back to an open, honest, level keel seemed too complicated now.

Binnie had probably relished the idea for years. Yet when the moment came, to give him his due, he seemed to find it difficult. "Maddy, you work hard and play hard, I've always admired that in you—"

Liar. He thought she was pushy and reckless.

"Always been envious of it, truth to tell."

That was nearer the mark.

"I've said before that you should take the holidays owed you, that there's no need to stay in late every night. There was bound to come a burnout point."

Maddy decided not to say much until she knew the extent of the damage. Was she being reprimanded? Taken off the Kelvingrove and Bearsden cases? Sacked?

"You've been far too good a lawyer for us to lose you now. Your judgement's been a bit impaired recently, let's leave it at that."

"Sorry, sir. Judgement?"

"Quite apart from stating openly to the police that you do not believe their case – there are *procedures* for such circumstances! – a witness has been living with you and—"

"Hardly *living*! Nor strictly speaking a witness—"

"And that another *witness*, being searched for by the police, made contact with you and you failed to report it."

"There was a perfectly good—"

"Ms Shannon! Please don't make matters worse. Take till the end of this week reorienting yourself with the Petrus case. You can take some holidays due to you. Kindly brief Mr. McKillop on the murders before the end of the week." *Now* the old bastard was enjoying himself. "*Including* any information you may be in possession of but have failed to report to the police."

Sorry. Things got out of hand this end. Hope you can sort everything at yours. I'll help in any way I can. Alan.

She turned off her email. He had dobbed her in. End of.

Dan sat outside typing solemnly. Izzie and Manda found reasons to come in to her office – tea, some little piece of information on a variety of pending cases, diary dates. The rumour mill had turned smoothly. She wasn't quite sure *what* they knew, but they knew she was in deep shit. Dan, presumably, had been informed of his new caseload. Dan was a loyal friend, but he was also a diligent and ambitious lawyer.

She had promised Belinda she would attend Paul's funeral. She'd have to go now as a friend, not an avenging angel of the law. She came out of her glass cubicle. "Think I might need a drink after the crematorium. Could bring you up to speed then, Dan. Vicky Bar at five anyone?"

No takers. Dan had a meeting. Didn't quite say who with – Binnie, or Coulter, or Deena Gajendra. Or the lawyer assigned to the case, Mark Alexander. She couldn't see the two of *them* getting on like a house on fire. Whatever, Dan was hitting the ground running. Izzie was meeting her mother. Manda didn't seem to have a reason.

"Tomorrow, Maddy, eh?" she said, and Dan and Izzie concurred enthusiastically. Maybe they had her welfare in mind. On black days like these she'd been known to drink too much, say too much, make matters worse. Better all round if she had an early night. Scream at the world in the privacy of your own home. Before leaving she checked her emails again. Couple more from Alan. She didn't open them. Two new ones concerning Petrus. She forwarded them to her home computer. A press release from the Police Department concerning the child murders. She opened that.

After today's ecumencial service for the repose of the souls of the poor victims, the Churches had agreed to become more proactive in the moral lives of the young. The Moderator of the Church of Scotland and a leading Islamic leader had agreed to join the Parliamentary Steering Group on Youth and Delinquency, as had a senior representative of the Roman Catholic church, Monsignor Patrick Connolly.

She was open to every passing emotion. Sorrow, pity, guilt, as Paul's coffin slipped into the hidden fire. Affection, compassion, even sisterhood, for Belinda, as she addressed the mourners.

The woman spoke of her son like he was a saint, a youthful sage, a spirit so bright and hopeful that the dark world just had to put it out. As if his death was proof of his extraordinariness – if he had lived, he'd have dwindled into ordinariness.

"The Aborigines' land," Belinda said, "is marked out by sacred places. People learn of them in songs, and can travel the world, following their songlines. Paolo's life is a note in a songline. He died in a garden and, no matter how dark and brutal his death might have been, I cannot believe that that was mere chance. My son lived to die among flowers."

The young priest did a better job than the mother, Maddy thought vaguely, as she zoned in and out of his sermon, too. "Humanists believe that, at death, we fade and vanish like dry leaves. What a terrible idea. Paul Pacchini is not some piece of biodegradable waste. He is, like the rest of us, soul as well as body. We believe he is in heaven, and that all the youthfulness and energy and potential denied him on this earth will be fulfilled in the next. An innocent will be dearly cherished on high."

They caught up with Tony Kennedy on Dumbarton Road.

The lock-up where he kept his van was down off a side street.

"You left the wake early, Tony."

"What's the point? Can't bring Sy back, can I?"

"Maybe the missus could have done with your support."

"Don't think so."

"Straight back to work. The day they bury your son."

"Where'd you get the cuts and bruises, Tony?"

"Fight. In the pub the other night."

"About what?"

"Who knows. Some shite. Hayburn Vaults. Go and ask."

Alan Coulter got in between Russell and Kennedy. "You been paid a visit by anyone recently, Tony? An unwelcome face from the past?"

"Nuh. How?"

"Did Ian Lennon come looking for you?"

"No."

"What for?"

"I said – he didn't come."

"Before – when you took a message for him. It wasn't just about gardening, was it? Who else did you go and see?"

"Nobody. Leave me alone."

"We can protect you from him."

Tony slinked between the two of them, and headed off down the street.

Coulter and Russell went back to their car. A fortnight ago, they thought they had more or less wound this case up. Their boss still thinks they have. Robertson seems quite happy about the whole affair, convinced Lennon will be pulled from under his slimy rock sooner or later. The public think the same. As does every editor, politician and TV pundit. The brute is guilty ten times over and his vanishing proves it. If he hasn't topped himself, he'll be killed in a shoot-out with armed police when they finally discover his hide-out.

Loyalists in Northern Ireland are using him for political

leverage; victims of IRA violence flag him up as an example of brutal criminal oppression. Moral panickers point to him as the demonic stealer of childhood and innocence… Everyone has a stake in seeing a bloody end to Mr. Lennon.

But Coulter had begun to worry. He emailed Maddy to tell her that he tried all he could to protect her. It was Russell who shopped her. Coulter pleaded her case with the Chief Constable, Robertson. She never got back to him. Probably never even read his notes.

If only they could pick up his trail. Find a connection between Lennon and Paul Pacchini – complete the picture that connected the accused to all the victims. How had these kids got in his way?

Russell had no doubts at all. Lennon had been his man from Day One. Had Coulter been blinded by the absolute belief of everyone around him? His own desire to have the case solved, so he could go back to the wife and kids, sort out life at home?

It was as if the pores of her mind were wide open; her emotional immune system stalled. Her mother's dread infected her the minute she walked into the ward. She felt the boredom and false empathy of a blank-faced burly nurse who'd spent too many years among the dying and the grieving.

"The doctor says they don't understand his condition perfectly," Rosa told her. "It's possible his body and his mind are just healing themselves. That he'll return to us fine."

Maddy squeezed her mother's hand and the two of them sat in silence for half an hour together. The feeling she should have had in church came to her now, a grace, connectedness, sitting there, hands folded and head bent before her grandfather fighting serenely for his life. She fell into a meditative state. The boys in the park, reaching out for one another, Frances in her deathbed of flowers, Belinda astral-planing over the brute realities of her own life, Jackie and Anne two Maters Dolorosas. She wasn't trying to make sense of it all. Not going round in circles, thinking of all the clues and suspects and circumstances. Just letting the thoughts come to her, as she looked at Nonno's calm, composed face. Until she heard herself say, "No one's ever mentioned that."

"What, dear?"

"Nothing. Sorry. Thinking out loud."

She had to listen in to her own head to find out herself what it was no one had ever mentioned.

"They're all religious."

"Who are?" Rosa was getting irked.

Sy and Paul and Frances, Catholic, to varying degrees. Frances and Sy by schooling, if nothing else. Paul through his stepmother. And, through his natural mother, spiritual; unorthodox, but still religious.

Nonno lay with his eyes shut, but his face looking up to heaven, head tilted back. Rosa stared at her daughter but, getting no response, turned back to gaze out at the Necropolis beyond.

V

Drums keep pounding a rhythm to the brain

Half-past six and Maddy has a glass of wine in her hand and a ciggie burning in the ashtray, CD turned up full pelt. She's been knocking on Louis Casci's chat-room door for an hour. Nobody home. Buddy Rich's twelve-year-old daughter singing like a woman who's seen all the hell and all the indulgence the world can offer. *Little girls still break their hearts, a-ha*

The bottle of Navarra tempranillo is half finished already. She flicks from Horseboy Paisley to Lovin' Couple Glasgow. Patti from Kilmarnock likes to do a slow strip in her bedroom, in a series of photos, from a top layer of cardigan and slippers down to Littlewoods tights and six-in-a-pack size 38 knickers. Maddy couldn't believe the woman's choice of curtains – totally clashed with the wallpaper. Muscleman from Musselburgh only had one muscle of any note, but his wife was a better mixer of fabrics than Patti. *And the beat goes on*

Perhaps Maddy shouldn't be looking for Elaine or her husband or Whyte at all. There was somebody else in amongst all these files. Maybe that was what Whyte was scared of.

Then *who?* She took another gulp of wine. Lennon? Christ, she couldn't see him in here. *Think*, Maddy. What about her religious theory? Was Monsignor Connolly in here?! God, wouldn't *that* be something? She felt queasy. She hadn't had anything to eat. Should do something about that. She heaved herself up and went to the kitchen, singing at the top of her voice to compete with Kathy Rich.

Men still keep marching off to war

She returned with tortilla chips and cheese and chutney,

home-made by her mother, a spoon, and another bottle of wine. A Petrus print-out was lying on the tray. Statistics proving that cancer rates both amongst Petrus workers deployed on or near the landfill, *and* in neighbouring housing estates, had gone sky-high since the dump. Skin disorders, too – eczemas, melanomas, you name it. Lawyers on stellar salaries are happily protecting the bastards who caused all this. Using the same Law Maddy applies, studies, works with. *And the beat goes on*

Then, it was there.

She'd been clicking her mouse, going through the ScotEx site almost unconsciously. She looked up and there was Elaine. Lying across a bed, not quite naked, breasts exposed, looking at a man in front of her. Her face had been digitally smudged, but you could still see it was her. In one in particular, definitely Elaine Docherty: heavy-lidded, full-lipped. Of the man she was looking at, only his bare back and backside was visible to the camera. A young man. Well, a slim and fit one anyway.

Sy?

There were about ten photographs in this session – and a couple of previous sessions on separate files. The earlier ones didn't seem to feature the young man. At the centre of each image was Elaine. Only her body was shown in full. But she was always with at least one other man. Hands came at her from every side.

In a few images, the back of one of the men's head was seen. Undoubtedly, her husband. Long thin arms, the elegant artist's fingers. The legs of his specs over his ears. The other set of hands belonged to the photographer, extending out from behind into frame. Darker skinned, hairier. From a ring on his finger and his watch it would be easy to prove if it was indeed Martin Whyte.

But was the young man Sy? He *could* be the same age. He was the centre of attention, especially Elaine's, who stared and smiled and pouted at him. His frame was that of a very young man, possibly a boy. The odd glimpse of his head showed he was closely cropped, but the hair colour was hard to discern. Maddy would have searched harder, but staring at those images made her deeply uneasy. There was something attractive in them – the stranger's skin, the way Elaine's nakedness reclined, abandoned, across the bed, her expensive lingerie, the hands coming at her from all sides…

Then Maddy recognised the room. About the only hotel she'd stayed in in Glasgow in her life. The place she'd spent her last night with Louis. Behind the Botanics.

She tried to get hold of Coulter. Must be between office and home; somewhere his mobile doesn't work. She left messages for him to phone back.

Belinda arrived back to collect her things. She had made some vague mention of a lift up to Dundee but had settled down, squatting on the floor beside Maddy. "You okay?"

Maddy'd drunk too much, eaten too little, was dishevelled, her makeup smeared and eyes red from weeping. Belinda hardly needed to ask. "Kids who end up dead or have to pimp for their mothers and old people dying and jobs and arsehole bosses and me screwing everything up and the world being totally fucked up–'" She drew breath and they both laughed. Sort of.

"Christ – how can you people become *parents*? I'd just sit in a corner terrified."

"I'm not really one to take credit for much parenting," Belinda replied.

For the first time, Maddy saw a softness in her, a failure of that sublime earth-given confidence. Maddy would have liked to confide in her about Elaine and the boy who might be Sy. But she couldn't do that – Belinda's own son was killed with Sy. Were the Dochertys and Whyte much greater monsters than those photos suggested? Did they kill the boys after they had ensnared them in hotel rooms? There was no sign of anything S&M or violent about

228

the images.... Was it just *this* photo shoot that had gone wrong? Or were Elaine and Jim and Martin mixed up in a much bigger story altogether?

Belinda poured them both another generous glass of wine.

"You and Father Mike got on well," Maddy said.

"He's okay. Typical orthodox type – can't think for himself. It's all learned in books."

"I suppose it depends on the books you learn from."

"The moment anything's written down, it loses its energy, its truth."

"What – you never *read* anything?"

"Only if I have to. I believe in human communication. What we're doing now."

Maddy had much less faith in the ability of talking to communicate *anything* – especially after nearly two bottles of wine.

"How Catholic was Paul?"

"Not at all when he was with us. Veronica, though, is old school. Giorgio's parents were too. I was raised an athiest myself. I'd rather my child be brought up in *any* religion than the emptiness of that. Imagine – no possibility, no *dream* even, of transcendence. My parents weren't even political. They just lived. Existed."

Every now and then, Maddy noticed Belinda glancing at the trees outside the window. And the woman didn't even know about Ian Lennon and his two plastic bags hiding, waiting, camouflaged high in the leaves. Their glasses empty, Maddy went to get another bottle from her hoard of supermarket bargains.

Coulter and Russell were interviewing Des and Veronica Kane one last time before they headed back to Pennyvale.

"Paul had trouble settling down. After the chaotic life with his parents in Glasgow, the split, his dad's move to Manchester... Giorgio let him bunk off whenever he wanted." Des shook his head sadly – the cruel irony of a man like Giorgio Pacchini having a son, while he and Nicky had tried for so many years. "We decided – with Paul's agreement – that he couldn't cope with school straight away. We moved out to the country. A smaller, safer community. A friend of Nicky's it was who suggested home schooling. We found out about it – and, between the three of us, decided to go ahead. For a year or two at first. Until the boy had settled down. We'd thought that maybe next year…"

The home schooling organisation they worked with turned out to have a base in Edinburgh. Coulter was just about to find out more, when the call from the hospital came in. He asked the Kanes to leave contact details for themselves and the educational organisation with the desk sergeant. He'd try to see them again tomorrow.

Tony Kennedy had been found by passers-by in a lane near his lock-up. Severely battered. No one had seen what had happened or who had done it. There were reports of shouts and footsteps running along the lane, then of screams and thumps. Coulter ordered a fingertip search of the lane. There was no point in going to the hospital: Kennedy had been given heavy-duty painkillers on arrival, and then a pre-med. They were taking him into surgery to fix some broken facial bones and stem internal bleeding.

Coulter's mobile went while they were trying to get more info from the medical staff. Maddy. He put it back in his pocket. He wanted a bit more space and time for *that* call.

There was only one good witness to the attack on Tony willing to talk. Guy relieving himself round the back of a Dumbarton Road pub. For once officers of the law were delighted that a punter had a pish up a lane. Malcolm Turner was brought in immediately to describe what he had seen.

"It was the guy in the papers, I'm telling you."

"The man who attacked Tony Kennedy? Did he have a Northern Irish accent?"

"I didn't have to hear him. It was Lennon. I've seen his picture in the papers. Killed those youngsters."

Turner had heard one set of footsteps, running, followed by shouting and threats. Then a second lot of footsteps, giving chase. He identified from photographs Tony Kennedy as the man being chased. Turner had slid further back into the doorway he'd been relieving himself in. It didn't take long for the bigger man – Lennon, he was certain – to catch up with Kennedy.

"When he did, he stopped him. Spat in his face. Said something—"

"What?"

"Didn't catch it. Nothing Shakespearean I wouldn't have thought. General insults and expletives. The other chap was shouting for help all the time – screaming, really. But your murderer swung just one massive punch, and the little guy fell, still shouting. Lennon runs off, up the lane, past me, towards the backs of the shops."

Where the hell had Lennon come from? Why did he make a beeline for Kennedy? Coulter was relieved that they had at least located the Irishman. But where was he now, and what had been going on between him and the father of one of his victims? It would be hours – maybe even days – before Kennedy was going to be able to answer any of these questions.

"He was in a hell of a state, the fellow."

"Mr. Kennedy is being well looked after in the Western Infirmary, Mr Turner."

"Not him. Lennon. He'd been in the wars. All bloody and messed up. Went limping off down that lane like Mary Shelley's Creature."

Three Uniforms were sent to search Tony Kennedy's lock-up and the lane round about it for the third time that night. Glasgow's police were like a man looking manically for his car keys, going over the same places time and again. This time, one of the officers *did* see something new. Right along at the end of the lane, several lock-ups along from Tony's and on the other side, one of the roll-down doors was open at the bottom.

"Not open enough for two men to coming belting out of."

"And neither one was likely to take the time to turn and even half-close it."

"Maybe you could roll out through that gap, though."

That must have been what happened. Somebody managed to get the door open, or forced the other to open it for him. Either Kennedy or Lennon rolled under, and the other did the same, giving chase.

Did Kennedy have *two* lock-ups? When the officers opened the door wide, they knew for certain that something unpleasant had been happening in there.

"When did you find *this* out? *How* did you find out?" Coulter had hoped that this would be a make-up call. It was proving quite the opposite.

"Alan – I've been trying to get you all night!" Maddy could hear the defensiveness in her own voice.

Coulter was agitated enough. A witness still in the interview room with Russell saying that *both* Kennedy and Lennon were bloodied in whatever had gone down between them. And officers phoning the station every few minutes from the lock-ups with new information. Now there was *this* to deal with… "There are pictures to prove it? Definitely Elaine Docherty and Sy Kennedy?"

"You can't see Sy's face. But it's him. In one photograph you can make out Jim Docherty."

"And Whyte?"

"I think he's the one taking the pictures. Check his ring finger. Some kind of gold band on his right hand index… You haven't caught up with him yet, have you?"

"We're checking hotels and B&B's in the Merchant City. There've been a couple of possible sightings." Too much was happening at once – Whyte still missing, Lennon apparently reappearing in a bust-up with one of the victim's fathers. "Shit, Maddy. This changes everything. I'll get WPC Dalgarno to ring you. Get details of the site. *Don't* – please, Maddy – busy up your line. She'll call any minute."

"Alan. If it is Paul Pacchini in these pictures then it's appalling what they're doing – criminal. He's underage apart from anything else. He's only a boy. But... there's nothing *violent* in the images. If anything, they're a bit dull and unimaginative."

"What do you want, Maddy? Chains and knives and blood?" He took a breath. "Maybe they're old pictures. Things got worse as they went along."

"They were posted about four months ago."

"Maybe Sy's death's not related directly to the pictures. But, it seems like Whyte and the Docherties mixed him up in something illegal."

"And knew him – intimately. Where does that leave your Lennon theory?" She tried to keep her tone neutral.

"God knows. But on that – stuff happening there too. I'll fill you in later. Got to go. Shit."

The living-room door was knocked dead on cue, just as Maddy put the phone down. She had kept her voice low and the door closed. "Come on in."

Belinda had a glass in one hand, a plate with food and a plastic box in the other. "Cheese, celery, apple, oatcakes. Celery is a natural calmative." She opened the little plastic box. "Ashwagandha. An Indian herb. Don't look at me like that. It does the trick, believe me. Two of these. A snack and a long drink of water and you won't believe the difference."

Maddy sat down on the couch and let Belinda pull up the coffee table and serve her. But she grabbed her half-full glass of wine. "Let me just finish off my course of medicine first." She drained it, and picked up the pills. They were huge.

"Aren't these for horses?"

Before Belinda could answer, Maddy's computer made a noise she'd never heard before. She got up and turned on the monitor. Strange, like your real life was being fictionalised and put on a screen: Louis's face was inside a stamp-like square. His movements were uneven, time-lapsed. Like a war correspondent in some far-flung conflict.

<Wht time is t there?>

Maddy checked the clock – later than she thought. <Half one in the morning>

<Ive left messges with coulter. when its morning you culd get him t ring me.>

<He's not in his bed, that's for sure. Things are happening this end.>

<like what?>

As she typed in some very basic details, mentioning no names – never trust computers or the internet, especially having seen ScotEx – Belinda cleared up behind her. Her cure hadn't quite worked. Maddy had drunk half the water, taken a single bite out of the celery and swallowed the pills. But she'd poured herself yet another half-glass of red and bitten two chunks out the cheese. Thank goodness she hadn't had time to try and set up her camera, this end, after all. She must be a sight. Her news about Lennon and Kennedy she knew was already old – things were happening out there right now.

<Dont know hw any of that fits into my pciture, but theres stuff going donw here too.>

Whatever it was that created the low-detail image of him – too few pixels or something – had the same effect as being back-lit. It edited out little details and simplified the human face. As a result, Louis looked half his age. His hair was uniformly dark and his eyes, in a pop-video stop-start way, darted and flashed. He looked beautiful. When Belinda was away washing dishes, Maddy stroked the tiny image of the man who had bulked her bed. Only a few weeks ago, yet she felt as if she herself had faded since then, vanishing from her own life.

<jordan Murdock spoke to friends about a foreigner. Called him a "contact", acting the big guy>

<A Brit?>

<An old brit>

<Old to a teenager could mean anyone over twenty two.>

<Maybe not Brit. Jordan told folk his contact had a irish acent.>

Maddy glanced round instinctively at the trees outside her window. There was no doubt Lennon was a killer, and that he had long-running dealings in the States. But could he possibly have killed this Jordan Murdock boy only a few days ago? If he *had*, then at least he wasn't outside her house right now.

She stared hard at the little image of the jumpy, bobbing Louis, trying to see behind him, pick up some clues about his home life. There was a square – a curtained window? Maybe a bookcase underneath it. The camera angle was too close-in. He might not even be at home.

<another weird thing. maybe you could check this out your end. Jordans sister says he mntioned a few times something about sy nite>

<Your typing's getting worse, Commander. Sy Nite?>

<Sth like that. She spoke it, not write it. some big secret of her brothers. Sy – like in your victims name – and night or neat. Sy neat?>

<Knight? Sigh?>

<dunno. Don't even knwo if its a person or a place or what the freak it is>

A warm glow was beginning to come over Maddy. She relaxed a bit, sitting here, talking quietly to Louis, glass of wine in her hand, about the big case right now in her life. The fact that it was just a computer image beamed across the Atlantic, that she was off the case, and that the bottle was empty, she chose not to dwell on. She began to feel sleepy, dreamy.

<How are you doing, *really*, Louis?>

<I'm good. Its you i'm worried about. I hear you're onto another –>

The connection was cut. The gods of cyberspace weren't letting her have her intimate moment with a virtual Louis. Her computer froze, and then told her she'd performed an illegal action.

It was turning out to be one of those nights when the power to be in two or more places at the one time would have been handy. As it was, he'd left Russell – which wasn't quite the same thing – back at the station, directing a quadruple search. Whyte they'd get soon enough – he'd been spotted twice around Candleriggs earlier this evening. They'd been keeping tabs on the Docherties, so they knew they were en route back down from a meeting in Inverness. They'd pick them up along the A9.

Coulter stepped inside the lock-up. Was Tony cute enough to keep an extra den to himself without letting on to anyone? More Lennon's style, that. And were people *normally* kept chained up here?! Two sturdy chains were attached to a wooden frame on the wall. One side of the frame had been splintered, which was probably how the captive got free. There were ropes, too, which he must have wriggled out of, or which perhaps weren't properly tied in the first place.

But who was the captive, and who captor? Coulter couldn't see little Tony Kennedy getting Lennon into the lock-up let alone tying him up. Unless he had a gun. *The* gun – the one that killed Paul and Frances? And his own son. Surely not.

Or was Lennon the imprisoner? Did Tony manage to wriggle free and make a bid for freedom, only to be felled by the bigger man halfway down a dark lane? But then why didn't Lennon drag him back? Because he'd been seen. He'd had to make a run for it.

Patterson Webb was making a beeline for him, talking urgently into his radio.

"Inspector. It's Whyte."

"At last. We've picked him up?"

"He's dead, sir."

Maddy half-woke. She remembered lying out on the couch, but not covering herself with the duvet. Or putting a pillow under her head. She turned her head round – a red wine hangover was beginning to kick in. She still felt exhausted. Drowsy. Belinda Laird was sitting up straight, her eyes closed, on the armchair. She had one of Maddy's books lying open, cover-up, on her knee. *The Leopard.* The computer had been turned off. Louis had been sent back up the tunnel to far America.

Part of her wanted to get up. Try and get the connection back with Louis. Listen out for Coulter's calls. Keep an eye on those trees out there. But the duvet was too comfy and that Ashwagandha strong stuff. Maddy let herself slip back down into sleep again.

It was like the Death of Marat. The bathroom had been lined with a hundred little candles; more than half of them still burning, their smoke staged dry ice. Radio 3 played through from the radio in the hotel room itself – some noisy, bustling Copland piece, totally inappropriate. Perhaps when Whyte was lying dying it had been something gentler. Coulter didn't know yet if Martin Whyte could officially be called a child abuser or not, but he found himself hoping for more fitting music for the poor bastard anyway.

Whyte had swallowed a cocktail of pills – valium, over-the-counter sleeping pills, painkillers. The bottles and a few pills lay scattered about the floor. Then he'd opened his wrists, and the blood tinted the deep bathwater pink.

Streaks ran down the enamel side of the tub, spilled out onto the floor. Suicides are always nasty, but Coulter couldn't help thinking that gay Glasgow artists make a better job of it than most. To complete the Marat scenario, Whyte had written a couple of suicide notes. One before he'd cut his veins, left tidily on the shelf above the sink, addressed to his mother. The other lying on the floor, soaked and blood-stained.

"I am sorry," it said, addressed to no one. "But the world should be too."

Coulter's empathy for him popped like a soap bubble.

Dan McKillop entered – Assistant Procurator Fiscal making things official. Coulter felt a pang of conscience – he was one of the reasons why it wasn't Maddy taking charge. Then he reminded himself that Maddy herself was the real cause of her not being here, missing a crucial moment in the biggest case of her life. McKillop on the other hand was perfectly composed and professional. He turned to a uniformed officer. "Get me some gloves."

"Hard to read it any other way than suicide," he said to McKillop.

"Still, we have to proceed cautiously."

The two men were cagey with each other – their worlds, their approaches, fundamentally different. When the Uniform brought a pair of plastic gloves, Coulter nodded towards the sink, seeking the PFs permission to retrieve the envelope addressed to Whyte's mother.

"Carry on," said Dan McKillop, shaking bathwater from the hem of his suit trousers. Coulter tapped the police photographer's shoulder. He wanted to be snapped opening the letter. Belt and braces. They weren't suited up for this, but he needed to see that note now.

"Mum. This is not as dire as it seems…"

A little respect for the dead man crept back into Coulter's mood. There was nothing in the letter – at first glance anyway – of any relevance to the manner of the author's death. It was a straightforward attempt to assuage a mother's agony. Course, it would have been better still not to have topped himself. And not to have done whatever things he had done that led to such a drastic end. As if reading his mind, McKillop stepped closer to him. "You have some notion why he did this?"

Coulter nodded. He almost said "ask your boss" but stopped himself in time. The two men went out into the corridor so that Coulter could tell the Fiscal the whole story to date. As he followed the tall, beefy McKillop out, Coulter felt like a turncoat about to earn his thirty shillings.

She had to blink several times, thinking it was a weird dream. She was still on the sofa, Duvet pulled up tight under her chin. There was a faint glow from the window, a hint of dawn. Belinda was still in her chair, but sitting up nice and straight like a good girl, eyes open. But she was talking to someone now. And – like Maddy was dreaming again – the man was a black-cloaked shaman. Worse, Father Mike Jamieson. Cup of tea on his lap as if he was visiting a poorly parishioner on a Sunday afternoon.

It was too absurd. Maddy closed her eyes again. What time would it be? Must be the middle of the night, and there's a chichi Catholic priest in your house chatting quietly to a New Age druid.

"It's like asking a clever spaniel to understand history. It's beyond their ken," the pubescent priest said to the pagan. Seemingly serious.

Jesus. Why'd they choose *her* house to talk like this! Belinda sounded as if she'd been on a roll and was reaching the climax of her statement. "We get glimpses of something bigger, stranger, but only glimpses. To weave that big story of yours about a bearded God and rebelling angels and the Son of Man, and pass it all off as irrevocable truth is simply dishonest."

"You're like an occasional smoker, Belinda," Mike was

saying. "You think you're in a better position than a heavy smoker, but actually your addiction's worse." Maddy was waking up properly now, intrigued to hear where this could possibly lead. "You get 'glimpses' but you refuse to follow them up, see where they lead. You haven't the courage to leave the fug-filled smoking room. The gift of Faith, Belinda. You haven't quite got it yet. You haven't tasted clean air."

Belinda had her mouth opened, ready to reply, but Maddy couldn't stand it a moment longer.

"Shut up!"

Fr. Mike and Belinda looked round – apparently surprised to see Maddy in her own home. But as she swung her legs round and sat up, they glanced at one another. There might be an ocean of difference between them theologically, but faced with as muddled and unspiritual a soul as Maddy Shannon, they bonded.

"How do you feel?"

"Like Mia Farrow in *Rosemary's Baby*. When does the Black Mass begin?"

"Not even in jest," said the young priest sternly.

"What the fuck are you *doing* here?"

Jamieson manfully shouldered the swear word, "Belinda told me you were going through a dark night of the soul. She thought – and I hope she's right – that you would be more open to *my* spiritual balm than her own brand."

"Dark night of the soul?" The attractive thing about religion, Maddy thought, was how it made little lives bigger, more dramatic. "I have one of those most nights, Father. Especially if I've cheapskated on the wine. Like Jesus at Cana."

"Cana?" Mike Jamieson was perplexed.

"Surely you know what happened the day after the wedding feast, Father? Joseph woke up the worse for wear and called through from his bed, "Mary, bring us a glass of water. And don't let that boy near it.""

Mike and Belinda looked at her, uncomprehending. More so when Maddy began to laugh, a little madly, at the old joke of her dad's.

"These have been difficult days for you, Maddalena." Fr. Mike thinks of her as a modern-day Mary Magdalen. He uses her full name to get to some part of her he thinks exists without her knowing it. "Nothing more difficult to come to terms with than dead children. A dying grandfather is hard enough, but I understand there have been upheavals in your professional life... and your personal life."

"Upheaval in one's personal life" was clearly theologese for shagging a man who's hightailed back across the Atlantic. Maddy got up and went to the coffee pot that sat on the hearth. At least her uninvited guests had been worldly enough to organise a brew. Must be for Mike; Belinda never touches caffeine.

"It's important that you use these low episodes you experience. View them as gifts, opportunities to reassess where you are and where you wish to go to from here."

Maddy zoned out automatically at the sound of Jamieson's voice, falling into a Sunday morning sermon daydream. She kept a semi-interested look on her face but let the words pass her by, and picked up the telephone. When she started dialling, Jamieson faltered, but she turned to him with that practised expression and he carried on. "The darkness is there for a reason. It doesn't just exist of its own accord."

"It's like dark matter in space," Belinda put in her twopenceworth. "It has a function." The priest didn't look at her, disliking the comparison. "God only allows the Devil to exist to serve His – and our – needs."

Coulter's answerphone again. Damn. She considered leaving some garbled message about Irish accents and Sy Knight, but thought better of it in front of these two. She shouldn't have fallen asleep. Louis's information might not have any relevance, but she'd already erred too far on the side of reticence She should throw these idiots out of her house and get back to her own life.

"Mike thinks, Maddy – and I agree with him – that you could do with some time away from it all."

"Away?"

"I've got my car outside," Jamieson said. "There's a beautiful monastery only an hour from here. In the Lomond Hills."

"I've been there, Maddy. The views, and the grounds! It's a healing place."

"You don't have to take part in any of the services. No one's trying to proselytise. Belinda's prepared a case for you."

His eye glanced to the side of the hearth. True enough, one of Maddy's cases had been packed for her.

"I took the liberty of throwing a few things together," Belinda beamed, "while you were sleeping."

Tony Kennedy spoke out of the corner of his mouth. DC Russell couldn't see why. He had bruises everywhere, but not around his lips. He was connected to drips and wires and monitors, but Russell knew there was nothing seriously wrong with him, nothing vital damaged. In this job you got to know who was dying and who was getting a few cushy weeks in hospital.

"I took him to the lock-up."

"Hang on, Tony. No offence, but you're a half pint o' nothing compared to Lennon. What d'you mean you *took* him?"

"I hit him over the head first."

It took some time to get a coherent story out of Tony Kennedy. Partly because he insisted in speaking out of the side of his mouth, partly because he ran out of breath or energy every few words. But mainly because the man wasn't capable of stringing three words together in the first place. Eventually, however, John Russell managed to construct a picture.

Lennon had gone straight home after being released from

the cells. Kennedy had heard through the grapevine that he had been bailed. He'd gone round to his house, broken in through a back window, and had a crowbar handy, waiting for him.

"And you knocked him out? In one blow, Tony? Let's say that actually happened... And exactly how did a little fella like you get a big lunk like him out the house and into your van?"

"Took fuckin' ages. Can't believe nobody saw me! He won't be happy when he sees his roses."

He had to hit Lennon once more in the van to keep him unconscious until he drove into the secret lock-up and got him tied up.

"What were you intending to do with him?"

Kennedy stared up at the ceiling. He had no idea. Never had a plan. All he knew was that Lennon killed his son. He wanted answers from him. Why? What connection did he have with his son? Did Tony Kennedy have reason to believe that Ian Lennon had killed Sy? If so, he didn't want to just kill him, he wanted to make it slow, punish him.

"Why didn't you finish him off, Tony?"

Tony glanced down from the ceiling and stared vacantly at Russell. "He said it wasn't him. He didn't kill my son."

Russell's jaw dropped. "That's all? He *told* you... and you believed him?"

"I shouldn't have let him talk."

"He's a trained killer, Tony. You can't guess how many people he's executed, in cold blood. Just because someone told him to."

Patterson Webb came into the hospital room; McKillop, Shannon's underling, with him. Shirtlifter, Russell had heard. Coulter was out in the hall, giving some Uniforms orders. He'd try and take over in here in a moment. Start the whole process over.

"Lennon's got no corroboration of alibi for the time of

your son's death, Tony." Russell tried to speed things up. "Forensic evidence ties him directly to the scene."

"The dog hair? He spoke about that. Easy to set up. Someone wants to link him to the murder, pats the dog in the street and puts a hair on the bodies. Christ, could even have happened by accident."

Unlikely, Russell thought. But Kennedy had a point about the framing. Find a house Lennon gardens at that's got a dog. Follow it one day and give it a pat... He could feel Lennon slip from their fingers. Fine by Russell – Lennon was always his boss's hunch. And things were developing by the minute on Whyte and the Dochertys – Russell's own preference.

Russell went off to bring Coulter up to speed on Tony's story. He didn't think he'd ever seen the man quite so hassled.

"Get Lennon. Get more men onto it if you have to."

"That's one hell of a liberty, Linda. Did you help, Father?"

"Course not."

"Maybe suggest knicker and bra combinations? What's right for a monastery? Sackcloth thong?"

"It's the only response the modern age has to faith and doctrine – cheap jokes."

Another time, another place, Maddy would have set about him. Right now all she wanted was to get Laird and Jamieson out of her house, and Coulter and Casci on the phone. She had a sense of urgency she couldn't quite connect to any single event or piece of information.

"Maddy. I'm sorry. I was only trying to help."

"Forgive my directness, Linda – but *you're* the grieving mother."

She flinched a little, but took hold firmly of Maddy's arm. "You need rest. Time out. Get back in touch with... *something.*"

Perhaps it was the woman's fingers on her skin, or just

weariness, but Maddy suddenly became aware of that big black line around her. Not only that, she felt that Belinda could see it, too. Sense it.

They had a point, the Pagan and the Priest. She did feel lost. Her life was a decade of broken rosary beads. Disconnected pellets of people, happenings. Nonno. Casci. Children dead in a park under cherry blossom. Wee lassie laid out in a posh garden. How do you keep going every day with all that spinning round you? She looked, quietly, for a moment at Belinda, who smiled. Then at Mike, not much more than a dark and concerned child himself.

"You've got a car and a driver now, Linda. And if *you*, Father, haven't got enough money for the petrol to Dundee, I'll lend you it." She crossed the room to turn on her computer, aware of Jamieson following her. She imagined him stamping his foot.

"I didn't need to come here tonight! I have people in my parish who need me. People can't be saved from themselves unless they put in a little effort too!"

"What if I don't want to be "saved from myself"? I might not actually *like* this burly, badly dressed mess of woman I've become, but we've reached an understanding."

"Come on, Mike," said Belinda, a huffy side to her showing for the first time. "I thought she'd be more receptive. I overestimated her."

Maddy felt like crying. She was coming out fighting, but throwaway lines like that were hitting a mark somewhere. Perhaps she did live in a swill of ignorance and blindness. She clicked on Messenger when her PC fired up. Nothing. No new messages.

"Some people can't read the signs that are sent to them." He was facing Belinda, but he was talking at Maddy. "It's why the mass of people can't understand miracles, or grace... they don't have the apparatus for it."

Maddy looked around for a cigarette. She'd had some in an old handbag. Did she throw that into one of the packing boxes? She'd decided weeks ago she wasn't ready to move yet she'd continued to fill boxes with stuff.

"It's because I'm a fish."

Belinda looked at her, as if this time she really had flipped.

"She's laughing at the Monsignor," Jamieson explained, then turned to Maddy. "Those who choose to see only darkness, *will* see only darkness. The Monsignor is a great mind, an acclaimed theologian throughout the Christian world!"

Maddy stopped, and looked at him. The priest, who had been leaning forward, like a soldier heading into batle, straightened up. She took a step closer to him.

"He travels, doesn't he?"

Jamieson nodded.

"Irish." It wasn't a question.

Jamieson turned to Belinda, hoping for help, an explanation of Maddy's strange words.

"Has he been travelling recently?"

"He was in Rome last week."

"And last month?"

"He goes all over the place. Spain. The States—"

He stopped when Maddy rushed out of the room. Belinda followed, calling after her.

"Maddy, please. Stop. Let me help you."

The Lomond Hills flex and stretch at dawn, the loch below rousing, rippling. The summit of Ben Lomond emerges from clouds like a sleepy eye opening.

Duncryne Hill affords one of the best views in Scotland in exchange for the least effort. Fifteen-minute walk from car to top. Elaine and Jim Docherty sat and waited for the police to arrive. If they'd danced up and down they couldn't have been more conspicuous. They'd made no attempt to conceal their car. It lay at the foot of the hill, unlocked.

Turn your back on the loch and you can see the beginnings of the city. It rises in clefts in the landscape, like a skin rash. The wind funnelling up the valley from the sea still stings, freezing the tears to Elaine's face.

They were conspicuous up there: Duncryne hill is not high, drivers coming in from Stirling noticed them up there. A romancing couple perhaps, or recently bereaved scattering ashes. Finally it was a local farmer who phoned the police – something suspicious about them.

Jim and Elaine waited to be found, locked up, interrogated and be labelled, if not vicious murderers, then dangerous sex monsters.

Coulter and Russell were pacing up and down in front of the Incident Board. The Docherties would be brought in any moment. Amy Dalgarno was hard at work on a phone – noising folk up before the clock struck seven. "The home schooling outfit's called Faith and Family. There's a helpline number on their answering machine—"

"An 0800?" Coulter looked at Amy like seeing her for the first time. She'd been seconded to CID for over a month but this was the first time he'd seen her without a uniform. Still in her twenties but she had an authority about her. Dressed well for work – modestly enough and smart, nothing that would make her stand out too much. Thick, fair hair tied back. "No, 01968. Down near Peebles somewhere. Finally got an answer to it this morning. Woke some poor sod up. He was a bit confused. Anyway, it appears that Faith and Family are more than just an educational organisation. According to this guy—"

"Called?"

"Sturgeon. Raymond Sturgeon. They're into lobbying, public education—"

"Lobbying for what?"

"Whole gamut of issues – anti-abortion, anti-sex education, AIDS, crime, Third World, immigration. They have offices in Edinburgh and London. And according to their website, affiliated organisations throughout the world."

"What denomination? Born agains?"

"RC. As Catholic as you can get, from the sound of it. Think Benedict might have trouble getting membership."

"Can we get a leading light of this crowd to talk to us? Someone from the schooling side. Did Paul Pacchini get tutors through them? Would he have paid anyone a visit when he came up here?"

"Sturgeon says they don't have bosses at Faith and Family – except for Jesus."

Coulter sighed. Russell put down his phone and called over to him: "That's our hillwalkers in now."

Walking out the incident room Coulter took a call from Maddy. "Where are you?"

"It's a long story. I'm driving. Listen – I spoke to Casci last night. He should have emailed you."

"Didn't check my inbox. I'll get someone to do it now. What'd he say?"

"Jordan Murdock – he's the kid who was killed—"

"Maddy! *I'm* the one working on this case. I *know* who Murdock is!"

"Murdock told people he had a contact from over here. A "Brit" he called him. But, with an Irish accent. Referred to him as an "old guy".

Coulter could hear his own groan echoed back to him through the earpiece. "But now it looks unlikely Lennon was over there. And I don't think he'd appreciate being called a Brit."

"You've got him? Thanks, Alan, for letting me know." He could hear tyres squealing. She was driving angrily.

"Actually, we haven't quite got him. But we know he's here and probably has been since he skipped bail."

"I think we're nearly quits, you and me, Coulter, on the cock-up stakes." A horn blared somewhere near her. 7 AM and already she was causing chaos. "Anyway Murdock wasn't talking about last week. He's been talking about this old Irish guy since last year."

Coulter stopped short of the interview room where Russell was waiting for him at the open door. Inside, the Dochertics' lawyer was already there, and a uniform sergeant. "We'll get Lennon anyway. Have to go, Maddy."

"Anything else I should know?" As things stood she had nothing to do with this enquiry now, but she still knew as much about it, if not more, than him or Russell. Best to keep her up to speed. "We're chasing up Pacchini's home-schooling guys."

"They religious by any chance?"

"Yes. Why? Listen, Maddy, where *are* you?"

"You don't want to know."

"An old Irish man?" Father Jamieson was shaking his head in smiling disbelief. "You *surely* don't think—" He was squeezed into the back seat beside a glowering Belinda. Much as she had wanted to be rid of them, Maddy had decided at the last minute to take them with her. Jamieson might come in handy. But she was ignoring him just now. Having just put the phone back on its cradle, it rang again. A long number she didn't recognise.

"Maddy. It's me."

Technology was bringing Louis back to her in pieces. First read his words, then saw his face on-screen. Now she was hearing his thick, low voice for the first time in an age. He wasn't sounding sociable though, so she suppressed her delight.

"Just a quick call – to see if anything chimes with you. I'm on the move, over the bridge right now to the Bronx."

"Why? What's there?"

"We've followed up some leads. Several of our victims, including Murdock and Braithewaite, might have been mixed up with some religious cranks."

"Louis? I'm making the exact same journey! Except it's

the Kingston Bridge, not the Brooklyn. And Cathcart, not the Bronx. But I've got my fair share of cranks." In the rear-view mirror she smiled at sullen Belinda and Mike.

"We think Murdock's Irishman might be a regular visitor. We've picked up other references, elsewhere. There's some kind of chain thing going on. Murdock had connections with Braithewaite. Braithewaite knew people who were connected to Plissard and Goodman Lane..."

Maddy remembered the names but had never quite got who they all were or what they had in common. "Louis, you told Coulter all this?"

"His phone's off. So's his sidekick's."

"Try asking for Amy Dalgarno."

"Haven't got the time right now."

Somebody was shouting to him in the car. He said his goodbyes and stopped, and Maddy immediately felt lonely.

Within minutes Coulter was convinced he was wasting his time with the Docherties. He had his mobile on to vibrate. He was begining to feel like a perv with it going off every couple of minutes in his trouser pocket.

They were both in tears. They confessed to the photography session with Sy Kennedy. First time they had ever done something like that. Would never do it again. Didn't realise what age Sy was. They didn't mean him any harm, and they swore they never saw him again. Were sure he was five years older. *He* came to them. He made the suggestion. And Martin Whyte set the thing up. Him and the Kennedy boy between them. Maybe Whyte had even done stuff like that before.

"Why did you hand yourselves in?"

"We knew that the minute you tracked Martin down, he'd tell everything," Jim Docherty said. "He was frightened. He might have tried to blame us more."

Elaine added, "And that woman lawyer took the files from my desk."

That was a complication Coulter knew he was going to hate. Inadmissible evidence, acquired without a warrant. Worse, stolen. By a Fiscal.

"We thought we saw police cars," said Jim Docherty. "On the lookout for us. Did you find Martin?"

Someone with more time on their hands could tell them about their pal's suicide. Coulter's phone shivered again in his pocket. "Do you know any Irish people?"

Monsignor Connolly glared at her like she were a vision, an incubus sent to torment him.

"I thought you were a prosecution lawyer." The question was rhetorical, so she just stared him out. "They don't normally ask questions like policemen, do they? Not out of court."

"I can get a policeman here now, if you like. I could get a couple of dozen. Sirens, warrants, guns, the full bhoona."

"Actually, I'm not sure you could, Miss Shannon. As I recall from the last Delinquency Committee meeting, you're *persona non grata* presently."

"You get told stuff like that at committee meetings?" She comes out of this with any career left and Binnie's head will roll. She'll make sure of it. "Have you been in New York in the last few months, Monsignor? You *do* know about the Potter's Field murders? "

"You strike me, Miss, to be in some kind of crisis."

"Don't you start."

Mike Jamieson smiled knowingly at the old man, who didn't return the compliment. Belinda, leaning against the door frame, didn't react at all. Maddy had expected her to vanish at some point, but she seemed to be hanging in for the ride.

Connolly was right, though – she must look like a woman demented. She'd slept on the sofa, a bottle and a half of cheap red in her; she was uncombed, stilll in yesterday's clothes, no makeup, wobbly high heels. She was about to ask another question when the old man smiled, and decided to play along with her.

"You want to know if I go to America often? Amongst other places, yes."

"Do you work with black kids over there?"

Jamieson laughed. "The Monsignor is a very important man, Maddalena."

"Well, Father," Connolly said without turning to him, "we all say Mass. And meet our parishioners. So, yes, I come across all shapes and sizes – and ages." He was keeping his tone light, but with effort. It wasn't Connolly's natural medium, lightness. Maddy could feel the man's intensity, straining beneath the condescending smile.

"Who or what is Sy Knight?"

The old man repeated the words, and they sounded even stranger in his Donegal accent. Like *cyanide*.

Belinda, Maddy noticed, had gone outside. She could see her through the window, sitting on the top step of the parish house, face tilted to the warm, clear morning sun.

"What about Lennon? Do you know anything about *his* trips to the States?"

She was flailing around. She could feel Jamieson become smug again, watching her. She had rushed out of the house an hour ago so full of questions and possibilities and hunches. Jamieson and Belinda had got caught up in her frenzy. But it was all melting away under Connolly's hot stare. Her questions seemed stupid, random. The old haze of the last few days replacing the sense of urgency. She tried a few more questions on the old man, but he fielded them expertly.

She walked towards the door, defeated. Jamieson stepped back from it, secure in his home patch, letting her loose, useless, on the world.

"I did try to help," said Father Mike, a syrupy, sorry smile on his face.

Connolly never took his eyes off her. They were light

brown, but felt darker. He gave the impression of a man who knew things ordinary folk didn't know existed. She opened the door of the little ante-room they were in.

"Sy Knight?" Connolly swirled the words in his mouth like an iffy wine. "Could be mispronounced. *Sinite?* Possibly. *Sinite parvulos.*"

"What's that?"

"*Sinite parvulos venire ad me.*"

Jamieson stared at him, too. Perhaps they didn't teach young priests Latin any more.

"'And they brought young children to him, that he should touch them, and his disciples rebuked those that brought them.' I'm a devotee of the King James version, you'll have noticed. 'But when Jesus saw it, he was much displeased and said unto them.' *Sinite parvulos*... Suffer the little children to come unto me... *Et ne prohibueritis eos talium est enim regnum Dei...* and forbid them not for of such is the Kingdom of God."

There was a moment's silence. Maddy realised that Belinda had left her doorstep and was now inside. Maddy turned back to Connolly. "You never knew Sy Kennedy or Frances Mullholland, Monsignor, did you?"

"No, Miss Shannon, I did not."

"Or Paul Pacchini? The son of Mrs Laird here. He was home-schooled by a religious order. His foster parents are Catholic."

Connolly kept his eyes on her, but he was thinking. Trying to remember something, perhaps, or deciding what to say. Eventually, he said "Faith and Family."

"What exactly is that?"

"Idiots." Connolly's expressions until now had been variations of storminess. But he could sneer, too. "They say that every institution must have its diehards. Its Praetorian Guard. Like animals need backbones."

"Extreme Catholics. Who are they?"

"Nobodies. Theologically speaking. Businessmen,

housewives, maybe a few teachers, lawyers. Aspiring professionals. They'd never admit it, but they use organisations
like that as Masonic lodges. You scratch my fanatic back
and I'll scratch yours."

Belinda stood listening quietly, but Jamieson busied himself tinkering inside a drawer. "Don't get me wrong. On
plenty of issues I'm in agreement with them. On abortion
and contraception. It's their means I dislike, overtly political. Right-wing. Half their members aren't even Catholics.
They've either been thrown out of other denominations,
or they've been excommunicated. Or should be."

"Who funds them?"

"Rich like-minded individuals. Big companies."

"Could any of these people have known Paul or Frances
or Sy?"

"I'd have thought they'd prefer to stay out of the way
of those kinds of kids. But they do have their educational
arm. I know nothing about it."

Maddy looked at Belinda, whose eyes were still full of
horror at the Monsignor's words.

"You'll have read about Ian Lennon in the papers - could
he be a member of this Faith and Family?"

"Isn't he IRA? Unlikely. Most of them hate the Church
more than a Loyalist bandsman does." Connolly turned
his body fully round to face Fr. Mike. Maddy wondered if
he had some kind of bone or muscle disease – no part of
him seemed capable of independent movement. "*You* never
came across anyone overly zealous out in Drumchapel,
Michael, did you?"

Mike immediately glanced over at Maddy.

"You were a priest in Drumchapel?"

"No no. A year or so back the priest there was ill and
I filled in for him from time to time. A couple of us did.
Paul Hughes over in St. Gregory's, and Jack Vittesse at St
Jude's."

"Father Jamieson also does some sterling work in

schools." Maddy somehow got the impression that the Monsignor wasn't wildly impressed with the curate's "sterling work".

"Ah, hardly ever in Drumchapel, Monsignor. Once or twice. Never long enough to know who was who."

Maddy had to get out of here. Her half-baked theory about Connolly was either way off the mark or the man was clever in ways she couldn't figure out. She'd arrived with one theory and a suspect in mind and was leaving with a new theory and a new suspect. Between the police and her how many suspects did they have altogether? Must be half a bloody dozen.

She had no idea where to turn now, what the logical next move was. She should leave this to the professionals. Her place was in an office making sense of others' detective work, or in a courtroom, stringing facts and possibilities into a story whose end she already knew. She headed for the front door, following the thin draught of cool, fresh morning air. She needed to breathe deeply. And she wanted to talk to Alan Coulter.

Lennon had been spotted. An unmistakeable description. Big, stooped, balding, covered in blood, limping, seen from a window ten minutes ago. What's more, he was walking along by the canal – the very same stretch that Pacchini and Kennedy had been marched over towards their execution.

Coulter should have stayed at the station. Keep up with Amy, still madly chasing down this Faith and Family outfit. They were a key, without a doubt. Could Lennon have *any* connection with them? He should be in the HOLMES room, waiting for the computers to churn out anything new. Background on Sturgeon, Babbington, Simon Knight. Casci had emailed a couple of times – he was getting new leads that might, or might not, apply to Coulter's case as well.

But he needed to get out. He'd keep his mobile on him.

For over a month he'd convinced himself more and more of Lennon's guilt. The vicious old bastard had given him the runaround for too long. He had to *be* there when he was finally collared. Everyone had got wind that things were happening this morning. Chief Constable Crawford Robertson was upstairs with half the Force's top brass. Members of the Youth Crime Committee there too, including the Czar himself no doubt. Glasgow's chair of the Police Committee, the Moderator of the Church of Scotland – who more than likely make up the four ball with Robertson and MacDougall – had been spotted coming in the building with the crime editor of the *Daily Record*. Cosy or what?

Amy, handling two phones at once, saw him put on his jacket. "You remembering the Kanes are coming back in at ten? Before they disappear back to England."

"Of course." He hadn't. "I'll be well back then."

Walking down the corridor he took a call from an agitated Maddy. "Alan, Louis is right. Faith and Family. Connolly knows all about it—"

"You've been to see Monsignor Connolly? Christ, Maddy, could you just go home to your bed for a day or so? That old codger's got connections. You're in enough trouble. Don't start throwing around accusations!"

"I'm not accusing him of anything. Yet. It's Mike Jamieson you need to look into. He's a priest. Young guy. He's worked out at Drumchapel and never told us."

"Ministering to the needy in the Drum might be a thankless task, but it's not a crime."

"Just go talk to him."

"Why don't *you*? You're talking to bloody everybody else!"

"I'm getting mixed messages here, inspector."

"I was joking. Remember that?"

"Seriously, Alan – find out about him. Go see him."

"Okay, okay. If you promise. Go home, *now*."

256

"Absolutely."

She hadn't even *tried* to lie with conviction.

She hadn't managed to shake off Belinda Laird. Either this woman had a serious gap in her life – no place she had to be, no one waiting for her. More likely, she was a mother in pain who didn't know how to show it. Who needed to find out what really happened to her son.

They were heading for Lochgilvie House. Under a perfect Caledonian sky, Saltire blue and paddling-pool bright. "Some kind of chain thing going on." Casci's phrase had stuck in her mind. He wasn't the most eloquent of speakers at the best of times, but she knew what he meant. Sort of. All the New York victims turned out to have connections, and some elderly Irishman was in the centre of them all. Over here Sy Kennedy knew Paul Pacchini, so the chances are one of them had a connection with Frances Mulholland. And the only person she could think of who might shine any light on that was Franny's big brother Darren.

She didn't explain any of this to Belinda. Belinda didn't seem to want explanations. The haze that had surrounded Maddy – that was still lurking somewhere in the back of her head like haar just beyond the shore – had engulfed the woman in the passenger seat. She sat staring straight ahead, silent as the sky.

Ten o'clock. Maddy dialled a number, and let it ring this time over the car's speakers.

"Mama. It's me. Any change?"

"Nothing." Rosa di Rio sounded exhausted. Hopeless. For the first time it flashed through Maddy's mind that it might be better for everyone if Nonno died.

"How are you?"

"I'm fine," her mother said, miserably. "I don't suppose you can..."

"This afternoon. I promise." This time, she meant it.

She dialled again, to make sure that Darren was still

in the Home and that he was going to be around in ten minutes. Janet Bateman wasn't there. She spoke to David Simons.

"Sorry. Darren checked himself out yesterday. Against our advice, but he's a free agent."

Maddy swung the car just in time to get the last exit before the M8 took her onto the A77 and carried her south to Ayrshire. Girvan. Go there, and she might never come back.

Ten in the morning and the sun was already strong. Even the canal looked good, flowing quietly between trees. There was a heron standing on the opposite bank, but no one in the party liked to mention it. Coulter, Russell, Webb, a couple of Uniforms. They were all being serious men on an important mission. Can't go pointing out cute wildlife.

Lennon's house was in Westlands – one of the new houses just over the back of the canal and the railway track. They'd had that covered night and day for weeks now. Coulter had sent another group to come down to the track from the murder scene. Webb's crackling radio was keeping them informed. Coulter wished the frigging heron would fly off. Something unsettling about those birds. They seemed to know something. Something ancient, horrible.

The hit man had disappeared again. Apart from anything else, this was getting embarrassing. If what the Corrigan woman said was true he could be sitting on a high branch watching them right now. Could survive for a decade without shifting from the same tree.

Coulter had uniforms fanning out from every exit off the track. Up onto Maryhill Road, Great Western Road, down into "the Valley", a tough little pocket of houses just north of them. He had resisted dredging the canal for the murder weapon. So expensive and ridiculous odds.

Coulter knew in his bones he wasn't going to find

Lennon. He should have stayed in the station. But the morning air was helping him think.

Take Lennon out of the equation… Could Whyte have killed Sy Kennedy? The Docherties – how did they fit in with Pacchini and the Mulholland girl? Kids like that. God knows the stuff that must happen. The Kanes – he'll give them the grilling of their life in an hour, dead foster son or no. Kennedy simply an avenging father? And then Casci's near-illegible emails and unintelligible phone messages about chain reactions or something. Coulter had tried to get back to him ten times this morning, but he was incommunicado. And Irish priests. Casci and Maddy. *Connolly* was Irish, not Jamieson.

He checked his watch. He'd have time to pass by Connolly and Jamieson's church, before giving the Kanes a going-over. He nodded to Russell to about-turn. Russell was loving his boss's confusion. All this running from pillar to post for nothing. So was the heron. Staring at him, like he was the dumbest animal in the world.

"Chapel? Darren? You mad?"

Jackie Mulholland had cleaned up the flat, spruced herself up a little. The ashtray in front of her was still full to brimming and the air in the room post-nuclear fallout. Ricky Graham was still a fixture, too. He hadn't made the same effort as Jackie – he looked as if he hadn't washed in a week.

"Matter of fact, Jacks, I think he did."

"What?"

"Your Darren. Snuck about the Pineapple. I saw him. Couple o' times."

"What were *you* doing down by the chapel?"

Ricky's eyes darted from Maddy to Jackie to Belinda. Belinda in particular seemed to intimidate him. "It's next to the pub. Outside having a fag, I seen him once coming oot."

"Darren? In the *church?*"

If they'd told her her son unzipped up the back and was really a lizard from space she couldn't have been more surprised. She took a long hard drag on her fag and shook her head slowly from side to side. What a world.

Hip-hop music came from down the hall, from Darren's room, where he was getting dressed after a shower. He'd just come home and he was going straight back out. Jackie didn't know where.

"Be in in a minute."

They sat in awkward silence, like a lull in conversation at a dinner party. Maddy was in no mood for patience, or lulls. She was following a trail of events, like a tracker Indian sniffing and listening to the earth. Is this what Coulter feels when he's close to a catch? What a fox or a hunting dog senses, in their skin, their bowels. "So, Jackie," she made a supreme effort, "you're looking well."

The woman's daughter wasn't long buried, but Jackie Mulholland got so few compliments that she beamed happily. "Ta. Trying to cut down on the bevvy and that. Less chips. Taking a bit o' pride in myself. Franny always telt me I should." At the uttering of her child's name, her eyes filled, and she became confused and desperate again.

Frances telling her mum to find some self-esteem. Maddy saw a cycle of tragedy being acted out in this house. Mother, daughter and son each urging the other to be good to themselves, to improve. While each, on their own, sank further into their own little hell.

"Will I make a cuppa?"

"Don't bother. He'll be here now, eh?" Maddy got up and walked to the door. The tingle in her skin was saying if she didn't move quick she'd miss whatever it was she was following. "Darren?" She shouted out.

No answer. The radio had stopped playing noisy rap. She went out into the hall, shouted over him. The door was ajar. She could see the bed and floor was a jumble of clothes, magazines, CD boxes. On the wall, posters of Henrik Larssen and Craig Bellamy, Marilyn Manson, a couple of women pop stars gyno-gyrating. "Darren! You decent? Can I come in?"

No reply. She pushed the door further open. Darren had gone. Maddy about-turned, rushed out, up the hall, towards the door. Belinda joined her. Jackie and Graham just stood in the hallway and let them go. One mother needed to know what happened to her son. Another shrank back from the hell of something happening to *both* her children. "Miss?" she said as Maddy was half out of the front door, "he's wearing his trackies."

La Signora Rosa di Rio walked through the graves of the Necropolis. Strange that a place of death can be so beautiful. Especially when the summer sun is rising high in the sky and you have the person you've loved most in your life dying. Just through there – through that window at eye level to her where she stands on a little mound behind John Knox's tomb.

She had sat for days now, by Nonno's bedside. Papà's bedside. They'd all called him granddad since Maddy was wee, but Vittore was Rosa's daddy. By any book you could read on the subject he was lousy at it. Worked too hard, didn't spend much time with her, got her working in the chippy when she should have been studying for exams, had a temper on him... But she worshipped the ground he walked on. His heart, his smile, his songs. And the fact that he was always *there*.

Yet he was beautiful. The daft songs he'd sing. Putting her on his feet to dance when she was wee. Embarrassing her with his stupid patter but making all her friends howl with laughter. The lovely, mysterious songs he sang from the old country. Taking her for walks along the beach. Giving Packy – her ill-chosen mate – a hard time, then easing up on him when he saw she wasn't going to change her mind, though he still knew it was a disaster.

Creating *two* worlds for her – not just one. The security and realness of a home, an income, a place to belong. Holiday Girvan. The Rimini of the Lower Clyde, bustling and fast and a place where you could make a living. He had the whole family working like pit ponies non-stop for two years, saving up, and then they'd go, with fistfuls of lire, back to Italy. For a month every two years, they were kings over there. Rosa, a princess. An exotic princess in a castle on a hill in Elba.

But Italy was more than that. Nonno had given them a mythical home. There was more to her than there was to other people. Rosa di Rio had an entire world the others knew nothing of. Italy was lodged inside her, like an extra engine, a secret heart. She had a heaven to go to.

And now the man who gave her all that was dying. Just over there. Might even be dead by now. She was sixty years old. A mother. A divorcee. She was fine for money. She had a wonderful, successful daughter who was good to her, who was a friend. She had other friends and other interests. But, without Nonno, Rosa didn't think she could live. She stood on the hill in the Necropolis beside John Knox's tomb, and bubbled like a baby. Not Nonno... Not her daddy. Babbo couldn't just leave her.

There had been no answer at the parish house. Coulter, Russell and Webb tried the church door. It was open. Russell was like Indiana Jones entering the Temple of Doom. The riches it held, the fascination – and the lair of everything Popish, scheming, malevolent..

The place was in darkness. It was an old church – high and cold and, in the dark, vast. Once their eyes got used to the gloom, they could make out the altar, miles ahead. A little light there, an electric candle. Coulter remembered hearing something about the light that never goes out. The three men stood in silence, listening. Not a sound. Russell turned to go, but Coulter remained still.

"This place isn't empty."

"What," said Russell, in wonder. "You mean... there's a *presence?*"

Coulter looked at him. "No, you moron. People."

It wasn't a hunch or a detective's sixth sense. It was good hearing. Sounds from the far wall. He walked towards them, Webb behind, Russell trailing. Voices, half-whispering, secretive. Crossing the main aisle they could see the doors clearly.

"Confessionals." John Russell hissed, as though he'd just spied a porthole to the abyss.

They walked as quietly as they could manage – which on tiles in a huge echoing church wasn't too quiet at all. Eventually, Coulter could make out one of the voices.

"Yes you fucking will."

"What did he say?" asked Russell. The unexpected words, spat out with venom, hollow-sounding in the ghostly acoustics, felt as if they came from inside Coulter's head. He moved closer still, Webb and Russell tiptoeing behind, like a Vaudeville comedy routine.

"They're here now," said the bitter voice.

"They are of no concern to me." This second voice was a higher vibrato, constricted.

"Render unto Caesar." The first voice was calmer now, but still full of contempt.

Coulter opened the door warily. Mike Jamieson was kneeling back in the shadows. Coulter could interpret the scene from what he knew about confessionals. There was a grille in the far wall. The young priest was kneeling beside it. It took a second or two longer for him to realise that the grille was not only open but that an arm protruded from behind it, and held Jamieson firmly by the neck. The young priest's eyes were popping and his voice was strangulated: "It is the Confessor's duty to give penance and absolution."

He squinted round desperately at Coulter as if asking for confirmation of the theological point.

The arm, sleeve rolled up to reveal knots of hard, hairy muscle, tightened more. The voice was ironic. "Not until the Confessor knows you are genuinely repentant and that you mean to make amends. You little prick."

"Another man can't judge that," Jamieson wheezed. "Only God can."

It wasn't any sense of the divine or mystical that kept the three policemen still and watching the extraordinary little scene. Nor even a hunch that something was going to be revealed, but the sheer freakishness of the situation.

"Then I'll absolve myself."

The hidden tormentor laughed. "First you have to tell yourself your sins. Out loud. Go on, tell us, 'I have sinned in thought, word and deed...' " The fist's grip got harder yet, and Jamieson struggled to breathe at all.

"Not the sin *you* think. I acted in good faith."

"You're a horse's arse." The Irish accent was full of disdain. Then the tone changed, becoming pleasanter, almost conversational. "Did I hear visitors enter? Miss Shannon?"

"This is Detective Inspector Coulter," Coulter said to the hairy arm, like he was addressing some vengeful, disembodied power.

"Better still. Inspector, Michael Jamieson is guilty of murder."

The fist let go of the young priest's throat and withdrew back inside the grille. Jamieson nursed his neck and, still rasping, said "I've never killed anyone in my life."

Coulter still wasn't sure whether to make a move or not. Russell fidgeted behind him, his worst nightmare of chapels come true.

"I was dragged in here against my will. Violently."

"Directly or indirectly," the Monsignor continued unconcerned, "he's not prepared even to tell God. But murder certainly, and perhaps more than one."

Jamieson looked down at the floor for a moment, then stood up, took a deep breath, and did something none of the policemen had ever seen before. With his thumb he touched the top of his lip, then his chin, then either side of his mouth. Then he walked to the door. Coulter, Russell and Webb stood back to let him pass.

"I am guilty of no crime. Not in your book, or in God's." He stood, stooped and coughed, supported himself with one hand on the back of the last pew, the other loosening his dog-collar, pulling it back from the lesions Connolly's gnarled old hands had made on his neck. He spoke to the policemen but looked directly ahead, towards the altar and the flicker of electric candlelight. "*You* are the murderers."

Coulter, Webb and Russell looked at one another, knocked a little off balance by the accusation. "Come again?" said John Russell.

"You. Your world. The world that despises children. That condemns them to the gutter. That abuses them morally, physically—"

"And you *don't* live in this world," Coulter cut the sermon short.

"I oppose it. I try to help."

"Not everyone would appreciate your particular brand of assistance, Michael." Connolly had appeared behind them, emerging out of an unseen door. His arms lay at his sides, but his fists were still red and clenched. He turned his back on the young priest to speak to Coulter.

"Michael told me about a young girl—"

"You made a vow, Brendan!" For the first time, free of the older man's physical threat, Jamieson managed to regain some authority in his tone. The use of the Christian name and the haughty manner sounded like a confident new generation shaking off the Old Guard. Connolly ignored him and spoke to Coulter. "I do not believe my colleague's confession was made with the necessary humility and contrition. But the only part of it I need to reveal is a name."

"You may *not* break the sacred seal of the sacrament, Monsignor."

"No confession was made here, Michael. You just admitted it yourself – I dragged you in there."

"What is a true confession and what is not isn't a judgement for you to make! Have you forgotten the vows you took and what they mean?"

Connolly thought for a moment, and replied. "Perhaps I have. And I believe my judgement to be the right one." He turned to Coulter. "During our... *discussion*, Michael Jamieson refused to elucidate on certain questions I asked him. Questions that I needed the answers to after a visit from a colleague of yours."

"Maddy Shannon."

"Michael was... reticent. Though he seemed to think that he could convince me of certain theological points. But he gave me enough information for me to make a full written statement, which may be of use to you."

"You mentioned a name, Monsignor."

"I deny ever having had this conversation with you!" Jamieson sounded very sure of his ground. "Do not believe a word he says. He is an old man, easily confused." He moved away from his pew to stop Connolly saying any more, but all the older man needed to do was raise his arm halfway to his chest for the younger to back away.

"Father Michael knew Frances Mullholland." The Monsignor looked at the ground, as though it was *he* who had confessed something dreadful. "I'd heard Michael complain of the girl's behaviour. With good reason. But I never realised..." He shook his head at himself.

"You should have seen her," Jamieson said, quietly, his voice even. "Well you can. Walk down any street in this city..." He looked as if he might stop talking, so Coulter nudged him on. "Children out of control. You can't pass a group bigger than two or three without being threatened, spat at. Mocked."

"So what was so special about Frances?"

"They all sneer and scorn at everything sent to help them. Everything beautiful. On a higher plane. It doesn't have to be like that. We should all be helping them, pulling them out of this rut, this.... Hell they're in. Saving them from themselves. I tried to help her. Frances. Her and her brother. Her whole family—"

"You also know Darren Mullholland?"

"He came to see me. After I spoke in his school. I spotted him immediately, the sorry state of him. He told me he had trouble at home. He was worried about his mother and his sister. And then I met her, Frances, and it was like meeting a child possessed." He clasped his hands on the back of the pew, as if praying for release. "She swore at me. And laughed – laughed outright at my cross. She called on her friends, and they laughed and sneered and spat too."

"You think this is a new phenomenon?" Connolly stared in disgust at him. "You are really so easily offended?"

"I wasn't offended. Not for myself. I was offended on behalf of Our Lord, of the Church. Dismayed, deeply troubled for the soul of that poor child and her Hellish cohort." He chose now to look past Coulter and for the first time address Russell and Webb, that they might understand. "We'll keep sliding downhill until someone has the bravery, the... *decency* to stop it. To tackle the evil."

"Evil. Being cheeky to your elders."

"Violence, Monsignor. Drugs. Lost souls, utterly lost. Sexualised before they're into their teens. What hope have they got." Jamieson turned back to Coulter. "Frances was as bad as I've seen. She and her friends. Every word they spoke an insult to the Lord, and a cancer on their souls. They blew smoke in my face. Every time I went to the school or the Parish they pursued me. They pursued the *Church*. Christ himself. One of them bared her breasts at me. Frances lifted her skirt." Jamieson put his head on his clasped hands, shaking in disbelief. "It only showed how *young* she was. How innocent that demon child *should* have been."

"Organisations like Faith and Family, gentlemen," Connolly broke the silence, his tone even, almost light, "began in Brazil and spread quickly to other predominantly Catholic countries. Tragically, they've found willing disciples here now."

"Look into her eyes and you could see the real Frances, the true girl. Faint, but still there. A shining innocence, drowning in a sea of filth and hate and despair."

Connolly ignored him. "They believe that a baptised child will go to Limbo in death, no matter what crimes it has committed."

"And you don't?!" Jamieson swivelled round to glare up at the old man.

"The subject, as you should know, Michael, of the nature and traditions surrounding *Limbus Infantium* is being deliberated upon in Rome now and throughout the Church. But, even if I do accept the doctrine, I do not believe I have the power or the right to *send* them there."

"They harm not only themselves," Jamieson cried out, exasperated. He looked at each of them in turn, Coulter, Russell, Webb, then back at the Monsignor, as if they were a class of fools who couldn't see the obvious. "But others. All of us. An innocent is corrupted, so she will go on and corrupt another, another ten, more. The cycle goes on."

Coulter took a step closer to Jamieson. "Are you telling me that... you *killed* Frances Mulholland?"

Jamieson shook his head forcefully from side to side. "I did not lay a finger on her."

"Murder is a mortal sin," explained the Monsignor. "A responsible adult would not have the option of Limbo. Or even Purgatory. Especially if he has not made a good confession." The meaning of his words was perfectly clear, yet there was silence in the dark church, until Coulter managed to say the words.

"You needed another child." He looked up at the distant altar. Silence reigned in the church, none of the five men present looking at one another. "But who?" Coulter turned to Jamieson, eyes scorched with fury. "*Who?*"

Jamieson held his gaze defiantly.

"Jesus – not *Darren?*" Behind Coulter, Russell made to lunge at the priest, but was held back by Sergeant Webb.

"You told Darren to kill her."

Jamieson shook his head again. "He couldn't."

"But you suggested it to him? His own sister."

A Mr. Mark Deveny and Mr. Robert Wilson, both of Stratheaton, Lanarkshire, had been arrested on charges related to the assault of Mr and Mrs Baxter in June earlier this year which led to the death of Mrs. Baxter and the continued ill-health and trauma suffered by her husband.

Deveny and Wilson were hardly newcomers to the police or the courts and all the paraphernalia of Scots law. They *would* be new, however, to the publicity that was about to befall them. The Consultative Steering Committee on Delinquency and Crime had decided – if not in quite so many words – to make an example of this pair. Thieves, drug-dealers, thugs. Deveny and Wilson were everything that was wrong with modern Britain.

Deveny was accused three years ago, when he was only fifteen, of raping and robbing an aunt. The victim turned out not to be related but a friend of the family and the case was dropped due to lack of evidence, but the story got out. Wilson had been moved from school to institution and back to school again for consistently disruptive and violent behaviour, just not quite disruptive or violent enough for the criminal justice system. Local children told tearfully of Wilson and Deveny's bullying, extortion, and victimisation. One twelve-year-old boy's house had every single window broken by the pair – twice. There was proof of their bullying: pictures on their phone cameras. Deveney and Wilson were happy slappers – punching folk, sometimes strangers in the street, and taking a photograph, sending it out to their peers.

A press call had been arranged for 12.00 midday outside Glasgow's police headquarters. The head of the investigative team from Lanarkshire Police had already spent all of yesterday in Glasgow. The Deputy First Minister herself would be present, alongside the Ministers for Justice and Education and Young People. Members of the Youth Crime and Delinquency Committee would be available for questioning, including its founder, Steven Murray MSP, its chair John MacDougall, and Procurator Maxwell Binnie. Chief Constable Robertson and Malcolm Henderson – Strathclyde Police's ACC – and senior colleagues from Lanarkshire, would also take questions on the Deveny/Wilson case, and the youth crime problem in general.

The Ministers' cars were at this moment approaching the city centre on the M8, relatively free of snarl-ups this morning. Those who had been meeting upstairs came down into the car park a little early, their business finished, statements agreed, and the day being pleasantly warm. They stood at the door, letting the smokers have a last puff before walking over to the assembled press. Maxwell Binnie grumbled to the Moderator that there weren't quite as many cameras, microphones, or hacks as he'd expected.

Along through the cars, behind the BBC outside-broadcast van, walked a young man. His hair combed tidily back, his tracksuit gleaming, and his hands held deep in his pockets.

Maddy was showing her card to the policeman on duty at the car park barrier, Dan's voice still speaking over the hands-free system. "He had a reputation, Maddy, that's all. No action taken against him." All the time she was keeping a eye on Darren Mullholland's progress through the lines of cars towards the station building.

"How did you know he'd be here?" Belinda asked. She

had never seen Darren before, but knew at once who he must be.

"The radio in his room," Maddy said, when the policeman had waved them in. "The news."

The bewildered expression didn't lift from Belinda's face. "They announced this press conference." Maddy's eyes flicked between finding a space for the car, the approaching Darren, and the assembled worthies outside the station.

"It's not an Irish accent, though the Americans might mistake it for one." Then, unhooking the mobile from its cradle, she spoke again to Dan: "What did you get?"

MacDougall looked over – whether at Maddy parking or Darren walking it was hard to tell. A moment later Binnie looked up too – in his case, quite definitely at Maddy. MacDougall merged back in with the suits and chatted to the uniformed honcho from Lanark.

By the time Maddy had parked and got out the car it was too late to head Darren off. He was ahead of her now and would reach the group first. A shout went up and the journos and technicians got ready for the conference. MacDougall, Binnie, CC Robertson and the rest walked towards the waiting cameras.

Pattison Webb had found a pew up near the altar to phone into the station: Darren Mulholland had to be found, as quickly as possible. Take men off the search for Ian Lennon, every car and constable available to find the boy.

Mike Jamieson was sitting now on the back pew, a saintly look on his face like he was communing with powers the rest of them couldn't comprehend. He was also sweating.

"Where's Darren!" If he could have, Coulter would have kicked seven colours of shit out him to get the answer. Connolly came between them. He brushed Coulter's arm and gently made him stand back. He put his hand on Jamieson's shoulder.

"Father," it sounded odd, from this elderly man to

Jamieson who looked every minute more like a hurt child, "you and I believe in the truth. There's a cycle of virtue, as well as evil. We are with Christ in fighting corruption and decay. You must say now where this boy is. You loved him, didn't you?"

Jamieson nodded.

He still had that beatific look in his eye. "It was too much to ask. To save the soul of your own sister. Of course it was. It would be better to exchange them. *I* suggested that." He was unravelling before their eyes, his shaking getting worse, his voice crackling, but he was still proud of his ingenuity.

"You suggested someone else should kill Frances? Who? Who did you suggest it to?" The Monsignor kept his voice soft and low.

Jamieson held his head high, his mouth closed. Like St. Peter, resisting the temptation to betray. Coulter couldn't take it. "Who killed Frances?!" He stood towering over Jamieson. "Was it Sy? Or Paul? Is that how it works – the crime is done by another already lost soul?"

"Come on Father – you're making a better confession now." Connolly massaged the young priest's shoulder. Jamieson nodded. And mouthed one word: "Paul."

"Who else is part of this?"

Before he could answer, Webb called over. "Alan. Darren Mullholland's been spotted at the press conference back at the station. So has Maddy Shannon, and Paul Pacchini's mother."

At the police station? *Why?* Coulter knew he would get nothing out of Jamieson. "Ask him," he said to Connolly, "has Ian Lennon anything to do with this? We have evidence of his presence in both crime scenes."

Connolly merely looked at Jamieson, who shook his head. "I was only told to get a hair off that dog, give it to Darren."

Connolly got down on his knees beside the weeping Jamieson. *"Ego te absolvo a peccatis—"*

"What are you doing?" Russell spat the words out at the Monsignor.

"As I said. We believe in breaking vicious circles." And he turned back to Jamieson, who was slumped now over the pew in front like a drunk at midnight Mass. Coulter stared as the old man made that little sign of the cross again on Michael Jamieson's lips.

The two constables thanked old Mrs Mackay for the cup of tea and got up from the table.

"I never realised police work could be so... tedious," she said, sympathetic.

"Has its ups and downs. Like any other job, I s'pose." Uniformed officers had been positioned outside her house for over a week now. The taller of the two on duty today collected his own cup and saucer and those of his colleague and carried them over to the window. But he stopped dead before getting to the sink.

"Just put them on the sideboard, dear," the old lady said.

"Good God," said the officer.

His partner got up and stood beside him – stock still too, petrified, as though some spell was operating in that half of the room. Helena made her way to where they were, staring out the window.

Out in the garden, clearly aware of their presence and the fact that he was being watched, but not taking his eyes off his work, was Ian Lennon, digging. He looked as if he'd been there all morning. In a groove, a rhythm of work achieved only after time and with concentration, serenity.

"What's he *doing*?" asked one of the officers.

"Turning the earth around the roses, dear," said Mrs Mackay, easing the cups and saucers out his grip. The other one managed to come round enough to get his phone out. As he raised it to his ear, Lennon half looked up, glanced at the policeman through the window. Only then were the bruises and stains of blood not properly washed away evident. He gave the faintest of smiles, then nodded towards Mrs Mackay. The old lady waved merrily back, and began humming as she washed the dishes.

Desmond and Veronica Kane knew a little about Faith and Family. The organisation – a registered charity – had matched the funding for Paul's schooling that they themselves had put in. "Not an inconsiderable amount, Miss."

Amy Dalgarno couldn't be sure if they were lying about having no idea of the organisation's darker side. They knew it was international – that really helped Paul with his school work. For geography or history essays, there was always an email contact who could help, in France or Venezuela or America. They knew it was religious – it was through a fellow parishioner that Des and Nicky first got in touch with them.

They were more forthcoming about John MacDougall. "Yes, we know him," said Nicky, smiling. "He came to see how Paul was getting on."

"Twice," added Des.

"Did you know that Mr. MacDougall's recently become a public figure up here? In Scotland."

They had no notion of that. Never heard the term "School Czar". They only knew him as an educator, a kind of inspector they had thought. They didn't even realise he was Faith and Family. "We thought he was appointed by the Education Department." When pressed, they hadn't even been sure that his name was MacDougall. "Wasn't it MacDonald, Des?"

"Paul just told us he was coming. It was fine by us."

"Are you sure he's a Catholic, dear?" Veronica wondered out loud to Amy. "MacDougall. Doesn't sound it."

"He's from the Uists, or a convert." Amy explained, merely repeating something she'd been told.

"Paul had met him before we had."

Amy took notes as, between them, Des and Veronica

explained briefly how Paul had been in the habit of going off to Day School sessions. "Nearby," Veronica said quickly. "And only once a term or so."

"To meet tutors," Des said.

"He must have been lonely," Amy asked "with no schoolmates?"

"Why should he be?" Des replied, but she detected a note of doubt in his voice. "He was a very serious boy. He liked his own company."

"He never got over his father dying," Veronica shook her head sadly. "No matter what we did or said, he still blamed himself. He was with him you know, the day his dad was knocked over by that car."

"He was awful hard on himself, the poor lad."

The Kanes, thought PC Dalgarno, were as bad as the natural parents Geo and Belinda. Paul Pacchini, born Laird, had been shunted from addiction and mysticism, to wealth and good intentions. What he really needed was someone who knew what it's like to be young and sad and scared.

Chief Constable Crawford Robertson was trying to get off the subject of Kelvingrove and the suicide, hinted at in this morning's papers, of a leading suspect.

"Have you arrested two others as well, sir?"

"Yes, a man and a woman, helping us with our enquiries, but that's not—"

"Is it true there's a child sex ring involved in this?"

"I can't comment on that just now. We're here today to discuss the Stratheaton case—"

Belinda followed Maddy up to the group of people listening to the press conference, both of them scanning the scene for Darren. He wouldn't be that hard to spot, kid in white trackies among dark-suited middle-aged men.

He appeared to the left of the speakers and cameras. Maddy, as luck would have it, was towards the right. There were about a hundred people now plus cables and wires and cameras everywhere. She could recognise even from there, though, that his track suit jacket wasn't Coq Sportif. Another wrong theory.

The boy gave off no sense of rush. He stood firmly, his back to the cameras, facing the assembled worthies. He took one step forward. John MacDougall stepped out from behind Robertson. There was a moment's silence before he spoke in his best headmaster's voice.

"Stay right where you are. Turn around, and go home."

Darren stared up at him, as if he hadn't quite understood. No policeman moved. Like some kind of collective decision had been made to let MacDougall's natural authority deal with the situation, like a true Czar.

"I won't say it again, son. Away home."

MacDougall took a step towards him, and Maddy watched the boy's hand drop towards his pocket. She was too far away to do anything about it directly. She stepped out from the crowd

"That's what these lads need, sir. Good old-fashioned teaching methods."

MacDougall, together with everyone else, turned to look at her.

"Excuse me?"

"Proper teaching. Like you used to do. Rules. Kids knew their boundaries then. You were famous for it, Mr. MacDougall. Every school you were in –teacher, deputy head, head, Convener." She smiled warmly at him.

MacDougall peered at her, unsure of her meaning or intentions. But everyone else looked back towards Darren, to see if she was right – if the pupil *would* do what he was told. Darren looked confused for a moment, aware for the first time of the exposed, public position he was in. He glanced towards Maddy, then back at MacDougall. But he didn't take a single step back.

"You told me I'd feel better. Cleaner."

"What are you *talking* about, son? On your way. This is no place for you."

Maddy kept advancing, the only moving body in the scene. "Didn't you hear the man? Don't you ever do as you're told?" Her tone perplexed everyone – not least Darren. Though the words were strict, taking MacDougall's side, her tone was light, not quite sarcastic. She smiled as warmly at Darren as she had at MacDougall, all the while keeping moving until she had placed herself directly between boy and man.

"You said I was marking them out." Darren had to squint his head round her. "So God would know them." His hand dangled at his side, near his pocket. Perhaps innocently, but Maddy wasn't going to take the chance.

MacDougall stiffened. "Look son, I don't know who you are, but if there's something I can help you with, I'd be glad to. But not now. We've important business here."

"Maybe I can help," Maddy said.

Darren looked past her, as though she weren't there. "You said it would make up for Frances and my Ma and everything I'd done before…"

Now a kind of minimalist choreography began. Everyone moved slightly. The cameramen to get a better angle of both MacDougall and Mulholland. Uniformed officers made a move towards their weapons. Everyone else shuffled, or began to put their hand to their mouth. But it was all slowed by fascination. A need to see where this unexpected story would end.

"It's my turn next, isn't it?"

MacDougall smiled and shook his head – daft boys in schools could make you laugh sometimes. "That's enough." He turned to the people around him, like they were unresourceful staff members. "Get him out of here."

"Who have you got lined up for that?"

The Chief Constable stepped back from the School Czar's side. Policemen moved closer in but they still weren't sure what was expected of them.

"Could *somebody* get the little prick out of here!"

Darren put his hand in his pocket and suddenly the dance livened up. Maddy made her dash for him. A shot thudded clumsily in the air, hitting no one. A nervous young Uniform looked at his gun as though it had fired itself. When they all looked back, Darren had a gun in his hand, but was pointing it at the ground.

"It's okay," said MacDougall, stepping closer to him. "Everyone relax. He won't use it." There was a smile on his face but his voice had taken on a harder, bitterer quality. "Now where did you get that?"

"From where you made me throw it. By the canal path."

MacDougall spoke over his head to the crowd. "Do you know what kind of a kid this is? The kind of life he leads?"

He was stopped by Coulter's car wheeling up to the car park barrier and screeching to a stop.

"He's like the rest of them. No-hopers."

MacDougall took a step away from Darren. Maddy reached Darren at the same time as the nearest Uniform. But there was no gun in his hand. They looked at the ground to see where he'd dropped it. DS Russell had jumped out the car and was running straight at them.

"They live subhuman lives." In a sing-song accent you'd normally associate with islands and soul and rain.

Coulter was at the ex-head teacher's side now. The two men looked at each other, Coulter put his arm on his shoulder. "Don't be ridiculous, man," MacDougall said.

Then the smile suddenly vanished from his lips. Every expression dissolved; for a moment his face was so blank as to be inhuman, void of any character, benign or malign. Only then came the crack, like thunder. Nobody had been watching Belinda Laird. She stood next to Darren, his gun in her hand, her face focused, poised, purposeful and clear.

An angelus bell nearby struck, and the morning was lost.

VI

His father sat him on a wall and looked straight into his eyes. Vittore could see the reflection of the sea and the sand in dad's dark shining pupils. But it wasn't *this* sea and sand around them now. The scene in his father's eyes didn't have the wet sting the boy could feel in his hands, his cheeks, and below the knees of his short trousers. The twin suns in Papà's eyes were Elba's sun. The sand lay below a hill – the hill their old house sits upon. Nonno and Nonna still there, on the parched earth, keeping Carlo company.

"You made very good," his father said. He was trying to teach himself, and Vittore, English. "A hard journey. You made good."

Vittore looked away, at the new beach that surrounded them. It was as if *this* was the reflection. It looked odd, out of shape, discoloured. The beach dulled and curled. The sea stretched too high towards the horizon before meeting the sky. The colours were all wrong – the sand was dark, the sea silver, and the sky was creamy, like French cheese. As if a child had mixed up the crayons.

"I Am..." Papà was struggling to find the right words in English. "I am Proud Of You."

He put his hand on Vittore's head and it felt like God had reached out of the curdled sky.

"Look."

Ettore stood aside, but Vittore saw nothing. Just an endless ribbon of early morning sand, sky and ocean. Three strands of silver. He wasn't even sure where he was. Since London – which they had more or less bypassed – his father had said almost nothing about where they were or where they were headed. Quiet, but not morose or moody any more. When either one of them mentioned Carlo they had

had to fight off tears together. Papa'd ruffle his hair and say, "Carlo, eh?"

Vittore knew they were in *Scozia*, and he knew that their new home was by the sea. But whether they had arrived there or not he wasn't sure. They had passed through a few seaside towns yesterday and this morning. Big solid houses glowing red or pale like sentries around the bays. Men with caps, ladies with bags. Narrow, rangy boys in caps and heavy shoes, white-skinned and dark-eyed. They held little Vittore's attention when they passed, like street performers. They frightened him, but fascinated him more.

Then he saw. She came moving across the sand, in full skirts, dressed for a ball, her hair tied back, a pretty blue bonnet on her head, her hair as dark and rich as the galaxies. She didn't float, as he had daydreamed she would. Didn't glide above the ground like a vision. Her walk was buoyant and hearty. He could see her feet work against the sand in her good shoes, her legs against the blowing breeze, sending loose hairs up into black, waving tendrils. As she got closer he could hear her breathing. His mamma was no angel, no vision, but a solid, fleshy, breathy, moving body. There was joy and sadness in her at the same time the way only earthbound creatures are. She stumbled the last step or two as she hurried to reach him. Vittore couldn't move, transfixed by this spectacular moment. She laughed when she almost fell into him. So did his father. The noise they made between them – high and low, sad, happy, strong and weak. Vittore's whole world in that one, complex sound.

And when her arms finally enfolded him, the universe ordered itself. When her breast crushed tight against his own small, fragile frame, the planets fell into line and everything made sense. The dry, grudging land of before, the strange colours of this new world. Carlo and Carlo dying. It was all fine. Papa's moods, Vittore's own worst fears and nightmares. The touch of her skin, the scent of her hair, her breath – death and defeat and fear vanquished. The fact that this one person existed made sense of his own and everybody else's existence. She lifted him. She was strong, but Papa helped too. They raised him up like an offering to the sky.

The decluttttering had gone further than she'd ever intended. It had taken on a force of its own, making her fill boxes with pictures and letters and disks and old ribbons and dresses that she wasn't at all sure she no longer needed or wanted. But she had time on her hands and it was a good way of killing an afternoon.

Next week she'd be back at work – fully reinstated after the most cursory of internal inquiries. There had been too many questions all round on the police's, the procurator's, even the parliament's, relations with murderers and accessories to murder, for Maddy's peccadilloes to matter much. A couple of tabloids had dubbed her a heroine, for putting herself in the line of fire. Monsignor Connolly hailed her, randomly she thought, as an agent of the divine.

The two cases of murder she had been working on a month ago had spiralled into several cases and a couple of dozen charges against Convener MacDougall, Father Jamieson and collaborators yet unknown. Maddalena Shannon would be prosecuting none of them. But her visits to Darren in hospital and Belinda in prison were readily granted.

The images never stopped playing in Maddy's mind. Two kids walking along a summer street in a dusty scheme. Darren kicks a can, Frances hits a stick off railings and car bumpers and bonnets. If they say anything at all to each other, Maddy can't hear it. At the hospital, Darren couldn't remember exactly what happened the day he took his sister to see the priest. But he knew what was going to happen. And he thought the priest was right. He couldn't stand another minute of watching his wee sister take drugs, get into fights, give in to the abuse of every brutal male prepared to exploit whatever power they wielded. He remembers he wasn't nervous or crying – that it was like going to church.

The odd car passes by; they meet the occasional friend or acquaintance along the way. One little event could have changed the outcome. A car offering them a lift, a quick word with anyone – just enough to break Darren's resolve. Some excuse for Franny to go off, leave her nice but boring, too-serious brother behind. Skip off in the other direction, laughing that laugh of hers, calling him names, but smiling. If ever a boy needed to laugh...

There's a smile waiting for them round the corner. A beatific smile, on the attractive face of the dark-haired little priest. Franny turns to her big brother and shakes her head, amused. She has nothing against the priest, but guys like that need noised up. Priests, teachers, shopkeepers, they hated Franny and her friends, Franny's mum; they hated Darren too, but Darren couldn't see that. So Franny struts, bold as you like, a swagger on her hips, up to the priest. They're behind a row of condemned houses, the wall of a now disappeared school hiding them from the posh houses in Bearsden two football pitches' lengths away. She hasn't time to reflect on the bizarre choice of rendezvous before the priest raises his hand to make a sign of the cross over her head.

Maddy can see, from her front-row seat in her mind, that the gesture enrages Franny. So full of arrogance and presumption. He's judging her. *Nobody* judges Frances Mulholland. Teachers and dinner ladies and bus drivers have tried that before and it didn't get them very fucking far. This smug little bamstick is just asking for a bawling out. She's just about to let rip when another figure steps out from behind the wall.

This one's young, good-looking, long-haired, hippy-ish. Franny's no idea who he is or where he comes from but she likes him. She recognises him. He's one of her kind. He's got that depth in his dark eyes, that rigid way of holding your body against the world. His smile is so wide and edgy that she takes no notice of the little priest falling to his knees, dragging Darren down there with him, making him pray. She sees how ridiculous her brother and the man in black look, their knees on the litter and dirt and broken glass. She opens her mouth to laugh. The tall, dark boy takes a step towards her. It's the evening of a sunny day and everything is outlined to perfection. Even though she wants to, Maddy can't miss anything in the scene. It's been beautifully shot. The boy reaches inside his shirt. There's a scream. Darren's. Then there's another.

The priest is dragging Darren away. The boy with the gun is strong – he can pick the deadweight of Frances Mulholland up without too much hefting. As he walks away, towards the big houses over by, the priest makes the sign of the cross on his own lips and glances at Franny's face. Paul Pacchini nods. He drags her, hanging from one arm, as though she were drunk or stoned. Nobody bats an eyelid at a junked-up or spaced-out thirteen year old. Not round here.

There are old photographs. Boxes of them. Dad always fancied himself as a chronicler of his times. Snaps of amusement arcades in Girvan in the sixties. Kids' motorboats in the pond at the front – Maddy could still smell their petrol, hear their too-loud noise as they struggle through the mucky water. There are seascapes, at dawn and at dusk, pictures of the Carrick hills – from the ground only, Packy was never one for walking up slopes. Family groups. Nine, ten, thirteen, fifteen-year-old Maddalena with Mamma and dad, seldom with them both, and with Nonno.

She tried hard to keep these pictures in her mind instead of this horror film on a loop... The handsome boy again now with Sy Kennedy walking along a canal path as an early June sun shins high up into the sky like an athlete scaling a tree.

Nobody's yet sure exactly how Paul and Sy met. There are plenty of places two school-dogging, runaway, bad boys might meet. Quite possibly a dodgy B&B behind the University. One of the places Sy took couples, or lone ladies – never men by themselves. He had suggested the place to Elaine and Jim Docherty, on-line, for a wee money-making scam.

MacDougall was still denying any knowledge of the Pacchini boy. Despite literally scores of testimonies, sightings, even photographs. It wasn't, Maddy knew, the last defence of a madman, but the advice of lawyers who knew where their only judicial hope lay.

Maddy sees the scene from Darren's POV... He's alone, behind bushes somewhere. There's someone behind him. Dawn lifts softly, a glorious morning of pink blossoms.

She hears them before she sees them. The raucous sound of two lads approaching, one's voice deeper and more rasping than the other. Abrupt bursts of guttural laughter, skirmish of feet as they suddenly indulge in a spot of horse-play. The sounds funnel up along the canal, filter through the bushes and out into the quiet park.

Then she sees them, as Darren did. Paul is virtually unrecognisable. He's had his hair shorn off – most likely by his new pal, Sy. He's wearing trackies. Sy Kennedy, as far as anyone can figure out, had no connection with Father Jamieson or John MacDougall. He simply had the bad luck to become a friend of Paul Pacchini's at the wrong time. Paul was already the friend of another boy, waiting in the bushes with a shaky hand and a loaded gun.

There's a movement behind Maddy. A voice close to her ear; close to Darren Mulholland's ear. She can't make out the exact words, but the voice is urging Darren onwards. Darren knows what he has to do. Knows how it works. His sister's soul has been saved. Now it's time to save the soul of another, and in so doing, commending himself unto God. God will love them all. *Though he may die, he shall live.*

When they get to the other side, the Infant Jesus of Prague will smile upon them. He'll understand and love Darren all the more for the difficult thing he is about to do.

But there are *two* boys on the canal path, and Darren wasn't really ready for one, let alone a total stranger. The man behind is angry, too. From what the investigation can gather, Pacchini knew he was walking to his martyrdom that morning. Whether he brought Kennedy along for company, or to stop it happening, nobody will ever know.

The boys are laughing and the old man is outraged and praying. Telling God to free his children from this terrible corrupting flesh, this evil world. When Darren remains frozen, terrified, and Paul spots them, MacDougall grabs Darren's arm from behind, raises the gun, puts his own finger over the boy's, and pulls the trigger for him. Twice.

What happens next is blurry in Maddy's mind. Like the closing titles are hiding the full picture. MacDougall is pushing the bodies into the bushes, swearing and praying, then going back for Darren, grabbing him by the wrist, pulling him away. There's a tiny bit of life left in Paul: when MacDougall's back is turned, restraining the traumatised Darren, Paul reaches out for Sy's hand. He hasn't the strength to quite make contact. MacDougall shoves Darren to his knees. Throws a knife beside him, and makes the Sign of the Cross roughly on the living boy's lips with his thumb. Darren turns, knife shaking in his hand, and looks down through tears at the dead faces and lips.

Maddy pours herself another gin and stares at a photograph of her eleven-year-old self and her granddad, trying to superimpose the image.

<Quik Hi. Talk l8r. OK?>

Louis gets in touch regularly. Usually by email or text. On the phone, voice to voice, they're awkward. It reminds them of being back in her darkened room, naked.

NYPD haven't made a single arrest yet – though they'll

be over in a week or two with their own indictments against John MacDougall. They can positively place him twice in the US in the last three years, on each occasion just before a murder. But they can only make tenuous connections with the victims.

<We have an outfit called God and Poperty wld you believe>

<God and Popery?>

<Property. they share compter files and links with yur Faith and Famly mob. The two memberships dovetail here and there.>

When she does phone, she keeps the tone light. "Will you be coming over, Louis?"

"Doubt it. The legal eagles will get the jaunt this time, is my guess. There's stuff over here for you guys to investigate."

She bought herself a phone with a camera on it, just to send across pictures of hairy cows.

Alan Coulter hardly got out of the station. It felt like *he* was the criminal. Being questioned – interrogated. By everyone. Every rung on his own chain of command, plus anyone with an epaulette and a need to stick his nose in. Procurator Fiscal never off the phone trying to get the story straight on Maddy Shannon. Journalists, apologists for the Scottish Parliament, minor members of the Committee on Youth and Crime...

And lawyers. Lawyers coming out of his ears. This new posh bloke from the Lord Advocate's in Edinburgh doing his head with quaint old Scots law phrases – *Jus Federale*, anyone? McKillop, Maddy's colleague, said to him, "LFC we call them. Learned Fucking Counsel. You get the pistol for them, prime it, load the chamber, uncock the safety catch, aim it for them in court directly at the guilty party – and the LFC twat still misses."

A special operations team was being funded to research

every child missing in areas where Family and Faith operated, and places where MacDougall was known to have visited regularly. It was Coulter's own – maybe hopeful – opinion that they had caught MacDougall early. Not quite early enough, but before he could recruit any more Father Jamiesons or Paul Pacchinis.

Maddy had emailed him – going out for her first public drink. He couldn't *not* go. He owed her that much at least. She'd solved this one before him. Anyway, they were old friends. Soon be colleagues again, now that she'd been reinstated. Beth and Jen would be out tonight; Martha will have gone round to Lauren's – the one place her headaches seemed to leave her alone.

At the hospital, Rosa di Rio Shannon held her father's hand. No change, for good or ill, in nearly a month. She had reconciled herself to it. Nonno wasn't outstaying his welcome. Wasn't hanging on, frightened to move over to whatever lay beyond. He was giving everyone a chance to make their farewells. Family man to the end.

Every cousin and half cousin and third cousin four times removed from Elba to Edinburgh, London to Girvan had been to visit. Every friend still alive, and the children of several others, had passed by. Rosa was still scared at the prospect of being without him entirely, and at times her tears still ran free, but he had given her time to prepare herself. She would live. She would carry him inside her, just as he carried Mama, and his own parents, and the brother he lost as a child. He'd given his granddaughter time, too, to get through her personal little hell, so that she could come to him and say a proper goodbye. "You always said she'd be trouble," Rosa squeezed his hand.

That priest, Father Jamieson. Seemed so nice and holy. She was a silly, lonely woman, who took friendship in ridiculous places. "You always kept them at arm's length, Papà. The clerics. God's politicians you said, and the king's. If

287

I'd been that woman, I'd have shot the whole bloody lot of them." She squeezed her daddy's hand tighter.

Dan McKillop put a long, cold G&T on the table. "Get that down you, boss."

It was warm again outside, a couple of days of cloud and smir nearly washing away the memory of a half decent spring and summer. Walking down from the hospital, Maddy had felt her spirits rise unaccountably – a bit of sun and you start whistling away all the bad stuff, all the crap. In sunlight her city becomes a good-time girl.

Izzie glowed perfectly in the snug of the Vicky bar, a light floral dress that made her look like a Lewis Carroll fantasy of a girl-woman. Manda's latest look was Glaswegian Björk – some weird fluffy top made of god-knows-what over a skirt so short she had to splay her Roman-sandalled feet to keep her thighs modestly shut. Dan had ventured out of a suit into matching jacket and trousers that might as well be a suit. They all raised their glasses to Maddy.

"Welcome back."

"Poor Maxwell. You've got to see him. He has to sing your praises everywhere he goes."

"And pretend he'd never wanted to sideline you."

"A toast," said Izzie. "To Monday morning – and getting started again on Petrus."

The never-ending forest of legal thickets and procedural thorns still there to be hacked away at in order to get to the next set of murdering bastards.

"How's the boy?"

Maddy shrugged. How *was* Darren? Would he ever construct some kind of life for himself? If he was a haunted child, he'd be a man possessed. Though he and his mother seemed to be helping each other as much as they could. Jackie went to visit him every day; swore blind to anyone who would listen that she'd changed. That she was going to dedicate her life to making her son well again.

"And Belinda?"

Maddy played with her gin, thinking of Belinda in her prison clothes, the brightness in her eyes only marginally dimmed. "She's working something through: she took action, for her boy, delivered justice. She thinks now she can forgive everyone. Except herself. Not for killing MacDougall. For failing her son."

They all sipped quietly. Izzie put her hand on the table, close to Maddy's. "What about Louis?"

"Want me to do The Test on him?"

"I managed that all on my own this time, Dan, thanks," She chinked glasses with Dan, Manda, and Izzie. The dusk sun stooped to peer in the bar window. Maddy met it in the eye. Up the street, a familiar figure approached. Coulter, looking ten years younger than he ought to, but with the hesitant walk of an injured old man. The sun was still warm, thawing that black line that had grown around her. Red sandstone and evening blue sky. Closing her eyes to feel the city around her, she felt a fourth, invisible clink of her glass. Nonno.

Salute, Maddelena. We've come a long way, you and I. From the rocks of Monte Capanne to this town half a world away. Keep travelling, *principessa*, one foot after another. Maddy Shannon raised her glass into the air. Ciao Nonno, have a good journey yourself.